Extraordinary praise for Abraham Rodriguez's debut novel

"[Rodriguez] brings to life a variety of individual characters, enriching them with inflections of street speech and fashion, detailing the physical environments they move through. . . . *Spidertown* succeeds on the basis of its compelling subjective quality of its principal characters' search for individual integrity and choice in a world whose options seem almost predetermined." —*Los Angeles Weekly Reader*

"Electrifying . . . gritty and sexy"
—*Paper* magazine

"*Spidertown* . . . finds the sweetness in the doomed children of the crack world. It's very hard and touching, like Nelson Algren goes to the South Bronx, and catches you up in the lives of people you might cross the street to avoid meeting." —John Sayles, author of *Los Gusanos*

"The characters grab your elbow and pull you through a slit in the air to another landscape, and you can't leave until their voices end on the last page. What a talent!" —Susan Straight, author of *I Been in Sorrow's Kitchen and Licked Out All the Pots*

"Rodriguez uses the repetitiveness of life in the ghetto itself to make the tension and desperation of *Spidertown* achingly palpable."
—*People*

"Rodriguez writes with the authority of an insider . . . placing himself in the tradition of Dostoevsky and Richard Wright as an author who will look at and bring into the open a side of society that might otherwise remain hidden." —*Library Journal*

"Rodriguez is a fascinating combination of raw intelligence, street smarts, and charm." —*Seattle Weekly*

"An authentic voice of today's America. An eye-opener in its honesty. Abraham Rodriguez not only writes from the guts, but also from the heart. The best kind of novel."
—Joel Rose, author of *Kill the Poor*

PENGUIN BOOKS

SPIDERTOWN

Abraham Rodriguez, Jr., was born and raised in the South Bronx. His work has appeared in *Story* and in *Best Stories from New Writers*. He is the author of a short story collection, *The Boy Without a Flag*, which *The Village Voice* described as "the most nervy, anxious, and brilliant writing by a New York Puerto Rican since Piri Thomas's *Down These Mean Streets*."

SPIDERTOWN

A NOVEL BY

Abraham Rodriguez, Jr.

PENGUIN BOOKS

PENGUIN BOOKS
Published by the Penguin Group
Penguin Books USA Inc., 375 Hudson Street, New York, New York 10014, U.S.A.
Penguin Books Ltd, 27 Wrights Lane, London W8 5TZ, England
Penguin Books Australia Ltd, Ringwood, Victoria, Australia
Penguin Books Canada Ltd, 10 Alcorn Avenue, Toronto, Ontario, Canada M4V 3B2
Penguin Books (N.Z.) Ltd, 182–190 Wairau Road, Auckland 10, New Zealand

Penguin Books Ltd, Registered Offices: Harmondsworth, Middlesex, England

First published in the United States of America by Hyperion 1993
Reprinted by arrangement with Hyperion
Published in Penguin Books 1994

10 9 8 7 6 5 4 3 2

PUBLISHER'S NOTE
This is a work of fiction. Names, characters, places,
and incidents either are the product of the author's imagination
or are used fictitiously, and any resemblance to actual persons,
living or dead, events, or locales is entirely coincidental.

THE LIBRARY OF CONGRESS HAS CATALOGUED THE HARDCOVER AS FOLLOWS:
Rodriguez, Abraham.
Spidertown: a novel/by Abraham Rodriguez, Jr.
p.   cm.
ISBN 1-56282-845-2 (hc.)
ISBN 0 14 02.3838 7 (pbk.)
I. Title.
PS3568.034876S67   1993
813´54—dc20   92–34088

Printed in the United States of America
Set in Transitional

TO LYNETTE

Special thanks to Lois Rosenthal, Richard Parks, and Pat Mulcahy,

for believing I could pull it off.

SPIDERTOWN

They were both sitting on the floor in the half-dark. Cold air seeped in through the shattered window with a moan.

Firebug had the bottle up against his lips, but he wasn't drinking. A thought was forming in his mind. He had eyes like an Arab; large, bright hazel, bottomless. "You know what?" he asked with a hoarse laugh, now swigging from the bottle.

"No. What." The words brought Miguel back to the now. His mind had sailed far beyond the stale plaster and the roaches that darted from craggy nooks along the far wall.

"They got this perfume f' faggits, man." Firebug regarded him with a solemn expression, making Miguel laugh. "Nah, I'm serious, bro'. A perfume f' faggits. I saw it on Amelia's TV an' shit."

Amelia. Curly-haired, crater-faced, too much eyeliner. City College. Psychology major. Crack pipes in her drawers. A mind is a terrible thing to waste.

"I'm serious, man. Faggit perfume."

"No way, man."

"Yeah man! I saw it. It say 'Parfoom por le homo' right on the bottle."

Miguel let the laughter burst right out of him. It sounded brittle, like paper being torn into strips.

"It means 'man,' " he said. "I think thass paisano talk."

"Maan. Only patos wear that shit. Is that wha' thum blancos need t' score some pussy? No Latino need shit like that. Latinos can walk into a room smellin' like puro sobaco an' still get pussy galore."

Miguel laughed. He had been with scores of girls, had fucked them and blown them off, and none of it mattered. Now he felt like some old man—sixteen and a half. "Love" had been another word for "fuck." Then he met Cristalena: a girl with a name like a poem.

He took a swig from the bottle, squatting on the floor like a Hindu. When the candle went out Firebug got up and stuffed some more rags into the hole in the window so the cold wouldn't blow in so strong. Then he lit the candle again, staring at the wiggling flame with loving eyes, shielding it with his hands as though it were a pet.

Firebug's hand almost caressed the dancing tonguelet. In school, Firebug used to carry a can of lighter fluid, to set scrunchballs alight and toss them at teachers. Gave Mrs. Grote a heart attack. She'd been up there doing math, writing out a problem, when the flaming balls struck the blackboard and bounced into her face. She screamed and thrashed and collapsed while the class erupted in a violent laughing fit. They took her to Lincoln Hospital, and she was never heard from again. Despite that, Firebug wasn't put on probation; setting that girl on fire in science class, that's what did it.

The girl's name was Anna Mercado. Firebug had a crush on her right up to the day she called him "a walking moco." He took that personally, so during an unguarded moment in class, he shot her with some fluid and set her on fire. The class howled in glee as she spun and screamed and beat at her burning dress. Everyone applauded while the teacher, a bald-eagle type named Mr. Sandstone, stood there pale and gaping. Firebug tried to explain that it was just lighter fluid, that it wouldn't even hurt, that the flames don't last long, but they put him on probation anyway and gave him a month of detention, which meant getting locked up in a padded room in the basement for hours and hours each day.

Firebug's glassy eyes glowed with the flame, as if it gave him safety. "My father," he said softly, "he used t' throw these parties on this lot on Tinton. He used t' build thum big fires an' shit, an' cook lechon an' burgers. A real wienie roast, right? He used t' make me an' my brothas jump the flame. It was like the Olympics, man. Everybody would line up t' watch. An' each time, he'd build the fire up higher an' higher, he had a way of doin' that, the fire would obey him. People used t' place bets." Firebug thrust a finger into the flame. "My two brothers, they were good, but not as good as me. They used t' get burned, an' quit. But not me. The fire never hurt me." He looked at Miguel as though he were a priest talking about having found a burning bush. "My father said the fire respects me."

Miguel had met Firebug's father once. He was a large man with a face that looked like it had been melted, skin charred and blackened with patches of pink that resembled plastic. He used to work in a junkyard on Gun Hill Road, melting down metal in a huge furnace. Ten years he had worked there without a problem. One day something went wrong. The furnace exploded. After that he went on welfare because of the headaches and the hearing problems and the methadone, because he claimed to still be in pain, two years later. Miguel could understand why Firebug preferred to be away from him.

"There's a wienie roast tonight," Firebug whispered, eyes luminous. "You inta comin'? I wanna know if you can pick Amelia up f' me like always."

Miguel leaned against the cold wall. "You got another one?"

"Yup. I'm a real busy man."

Miguel thought for a moment about the big fire he had seen two nights ago, the big tenement on Jackson Avenue. Rolling clouds of black smoke blotted out the sky while brilliant sheaths of flame slithered out of every window. Rows of engines clogged the streets, red lights pulsing like strobes in a disco. Miguel and Amelia sat on the hood of his Impala, his '68 four-door cherry leather Impala. They had been two blocks away, across an empty lot, and they could still feel the heat on their faces.

"He's gettin' better," Amelia had said, munching loudly. She passed him the bag of popcorn and he handed her the bottle of beer, while small clusters of grieving tenants clutched blankets and stood out in the cold, some barefoot, some in ragged slippers and tattered robes, some crying, screaming, yelling anxiously for their children, a fat mother with steel-wool hair frantically counting heads. Amelia had pointed out a man who stood by a lamppost, clad only in underwear, his thin legs trembling. She laughed and laughed. There was a time when Miguel used to laugh too, enjoying the show from his front-row seat. Now he felt disgusted. He tried to hide it behind a smirk, but Amelia caught it. It was all because of Cristalena.

Take the apartment, up on the top floor of a smelly tenement on Prospect Avenue. When Miguel had first laid eyes on the place, it was the fucking Garden of Eden. Now it was like living in a sewer. There was hardly any heat. Most of the rooms didn't have light fixtures. Miguel had bought all the furniture in the place; Firebug didn't believe in furniture. He bought a dresser, a pair of night tables, two bookcases for his books and records. There was his stereo rack system. The rest of the place was empty. It was the way Firebug wanted it. Miguel had kept from buying himself a bed only because Firebug had a fit. They both slept on the floor on old gym mats. Firebug didn't need furniture. He had a box to hear music and a backpack for his stuff. What else did he need? "You have to live light in our kinda business," he lectured Miguel time and time again. "Don't wanna get too comfortable." He lived out of a matchbox, laughed at Miguel's books, records, his boxes of clothes. He did give in long enough to help Miguel drag a large car seat they had spotted in an abandoned van up the five flights. "A real living-room couch," they had announced to the empty room, laughing insanely as they slid the thing from one end of the room to the other. Encouraged, thinking maybe it was just new things Firebug didn't like, Miguel began to rummage all over the big empty lot on Fox Street, where all the stolen cars were dumped, stripped, and burned. There he found a small writing table with a busted leg. He fixed it, varnished and painted it. Firebug stared at the finished product. "Put it in yuh room," he ordered.

Miguel had glared at him, holding the wet paintbrush like he would sock him with it.

"I meant put it where you want," Firebug said, retreating. He could only shrug. "I don't know wha'chu gonna do when we gotta do a sudden fade-out. It happens in this biz."

"We ain't goin' nowhere," Miguel told him, picking a spot opposite the car seat for the desk. He wasn't some fucken gypsy. He wanted to live somewhere, period. The idea that they had to be ready to be on the move at a moment's notice had always been exciting to him, a crazy hint of danger and urgency. He felt like his life was his own. He could party as late as he wanted, come and go as he pleased. No parents, no rules, no homework. On his own, with his own place, a dope car, money, and an exciting job, not the fucken four-dollar-an-hour shit some of his schoolmates might be making at McDonald's. Miguel was into something good, and it had felt good for a long time. Then it had worn off. Suddenly he was uptight about his life: He wanted to have a real apartment, with real furniture, so people would know he was making it. He had more money than most of them, didn't he? It was pretty dope that a sixteen-and-a-half-year-old brat like him could save up seven thousand dollars while not even being able to get a bank card.

So he'd scrounged over the empty lot and found a framed metal sheet, the kind they use to board up windows on abandoned buildings facing the expressway. It had shutters and a flowerpot on a fake sill painted right on it. Miguel had put it up on the wall like a painting. When he stared at the fake windowsill with the fake shutters and the fake potted petunias he felt waves of depression washing over him.

"Whassup?"

The question brought him back from the unknown. He grinned and took another drink, passing the bottle to Firebug as he sat by him.

"Jus' thinkin' 'bout the wienie roast."

"Cool." Firebug stared at him. He was a suspicious cat, wary of people getting pensive. He was always watching his back. Six months as a teen crack dealer taught him that much. Miguel could see the mistrust in his eyes.

"It's gonna be a serious party," Firebug said.

"Yeah man."

"So you think you gonna be pickin' Amelia up?"

Miguel checked his watch, rising sluggishly. Some of the brown stuff was sloshing around behind his pupils there, making things look a little blurry. "Yeah, but I gotta meet Spider. I gotta meet him now. When's the party?"

"Ten. About ten it should go off."

It was a ritual. Miguel would pick Amelia up and they would be Firebug's appreciative audience. (Firebug never attended. He considered it bad luck.) After the "wienie roast" they'd drive over to Mongo's bar on Longwood Avenue to celebrate, him and Amelia and his posse of teenagers who cheered him on with descriptions of the show. (Mongo kept the cops well paid so that all the kids drinking in there wouldn't get his license revoked.) Firebug looked older than all of them, with his unshaven, pockmarked face, his eyes hollow like a soldier's. He had just hooked up with Amelia when Miguel had moved in with him, so Miguel's first wienie roast was her first, too. "I want huh t' see it, it'll blow huh mind," Firebug had told him. He asked Miguel to pick her up at her father's Cuban sandwich shop on Kelly Street. Right off, Miguel didn't like her, because that first time she lit her crack pipe in his car. He braked with a violent jerk, making her smack the dash with an outraged "Hey!" He leaned over and opened the door for her.

"Out," he said.

"Whass that mean, man? Where you come from with this snotty shit? You in the business an' you won't let me light up?"

"Not in my car. You wanna ride with me, you don't light up."

She stared at him with a strange twinkling intelligence in her eyes, the corners of her mouth twisting upward. "Wow. Little boy got himself in an uproar, ah? The kid don't make sense. I like that in a man." She was fiddling with her pipe. "Have you had this contradictory nature for very long? I'm a psych major, you know. I could help you."

"You holdin' that pipe an' you wanna help me?"

"Ohhh baby, I sense holier-than-thou. Wow, you could be a pretty interesting case."

"Is that what Firebug is, a case?"

"No. I fuck him because he has a big dick."

"Don't light that in here, I swear. Go out an' do it."

"Fine. You wait f' me." She scooted out of the car and disappeared into one of the dingy vestibules along the street. Moments later she hopped back into the car and slammed the door. "There," she said breathlessly. "You happy?" Her eyes challenged him.

"You don't understand," Miguel said, shifting the car with a jerk. "A man's car, it's sacred. You don't do junk in yuh car. Thass obscene. Lookit this cherry-red leather upholstery. Feel it. The fucken shit breathes."

She leaned back, staring at him, her eyes looking darker, as if she had gone into the vestibule to add more eyeliner.

"An' who'dju have to kill to get this car?"

"I didn't kill nobody."

"Yeah? Look, I know you sixteen. It's why you got the tinted glass, right, so the cops won't spot'chu?"

"The tinted glass is dope. The four mags gimme speed an' sleekness. Whisper quiet."

She grimaced. "The four what?"

"The magnum alloy tires. An' that red color? Thass magenta. I had it painted like that with the black trim. You try an' find another car like it, man. I tell you, it's my tag."

"An' those words you got written on the car's ass?"

Miguel frowned at the way she said it. "On the trunk. In pretty script. Cost me a bitch, man." He played with the gold chains around his neck. "It say, 'My Baby does the hanky-panky.' Thass a song."

She laughed, clapping her hands with delight. "He got his own thing together."

"Is that what that crack shit does, make you talk all stupid?"

"Look," she said, as if trying to reason with him, "you work for Spider, jus' like Firebug used to. An' yet you don't want me to light up in your car. Don'chu think that's a little . . . well, contradictory?"

"I don't go t' college like you," he said through a sneer, "an' I don't do crack. You go t' college an' you do crack. Now wun'chu say thass a little . . . well, contradictory?"

She stared through the windshield, chewing on the inside of her mouth. "Not necessarily," she said after a pause.

"You should have more brains than to smoke that shit."

"Oh?" she thundered. "An' what makes you think you have the brains to know better?"

"With me it's the money thing. I'm a runner. I do my bit, get it here, drop it there, duck some bullets. I get paid. I don't need t' be smokin' that shit. I seen the kids that smoke it, man."

"Well, I ain't in the business," she snarled. "I just smoke it. I don't have to think maybe I'm helpin' somebody kill himself."

"Is that wha'chu tryin'na do? Kill yuhself?"

She sighed, slapping her hands against her thighs. "You're missing the point."

"Nah, I think I made my point real good. Look. We almost there."

They stared up at the large building, plumes of black smoke billowing from its windows. "Wow," she said, sucking in air. "I didn't know he was doing this!" Her eyes opened with twisted delight. "Is this him, really?"

"Yeah," Miguel said, mystified. They ran out of the car, holding hands like children, stepping over rows of hoses that lay on the wet street, buying popcorn and beer, cheering when the water gun on a pumper nailed the building with a loud crash that sent bits of metal and wood flying, flames scurrying away. And then he started to like her, seeing that she was funny and twisted and sometimes sad in a way that bothered him. On those nights when Miguel hadn't bothered to find himself some pussy, he could hear Firebug fucking her, could hear her crying and pleading and panting and giggling. He wondered about her. She knew it. One night, after she had fucked Firebug into unconsciousness, she had appeared at Miguel's door, clad only in panties. She squinted from the lamplight. Out there Firebug only used candles. She leaned against the door for a while, staring at him as he lay on the gym mat, smoking. She threw a T-shirt over the lampshade, arranging it to soften the light.

"You were listening," she said.

"Who could help it? They could hear you in Newark. You should be more considerate, think of others."

"I was thinking of others."

He paused to think about that. He was lying there in his jeans, tracing letters in the air with his cigarette. His eyes were far away, almost like he hadn't noticed her standing there half naked. It was a new sensation for her. She sat beside him on the mat, resting a cheek on her knees to stare at him.

"So wha'chu want." He wasn't even looking at her.

"You read books," she said.

He still wasn't looking at her.

"My father hated books," he said, playing with the ash on the tip of his cigarette. It collapsed onto a fingernail. He flicked it away. "He thought they were a waste of time. So I read books."

She passed a finger over the books on a shelf by the nightstand. "An' you read all these books?"

"Yeah." Careless shrug.

"H. G. Wells? Dickens? Oh shit, you got Tolstoy." She pulled out a fat paperback, flipped through its pages.

"Okay, I didn't finish that one. Guy put me t' sleep."

She suddenly reached over and took the cigarette from his mouth. He had to look at her then, and the thought crashed through him: This ain't no girl. This is a woman, a fucken college woman, twenty years old, what girls grow into. He was staring at her tits now. She noticed and grinned approvingly.

"You got real pretty tits," he said. He lit another cigarette because she was smoking his.

"They're real soft, too." She smiled softly, her eyes glazed over as if she were daydreaming. She sat a little closer, her calf scraping up against his. "So why'dju quit school? Din'chu like it?"

He smirked as if he was looking at a guidance counselor who was asking all the stupidest questions.

"My father was right," he said, but then his words seemed to get all tangled up. He cleared his throat. "I mean fuck it, I make more money this way."

"Yeah, but what about tomorrow, baby?" Her voice was a soft caress. "This ain't gonna get'chu nowhere."

He forced a laugh, cigarette smoke stinging his eyes. "I'm someplace now I wasn't before."

"Yeah, but tomorrow, honey, think about tomorrow. Every kid starts out this way. But you can't stay too long. Gotta know when to cut out. Even Spider's countin' the days on one hand. Someday soon he'll tip. Just like a poof. Wha'chu gonna do with your life then?" Her eyes looked concerned. It spooked him a little. She sensed that, and moved closer, the gym mat making tearing sounds.

"What about'chu? What about yuh tomorrow? You can't be makin' no heavy plans if you be suckin' on that pipe."

She fought the grin, her thin lips trembling. "Nobody cares about me," she said, "but I keep hopin' someday I find somebody who cares. Who asks me, 'What about'chu?'" She put a warm hand on his naked shoulder. It slowly worked its way up to his neck.

"Firebug is my friend," he said, not looking at her.

She sighed, shook her head, clicked her tongue, grinned, took her cigarette and gently placed it back between his lips by the other one. "What a heart on you," she said, as if she were taking pity on him. Then she left.

After that he was always uneasy around her, as if she knew some secret about him. Her questions disturbed him, her knowing looks unnerved him, almost as if she had figured him out and knew all the answers. At the last wienie roast, she had picked up on his disgust, teased him about how he wasn't wearing his gold chains or his beat-boy clothes, and he resented that she saw it. They'd been sitting on the hood of his Baby, watching the flames tease the dark rolling clouds.

"So why you so pensive?" she asked bluntly.

"Nothin'." He wasn't going to talk about Cristalena.

She munched on some popcorn. "Maybe it's all gettin'na you. Maybe you ain't so fucken tough." She didn't look at him, flames making her face glow with defiance.

"Shut up."

"I can tell when something's up wit'chu," she said with that smug grin. "You can't hide it from me. Your face is too deep. Too much character. I can see the feelings pulse on it like a strobe. Firebug? He has that blank muskrat face. He don't feel shit. Only time his face looks inhabited is when I'm fucken 'im."

"Can'chu jus' shut up an' enjoy the show?" He shoved a fistful of popcorn into his mouth angrily, spilling kernels everywhere. "All this goddamn talk."

He had walked away from her, over fire hoses and foamy streams of water. He didn't want to be a part of this anymore. It was all Cristalena's fault. Hi, Cristalena, my roommate's an arsonist, he burns down buildings for a living an' we all show up like it's a movie premiere. We chomp on popcorn an' pass beer around an' even rate the fires. ("This one's a seven," Amelia announced from behind him, having followed him, reminding him he had to walk farther.) I'm a drug runner, girl. I work for this gremlin named Spider. I'm sixteen and a half and I have seven thousand dollars. I got these freaks beat, man. I laugh at 'um every mornin' when I see 'um goin' off t' work. I make more money than they do. Dig it, my father, my own fucken father, wha'chu think, he was a self-made man? Nah, I'M A SELF-MADE MAN. He's a self-made mess. Works as a construction man, a bag of muscles, two hands to carry yuh bricks. Gets treated like a sack a' shit all day, comes home, screams and takes it out on the family. My sister was smart. She got pregnant, went off to live with this dumb spick named Jose, now has two kids and welfare, an' where's Jose? But fuck it, at least she got out, right? With huh gone, the ol' man only had me to yell at, t' get whacked by those huge hands that pounded my mother's face into new shapes, but she got back at him, yeah, she became a putona—you know what that is? Thass cocksucking fuck me in the ass whore. She fucked everybody an' everything in sight, in the building, on the block, in the shanty on the empty lot across the street, even jerked a man off once on the BX-17. Like she hadda show him other men wanted huh but my father he wasn't gonna be what white people call a cuckhole a cuckood a Cuckold no sir man, he did what any man woulda done, he left. Took his shit an' booked. The fucken loser would drop a real brick if he saw me sailin' by him in my magenta Baby, the bastid would jus' croak. All he ever had was a beat-up old Falcon. All that car did was whine.

When he flew the coop my ma cried an' cried she was so HAPPY an' then she started makin' it with this guy named Nelo. Yeah, Nelo. Sounds like some kinda doughnut flavor. The fat pig came outta nowhere an' then he was sleepin' in huh bed an' the two of 'um makin' those pig noises all night like that, I couldn't stay there, *fuck that shit.* Like sure I hightailed it outta that shit, into my own shit. Into life on the street an' hangin' out an' creepin' reefa around (nickel bag part reefa, part rug fibers dash oregano with a little roach spray f' flavor), an' then I met Firebug the man who set me (ah-hem) THE MAN WHO SET ME ON THE PATH. Which is why I can never leave it, I can't give it up, I could never leave it I could

Amelia had laughed, tugging on his arm. "You're not made for this," she'd said, caressing Miguel's face, like he was some kind of baby soldier. He remembered the look on her face, suddenly noticed something like it on Firebug's face now, although Firebug seemed annoyed that he was so deep in thought.

"Look, man, you shun't think so much," he said gruffly. "I mean that, bro'. It's nah good in our biz."

"Is that some kinda threat?"

Firebug laughed, his teeth glistening in the candlelight. "I jus' know that thinkin' don't mean shit. Lookit Amelia. That bitch, she thinkin' alla time. Won't shut up with huh shit about life an' love an' whass it get huh? She's just a ravin' bitch. You wanna end up like that?"

Miguel wanted to tell him to shove his goddamn wienie roast, but that's not what came out. "Look, I'll be there," he said roughly. Firebug gave him the address as he rushed out of the apartment and down the stairs on woozy legs. Miguel was grateful for the cold wind biting his face. He buttoned up his Marine coat and walked down Prospect Avenue to where his Baby was parked. He got inside and sat there for a moment in the semi-dark, fingering the pair of furry red dice hanging from the rearview mirror. Already, the car reminded him of Cristalena, as if she had taken it over. She had loved his car, fingered the dice, petted the dash, the string of blue Christmas lights underneath making her pantyhose shimmer electrically. He could feel her presence in the car. That first date, he had driven her down Southern Boulevard from her cousin's house, past a few busy corners where dealers hopped from foot to foot, anxiously dispensing their wares. Miguel even knew some of them. Cristalena's eyes had filled with venom. It was so strong that he had to ask whassup.

"Nothing," she said, looking at him as her face softened. She turned away. "It's just those lowlifes selling that shit. Makes me wish I had a machine gun so I could knock 'um off."

He laughed, something in him touched, while the rest of him stiffened. He shrugged. "It's just business," he said lightly.

"Business nothing. This block used to be nice once, little kids playing, old men playing dominoes. You could hang out. Not now, not anymore. These creeps have stolen it, killed it."

Her righteous anger moved him, filled him with a weird sense of shame that jarred him. He felt remorse; maybe he shouldn't even be going out with someone like her. He stared at her, trying to zero in on her imperfections, but there weren't any. She was a bright-eyed beautiful girl, young and hopeful, untouched by the streets, not out there toking on joints and getting felt up by the posse. Not tarting around in tight-ass putona gear. She was straight and beautiful straight, the first girl he felt it for. He tried to dislike her, but the first date had been like some strawberry-coated fantasy. Her kisses were passionate, her eyes probed him trustingly. There was something about the way they clutched at each other right from the beginning that moved him, made him feel that what they had went far beyond words. He had never experienced that. It forced him to look at his life and what he was a part of. "I'm getting out of this place as soon as I can," she had said, casting worried glances at the dark streets, and he worried for her, saw how she was in danger, how His business had encroached on her. She bit her lip and stared pensively out past raindrops that clung to the windshield in rainbow colors. She didn't know she was sitting beside one of *those* people.

No, Miguel thought, I ain't one a' those people. He turned the engine over, the warm rumble of his Baby rejuvenating him. I'm jus' a runner. A high-paid messenger, a transit man. I hardly even touch the stuff. He imagined himself telling her, and saw her tiny face falling, shattering on the sidewalk like a small mirror.

The car was sluggish, as if his thoughts had seeped into the car through his hands. There was no relief in the driving tonight as he barreled down dark streets, huddled dark masses on corners cringing from his headlights. He grabbed a parking space, his brake lights making bloody stains on the car grille behind. The car idled softly as he messed with the heater vents. A dingy shadow walked up to his window.

"Wha'chu need, bro'?" The voice quivered, from crack or cold, Miguel couldn't tell which. He rolled down his window. "Spider," he said.

The guy stepped back, giving him the reptile eyes. He was new. He took too long. You never take too long on the street because there's always some dude right behind you, waiting to cop your sale. Then there's the cornerboy, a kind of on-site supervisor who watches the personnel and ensures a steady flow of cash and product. It was the cornerboy who came over now, pulling the first kid away from the car with a contemptuous jerk. The others ran forward, chanting, their faces contorted. " 'Ey buoy! Right here, man! Yo yo yo! I got it yaw, jus' wha'chu nee', bruthaa . . ." The cornerboy leaned into the car, his calm voice like a narrator's voice-over.

"Whassup, Miguel? Lookin' f' Spider?"

Miguel clasped his hand. The cornerboy yelled for everybody around him to chill. He rolled his eyes. "Fucken chumps gonna fuck up tonight, I jus' know it. I can feel the shit inna air. They too young f' this shit."

"You tell Spider?"

"Yeah, but'chu know . . . the guy like 'um young." They shared a quiet laugh, then the cornerboy went off to get Spider, who was making the rounds. It was payday. Spider would be a walking armory tonight. Miguel eased his car forward a little and slipped into a dark spot by a gurgling hydrant. The car rolled over a puddle of ice that crackled.

Miguel lit a cigarette. He welcomed the familiar tenseness like an old friend. His mind played him images of his own murder, machine-gun slugs ripping through the car, windshield punctured with holes, glass flying around him like dust, Miguel blindly grasping with hands flailing as the bullets stitched through him. Not teenybopper .22s, but gargantuan automatic-rifle slugs that tumbled into his chest cavity and ripped savagely through lungs, cracking ribs, forcing his stomach out through the gaping rips, tearing huge exit wounds that splattered blood on the windshield like finger paint. Miguel could hear distant sirens, muffled screams, the chink and crackle of falling glass. And dripping. His blood, pouring all over his cherry-red leather seats. He was being wheeled into an operating room, the lights like huge orbiting moons.

There was yelling.

Miguel rolled down his window, tossing out his cigarette. There were dealers all around, their chatter a frantic bellowing that seemed to come from some monkey house. It was the kind of haggling that sometimes was punctuated by gunfire. He lit another cigarette, feeling like a soldier in a foxhole, waiting for the barrage. When Spider tapped on a window, Miguel gave an involuntary jump. He leaned over and unlocked the door. Spider jumped in quickly and slammed it shut. They'll wait 'til he's trapped in my car, Miguel thought, and they'll surround it quickly an' pump it fulla shells.

Spider let out a string of curses. His dark curly hair seemed tangled, the stubble on his cheeks and chin turning into real beard growth. His large anxious eyes glittered as they darted from spot to spot along the street. "Shit," he said, leaning back, sneakered foot up on the dash. He passed Miguel his hand and Miguel squeezed it for a while. "I don't believe these crazy li'l shits, man. Everythin' goin' crazy, pana. I think there's gonna be trouble." Spider gave Miguel a solid stare with his dark, troubled eyes.

"What kinda trouble?" Miguel felt a tremor run through him. He dragged on his cigarette long and hard, sending ashes fluttering down onto his pants like tiny leaves.

"One a' thum kids, man. I tell you. You see why I gotta be careful? I take on everybody sometimes. I'm too trustin'. The kid's been wif' me f' two months, a good kid. He's been runnin' some shit f' me. So this week I gave him the pad. A small one—five grand." Spider paused for effect. "Would'ju believe that brat took off wif' it? He musta been a crackhead, man, I don't see how that got past me. Now I got cops on my ass. They runnin' all over the place, lookin' f' trouble. All the kids out here is freakin'. A lotta thum is packin'. If they pull on a cop . . ."

"Did'ju tell the cops what happened?"

"Did I tell the . . ." Spider faded out, squinting past the windshield as some guy approached the car. Miguel froze, but it was nothing. "Course I tole the cops. You think they gonna believe me? Man, it's too bad about that kid." He shook his head, swiping Miguel's cigarette and puffing on it. "I hope he cleared out good." There was a weary sadness in his voice. Coupled with the beard, it made Spider seem old and wise in a bummy kind of way. "He gotta be an example, you read me?" He whispered hoarsely. "My ass is too precious t' me. He's gonna be an example. You understand that, right? 'Cause if he gets away with that, every li'l pancho be dickin' me up the ass. I can't risk it."

"So wha'chu gonna do?"

Spider frowned. He passed a hand through his hair, eyes scanning the streets. "But it's already outta my hands," he muttered, reaching into his army jacket and taking out a business envelope. He flicked it open, counting the bills inside. "You my pana, right? I mean, how you feelin'?"

"I'm feelin' okay." Miguel lit another cigarette because Spider kept his.

"Firebug's been tellin' me you in the dumps."

Miguel shrugged "No. I thought'chu an' Firebug was on the outs."

Spider grinned, still sifting through the envelope. "Ohh, I wun't say we friends. But sometimes you can say our business functions interact."

Miguel was waiting for more of the scoop, but there was nothing coming. He knew Firebug and Spider had been real tight. It was Firebug who recommended Miguel to Spider, got him working. The funny thing was that by that time, the two of them weren't so tight anymore. "We jus' ain't so tight like before," Firebug would say, shrugging it off every time Miguel brought it up. "Jus' a business thing." But if Miguel hung with Spider, Firebug refused to come along. The same went for Spider.

"Firebug say you gettin' all gloomy gus an' shit. I can see it on you now. You know all you gotta do is talk t' me. I'll help you out, bro'. We buddies, right?"

Miguel shrugged. "Sure."

"You need some bennies? I got bennies."

"Nah."

"Smoke, right? I got some good stuff."

"Nah man."

Spider sighed. "Bitches. You need some bitches? I know Firebug be hookin' you up wif' thum dogs he knows. But I know some real nice girls, gentle an' juicy, not crack babies. If you want, I—"

"Nah man. It ain't like that."

"Look, I known you f' how long? Seven months? Some shit like that, right? We don't go that far back, but'chu know what? I trus'ju. I trus'ju 'cause I can see what kinda kid'ju are. You are a more balanced kid than any kid I ever worked wif'. You got this balance in there that keeps you from bein' as stupid as these other putzes. You got brains, bro'. Not criminal brains; criminal brains, thass jus' bein' selfish an' crafty. I'm talkin' real brains, the kind can get'chu places. You can go far, fartha than me, even, but'chu need t' be tough, can't get there wif' all this thinkin' an' shit. Yeah, I think maybe yuh thinkin' too much. About the operation, about things. Maybe about things that gotta be done. You feelin' spooked?"

"Nah man, I ain't spooked."

"Runnin' is a tough business. Some people take t' it; others, well, mosta my runners don't make it this long. They move on t' another kinda work or they get tattooed by gunfire. You wanna talk about maybe doin' some other kinda work?"

"Nah man. This is it. It's got nothin' t' do with all that. It's jus' this ain't no kinda life, bro'."

Spider stared, cigarette tip burning bright. "Go ahead. I'm lis'nin'."

Miguel sighed. He couldn't explain about how he felt, about how he had been happy and nicely doped and there were bitches and parties and a wicked sense of pride and then he met Cristalena. Okay, fuck it, she's just some girl, he thought right away, trying to break her down into bite-size chunks he could handle. So what if she don't like what he does? Plenty of girls out there do, and he saw them, saw several after that first date with Cristalena, like he was trying to erase her image, wipe it out, make her into just another bitch, but it didn't work. The fact was there wasn't any other bitch. Cristalena had this hold on him. It was like voodoo. He hadn't known anything like that before. All he knew was that quick-fucking shit, lying there beside whass huh name? Ignoring the smell because it feels good, she standing lying sitting on the bed face down ass up thass the way I what was that pop? Did my gym hat break? Her lips going Gimme Gimme Gimme like you could buy them with a joint, some crack, some blow, or maybe that five-hundred-dollar watch a friend donated after that last favor. Sex was just another deal, another transaction, something that was available as long as your pocket bulged with money. So what? A year ago he was a desperate putz, say anything, do anything to get it. Now, who cares? You don't even have to like the bitch. It's what's in her pants, under her skirt. The rest of that shit is *disposable*. They know it sometimes, they get loud and shriek and maybe get violent, like that bitch Carmen who pulled a knife on Carlos last week. He threw her down two flights of stairs and kicked her up. Now Carmen has a new boy, some posse kid who's gunning for Carlos. Who needs that? Miguel got what he could, like everybody else, and he had maybe three girlfriends he was fucking regularly, bringing them smoke and pretty stones, and then three became five, because a man should have diversity, and those gold chains around his neck, man—they draw. The girls always ask if he has a piece. Miguel didn't have one, but he had a box full of blow, "snuff," he called it, like he was Napoleon. That was enough, and later, with fluttering eyelids and twitching arms, she'd be giving it up, pillow muffling her cries. What is it with these condoms popping all the time? And the next morning, there's some fat ass bitch lying there bloated with that face going, "Where's the blow?"

Cristalena was a dream compared to that, a real person. Skin like ice cream, black hair flowing down to her ass in shimmery waves, braided here and there with a piece of ribbon. Like a present, all wrapped up. Didn't want blow, blunt, crack, didn't ask if he had a piece, laughed at his gold chains. "Man, you actually wear those?" She laughed, tiny hand covering her mouth.

"They're dope," he said, fingering them, amused at her laughter.

"Naah, thass goofy," she said. "I never went out with a beat boy before."

"I ain't no beat boy."

"Yeah. You are." With a smug nod.

"Nah man."

"I insist."

The gold chains were gone now, too. He reached for them now, used to finger them while lost in thought, but they weren't there. Spider was staring at him.

"Look man," Spider said, "I'm in bad shape right now. Problems are everywhere. I'm surrounded by people I don't trust. I got posse wars, kids shootin' up my shit, other kids shootin' thum up. Now this dumb li'l fuck runnin' out on me, an' when they find 'im, they're gonna . . . I jus' need one person I can trust, man. Everything else is bullshit, but I need t' have people around me that I can count on. Somebody I can talk to. Thass all." He paused as if what he had just said made him uncomfortable. He looked out at the street. "Firebug, he was tellin' me about how you two guys was always in detention together, in school. Elmer Bogart, right?" He was smiling and nodding like a gypsy in a carnival booth. "I went there too, I was there before you, but I know that room. Man, I spent a lotta time in that room. No shit." He was lighting a cigarette of his own with his gold lighter. "The room wif' no windows. An' mattresses on the walls."

Miguel smiled at the memory. "Gym mats. They were like gym mats."

"It true that one time you an' Firebug was in there an' he set one a' thum mattresses on fire so you could break out?"

Miguel laughed, nodding slowly. The memory was like an old newsreel. They had been crazy not to frisk that boy. The fire got them both suspended.

"This is all some kinda fate, don'chu think so? I mean, us all comin' from the same place, meetin' up like this? Thass how I see it."

Miguel nodded, his eyes distant. Yeah, Firebug had been fate. Spider had been fate. Cristalena. *Fate.*

Spider handed him the envelope. "Boss man like you. He tole me I should sweeten it up this time, so there's some extra juice in there. Jus' so you know I take good care a' you." He grinned, his eyes twinkling wetly. He looked away.

"There's something else," he added reluctantly.

Miguel tightened his grip on the wheel. "Okay."

"This pad thing. We gotta double the take this time around, jus' a little insurance. I need somebody reliable t' handle this. You think maybe you could . . . ?"

Miguel sighed. "Yeah. Sure. No problem. When?"

There was relief on Spider's face. "Maan, you'll get in good f' this. Gonna be in real tight. I knew I could count on you, bro'. We talkin' ten grand. Who could I trus' wif' money like that?"

"How you wanna work this?"

Spider paused, stroking his beard. "I'll beep you. Okay?"

"All right."

"My pana."

Spider gave him a quick hug. "See yuh." He jumped out, slamming the door, shoulders hunched from the cold, another dark shadow scurrying from the light.

2

Amelia was sitting beside him in the car. She was quiet, which was the way Miguel wanted it. He wasn't into this wienie roast.

"Stop the car, please," Amelia said suddenly as they coursed up Union Avenue, dark and ugly from the busted streetlamps and the clusters of crackheads camping out on corners. It was like she had woken up from a trance, her dark eyes turned inward. Miguel couldn't understand it. She made him nervous when she talked and she made him nervous when she was quiet. He pulled over to the curb.

"We're already late," he said.

"So what. We seen this before. I won't be long." With a shrug and a hop she was outside, stepping over to a cluster of crackheads that she must've been in with. There were hugs and kisses from one girl who looked like her face had been bitten by an army of beetles. Her ratty hair hung down like seaweed. Amelia took her aside and they exchanged something. Then they both walked into an alley between a small pentecostal church and a rat-eaten shack advertising cheap tires. Miguel saw the flash of a lighter, the curling blue flame inside a glass pipe bowl. He frowned and honked impatiently.

Amelia returned to the car, slamming the door and throwing her head back, her eyes shut tight. "Don't say anything," she said.

"I don't give a fuck myself," Miguel said, stepping on the pedal. The car lurched.

"How can you be so proud of saying a thing like that?" She shook her head, eyes still shut.

"You should talk about pride."

She turned her gleaming eyes on him. "There you go again. You're such a snotty little shit. Okay, so I smoke crack. Big fucking deal. Am I the first? No, right? Ain't there enough of us out there?"

"Sure there are. But how many go to college?"

"Damn. Thass what bothers you, isn't it? I wonder why. It's like this hang-up you have, like I'm committing some kind of sacrilege. What about you, kiddo? Don'chu think a sixteen-and-a-half-year-old kid who reads Tolstoy who happens to be Latino is sacrilege?"

"Oh so what."

"It's not very typical I mean. So don't get all snotty with me. Yeah, I've gone to college. I took a leave, okay? I ain't been to college in six months and it don't look like I'm going to make the next semester. So what? What do you know about it? I've been to college. More of a reason to smoke crack than anything."

"I don't know what the fuck you talkin' about."

"I'm sayin'," she yelled, "tha'chu hardly got a right to talk about me! If I wanna destroy myself, it's my right, do you hear? I ain't out to destroy anyone else. Unlike you. You with your goddamn business."

"What? What the fuck is that?" Miguel grimaced, his foot down on the pedal. His Baby was careening down dark streets like a missile.

"I'm sayin' you ain't so innocent either. I'm sayin' you run around delivering crack shit all day so pathetic pieces a' shit like me can smoke it. You're worse than me."

"I don't wanna hear this shit in my car," Miguel snapped, starting to yell. "I ain't gonna get lectured by some crackhead!"

"Oh yeah, the kid knows, he's got ethics. Go ahead, act like you care about someone other than yourself."

"Where is that fucken shit from now? I mean, what the fuck are you talkin' about?"

"I'm sayin' if you don't give a fuck about me, then stop talkin' t' me about crack. Just say I'm an existentialist exercising her right to self-destruct, to plan an exit. All right?"

"But you don't . . ." Miguel stopped, gripping the wheel as he came to a red light. His neck throbbed with anger.

"I don't like crack," he said.

He suddenly felt like he was Cristalena, staring out resentfully through the windshield at all the hulking shapes she saw as the enemy.

"But thass your livelihood," Amelia said, lighting a cigarette. Her voice had softened with weariness.

"I don't like what it does," Miguel said, as if trying out new words. He felt he had said too much, even though there was more he wanted to say. He fumbled for the words but they didn't come. She smiled softly behind the swirling cigarette smoke.

"Your problem is you got heart, baby," she said tenderly. "You got too much heart f' this. I knew that about'chu! I wasn't a psych major f' nothing, you know. I had'ju pegged from the start. A real thinking loner. Out to get what he can, but filled with remorse. Sorta like the vampire in that Anne Rice book. You ever read her?"

"No."

"You should pick it up. Fuck, maybe I'll even lend you mine if you're nice t' me."

"I don't read books no more. They don't mean shit."

"You don't mean that."

"What do you know what I mean or don't? Whatayou, some translator?"

"You jus' don't, I can tell. You must have a hundred books in your room."

"My father was right, man. Books don't mean shit. I guess you only read them when you don't have experience. Lookit me now. The streets. Thass a education. Books din't teach me shit. Neither did school. They don't lead nowhere."

She smiled. "Double negative." She moved closer. "You're just mad now, and confused. I can see it. You don't belong on these streets doin' this. You're too sensitive. You're yearning for something better." She sat up a little with a funny, theatrical sigh. "You know, thass funny because so am I. You see how alike we are?"

"No." He didn't look at her, as if he were too busy driving.

"Lookit'chu. I can see it every day, changing more an' more. You don't even dress the same anymore. What happened to the gold chains, that gold watch you had on prominent display, hey lookout, here comes the big man? You look all dark-colored now, like you in mourning. That Marine coat is new. Where's your Raiders coat?"

He shrugged, searching the streets with his eyes. "Hey, Firebug said this place was on Jackson, right?"

She didn't answer, stubbing out her cigarette, seeming to curl up in her seat like a cat. She was in a white dress with lace stockings. He really hadn't thought of it until now, when she pulled her coat off and sent the bulky thing tumbling into the back seat. Her bony shoulders stuck out girlishly.

"Are you in love with someone, Miguel?" Her voice was soft and pleading.

Miguel didn't say anything. They seemed to be heading nowhere. He hit Jackson Avenue and reached the el on Westchester, watching the flash of a passing train.

"I just don't care about anything anymore," Amelia said, her voice bitter, petulant. "Just wanna get everything over with. You got heart like I used to have heart. But no more, you know? I mean, I still got some left, but I'm tearing it out. I mean methodically. I'm chipping away at it piece by piece. I'm not gonna be hurt anymore."

"Is all this about Firebug?"

She laughed silently, covering her face. There was something about the way her fingers fell over her face that made something tender pulse in him. She peeked at him with large, sleepy eyes, then shook hair from her face with a defiant motion.

"Are you serious? Firebug?" Her voice hardened. "You think I'm in love with him? You think he loves anyone? He's a gone maniac. He's a twisted little pipe stem."

Miguel shook his head, trying to concentrate on the streets. He didn't care if they found the wienie roast or not. "Where is this fucken place?"

"He's hurt me a hundred times. Now he can't hurt me anymore. I tol'ju, I'm growin' a rock-hard heart, man. Nobody can hurt me. Only I can hurt me. I do that better than anyone. But Firebug, he'll hurt anyone. He hurt me and he'll hurt you too, Miguel, I swear it. You shun't trust him so much."

Miguel shrugged. "He hasn't done anythin' to me. We go far back. I owe him."

"That won't matter. You'll see. You'll have to learn the hard way. I think you have heart, maybe thass why you hate this life. But Firebug, he don't have that. You either get harder than him or he'll eat'chu up. He loves this life. He's like some kind of insect. He's got that tough exoskeleton. His bones are all on the outside. He'll do anything; trick, bite, turn on anyone. His father used to burn him. Did he tell you that?"

"No." Miguel felt left out, like maybe he wasn't so tight with him after all. The car was hardly moving as he listened.

"His father was sick, got his head all fucked up. A furnace exploded all over him. He thought it was God punishing him. So whenever he got mad at Firebug, he'd take him over to the stove an' punish him." Her voice shook, her eyes glaring through the windshield. "Ain't that sick? To punish him. Just like God. I couldn't believe that."

Miguel stopped the car. He was looking in his pockets for that scrap of paper where he wrote the address of the building they were looking for.

"Firebug torches a building as if he were making a bonfire for his father to jump over. He looks up an' says, 'Take that, Pop.' But his father's never gonna jump it. His father don't even know. Maybe thass why Firebug don't like to hang around to watch. He's fighting his own war thing. He don't got time for love or friends. He's a kind of insect. He's a sick little leech. I hate him."

A shiver of disgust passed through her. She put her white lace feet up on the dash, toes gripping at the glove compartment lock.

"Then how come you with him?" Miguel said, wanting to shut her up already.

"I told you. He has a big dick."

The words caught him off guard. The laughter tumbled out of him in choppy spurts. He looked at her sitting there with her face looking slightly triumphant, and he liked her. "There's more to it than that," he said, fighting the laughter.

"No. Guys can feel that way, why not girls? Yeah, I like his dick. He has a good one. You can count on it to get'chu off. Don't think there's anything else he has to offer. He has nothing. No heart, no soul, nothing to cling to. An empty shell. You think I'm worried? I don't depend on him. I don't have expectations, so how can I get burned? You can get more burned than I can. He knows where your money is, did'ju know that? Why don'chu open a bank account someplace?"

Miguel stiffened. He could hear sirens wailing in the distance.

"Whass that mean?"

"You keep your money hidden in the apartment. Like if Firebug don't know where it is."

"Ahhh, come on."

"He laughs about it, about the way you trust him. Damn, even I know where you keep it."

"Yeah? Where?"

"In this old Kenneth Cole shoe box buried deep in your closet under some other shoe boxes. Firebug says you have them counted. Third one down on the left, something like that."

"Shit." He smacked the steering wheel. Why was she doing this? Adding more uncertainty. Sure, he had always suspected Firebug of digging up his stash. He had moved it around twice already after getting the feeling his money had been riffled through. There had been that sudden interrogation one Sunday when he had come home after fucking the Suarez Twins and found his money in a different order than how he had left it. He barged into Firebug's room, where he found him lying on his mat with the radio on, his glassy eyes staring at the ceiling.

"You know what?" Firebug said dreamily. "It's weird but when you look at the reflection of the street coming through the window, up on the ceiling, you can see those little shimmer things on the edge, on a real hot day, like flames."

"Did'ju go through my money?" Miguel yelled.

"Nah man, I swear man, I wun't do shit like that, bro', you like my brother . . ." His muskrat face had grown solemn, eyes huge and doglike in their humble suffering. Of course it had been him, who else? But what was Miguel going to do? He kept changing the hiding place. Now, sitting with Amelia, he realized he was going to have to change it again. He started the car, jumped into gear, sped down toward the el.

"Put it in a bank, Miguel."

"I can't get a fucken bank card! I can only get this passbook savings shit. Thass bullshit, man. What good is it f' me t' be my own man if the bank treats me like some li'l kid?"

"But'chu are a little kid."

He didn't look at her. A creepy thought went through his mind. What if Firebug had sent both of them on a fake wienie roast so he could grab Miguel's money? Sick thought.

"I think you should get out of this fucken business."

"Will you shut the fuck up? Haven't you done enough? Said enough? Goddamn. You should learn t' be more quiet. I'm still tryin'na find this place!"

"You went up the wrong street," Amelia said calmly. "It's just off Jackson. Look, there goes a fire engine."

He followed the speeding flashing red blur, wailing and honking as it careened up a side street, and then they saw it, a five-story building with bright yellow flames dancing wildly in every window. Clusters of people milled around, bumpy silhouettes that seemed to linger only for a moment on their way to more important scenes.

"Wow," Amelia said. "Another big one."

Miguel crawled up the street slowly, slipping into a parking spot a block down from the fire. He had already spotted some of Firebug's friends, leaning against a parked car right across the street, their faces glowing from the flames. Sammy, Jackie, that girl everybody called Two Ton because she had a fat ass, and that little pimp kid named Careta, who was Miguel's age but already had set up a fine stable of young rentable pussy. Miguel looked at them and sighed, not wanting to join them. He expected Amelia to hop up like she usually did and drag him over to where they were, so they could stand and watch with their beers in moist brown bags, cheering and booing like they were watching teams out on a field. They'd all end up at Mongo's, where Firebug would already be sitting at the bar with the juke blaring house music and his eyes spinning with booze, smoke, and pride. He would demand descriptions, basking in the glow, pausing to explain his technique like a tennis pro. Amelia would be in his lap, being cradled and caressed and kissed in that crazy lustful way Firebug had, more like rage than tenderness. That's when Firebug looked like a young kid again; forget the stubble and the dizzy red eyes. He would laugh and toss flaming scrunchballs and pump quarters into the blinking juke that squatted in the back like an old fat whore. Then Miguel would have to find pussy because he knew Firebug; he would head back to the apartment and they'd start fucking and he'd have to hear it. So he made it a tradition to find some pussy. If there wasn't one around at Mongo's, he could drive up to Tinton Avenue and maybe find one, like Yolanda or Maria or Rachel or that girl he fucked a hundred times, whass-huh-name, the one who dyed her hair blond but only succeeded in making it turn a crunchy bronze. Then Miguel would go up to the apartment with his catch and they'd all party for a while before Firebug and Amelia retired to the bedchamber for some fucking. Miguel would take *Whoever* into his room, and the fuckfest would begin, each trying to OUTLOUD the other, even past the blaring music (Miguel would move one of his stereo speakers out into the living room), all of it part of a wienie-roast tradition that had died for him. First he began to shy away from the crowd of young street thug arsonist gunslingers. Then he stopped with the fuck contests. Some nights he'd be lying in his room, listening to Amelia riding Firebug's cock, lying there absently staring at his cigarette and wondering about where he was going and what he was going to do.

She was right about him. He was weak, sensitive. Shouldn't be in the business. He wasn't cold enough. Maybe she wasn't either. She wanted to be cold, but she wasn't there yet. He stared at her as she sat there in her white dress, her legs folded all over the place in pretty lace. She noticed him staring, shifted position, tucking her legs under so she seemed to move closer. The wildly dancing flames illuminated them. It was like being in a rock club, surrounded by strobes and flashing lights.

"I wonder what they be sayin' about us," she said softly, gesturing at Firebug's friends. "Considering we're in the car alone, together. An' last time, too, pretty much. Until you ran off an' tried t' escape me."

Miguel half laughed. "You can go join 'um if you want."

"I'd rather stay here with you, Miguel."

He stared at her for a moment, until something intense in her eyes made him look away. Her voice sounded like she was making a commitment. It was then that Miguel realized that she had been getting prettier and prettier in obvious ways, with clothes and earrings and even painted nails, little frills that he noticed and commented on. "Thass a nice blouse." "Heey, you fucken painted yuh nails! I din't know that." She seemed to blush when he noticed, to laugh and on occasion curtsey. Her words to him now had become more intimate. She seemed to watch him carefully and had immediately picked up his sudden shifts of mood, almost as if she could read him, as if she knew him and anything that he could say would never surprise her. She always rated his girls. "So, tha' girl, she really your type?" Or maybe: "Hmmm. Another blonde." Or that last time, when his heart hadn't been in it because he had been trying to erase Cristalena from his mind: "It really looks t' me like you jus' scooped this one off the street. An' lookit'cha eyes, you don't look like you're here." He had walked away from her, trembling a little. How did she know him?

He took out his cigarettes. "I'm surprised you don't wanna be over there," he said, gesturing with his chin at their little Firebug booster crowd.

"I'm sick of them. I used to celebrate them, to make speeches, to say things nobody ever understood. Except you. You picked up on me right away, din'chu? The only person. That time when I made a toast to the spirit of Nero? An' nobody got it but'chu, you were laughing, an' then you said, 'We should get a fiddle an' shit.' I fell in love wit'chu on the spot."

The trumpet of a fire truck blared as it sped by with a truculent whoosh, lights blazing, brakes wheezing as the truck slowed. Another followed with even more noise, horns and sirens going like a mad kiddie tantrum. Miguel watched as big chunks of building came crashing down just beyond the engines. Beams and crackling wood careened down. Firebug's friends applauded and cheered appreciatively.

"I don't think you know what it's like to grow up being a Latino girl with brains. I don't mean that in a conceited way."

Miguel laughed. "I know you got brains."

"You don't understand. I grew up with three other sisters. A real Amazon tribe. Two of my sisters are already married, got married in their early twenties. Right on time. All they cared about was clothes and jewelry and being in vogue. Cooking classes. Meeting the right man kind of shit. My younger sister, she just started college. She's no psych major. She's going into hotel management, though I think that's only because of the guy she's in love with. You follow the man in my family. See, my pop, he's a good man, worked hard all his life, but he wanted boys. Never got 'um. Don't think he was ready f' girls. Taught us all how t' play baseball with him on Randalls Island. You should check out my curveball, bro'. I could strike you out."

"Get the fuck."

She leaned forward and stroked a cheek with her fingernails, softly.

"My father, he was scared f' us. I think he would've known what to do with boys, but girls? About the only thing he knew was that they should stay virgins and get married off as quick as possible. An' you know, so far he's got a good batting average, except f' me an' my younger sister Marta, though I think she's almost there. She's been working this guy she's with now for a year already. She's pleasing to the eye, runs to the kitchen at the first sign of a man. Can cook, sew, she loves to do laundry. Never argues with a man. Shit, she's almost like an oriental.

"Me, I came out different. I argued with guys. I was good at math. I was on the debating team. I didn't think much about clothes and makeup, I thought that shit was stupid. I thought I could make my life anything I wanted to, just because I had brains, but then I saw people just hated me because I wasn't like everybody else, I didn't accept stuff, I was always questioning it all. Girls thought I was snotty and strange, and guys avoided me. I ended up hanging with people nobody liked—junkies, winos, potheads, hookers. My father hated it. When I told him I wanted to be a therapist, he just glared at me. He didn't even want to hear about

City College. That's not where I belonged, I was wasting my time. So . . ."

She had pulled her legs up, her chin resting on her knees. Her face seemed calm and rested, almost delicate and tender in the flickering red lights of the fire trucks.

"That why you got out?"

She frowned. "I'm jus' tired. I get tired of things. Sometimes life is fulla shit. It's all self-deception. You ever read Sartre?"

"No."

"I guess the whole thing is the biggest self-deception there is. Just look at this street, man. All these people sucking on this shit and convincing themselves that it's life. Some people do it real good. The better you are at fooling yourself, the happier you'll be. Some people, they can't do it at all." She stared at him. "What's made you change, Miguel? Is it a girl?"

Miguel frowned. He had been holding the pack of cigarettes without doing anything. Now he took one out and lit it. "Yeah," he said.

"I knew it." There was a sad resignation in her voice. "But'chu can't be in love," she said, fighting it. "You're only sixteen. You don't even know wha'chu want."

She snatched his cigarette and took a few quick puffs.

"Yeah, but I'm startin' t' find out."

And he snatched the cigarette back.

After that there wasn't much talk. The fire died down, the crowd broke up and began heading for cars or else the long stroll over to Mongo's for the after-fire party. Miguel sped down Westchester Avenue, the wind moaning against the windows. When he got to the bar, she asked him if he was coming in. She was slipping on her flats reluctantly, as if waiting for him.

"Nah," he said, "I have to meet Spider."

She nodded, stepped out of the car. Right by the door of the bar, she turned to look at him, remorse on her face.

Miguel headed back to his apartment to check on his stash. He hadn't meant to lie to Amelia, but Firebug was getting pretty weird, staring at him funny, bitching to Spider; this was all news to him. He had to find another place to hide that money. It made a comforting pile as he lay it all on his mat, trying to figure out where to hide it next. He tucked the stuff back into its drawstring bag and walked out into the living room, feeling his room was already all cased out. He thought about hiding it in the car seat, but Firebug was always moving the thing around. Then he stared at the fake petunias up on the wall and got an idea.

He took the fake petunias down, noticing the wooden border around the back for support. He got some electrical tape and some newspaper and secured his bag to the board. He covered it in newspaper to flatten the bulge and to seal it up nicely. Then he put the fake petunias back up. There shouldn't be any way for the bastid to know.

The petunias reminded him of Cristalena. He didn't know why. He sank down into the car seat, staring at the fake flowers, thinking of getting her some real ones.

3

He knew her back then as Lena.

She used to sit in front of him in French class. She had the most perfect little ass he had ever seen, round and firm and perky in those blue slacks, tight as skin until they flared out gently at the calves. She wore them with Pro Keds.

Miguel used to bother her. He would stomp on her Keds to dirty them. He would throw scrunchballs at her. She would smack him with her fists, hard. "You asshole, you fucka, you bastid, lea' me the fuck alone." There was an intense anger flashing in her eyes that insulted him. He kept bothering her. There's nothing like a challenge.

One day he was in the schoolyard with Firebug when this guy named Raul came over. He was tall and thin and had all his regulation beat-boy gear in order. He was quiet, a loner type nobody fucked with too much because he had mauled a few faces up pretty good when he needed to. He came right over to Miguel, a plastic straw in his mouth. He pointed the nibbled end at him. "Miguel, right?"

Miguel nodded. He was leaning up against the chain link. "So?"

"I jus' ratha get it out inna open now than fuck around. If we gotta settle it, we settle it, man t' man, I don't care you got a crew o' what." He looked at Firebug, who was sitting at Miguel's feet like an arrogant Doberman.

"Yeah, I'm his crew," he said with mockery and defiance.

"This between him an' me," Raul said.

"Whass between you an' me?" Miguel's stomach began to tighten. He had been sucking face yesterday night in that vestibule on Tinton Avenue. Was this Rosa's boy? Or maybe he was Tina's? He had stuck half his hand up her pussy in the empty gym last week. There were others.

"You been hasslin' my girl. I wan'chu t' know, she spoken for."

Miguel's face twisted with derision. "What fucken girl?"

"Cristalena."

"Crissawhat?"

Firebug burst into laughter, clapping his hands.

"Cristalena, mothafucka."

"Ohhhh yeah, Lena. That homely girl in my French class."

Raul didn't laugh. He stepped closer. A granite hardness came over his face that killed the laughter. He's gonna bop me, Miguel thought.

"Call huh homely again," Raul said calmly.

"No."

"Come on."

"Fuck you, man."

"Fuck me?" Raul looked him up and down, eyes opened wide with derision. He laughed and shook his head. "You jus' leave huh alone, bee, you'll be all right." He walked away from him, still laughing.

"You think he's laughing at us?" Firebug asked, rising up as if he would run after him.

"Ahhh, who gives a fuck," Miguel said, shrugging it off. He had more girls than he knew what to do with. He chucked Cristalena right out of his mind after that as not being worth the risk. And that was pretty much it for her. Months later he would drop out of school and never see her again, at least not until that day two months ago, when they bumped into each other on Prospect Avenue. He was on his way to his Baby with a package of material when they spotted each other and froze simultaneously. She laughed, covered her mouth. Arrays of curvy dimples appeared, her eyes sparkling, her hair flowing down her back in a long ponytail that made her face seem small and serene, like the image on a cameo. She had on a puffy sweater and tight jeans. It was the same girl, the one that hadn't liked him, only she was twenty times more gorgeous now.

"Oh shit," he said, his eyes wide.

"Miguel, right? Damn, I feel like I'm sittin' in French class."

She remembered his name. "Lena," he said to her, holding out his hand. She clasped it quickly.

"You look different," she said.

"Yeah?"

"Yeah. You're kinda cute now." Her eyes widened as though she were shocked at herself. He laughed.

"Wow, man, you look almost the same."

They nodded to each other, not knowing how to continue. They fumbled for words, watching the traffic pass.

"Man, you look real good," he said, admiring her.

Cristalena smiled gratefully. She looked up the street and then she said, "So wha'chu been doin'?"

Miguel grinned proudly. "I'm doin' good, you know. I got a nice car, a heavy job, good money. How about'chu?"

She smirked. "I'm in high school. What else? I think I wanna be a dress designer." She shrugged. "I work part-time in a boutique." Her eyebrows knitted together. "So you're not in school?"

The question caught him off guard. He shifted his weight. "Nah, nah, I jus', you know, hadda go t' work, an' then I landed in a good situation, so I don't, you know . . ." She was squinting at him like she didn't understand a word. He shrugged and laughed. "Anyway, I got a good job."

He showed her his car. She laughed and said, "Yeah, right," because she knew he couldn't be very much older than she was, but he had keys, and he shoved his license under her pretty nose.

"No fucken way," she said, her voice all catty like the old days, when she used to push him away with her fists. She looked it up and down. "How'dju do it?"

He grinned and shrugged.

"You did some kinda trick," she said.

"The company I work for needs me t' have a car. So they swung it for me. But I can drive real good, I swear."

"I don't know if I wanna find out," she said, handing the card back. "But thass a beautiful car." She peered into it. He unlocked it and tossed his package into the back seat.

"Listen, you wanna lift?"

She looked at him. "Ohh no. Not with that license. I mean, who knows if you can even—"

"I can, trust me." He opened the door for her. She took a sniff of those leather seats, and that was it, she was in there, feeling them up. Any other girl, Miguel would've boasted about the many times he'd had the trunk fixed to cover up the bullet holes, but right away he sensed that Cristalena wasn't that kind of girl.

"My cousin's house is on 156th Street and Southern Boulevard. I was going there now."

"I'll drop you." He climbed in and sat behind the wheel. She was caressing the dash.

"This is a real pretty car."

He grinned with pride, turning on the tiny blue Christmas lights he had strung up under the dash. She laughed with delight. He turned the car over with a sweet rumble, and then he noticed he was nervous. The car managed like it was stuck in gooey caramel, because a car is like a horse sometimes. When you're tight with it, it senses your mood. Miguel's nervousness flowed into the car. With any other girl he'd be boasting by now, working his way around her to see what she wanted from him, what it would take to make her thighs part. Look, I make eight hundred dollars a week, I got a car, I live on my own, I got blow an' smoke. You like my chains? I even get shot at sometimes! Ain't that wild, man? Just like in the movies! But with Cristalena, he was tense. The ride was pretty quiet-going when she suddenly laughed softly and said, "My God, those chains."

He fingered them. "You like 'um?"

"Nah, they make you look like some pimp, or a crack dealer. Are you some posse boy?"

"No."

"Mostly posse boys wear that jacket right now."

"This eight-ball thing? Nah, it's jus' a fashion. I work by myself usually."

"So what is it you do, then."

He swallowed. "I work in this lumber place down Southern Boulevard. A friend a' the family runs it. It's like havin' a job f' life. I make good money an' I'm well connected." He leaned over, reached into the glove compartment, and gave her one of his cards, little jazzy things that Spider had printed up. (Spider loved all that corporate shit.) It had his name and his beeper number. And his specialty.

"Materials," she read, looking puzzled. "Whass that?"

"Thass what I do."

"Wow. Your own business card. Mr. Success. You doin' good. I don't know many kids from school are even halfway set up yet. You got a jump on everybody."

"I was lucky. I had good connections."

"You ever going back to school?"

He sighed. "Yeah," he said, without conviction.

"Hey, thass my stop." She pointed to an oncoming corner. Miguel pulled over.

"It was fun seein' you," he said awkwardly.

"Yeah, me too. Maybe I see you around?"

"Yeah."

He watched her scamper off across the street, charmed by the memories of her sweet caboose in those slacks, now an even more delicious vision. It was like she had returned from the past just to taunt him. Seeing her made him think he wanted a girl like that, someone clean and untainted, not someone rubbed raw by the streets. The next night he was fucking a girl named Dora, her ass a bumpy cushion for his thrusts, and he kept imagining it was Cristalena. None of the girls he had at hand even came close.

Maybe he would've gotten over meeting her if he had never seen her again, but now he kept running into her. On Southern Boulevard, in bodegas on 149th Street, on Prospect Avenue with her crinkle-haired cousin. It was never a quick hello or just a nod; they always walked right up to each other, no matter what the distance (she once ran two blocks to catch up with him), coughing self-consciously, struggling for words, lingering even when the words died and there was already a goodbye coming. They shared laughs and small jokes. One time in the Morales discount store, she grabbed his hand and steered him over to the lipstick counter.

"Okay, you gotta tell me which one," she said, grabbing a lipstick and daubing it on quickly. She checked herself in the little round mirror. "This one? Or is it too dark?"

Her cousin giggled and rolled her eyes.

"Thass nice," he said, dark red setting off her vanilla skin. "But maybe you should pucker."

Without batting a lash, she puckered at him while her cousin went into hysterics.

"Damn," he said.

Cristalena wiped it off. "Or this one. This one's lighter." She traced out the lovely curve of her lips in soft pink. "How about this one?"

"Well? I'm waiting."

She laughed, puckered, sweeping hair from her face like a pinup.

"I'll take it," he said, her eyes lighting up.

"Yeah?"

"Yeah. The light one's dope."

She bought it. They walked outside together. The orange sunlight fell between the tanned rows of tenements.

"So how come you never call me?" he asked her.

"A guy's supposed t' call the girl, right?"

"Well, whass yuh goddamn number?"

She rattled it off while her cousin pulled her away from him.

"Hey, no way," her cousin yelled, "thass my number!"

The first time he called, he got her cousin. "She ain't here, but she will be in about twenny. Can you call back?"

"Yeah." Twenty minutes later, she was there, a little breathless. Then she was sitting beside him in the car, a little close, her hand petting the dash.

"Damn, I love this car," she said, making him smile proudly. When the engine kicked in, there was a sweet roar like the opening barrage of a great battle. He pulled out of the parking, engine bubbling warmly, wheels gliding over the pavement as if in a dream. The exhilaration he usually felt while driving was multiplied by her being there.

"Do you ever drive, man? I mean, sometimes you drive an' it's like some dream, you don't even notice yuh doin' it." He shot her a mystified glance and noticed that she was looking at him funny.

"You look like a little kid an' a man at the same time," she said.

"Is that good o' bad?"

She smiled, looking as though she had just picked his pocket. Her hair was splattered all over the top of the seat. It was fucken gorgeous. He wanted to kiss her or something. She joked about his chains (he was still wearing a few, though less than usual), about the twirling furry dice, about cigarettes the minute he took his pack out to light one.

"You want one?" he asked. She curled her lip in mock disgust.

"D'you ever kiss somebody who smokes? I wun't kiss a guy who smokes. It's like licking an ashtray." She leaned back, her eyes twinkling maliciously. He put the cigarettes away.

"I'll make it up," she said, her words setting off brush fires.

They ate lasagna at the Venice Restaurant on 149th Street, sitting in a booth by the windows with a tiny candle in a glass cup that flickered weakly. There he asked her all the important questions.

"So who's yuh boyfriend?"

She laughed. "I don't got one. Would I be goin' out with you if I had one?"

"Maybe. Who knows."

"I ain't tha' kinda girl."

"What kinda girl are you, then?"

"I'm a good girl. My parents are pentecostal. My father was a pastor of his own church. It burned down. Now he stays home a lot and yells about God punishing him. He's a member of this other church but they don't let him preach very much. 'God's teaching me humility,' he says. My mother arranges her plates according to size. She hates pantyhose and makeup. I fought a war with her. Used to leave my house looking one way, then I'd change at my friend's house."

"Like into those ass-huggen blue pants you had? Mmmm."

She punched him.

"What about tha' Raul guy? The one you sicked on me?"

She laughed, covering her mouth, dimples making pretty creases.

"I didn't sick him on you. He was my first boyfriend. He was nice, but real stuck-up. He replaced me pretty fast."

"He must be sorry now." Miguel grinned. She made a little motion with her hand, as if to say, "Oh, stop."

They went to see *Nightmare on Elm Street III.* It was playing up on Fordham Road. (She had picked the movie.) Miguel sat through it, too wound up to concentrate, the sudden scenes of gore sending Cristalena into his arms many times. She gripped his hands, his shirt, burying her face in his chest, hiding and laughing at her own reaction. Was she just pretending to be scared? Miguel was suspicious, especially on those occasions where she'd bury herself in his chest and stare up at him with burning eyes. Face to face, her breath stroking his lips, she'd stare with determination.

"I was waitin' f' you to ax me out," she whispered, her eyes going from his eyes to his lips in quick leaps.

He wanted to kiss her. She felt it coming. She put a finger over his lips that smelled like popcorn.

"What's your girlfriend's name?" she asked, her eyes burning holes into him.

"She got a name like some poem," he said. "Huh name is Cristalena."

She pressed her lips against his softly, and then, amidst the rising cacophony of screams and screeching violins, she opened her lips, her tongue surprising him, her hands pressing his head closer as if she wanted to swallow him. They kissed deeply all through the screaming. It was only when the noise died down that they gently unhooked their lips to stare at each other. He had his hands on her waist, could feel the warmth throbbing right through her sweater. She looked at him a moment as if there were some kind of regret or shame fighting it out inside of her. He had his arm around her, but she suddenly seemed distant, lost in the movie.

In the car she was a little quiet, even though they strolled out of the theater like old lovers, arm in arm, almost in step, and when he bought cones, she gave him first lick of her chocolate one and took a chunk out of his vanilla. In the car she was pensive, as if she might be having second thoughts. He started chattering away, but nothing worked until he said, "I really like bein' with you, Cristalena."

She moved a little closer, holding her cone to his mouth. "I like you, too," she said. "But do you think I'm cheap?"

"What?"

"I mean because I kissed you like that. Because maybe now you think I'm cheap, some kinda putona o' something. I'm not, Miguel, I swear. I know this was a first date an' everything, I jus' met'chu, I shun'ta gone all crazy like that. What I mean is that I really like you so much an' I hope you can still respect me because I shoulda controlled myself more better."

He laughed softly, reaching over to pet her head. "You were fine."

"A guy don't respect a girl that gives it away like that." She wasn't looking at him, holding her cone in both hands as if it were some kind of chalice.

"Shut up with tha' shit, man."

"You think I'm a slut, a putona, right? All that stuff my parents said was true, about me, an' sin, an' how I was gonna end up."

She seemed really upset, her voice trembling a little. He pulled over by Crotona Park, and gave her a hug. She was still holding her cone. She took a few worried licks.

"Yuh fine, Lena. Yuh the finest girl I know. The finest girl I wanna know."

She looked up at him, her eyes still uncertain. "But I did it all on purpose! I jumped'ju. I wanted t' feel you. I don't know what woulda happened if the movie hadn't ended. My parents were right. They said I'd end up like some criminal in a dark theater, jumpin' on guys an' suckin' face."

Miguel's laughter put her at ease, her face softening as he caressed her hair. "It's okay if you wanna touch me. I hope you always do. Don't make that go away, okay?"

"Okay," she whispered, leaning up to peck him on the lips.

"Din'chu like kissin' me?" he asked.

"Hell yeah. I'm still all quivery."

He laughed. "Me too."

Things started to happen fast after that. Two nights later, he took her to dinner at another Italian place up near Fordham Road, with blue velvet curtains and candlelit tables, the streets outside crisscrossed with flashing neon and piercing car headlights. When he picked her up at her cousin's, she had on this pretty red skirt and black high heels and designer pantyhose. He immediately felt like going home to change, even though he wasn't wearing beat-boy shit. He had on a white silk shirt, black slacks, and black loafers. He had even put mousse in his hair. No chains, no baseball cap, no eight-ball jacket. He still felt less than her, even though when she first saw him, she fell against the door with a hand to her heart.

"Damn, boy," she said, sliding into his arms, rubbing her lips against his. Her cousin, also by the door to check out what was happening, looked shocked. It made them both laugh later, when they were in the restaurant. "Rosa's pretty wild herself," Cristalena said, "but she ain't like me. She got pride. An' scruples. Me, I see what I want, I go for it." She pressed her high heel against his calf.

" 'Ey man, you dirty my pants!"

When the food came, she said, "I was down Southern Boulevard the other day. I saw this big lumber place, an' I remembered you said your place was down there. So I went in an' axed for you, but nobody knew who you were."

A series of tremors struck Miguel, paralyzing him for a moment.

"Where is it you work, anyway?"

The candles wavered and blinked. Miguel exhaled and one of them went out, sending up a rolling squiggle of black.

"I didn't wanna tell you," he said quietly as he stabbed his Parmesan noodles smothered in bubbling sauce. "But uh . . ." He sighed, not looking at her. "I lost my job."

"Ahh Miguel. I'm sorry." She grabbed his hand and squeezed it. "I didn't mean to be so nosey."

"I didn't wanna say anything." He still couldn't look her in the face. "Right now I don't know what I'm gonna do. I've got a lotta money saved up."

She was rolling up this great ball of spaghetti on her fork, spinning it around and around. "Maybe you should go back to school," she said. First he shook his head, then he shrugged. He felt bad for lying, worse when she tried to console him, as she spoke he felt as if a huge canyon were opening up between them. If he never told her the truth, she couldn't be a part of him, couldn't even begin to understand his world and what he was up against. He reached for his pack of cigarettes but then remembered how she felt about smoking. He froze and lost his appetite.

"Uch, let's nah talk about it."

"Okay," she said with a little sigh. He could tell she wanted to know more, and he felt like he wanted to say more. But he couldn't.

They drove around in circles, Cristalena trying to wrestle the wheel away from him. She tried to step on the pedals, made jokes, sang him a Dominican song about a man with a fish for a cock that made Pepsi shoot up through his nose. It was like she sensed his sadness and fear and became ten times more zany. When he parked the car on a quiet street facing an empty schoolyard, she climbed into his lap and smothered him with long, deep kisses. Her arms closed tighter and tighter around him, her hips grinding slowly into his hard-on.

"Damn," he said, half laughing, running his hand up and down her nylon legs. The kisses became more furious. She emitted tiny, pleading squeals, her breath quickening, her hands slipping in under his shirt. Suddenly she stopped kissing to check in each of his eyes. "You think I'm crazy, right?" She was breathless, frantic, scared. He felt so drugged he couldn't respond, his whole body throbbing. Man, he had been with a lot of girls, but it had never felt like this.

"I better get'chu home," he whispered. She climbed off reluctantly, leaning against the door, putting her feather-soft foot in his lap. He grabbed it. It was like holding a squirming warm pigeon.

"Yuh beautiful," he said softly. He was in awe of her.

"So wha'chu gonna do about it?" She stretched her legs out, burying both feet in his crotch.

"You keep it up, bitch. You'll see what I do about it."

"Umm. Do I detect an offer?"

She wanted to go to his apartment. They could be alone there, she said, making his mind and cock twitch with the thought of that, but he couldn't take her there. Yet. He told her he lived in that big building on Prospect Avenue, the only one left there. It was surrounded by empty lots and a small cluster of businesses that clung desperately to the edge of the street.

"So when you gonna show me?"

He sighed. "It's a dump, I swear. Looks like shit. I din't mean t' give you the impression I was doin' so good. 'Cause I guess I'm not." There was a lump in his throat.

"But we could be alone there."

"It's a dump. Plus I got a roommate."

"A blond girl called Crissy? A dark hair girl called Janet?"

"No no. An ugly little junkie named Firebug."

She laughed, striking his chest with a pointed foot. "Get the fuck."

"I'm serious."

"Why they call him Firebug?"

He sighed. " 'Cause he likes playin' with matches. Used t' carry a can a' lighter fluid."

"Shit. I remember there was this guy at school like that. He almost burned it down. Set a fire in the detention room."

Miguel laughed, clapping his hands. "Thass him! Thass Firebug!"

"No shit!" She laughed. "He's famous. They still talk about that."

"I gotta make sure an' tell 'im."

He drove her home, leaving her down the block but watching her to make sure she got in okay. She didn't want anyone to spot her with him. Her parents didn't know about him. Supposedly she was at Rosa's, her cousin's. That was where she spent most of her time these days after the great pantyhose war. Rosa was her "beard." If Cristalena's mom called, Rosa covered for her, made up excuses. Cristalena's aunt was in on it. "Oh, they both went out," she would say, or maybe they fled next door. Cristalena's aunt was no pentecostal. She blared Alejandra Guzman records, went to Roseland regularly—owned every Madonna video, including that last nasty one. Who says divorce is a time of mourning? The story made Miguel laugh. "You should maybe get a beeper," he told her.

"Maybe I should," she said. They exchanged a look, like co-conspirators. It made him feel good to know she was living a secret life, just like he was. The painful difference was that she'd come clean to him. He had yet to admit all his secrets, and they haunted him.

They went to see *Sea of Love*. More frenzied kisses in the half-dark car. He felt her becoming a fixture, irreplaceable. Before saying good night they would stare into each other's eyes as if they would never see each other again. There was fear to share. The fear of loss, of the streets, of forever separation. You feel you are going to live forever until you fall in love. He fought the urge to tell her everything, even on those nights when they strolled up 149th Street and ran into Sammy, Careta, or Jokey and his three Flyboys, all of them armed with broomsticks that had been sharpened into spikes. Jokey and his boys circled the two of them approvingly, Jokey grinning and shrugging. "Please excuse the boys," he said in his Muppet voice to Cristalena, "but my boys don't hardly ever see a real lady."

They ran into Jimmy, a runty fourteen-year-old kid with chocolate stains around his mouth and a 9mm automatic that he whipped out to show Cristalena.

"Put tha' away, bro'," Miguel thundered, pulling Cristalena away from him.

"But I'm jus' tryin'na get a date," he said, eyes discouraged. Those weren't chocolate stains, Miguel explained to her later. When Jimmy was seven his mother had tried to cut out his mouth with a pair of scissors.

"Jesus," Cristalena cried in shock as they hurried across 149th, traffic lights blinking as cars roared closer. "How come you know those people?"

Miguel had wanted to tell her, but he could only shrug. "They jus' my friends, you know."

She clutched his arm. "You be careful, Miguel." Miguel thought she must suspect something, especially that time Sammy had said, " 'Ey bro', you don't hang out no more, you buy new threads, whassup? You too good f' us now, bro'?"

"I'm tryin'na get outta this shit," he told her, holding her close in the car, just a block from her house, the streets deserted and dark. The cold wind sent garbage tumbling across the street with sleighbell sounds. "I'm tryin'na get a better life goin'." It was as close to the truth as he could get right now. She pressed against his thumping heart. It was bothering her, he could tell. When you're sixteen and a half, life is supposed to be simpler, answers straight and clear. Her eyes probed him.

"Miguel, why don'chu live with your folks?" The way she asked made him think she had been wondering about it for a long time. No normal kid should be out on his own, right? She smelled a rat. He passed his hands through his hair, clutching the wheel silently, dashboard dials glowing. And without even thinking about it, he took out a cigarette and put it to his lips, pushing in the lighter with a click.

He frowned, as if the words forced their way out without his help. "My father's a bastid. He's a fucken bastid. I can hardly put it into words. He had a hard life on the island. Back then they used t' beat'chu jus' 'cause they could see you. He came over here screamin' about how his father was a nobody. He joined the Army. He learned to speak English an' shoot people. Then he got out an' all he knew how t' do was yell an' fuck an' use his fists. Beat me, beat my ma, beat my sister. Then my sister escaped, she got huhself married away. That only left me an' my ma." His words were all twisted up. "Look," he said, exasperated. "You said you had a war with yuh ma. I had one with my pa. I cun't stay around him 'cause he was always beatin' me. I dropped outta school. I met friends. I started to . . ." He stopped himself, his choppy words disjointed. The lighter popping out saved him. He lit his cigarette. His eyes were glued to the dash.

"I don't know where my father is. He left a year ago. My ma is livin' with some other guy in the same house. She was movin' when I cleared out. Thass all there is to it."

He looked at her and realized she was scared. She slid closer and gave him a hug, pressing her head into his chest. Then she pecked him on the cheek, slid across the seat, and left the car, quickly darting up the street and into her building.

4

He decided he would forget her.

It was a conscious decision. He figured once you're a man, you have to look at your life and see if you like where you are and move from there. Cristalena helped him look at his life. After having looked, he decided he was fucken pleased with his life. Crazy pleased he was. All he needed was to remind himself.

He had his usual Friday night. He put on his silk shirt with a few chains underneath. Moussed his hair. Wore his slacks and loafers. A new look. Big coat, like a detective from the 1940s. Mickey Spillane. He had liked his stuff.

He had four packages, Spider's voice on the phone reassuring.

"Hey, my pana, you ready f' action?"

"You got it."

"Pick up yuh stuff from Franco?"

Franco. Corner bodega on 156th Street. Hardworking Dominican family. They leave the stuff in the back, in a box in the right-hand corner marked CLOROX. Nicely bundled and bagged and tied together. Like dynamite. Don't you know how hard it is to make ends meet these days running your own bodega? A whole hell of a lot of overhead. This way, Lourdes can buy nice clothes and have boyfriends. And Marta, she bought three hundred dollars' worth of videocassettes. She's too old to go to movies. She likes the sexy ones. Pablo bought the large-screen TV he wanted, though he's still working on the sound system for it.

"Yeah, I got the stuff," Miguel said, bubble gum clacking in his mouth. The cold wind made him wince and stamp his feet.

"Good. Two by two, pana. Ritchie gets the green. Get Joey the red one, tha' should be a big one. An' drop by Petey with the yellow. Gotta do it all by midnight."

"No sweat. Get me on the beeper if there's anything."

"Pana, pana, hol' up. Listen, there might be trouble on Dawson. The posse up there been lookin' f' hassles. Some a' them dudes know yuh car. You sure you don't wanna borrow a Buick o' somethin'?"

"I go in my Baby," Miguel said, like a soldier attached to his tank. "Confianza, amigo!"

Spider laughed. "Good t' here you so up, man. You looked like shit the other night. I thought maybe you was gettin' second thoughts. I mean, I kinda expected it. You a thinkin' dude. But'chu know opportunity when it knocks, don'chu?"

"Everybody gets the blues, bro'. But now I'm ready t' kick it live. It's cold, bro'. Is there anything else? I wanna go run my ass."

"Jus' be chill on Dawson. Be a eyeball on Avenue St. John. Do yuh thing an' step. I don't wan'chu gettin' shroomed."

"Got'cha."

"You gotta party planned tonight?"

Miguel sighed. He needed a party. Needed some smoke. He could stop by Tinton, maybe Yolanda was around . . . nah, Yolanda was a fish, man, useless, she just lies there like some slab. You need a girl that moves, get that bucking action going . . .

"I wanna definitely party tonight. Friday night, bro'."

"Well, you know the place. I'm throwin' a little get together f' some a' my pana. I got some a' thum nice juicy tidbits comin' down. They nice, I'm tellin' you, not like those butch beasts Firebug be hangin' wif' . . ."

"You got smoke? I'm out."

"You been buyin' from Dusty, man. I heard tha' shit. I'll get'chu good stuff, why don'chu tell me? Dusty be sprayin' his shit wif' Raid, bro'. You don't wanna be smokin' that."

"I come down t' get some later?"

"Yeah, yeah, stop by, man. I'll have somethin' f' you. Now you be a fucken eyeball. Somebody behind'ju?"

Miguel glanced around him. The street was empty. There were a few people in the pizzeria nibbling on slices.

"Cut that out."

"Keep yuh eyes peeled. Be like Mr. Potato Head."

"Check. Later."

Back to the car, a half-run hop skip situation. Hands frozen. The heater up full blast. The windows fog up slowly. See heavy shadows approaching. Hollow slapping sounds, flickers of light and the windshield shatters up like a crystal spiderweb, and then Miguel jumps back with six or seven or a dozen thick speeding slugs bursting through him like he was made of paper and then

AND THEN

He checked the packages, put them by the front seat on the passenger side for quick handhold kinda shit don't wanna be fumbling for these because Spider sounded worried. Miguel had been shot at before. The car had been hit only twice in nearly half a dozen shootings. The first time some fuck with an automatic raspy drilled his car as he was making his getaway. The street cleared like a dream, the streetlight going out just as the shots spattered out. Before he ducked he actually saw the flashing gun muzzle in the window of a metallic-blue Mustang.

"Bro'! Fucken step!" Domino had yelled, beating his door and running. Domino was funny, with a face like someone shot darts into it. Some lookout he was; he spotted the car when it was almost on top of them. Fucken crackhead. The Mustang braked with a screech as Miguel spun his car sideways. He heard the rapid pokpokpokpokpok before he felt the crumpcrump shudderings and the tinkle of glass. That was all he remembered from that one. His rear window was like scraped ice. There was a funny pattern of bullet holes down the right side, stopping short of the doors, a smattering of holes running into the rear window. Boom. $1,800. A week without his Baby.

The second time they got the trunk. He was sitting in his car talking to Sammy on the corner of Longwood and Dawson, just shooting the shit, with Sammy leaning on his car door clutching a beer. They were still looking at each other when Miguel felt the car buck, and that thump-thumpthump.

"Oh shit!" Sammy yelled, ducking. The car roared past, its gun still barking as the car made a vicious turn down Longwood. Sammy reappeared, his hair looking new wave.

"You fuck!" Miguel screamed at him. "Thanks f' nothin'!"

"Wha'chu, wha'chu mean?" Sammy gasped in a falsetto. "Din'chu, din'chu see? I almost, they almost—"

It cost him six hundred dollars to get the holes in the trunk fixed.

He lit a cigarette, thinking about how sad Cristalena had looked when he had lit his cigarette, but he couldn't help it. He is what HE is. Shouldn't she accept him the way he is? The girl was turning everything upside down. She was a threat. You don't fall in love with a threat. And a snot, wasn't she a snot? The way she blew him off, ran out of the car, like she was deserting him to his life. He had felt confused enough to call her cousin's the next day.

"She's not here," came Rosa's response, sounding a little gruff.

"You tell huh t' call me?"

"Yeah." Like leaving a message for royalty. Was Rapunzel gonna let down huh fucken hair, or did he have to bring his grappling hooks? It wasn't like he had been waiting or anything, of course not, but she didn't call back. It pissed him off, that he had gone so far as to even call her so fast like that, like he had been hard-up. Fuck it. She could be replaced. He shoved her out of his mind, speeding down the streets with screeching tires. The night had just started, and already an empty can of beer. Five more to go.

He went by Tinton. Friday night, posse in effect, streets lined with kids in their colors, orange caps and red caps and big black coats and bright red jackets, all of them sharing the same sidewalk because the posse thing wasn't about turf. It was about being seen, about pulling the bitches and showing off your colors. The turf thing, that took place somewhere else. Tinton Avenue was like a posse social club. All the loudmouthed bitches were out in force in their FUCK-ME clothes. Where were the Suarez Twins? With Jackie? Who the fuck is Jackie? Man, just once he'd like to fuck a girl twice without having to make some kind of appointment. He was fuming about it when Yolanda hopped into his car, the sickly sweet stink of her perfume almost choking him. Her scarecrow eyes were big and droopy.

"Yo bro'," she rasped, "I ain't seen you." She slammed the door shut, like he was taking her someplace.

"No way man," he said. "I'm workin' now."

"You got any smoke? I was wif' Malo, tha' fucken cheapskate. Smoked a whole blunt an' only le' me get one hit."

"Nah. I don't."

"Fucken liar. Fuck you then. Don't come axin' f' me later." She opened the door with a shove and slammed it shut, the smell of her remaining. He rolled down his window. He cruised slowly, checking the streets for girls almost desperately, as if he had something to prove.

Scarred faces, hostile grimaces, grinning ghouls. The girls looked sick to him. It was the first time he had noticed it. The Yolanda stink was still in his car. He popped open another beer and sped away from Tinton, feeling like a dog that had been plowing through a garbage can. He pulled over, ran right to a phone while his Baby seethed.

"Hi. Is Cristalena there?"

Rosa sounded sick of him. "Nah, she's not."

"Could'ju tell huh t' call me? This is Miguel. You remember me, right?"

"Yup. I'll tell 'uh you called." Click.

The first stop was under the el on Intervale. Trains rumbled by like thunder, clusters of dark shadows everywhere. There were rows of streetlights knocked out by crackheads so they could do their thing in private. Miguel scoured the ranks of battered stoops with empty windows and broken doors. Joey was standing right by the boarded-up social club. There was a line there of shabbily dressed shuffling bodies. Joey ran right up to his window. Miguel cranked it down, not in the mood for talk.

"Yo baby, yo baby," Joey said, cigarette twitching with his words.

Miguel tossed him his package and pulled away, tires screaming.

"Damn mothafucka!" Joey screamed, dropping the package. "Nex' time take me wit'chu!"

Miguel was laughing insanely. Can of beer number three was already giving him a nice buzz. The steering wheel felt elastic and rubbery in his hands. Speeding down the el, posts flying by with sonic whooshes. The car responded like magic to his every twitch. Man and car, united as one. This made him sing.

> Why do birds magically appear
> everytiiiiiiime
> you be neeeeeeeeear?
> well jus' like meeeee
> they wanna beeeeeeeee
> close t' Jews!

An empty lot. He pulled over, struggling with the words to the classic song by that skinny girl who died in a closet. The Carpenters? Miguel got the serious giggles as he ran from the car, stumbling over bricks. The bitch about beer is all that pissing. He stood out on the empty lot, flickering lights of a passing train blessing him. He wagged his dick at it, all those lights flashing. Running back to his car, he wanted to hug his Baby, but it was too cold. When his beeper went off he took it out, then jumped into the car and drove over to another phone.

"Yeah, what?"

The voice was wheezy. "Yo, this is Miguel?" It sounded drunk, too.

"Yeah this is Miguel. So who the fuck this is?"

"Yo bro'. You don' reckanize me?"

"No I don't fucken reckanize you. Hurry up man, I'm workin'."

"Well nice t' know you workin' 'cause Spider, he tol' me I get my shit at midnight an' it's already . . . yo honey wha' time you got? Twelve-thirty, bucko."

"Oooohh I know you. Whassup, Ritchie? You should, you should, yo . . . lemme tell you somethin'. I ain't yuh bucko, man. You should learn t' treat people with some respeck."

"You get tha' shit over here fast, homey, or I'll be teachin' you some lessons all right."

"Yeah, yuh father." Miguel hung up. He got out of his warm Baby for this? Back in the car he turned the radio up to some throbbing DJ Mastermix stuff. Made him horny. He stopped underneath the Prospect Avenue train station when he saw these two dope bitches in tight-ass dresses, standing outside a tiny social club. He rolled down his window and started yelling at them about where he could take them. They looked startled, and exchanged glances. Then a guy in a black coat came out of nowhere and said, "Yo, keep movin', bro'. Keep movin'." Two others joined the chant. Then another guy appeared carrying what looked like a rifle. Stick? Baseball bat? Rifle? Miguel shot the fuck out of there, tossing an empty beer can at them.

He took a screeching left on East 156th Street, roaring down the crowded road. Lots of streetlamps were busted, his headlights making people scurry off the street, eyes glowing like cats.

He braked. The crack house just off Kelly Street was crowded, people milling around outside. There was a fight going on. Two big black guys were yelling, vapor bursting from their mouths.

"Where's Petey?" he yelled into the crowd. A young girl with glassy eyes stared at him and laughed. Suddenly he felt a series of thumps. He spun to look, and spotted Petey advancing toward him, whacking the car.

"Don't be whackin' my car!" Miguel screamed.

"You fuck! Where you been?" Petey had a face that glowed in the dark, it was so pale, with funny bumps on his cheeks. Miguel didn't say anything. He was checking his packages in the half-light while Petey screamed. "Jus' who the fuck you think you are? Ahh? You forgot'chu workin' f' us? Huh?"

Miguel tossed the package right into his face. Petey fell back, arms swinging. Miguel stepped on the gas and grinned. His Baby screamed and jolted away like a dog that's been kicked in the ass.

"What I wun't give f' some pussy," Miguel said to himself, drunk and lonely. He detached another beer from its plastic gasket. No way, man, he was through with that shit. If a girl couldn't understand his fucken life, that was tough shit. Why should he feel bad? He slowed the car, back to a phone.

"Hi. Cristalena there?" (He was going to tell her off good.)

There was a pause. "Is this Miguel?"

"You know it's Miguel. I mean, you know, right?"

"Don'chu know what time it is?" It was Rosa, all huffing and puffing like she was going to blow his house down.

"You knew I was gonna call!" he screamed.

"She ain't here, I tol'ju that. She don't live here, you know. You lucky I been up watchin' *Friday Night Videos.*"

"But'chu don't understand, Rosa Mariposa . . . I need t' talk t' huh."

Rosa's voice softened a little. "I tol' huh that. But huh father's sick. She cun't come over before. Ain't no way you'll get huh now, not this late."

"Well jus' gimme huh number an' I'll—"

"I can't do that."

"Ahh c'mon. This is important, man."

A string of shots stuttered nearby. Miguel looked around.

"I can't give you her number."

"You gonna feel like shit if I got shot out here."

She laughed. "I'll try an' live with myself."

"All right. Thanks." For nothing. Damn bitch.

Why was he trying to attach himself to people? He had always thought the more unattached he was, the happier he'd be, but Miguel hated to be alone. The more he needed people, the more he saw how unreliable they were.

Firebug? The guy would probably swipe his money, first chance he got. Amelia was right about him. He would have to keep hiding his money. Now he had fifteen hundred which he kept hidden in the car, in case of . . . in case of what? He didn't want to think about it.

His beeper was going again. He checked the code.

Fuck it.

Miguel raced down Longwood, turned into Dawson Street. A group of people stood on the corner, staring at his car. They were coming over in slow motion when he began to giggle, easing the car forward.

"Yo, yo! Hol' up!"

He kept driving up the block, giggling when he spotted Ritchie running behind him in the rearview mirror. Miguel suddenly braked, making Ritchie skid. Ritchie banged the trunk with his fist. "Mothafucka!"

Miguel reached over, grabbed Ritchie's packages. He rolled his window down and awaited the boy, still laughing. He fought down the giggles as Ritchie approached, his young face twisted up with anger.

"You fuck, you sonofabitch, who you think you are?"

"Come on, man, issa joke, can'chu take a fucken joke?" He rolled the packages over the edge of his window and watched them fall onto the street. Ritchie stopped in mid-step, his face changing color. This made Miguel really laugh. He was still laughing when car tires squealed loudly somewhere nearby. A pair of car lights swept across the avenue ahead like searchlights. A black man yelled. There was some kind of commotion, like a huge engine backfiring. Could've been a truck, a series of huge crates falling, or maybe a heavy semiautomatic. Miguel dropped his beer can.

"Shit shit shit!" Ritchie said desperately, trying to open Miguel's car door, but it was locked. Miguel shifted gear, car surging forward.

"Oh shit, wait!" Ritchie screamed, but Miguel had left him far behind by then, his outstretched arms flailing, his sneakers slapping the pavement. Then Ritchie fell, from sheer momentum or bullets, Miguel couldn't tell which. He wasn't going to stick around to find out. There were headlights behind him, growing larger, engine growling, and those swift stuttering barks kept coming. He turned sharply on East 156th, racing toward Southern Boulevard. The car wasn't behind him anymore. He was trembling a little, waiting for a green light, thinking he had lost them, when he heard that strange engine sound again, a nasal churning. He spotted a loaded-down Falcon speeding by on the boulevard, windows full of young laughing faces. Miguel realized with a tremor that this was the car that had done the shooting. When the light turned green, he kept going straight and got on the Bruckner Expressway.

He couldn't think. His arms felt numb and his head hurt. He came down 149th, zoomed up to Third Avenue, to a pizzeria he knew there for a couple of slices and a soda. He wolfed it all down without thinking. Then he called Spider. He was pissed off.

"The thing ain't the shootin', brother, I know that. The thing is tha'chu were late. I tol'ju before midnight, right? Din't I say that?"

"Yeah, I know, but—"

"You fucked up, bro'. I mean, what were you doin'? Whassup wit'-chu? You had some bad nights before, but it never affected yuh run before."

"I don't know, man. It was womp tonight." He felt tired. "Was anybody hurt?"

"One kid got hit, but it wasn't bad, didn't even have t' call the 5-0. But what woulda happened if you had been on time, bro'? Why'unchu thinkin' about that? They was all waitin' around f' you. Didn't I tell you before midnight? Do the Spider know or don't he?"

"Don't be yellin' at me, Spider. It ain't all my fault."

"Thass not what Ritchie said. You lucky it wasn't one a' his boys got hit."

Miguel sighed into the phone. He felt like crying. He didn't know why. Everything was just disappointing. "Well, sorry man. Sorry I didn't get my ass shot off f' you."

"Chill. Go home. I be in touch tomorrow. We still gotta do the cop drop, right?"

"Yeah, man."

"I can still trus'ju on that, right?"

"Well, wha'chu think?"

A pause. "Tomorrow, bro'. Get t' bed." The line went dead.

Miguel slammed down the phone. He felt fed up. He got in his car and thundered down to Tinton Avenue, thinking he was going to find himself a woman, but the streets were empty. No Suarez Twins, no crack babes, just a few dealers he knew, a couple of bums fighting over a pint, and Yolanda, who spotted his car the minute it turned up the street. She peered in through his window with a smile and a nervous tic that made her appear to be pleading. She tried his door but it was locked. She beat on the window.

"Hey!" she squealed, head tilted to one side like a bird's. "You got any smoke?" She supported herself against the car, her eyes unfocused.

Miguel stared at her. "No." He felt like he could smell her stink again, seeping into the car. He stepped on the gas suddenly. There was a shriek. She spun away like a top. In the rearview mirror he saw her fall to the street. Good.

He ended up on Union Avenue, where he stopped for a red light. A small kid ambled over to his window and pointed his shiny nine at him.

"Ahh shit!" Miguel screamed, recognizing Jimmy after a tense moment. "Wha'chu tryin'na do, man?"

Jimmy grinned delightedly, still pointing the gun. " 'Eyyy, check it out, it's Miguelo. You gonna hang out wif' us, o' do I gotta shoot?"

He parked on Union, shared a huge pair of blunts Jimmy whipped out. Jokey was there with one Flyboy (the other hand found a girl); they wrestled with each other, their broomsticks clacking as they lunged and swung and parried like gladiators. Jimmy watched them as he sat beside Miguel on the curb, then walked toward them as if hypnotized.

"Stop," he said, but the duel continued, Jokey grunting as his Flyboy parried a deep thrust. Jimmy drew his gun from under his thick coat.

"Oh shit," Miguel said, sensing something was going to go wrong. He wanted to get up but couldn't; his arms and legs wouldn't respond. He felt like he was weaving back and forth forever. He was moving in slow motion when Jimmy let off a sudden burst that sent chunks of sidewalk flying everywhere. The ground spurted up around Jokey and his Flyboy. They both dropped their sticks.

"WHAT THE FUCK?!" Jokey screamed, his Flyboy jumping back with shock.

"Stop," Jimmy said.

"I'M GONNA KILL YOU!!" Jokey picked up his stick.

"Yeah? You can't catch me," Jimmy sang, like a little kid that wanted to be chased.

"I'm gonna make you eat tha' gun, mothafucka!"

The Flyboy threw a bottle. It missed everybody but hit Miguel's Baby with a hollow thump.

"Hey!" he yelled, rising to his feet. It seemed to take ten years. Didn't look like he was going to drive very far now, he was too fucked up, but he wasn't going to stick around. He crawled into the front seat, found the ignition, turned on his car. Jimmy and Jokey and the Flyboy ran into the nearby empty lot, their laughter rebounding off the shattered brick walls all up and down the street. Miguel eased the car forward. He came down 150th Street, a block from his house. He wanted a woman. Where was he going to find one? It was too late. He thought of fucking Amelia. He knew she would fuck him in a minute. He was sure of it. So what about Firebug? The guy wanted to steal his money. Miguel should pay him back. But he knew where Amelia was tonight. It was the reason he didn't want to go up to his empty room without a woman of his own to drown Amelia out, but he wasn't finding a woman. A slow trip past Mongo's showed him all the best bitches got dates already, and a cruise up Tinton only showed him Yolanda, standing under a bodega awning like a lonely rag doll with big eyes.

He burst into the apartment, stumbling down the hallway. Right away he heard them. That was her now, crying out breathlessly, a giggle of pleasure slipping out as she fought for breath.

"Who's that?" Firebug yelled.

"Yuh mother." Miguel walked into his room, crashing down onto his mat without the strength to take off his coat. He lay there staring up at the ceiling, tired of himself and his life and his room, closing in on him in the half-darkness. Green and red wiggling worms danced in his sight like fireworks. For some reason, he saw Jimmy's mother, holding the kid down, trying to tear his mouth off with her bare hands, nails cutting deep, Jimmy screaming and screaming with arms flailing and scraping the walls. No, that don't work, she yelled, grabbing a pair of scissors so she could

do it   right

Miguel was immersed in total dark. He dreamt that Amelia was taking off his clothes. He could tell it was her because of the way she breathed, the way her hands touched him so gently. He could also catch glimpses of her curvy silhouette from the light that came in through the window.

"Firebug," he said. The sound passed through his lips as if it hadn't come from him.

"He sleeps like the dead," she said, lifting off his pants, her nails slowly raking up and down his calves, his knees, his thighs. "What were you tryin'na do tonight, get yourself killed?" Her hands softly massaged him into a dark kind of coma, of sleeping and not sleeping.

"Whatayou know." His lips weren't moving, were they?

"Spider told me." Her hands slowly caressed his chest. "Nothing but complaints about'chu tonight."

"Ahhhh . . . fuck off." He was rolling away from her, rolling forever down a steep hill. He was picking up speed. He was going to crash.

Amelia stood up. He was on a raft, tossing and turning. He was trying to lift his head when she sighed and said, "Some girl called."

He snapped out of a dark fog. Sunlight poured in through the windows, making him squint. He was in his underwear, his clothes folded neatly nearby.

5

The first thing he had done after getting up was scoot over to Kelly Street, where Amelia's pop had his sandwich shop. It was a small joint, all windows and stools and tiny tables that jiggled. There was a statue in the window of a wino leaning on a lamppost. Inside, not much business. Amelia was behind the counter. She looked cheerful and young in the sunlight.

"Well well well," she said, chin in palm. "The boy even got dressed for me." She leaned over the counter and pecked him on the lips. "You want coffee? You look like you need some."

"I'm nah stayin' tha' long."

"Coffee," she said, sliding a cup across to him, pouring in the hot steaming liquid from the glass pot, not taking her eyes off him. She added a little cream for him. "You look gorgeous," she said. "Like something out of a Ray Chandler film. You know Ray Chandler?"

He took out a cigarette, lit it fast, and was just about to savor the first puff when she swiped it from his lips.

"I'd like to think you came to see me," she said, puffing.

"You can dream all you want."

"You're a dream all right. You should see how you look. Much too good for those twisted little pipe stems you fuck every party night at Firebug's. You forget I've seen them, right? So right away I know something's up. The only time a boy dresses up is when he wants a girl to give him a real good significant fuck."

He laughed, sipping the coffee, loving the way words rolled out past her lips, so effortlessly, cigarette hand twirling, cigarette smoke hazy cloud cover for her face. "Speakin' a' dreams," he said, "I had this dream las' night where you was in my room, undressin' me."

She leaned close to whisper. "An' then I fucked your brains out?"

"No, you only took my clothes off."

"That was no dream, honey."

"You said a girl called. I was too far gone to get the scoop. What happened? When did she call?"

Amelia stared at him a moment, as if she was adding something up. "Ohhh, I get it." She grinned. "I guess I shoulda said THE girl called."

A small shiny-headed man with an unshaven face growled at her in Spanish. Amelia carried a plate of eggs and toast over to a man sitting in the back, poring through a newspaper. It made Miguel laugh to see her make like a real waitress. She darted back, sitting on a stool beside him. Chin in hand, she looked at him like she was tired, and returned the cigarette to his lips.

"You're just a baby," she said. "You don't know wha'chu want."

"When did this girl call?"

Amelia seemed to pout, playing with a salt shaker. She slid it along the counter toward him, making skidding sounds when it reached his arm. She spilled salt on his hand.

"An' here I was, thinking you came to see me."

"I did, I did. I came to see you about that call yesterday. The girl. Remember?" He grabbed her hand.

"You're holding my hand."

"Stop bein' silly!"

"All right. The bitch called three times, man, she wouldn't stop calling. What am I, your answering service? Don't I have better things t' do? I was gonna tell her to bug off, tha'chure my man an' that I'm gonna fuck 'er up."

"What did'ju tell huh? Amelia, wake up! What did'ju tell huh?" He nudged her, because Amelia started making like she was falling asleep.

"Chill, bastid. I told 'er you weren't there. That was the first time. Then the second time she asked again, I told 'er you still weren't back, could I take a message? So she says yeah, tell 'im Rutabaga called."

"Cristalena! Huh name is Cristalena!"

"An' a fine an' dandy name it is, worthy of all fine literature. But I knew that already, I was makin' funna you, see? It's called sarcasm. You know what that is? Because you see, the third time she called, I got everything I need. Name, number, all that shit. I could go over there an' get her anytime. You hear?"

"So she called me three times? Damn." It made him feel better.

"She said her father was sick. Like I gave a fuck. Then she got all snotty an' says, 'Who are you?' I told her who I was all right, you can bet on it. I—"

"Thanks," he said, slapping a sloppy kiss on her cheek and racing out of there.

"BUT I'M NOT FINISHED!!" she screamed.

The boutique where she worked was called Butterfly's. It was a small place on Third Avenue where purple glitter on the walls and racks of clothes surrounded you. Decapitated mannequins were everywhere, in lace teddies, striped halters, and bikini underwear. Long rows of legs in a variety of colored nylons stood like levers along the far wall.

Miguel was wearing one of his new silk shirts, baggy whites, and loafers. Since meeting her, he had rethought his wardrobe and had blown real cash on new clothes. No more chains and beat-boy posh. He even moussed his hair again because she liked it, darkly wet but still a little too curly. He felt pretty groggy, his legs weak. He walked around the racks, opening his Marine coat, then he spotted her standing by a dress rack, staring at him. She was wearing a black skirt and black tights, hair swept back from her face and flowing down her back in a long ponytail. It was a small, serene face, like on a cameo. He noticed that when she saw him, a tiny sparkle came into her eyes and her lips trembled a little. She had on this blood-red blouse that made her look real uptown. Miguel came right up to her as she leaned on a row of dresses. She was trying to play it cool. He stood in front of her.

"So," she said.

Miguel kissed her on the cheek. Her skin felt smooth and cool.

"I missed'ju yesterday," he said, grabbing one of her hands. She smiled warily, her hand limp.

"Who's Amelia?" she asked, like a domino player slapping down that last winning piece.

Michael laughed. "Ohhh shit," he said, and softly clapped. Cristalena was looking at him like she couldn't believe he was laughing.

"Miguel! This is trouble, I'm axin' you a question an' shit."

"Yeah, I know, hol' up."

She walked over to a tall woman whose hair was tied with a colorful bandanna. The woman sent Cristalena near the back to gather up some new garments, where she checked the items for tags and put them on the rack according to size. He watched her quietly, then he checked her work. "Hey, thass a small, dumbo," he said, tossing one back into the pile to annoy her. She swatted him away.

"You better nah get me fired," she said.

"I wun't get'chu fired. You supposed t' help the customers."

"So who's Amelia?" She searched a dress for its tag.

"She's Firebug's girl."

She grinned. "Thass a likely story."

"It's true, man."

"So where were you?"

"I went out with this girl. Everybody calls huh the Pump. You know why? 'Cause when she—"

"Thass it," Cristalena said, tossing down a dress.

He grabbed her suddenly, pushing her into one of the empty fitting rooms. He drew the curtain shut, pinning her to the wall, face to face.

"Now we alone."

She was resisting him only a little bit. "You gonna get me fired," she whispered, her hands on his waist, but she wasn't pushing. He kissed her softly. They were both trying to be quiet about it, but their lips made noises and they laughed.

"Damn Cristalena, I miss you."

"Me too." She seemed sorry about something.

"I tried to call you. I was runnin' around."

"I cun't go to my cousin's. My father was sick. I had to cook for my mother." He laid a row of tiny kisses on her quivering eyelids. Then her words seemed to hit home. He looked at her.

"You cook?"

"Fuck yeah."

"Less get married then." He was nibbling on her ear.

"Miguel!" She shivered with a hundred tiny tremblings, his lips sliding down her neck. "You shun't joke like that." She checked his eyes for sincerity.

"But I ain't jokin'," he said. "I'm in love with you an' shit."

She inhaled deeply, her face a little shocked. She threw herself against him, kissing him so deep and long that when it was over he had to sit down on the little bench in there. She drew the curtain aside and stepped out, putting dresses up on the rack as if trying to make up for lost time. She threw him a few nervous glances, then pulled him into the stockroom nearby, where she kissed him again, emitting tiny squeals. Her hands slipped under his shirt. She looked around, then she told him to wait there. She came back with a plastic cup of water that she handed him after taking a sip.

"I'm on my break," she said, kissing him again with wanton disregard, pushing him up against a stack of boxes so hard that they groaned. "It's my birthday next week," she breathed hotly into his ear. "Next Saturday."

"Yeah? Well, wha'chu want f' yuh birthday?"

She crinkled her nose. "I'm lookin' at what I want." Her hand brushed against his crotch lightly. She stepped back. "I wanna invite'cha to my sweet-sixteen party, at my cousin's house. I wanna show you off." She came close again. This time she stroked his balls.

"Hey."

"So will you come?"

"Yeah. But I'm serious, wha'chu want f' yuh birthday?"

She held both his hands. "I want two things. The first thing is a nice fat teddy bear, like the kind they got at Kiddie City on Hunts Point up on the second floor near where they got the board games."

Miguel laughed. "An' what else?"

She grinned and came close again, her hand brushing his crotch again. "I wanna go to your house. I wanna spend the night."

His blood froze. "My house is a mess."

"I'm not goin' there to inspect it. I wanna be alone with you."

"I have a roommate."

"So get rid of him. I wanna be with you, Miguel. No cars, no theaters, just you an' me. An' candles, we gotta get candles. Romantic. Some soft music."

He smirked. "You mean like Lionel Ritchie?"

She made a face.

"I'll bring something. You have a stereo?"

"Yeah. But how you gonna stay over when yuh parents are always so—"

"Rosa'll cover for me, she can say I'm staying over, I can even call from your place." Her eyes flashed suddenly. "Unless you don't want to," she added truculently. "If you don't want to, thass fine, too." She looked at her watch. "My break is almost up." She turned away from him, heading for the door. Miguel panicked. He grabbed her forcefully. For a split second, she struggled. He was holding her by the wrists.

"Don't do that," he said gently.

"Don't do what?" Her eyes simmered resentfully.

"Don't turn yuh back on me. We should be able to talk."

"Who can talk to you? You fucken scare me, Miguel. You want me to talk? Why don'chu talk? Last time you talked I still didn't know wha'chu about."

"Wha'chu mean?"

"I mean you ain't no mystery man. If you don't wanna be with me, just say so. But don't be actin' like you got all these fucken secrets. You think I can't see you dodgin' me?"

He let go of her wrists.

"I have to get back to work." She returned to her garments on the rack.

"I came here t' make things better, not worse."

"Jus' be straight with me, Miguel."

"All right," he said, coming right up to her. A lady customer at a nearby rack clutching a few ballet tees turned to watch them as if tuning in to a TV show.

"My life's screwed up," he whispered frantically. "I don't know where the fuck I'm goin'. What am I gonna do tomorrow? I'm on borrowed time an' some day my money run out an' then I'm fucked. An' no, I didn't wan'chu comin' up t' see how I live. I live like a fucken bum, my place ain't shit. I been tryin'na impress you."

"You don't gotta do that."

"I do, I do, you matter t' me."

"Well, you matter to me too . . ."

The lady with the ballet tees was now joined by an older lady with a small girl by the hand.

Cristalena stopped talking. "Can I help you with anything?"

"No," the older woman answered kindly. "Just looking." They kept staring.

Miguel sifted through the pile of dresses nervously. "I jus' don't wan'chu to get the wrong idea about me an' shit." He handed her two dresses. "These are small. I mean about who I am an' shit. I don't wanna be pegged f' somethin' I'm not. People are always tellin' me what I am, what I should be, where I could get to if only I this o' that. Jus' once I'd like t' find out f' myself."

The thin woman with the bandanna appeared. "Cristalena, I need'ju."

"Be right there." She looked at Miguel sadly. He pecked her on the cheek.

"Get to work," he said.

"Is that it? That the goodbye I get?"

Miguel laughed, hugged her. She gave him a passionate kiss, pressing him close.

"Ugh. You make noises when you kiss," he said.

"Nah, thass you."

"So can I call you later?"

"I'll be at my cousin's. You better call." She walked away from him toward the cashiers. "Do I get my presents, or not?"

"Yeah," Miguel said. "All of them."

She smiled, tossing her hair back as if deep down she had known she was going to win all along.

6

They started calling him Spider because he could climb up buildings. Right up the sides of them, without a ladder or rope or funny boots. Just his hands and his Keds. Some buildings looked harder than others. Kids would walk miles looking for a building they thought looked hard to climb, so they could place bets Spider couldn't do it. Spider would climb them. Three, four floors up, wind whipping at his clothes until the cops would come or somebody would freak out. At least, that's what Spider said. Miguel had a ninety-minute cassette of Spider talking about himself. He was listening to it now as he sat on his gym mat with the ten grand, tracing words in the air with his cigarette as Spider's alcoholic growl filled the room. It had been Spider's idea, because they had gotten on the thing about books and how Miguel read them and then got into Miguel's dead dream of wanting to be a writer. Miguel shouldn't have even blurted it out, because it was dumb. There weren't any Puerto Rican writers. Puerto Ricans didn't write books. Miguel had never even seen one. Miguel tried to tell Spider about how stupid it was, but to Miguel's amazement, Spider loved the idea.

"You should write about somebody real amazin', a real amazin' kinda life. Somebody people gonna go оннн sнiт!, somebody bigger than life. The only way there could be an amazin' spick writer be to write about amazin' lives. Why don'chu interview me, bro'? I'll talk about myself into a tape recorder an' you can write a book about it. Don't be laughin', I'm serious! Damn, no more smoke f' you, you gone. Lookit'chu laugh. I'm tellin' you, mines is a million-dolla' story. I can see it in the movies. Who you think they should get t' play me? Nah, don't be laughin', I'm serious, bro'!"

"Lou Diamond Philips."

"Naah. He ain't as pretty as me. Needs the curly hair like I got."

"They could curl it."

"No."

"How about the rapper Ice-T?"

"Damn, I ain't black, you know. I mean, I'm dark an' shit, you could say I got coffee skin. Could'ju write that? Coffee skin. But I ain't black."

"He got that street attitude down."

"Yeah. But we want a Latino brother. Blacks got they own expression, know wham sayin'? We should have our own."

"I don't know one Latino actor that could be you, Spider. Not in Hollywood. How about that guy that played the teacher? Edward James Homo?"

They both laughed.

"Come on, man. I'm serious. I'm gonna hafta play myself."

After that, Miguel never brought it up, but Spider always did. If he saw him on the street, he would ask him, "Yo, how's my book comin' along?" And Miguel would always laugh, so much so that one night Spider took him aside on the street. Miguel thought it was something important, like business, but it was about the book.

"The reason I bring it up, pana," Spider said, hand gripping his shoulder, "is 'cause it matters t' me that I leave somethin' behind in the world. This might be it, you know?"

"Spider," Miguel said, exasperated, "I don't write, man. It was just some dream. There ain't no spick writers."

"So you could be the first, man. Start a trend."

It made Miguel laugh that Spider was so hung up on it. One day, he dragged him over to one of his apartments on Tinton Avenue, a place they called India House, covered in rugs and throbbing with music and tinted lights. There, Spider rolled a thick blunt and took out a new Walkman.

"Oh shit," Miguel said, knowing what it was for. There were two ninety-minute cassettes sitting on the floor beside it. He started to laugh and laugh.

. . .

It was Firebug who brought them together. Firebug, not the same school kid with laughing eyes and a prankster hop. The kid who always got away with everything had turned into a gaunt ghost, spotted on the corner of Wales Avenue between bites of pizza as Miguel tried to figure out who he could call to put him up for the night. And there he was, hadn't seen him for more than a year, not since Miguel had quit school to become a gutter rat, to sell smoke and pal with street goons and be on his own, away from his mother and that new man she was with. Miguel had called out to him. Hugs and clutches. Wha'chu into, bro'? Just so happens Firebug's looking for a new roomie, just dumped the old one. Miguel says yeah EXCEPT THAT he don't have that much money, not even enough to buy a new lid so he could sell some. Firebug smiled. "Don'chu worry. You my friend. I know a place I could get'chu some work."

It was in that same room where Spider played with his Walkman that Miguel had first met him. Back then, Spider was a guru figure. He squatted on his haunches like a Chinaman, wearing thong sandals and a potato-sack shirt with baggy shorts. His large round eyes probed Miguel that first time, as if he could look inside with ease. Miguel hadn't been impressed with the decor. Mattresses without bed frames seemed to be the rage with these people.

"Firebug tells me you like books," Spider said after an awkward silence. It sounded contemptuous. Miguel shrugged.

"You ever read a book called *Oliver Twist?*"

Miguel nodded. "Yeah."

"An' what character would'ju say I'm more like?"

Miguel looked around like this was some kind of joke. He had never been asked a literary question, not even in school. "Fagin," he said.

Spider grinned at Firebug. "He read it okay. Gave me the best answer, too." He looked at Miguel. "Read tha' fucken book five times. My favorite. So which character are you, then? You see yuhself as a kinda Oliver?"

"Nah," Miguel said, rubbing his chin. "The Artful Dodger."

Spider looked pleased. He winked at Firebug, then he picked up a blunt and lit it. "Smoke with me, man."

After that, they became friends. Spider broke him in on small errands, buying supplies at a smoke shop on West Fourth Street, bartering for crack vials, and dropping off packages. It was chump change work. It got him enough money so he could buy some lids and sell enough weed to pay his share of the rent. At the first party Spider invited him to, Miguel brought it up.

"It ain't like I'm complainin'," he had said cautiously, because he didn't know how Spider would react, "but I need more work, more money."

"I don't know," Spider said with a tight-lipped grin. "You bein' a bookworm an' all, I don't wanna get'chu doin' shit tha' might prove too intense f' yuh sensitive nature."

"You cut that out."

The party residence was on the top floor of a private house on Tinton. There was loud music and tons of beat boys and posse boys and girls, all glassy-eyed. Thick rugs, beaded curtains, lava lamps, colored lights. Spider called it Turkish House. He introduced him to a girl named Wanda, who had platinum hair and big tits. She took him into a mirrored room in the back and fucked him. Later some posse grabbed her for a gang -bang but then Jenny took over, skinny, tinted black hair, thick like the hair on a plastic doll. Miguel remembered thinking he was living THE LIFE. Later, when the sun came up and people drifted off into the streets, Miguel lay beside Spider on the sofa.

"So, any complaints?" Spider asked, nudging him.

"I need more work," Miguel answered.

Spider lent him out to a friend who ran a candy store on Southern Boulevard. Way in the back was a fake electrical outlet through which people passed Miguel the money. He was on the other side of the wall, slipping nickel bags and dime bags through the slots. He worked there several days a week, on top of his deliveries. He ran around with Kenneth, a huge black runner who drove a Buick Skylark. Miguel was supposed to learn the ropes. After a few weeks, Spider asked him, "So, you like runnin'?"

"Yeah," Miguel said. "But I'd need a car, right?"

Spider grinned. "Thass no problem, pana. I could get'chu a car."

"No shit? Don't fuck with me, man!"

Kenneth gave him driving lessons. Two months after Miguel had started working for Spider, he had a car, a beat-up secondhand '68 Impala. It was cream-colored, no hubcaps, with torn seats and a battered trunk. He got it the same day he got the license. He drove it all day long, falling in love with every cough, clank, and knock of the engine.

He blew tons of money on it. He found hubcaps. He repainted the car a pretty magenta. He replaced the battered muffler and gave his Baby a new transmission. He reupholstered the seats and later bought tungsten camions. By the time he had monogrammed MY BABY DOES THE HANKY

PANKY on the trunk, his Baby was attracting attention. Now he felt like real hot shit driving down the streets with the girls on the stoops in their tight shorts smiling at him.

"How'dju get to do all this?" Miguel had asked Spider, in total awe.

Spider shrugged, handing him a blunt. "Those who deserve it get the best. Lookit right over there. A little supper f' you in appreciation of yuh work this week." He pointed to the Suarez Twins, who were standing by the window, munching on chips with their plump faces all dimpled.

"So, you like yuh life so far, Artful Dodger?"

"Yessuh, Missa Fagin, I like it real good."

What do they call them—lettuce days? Mixed salads? Miguel couldn't remember the phrase. It struck him how happy he had been then, and how lousy he felt now as he listened to Spider's drunken voice. It was as if Spider had died. When he had made the tape, they had been crazy stoned, people coming and going, music pumping, girls screaming way in the background. It was all there, a chunk of his life along with the man who made it possible.

"Nah man, you gotta be kiddin'," Miguel had said when he saw the Walkman, but Spider wasn't kidding. He was determined to be remembered, immortalized. He was an entrepreneur, what's this about being a criminal? Sure, he had to lie low now, dress like a hippie junkie, but the day will come when they'll see him in a three-piece suit like the successful businessman he IS and EVER SHALL BE, no epitaph yet, m'man, this one gone clear, sitting on top of that huge street empire employing hundreds of kids, KIDS ARE THE FUTURE and Spider's got the future locked right up. Hitler knew about kids, din'chu see that Hitler Youth special on TV, all thum tiny brats throwin' themselves in fronta machine guns? Maan, kids ARE TOMORROW an' I got tomorrow inna palm a' my hand. Where are their parents? Like that question on TV: It's ten P.M., do you know where your children are? YEAH. They're in the street, makin' more money per hour than they'd ever make peddling roasted animal flesh on sesame-seed buns. (Sounds of Miguel rolling on the floor in a coughing laughing fit.)

Spider says he can grab a ten-year-old kid and turn him into a success-ful businessman faster than IBM or ITT. He sounds like a proud camp counselor, talking about giving kids the chance they need, providing the incentive that gets them involved and functioning for themselves. "I activate their independent survival instinct," he says. No school, no company does that. He gets young kiddies to scour the streets looking for discarded crack vials that he pays them a dime apiece for. He knows the dream of every little kid is to have his own car, so he promises them one, an old Camaro, a battered Nova, with tinted windows. He shows off Danny, his resident poster child, eleven years old, with his own GTO, dope threads, and five girlfriends. A scar on his shoulder from where he claims a bullet nicked him. Every little kid that sees him goes WOW. Having a car is almost as dope as having a piece, and Spider can get those too. (Danny always displays his midget .32.) Kids that used to chase each other over rooftops now empty guns at each other across schoolyards, crowded or not, it doesn't matter, none of them can shoot straight, anyway. That's why there are so many innocent bystanders shot up. They call them "mushrooms." (Why mushrooms? Because they pop up in the line of fire. Ho ho ho.) If a kid goes home and sees his pop working fifty hours a week to come home with NADA while the kid makes more money on the street on his own working less, there goes that family. There goes respect and all the American Dream shit. Spider even had families working for him. He saw it as a kind of revolution. Pretty soon, he'd suit up like Che and head for other cities, to spread his operation out, to use the same principles that have worked so well here. Then he could dress up in a three-piece suit and appear on *Donahue.*_\

"The idea, Phil, is to inculcate in the youth the idea that they too can have big cars and guns and be Clint Eastwood and say MAKE MY DAY and have Robin Leach interview them while they lounge on their divan with a few blond beach bunnies. It's my job to open the world to them, to introduce them to the concept of business, free enterprise." NOT AS PRETTY AS GOTTI, *People* magazine piped, BUT LOOKIT HIS CLOTHES! Not the Dapper Don, but Spider the Slick! In his big private jet loaded with blond pink-skinned beauties in metal gear, the ones with the poofed-up hair and spandex and high heels and miniskirts that cling . . . THE CHUMP SHUTTLE. What the fuck?!? Why bother with the blond teasers? Throw them out over Akron or Denver, who needs the artificial flavors and preservatives? We got Latinas, tits overly riped from cattle fattener that slipped into the island's milk supply (remember the article in the *New York Post?* Lovely photos). Our girls PLEASE, boys, no major brains to get in the way, born to say ay papi, ay papi, aaaayy papii . . . grinding into your pale sickly white flesh until you wanna scream for mama and head back to the suburbs, for a nice calm Sunday fuck before brunch. After the release of *Spider: The Movie,* there'll be picket signs and marches and campaigns because white kids seeing movies about mafiosi is one thing, but a SPICK crime lord? OH NOO, before you know it all these white kids will be coming to the SOUTH BRONX because being POOR is cool, wanna talk like them dress like them DANCE like them say DOPE and CHILL all the time thinking nice thoughts about the big melting pot we all swim in when IN FACT the white cream keeps rising to the top while all us other people not of the lily white tumble down to the bottom of the cup like coffee grounds. Are poor people wrong to get money any way they can? THE WORLD IS A LOCKED DOOR. Ain't this war? It's a goddamn people's revolution! (Spider adjusts his beret.)

"Spider . . ." Miguel's voice sounded slightly hysterical and distorted, as if his lips were pressed against the mike. "Almost outta tape, bro'."

"So turn it over . . . Tha' was my pramble. Preamble. Now I get inta the good stuff. Hell bro', I should ax you what it's like t' work f' me."

Miguel giggles. There was laughter all over the place back then. Miguel replayed that part, trying to recognize some of the laughter. He could imagine Cristalena beside him, her eyes glaring at him.

"What makes people sick like that? How could'ju even sit next to a person thass so fucked up?"

IT WAS HIS FATHER, Miguel saw himself screaming at her. It's always the father! The parents hand their sickness down to the kids, right? He was waiting to hear it from Spider's own lips, tales of abuse and violence and heavy drinking, waiting because Miguel had never heard the whole tape. At the time Spider got heavy with his life's story on side two, he had lifted the machine and pressed it to his lips so that the speakers throbbed with his words. He remembered wandering off at that point because Wanda had come in looking for a face to sit on. He had left with her. Now he waited for the story from Spider's very own lips, as if he needed to know why. He was disappointed. The story didn't make any sense. It was going to make a stupid book.

"My father was always a quiet man," Spider said in a serious voice. "He married a loud woman who was always complainin' 'cause he was a quiet man. He worked f' the Post Office f' twenny-five years, retired, lived on this pension thing. Every day you could find 'im outside the bodega on Leggett Avenue playin' dominoes wif' his compadres, chewin' on my mother's bacalaitos. Always had that grin on his face, like everythin's okay wif' him." Spider paused here to puff on something. "Yeah . . . like everythin's okay."

Spider laughed softly. "What kinda man is that? The world is fallin' t' pieces, an' he's sittin' there suckin' on a pipe an' playin' dominoes. He didn't like me inna house. He thought it was bad f' me to be inna house so he set me free. My ma hated it. She wanted me in the house. He used t' wink at me. Used t' come back after dark all dirty an' grimy an' he used t' wink at me . . . Dint know I was sneakin' inta places, robbin' young kids, climbin' up buildings . . . The streets took me over. My parents, they seemed glad jus' t' get me outta they hair. I don't think they had planned on me . . ."

There was some laughter and noise. Spider put the cassette recorder down a moment, and then he came back, his words spilling out at a clip: "I wasn't gonna end up like him NAH I wasn't gonna be a happy nothin' playin' wif' my dominoes fat wife bored life no frills watchin' the wurl' roll by NAH I was boppin' up the street scam here scam there thass me hustlin' hubcaps runnin' a stolen car shop fencin' some shit YO I DINT STEAL IT, OFFICER, but here I am I got money in my pocket. YEAH I believe in CRACK I believe in it 'cause it saved me took me out gave me a hit on high life gave me a hit on power on the juice I got the JUICE don'chu know? My pop don't know nothin' he still sittin' outside tha' bodega still playin' his dominoes sometimes I drive by 'im jus' t' look like I GOTTA LOOK like I GOTTA tell myself THAT AIN'T ME, THAT AIN'T NEVER GONNA BE ME, MISTA SITTIN' BACK RELAXIN' INNA GHETTO the wurl' can go t' hell but I got my dominoes my wife my bacalaitos, bro', the spice of life . . .

"Yo, I don't hate 'im jus' like the same way he don't love me. It's the same can you reach that? I'm sayin' he's glad I'm a big boy I ain't in his way so now he can do the real relaxin'. But'chu know someday I'm gonna drive by in my LIMO an' I'm gonna STOP an' get out an' he gonna lookit me an' his jaw gonna drop, bro'. An' he gonna say YO, WHAT THE FUCK? An' I won't say a word, I passed him by man, jus' like that. I climbed. I came I saw I fucken FUCKED tha' bitch up the ass, Pop. Like did wha'chu didn't have the dick to do, Pop." Spider's voice was trembling with something. Bennies? A hit of crack? Spider didn't do that stuff, it must be something else, something hidden. More to the story than that, he thought, but Spider was an actor. He knew how to screw up his eyes when he had to frighten somebody. He was a Streetwise Patton, twirling his pearl-handled revolvers in front of a mirror to get the act right. He kept talking about the limo, the money the empire the women. It was the whole American Dream he was promoting. It was freedom and democrazy and MONEY. How could the law be after him? The only reason they didn't like him, he yelled, was because he was a Boricua. If he were white, that would be different. They'd make a movie about him, they'd assign a reporter to cover his activities from clubhouse to clubhouse. IF HE WERE WHITE. But he wasn't. And so he wasn't allowed to be good at his craft. Sooner or later, they'd get him.

"But they better move fast 'cause I'm movin' fast, my operation is movin' fast, before you know it I'll be in they backyard across the street in the condo in the house across the street an' then you'll see thum scared. Then you'll see 'um scream f' cops an' safety an' all that shit. But it's gonna be too late."

When he started singing the Carly Simon song "It's Too Late," Miguel shut off the machine, and went into the kitchen for a drink of orange juice, thinking about the ten grand that was sitting in that little book bag Spider had given him last night in the back room of Franco's bodega.

"Look man," Spider told him, voice trembling, "I'm gonna give you the stuff now. I know it's crazy, but I trust'ju. We gotta meet up again tomorrow an' I don't feel like gettin' up early. Don't wanna cut it close." He laughed, breathless from having run there. Miguel hadn't asked him why he ran.

"Thass it. Ten grand. You gonna give this t' the cops tomorrow mornin'. They gonna be parked in a squad car on Fox Street, right off Prospect. Right where you live, bro'."

"Yeah man."

"Eleven o'clock. Be sharp. Can't have 'um think we pullin' a fast one, or else we got big trouble."

"I'll be there." Miguel lit a cigarette. "They ain't gonna do nothin' weird, are they?"

Spider wasn't looking at him, just scanning the pile of boxes where Franco hid the packages. It was a plain-looking bodega, three dark fat men with Indian faces sitting at the counter in straw hats and guayaberas, sipping rum and talking in soft whispers. The store had more beer than anything else; most of the shelves were empty. On drop nights, Spider's boxes were marked by colored stickers and piled in the stockroom. To-night there were just boxes, empty. Spider seemed nervous. It made

Miguel edgy. He was going to ask what was up, but Spider pulled him back out onto the dark street. He waited until Miguel was back in his car and revved the engine. He tossed him the paper, which was folded open on the page where local crimes were unceremoniously listed like want ads. Miguel scanned it as Spider hopped away from the car with his bouncy street shuffle.

> Found murdered, unidentified eighteen-year old male in empty lot on Jackson Avenue, South Bronx. Victim had multiple stab wounds and was partially burned. Police familiar enough with the MO to believe homicide is drug-related.

"Fucken shit."

Miguel pounded the wheel of his car, spun around to see if he could spot Spider so he could yell at him, but Spider was gone. He was like a roach, could melt into the cracked recesses of the tenements all around. A dirty trick, a dirty fucken trick! All that talk about trust, and he lays this shit on me! Miguel roared out of the parking space.

He sat in the kitchen with his lips pressed against the juice carton. Waiting for eleven o'clock, getting crazy thoughts about the money. He could be at the airport, buying a ticket out. But a ticket where? Where could he go to make a life for himself? It wasn't going to get better no matter where he was. If he dropped out of the business, he'd be nothing, a young punk living on a grant, a crime subsidy that would soon run out. Then what? He'd be a regular seventeen-year-old brat trying to get a job at McDonald's shoveling fries and pushing a mop. He couldn't leave. He was dependent, like an addict. He couldn't go and he couldn't stay. There was probably somebody on the street assigned to watch him, just in case he did decide to jump into his car. It made him feel rotten. He wanted to be really trusted, and wanted to be able to trust someone completely. He didn't know anyone like that. The business hadn't brought him any-one like that, and Cristalena, well, he was lying to her. He just couldn't tell her. She probably trusted him, but he couldn't tell her the truth. Was that love? It made him want to get stoned, to forget about it all.

He had opened the book bag to see what ten grand looked like, but the stuff was wrapped in brown crackling paper, dozens of bundles. He put it all back in disgust, went over to his window to look out at the street. There was Fox Street, flanked by tall grass that shivered with cold. A cop car was already parked there. Miguel stared at the people on the street, trying to figure out which guy'd been assigned to watch him. Was it that thin ugly guy in the brown coat, leaning against the streetlight, his eyes scanning the windows? Or was it that short antsy guy in the tattered beret, shifting his weight from foot to foot as he stood behind the glass of the bus-stop shelter?

Miguel got dressed. He was thinking of taking a quick ride to see Cristalena, to give her a hug, to feel something warm and good up against him. She made him feel safe, home turf, but at the same time she confused him. There were so many things he had to tell her. Would she leave him? He knew she wasn't an idiot, that sooner or later she'd start to notice things. He'd have to tell her, and soon. He wanted to get it all off his chest. It would be a relief. But what would she do? Would she still be with him?

His thoughts circled like vultures. No, he'd see her afterward. Before, she might pick it up that he was worried, it was weird how girls could do that. He crossed the street, carrying the book bag by its drawstrings, heading for the parked cop car. The wind was vicious, tall grass gasping with distress. The car was packed, nothing but dark globs through the sunlit windows, badges on hats, badges on coats, brass buttons in pretty rows. The back door opened for him.

The first thing he noticed when he got inside was that the cop beside him had covered his shield numbers with some kind of elastic band. The two cops in the front seat didn't turn around right away. The one beside him looked like some Hispanic borough president, with a pudgy face, swollen eyes, and a well-clipped mustache. He didn't look at Miguel at first, not until he had closed the door. Then the cop looked at him, his lips pressed together so hard they were pale.

"So where's Valentino? Ahh?" The cop in the passenger seat spun around to stare with his cold blue eyes, his puffy moonscape face as pale as Monterey Jack cheese. "Ahh? Wha' happened t' the boy who thought he could have a little vacation with our money? Ahh?"

"Shut up with that," the cop behind the wheel rasped. He wasn't turning around no matter what. All Miguel could see were his malt-ball eyes in the rearview mirror. "Just get this shit over with."

The Latin Cop nudged Miguel with a finger. "So wha'chu got for us, posse boy?"

Miguel didn't like the way the man's lips puckered. He slid the book bag over to him. The cop peered in, then passed it to the guy in front, who began counting the bundles.

"What's your name?" the Latin Cop asked quietly, as if interviewing him.

Miguel felt his own eyes were on fire. He found it hard to focus on anything. "Miguel," he said.

" 'Ey Petey," the guy behind the wheel said hoarsely, "less get this over with, right? We got the dough, less blow." He turned on the engine with a swift, disgusted motion.

The cop beside him smacked him on the arm. "You fuckhead. Moron." He turned to look at Miguel, who noticed his badge number was covered too. " 'Ey Miguelito there. You din't hear him say Petey, now did'ju?" The eyes had something ugly in them. "Did'ju?"

Miguel was shrugging when the Latin nudged him again. "You didn't answer my question. I'm going to ask you again. What's your name?"

Miguel sighed. "I told'ju. Miguel."

"Miguel what."

"It's just Miguel, man."

Cheese Face whacked him on the knee with one of the bundles. "No, you didn't answer MY question. Did'ju hear this bozo say Petey or din'chu? Ahh?"

"No. I heard'ju say it twice already though."

The cop behind the wheel smothered a laugh. It made Cheese Face's eyes flash for a seond.

"Are you in school?" The Latin Cop continued his interview. Miguel started to hate him. He sounded like a goddamn guidance counselor.

"Yeah," Miguel said with contempt. "I'm in a work-study program."

"Cheez," the cop behind the wheel said.

"We should show this fuck what happens t' smart-aleck spick kids," Cheese Face said. He was ripping open the money packets.

"You shut up with that shit," the Latin Cop said forcefully. He turned to Miguel. "Why are you into this kind of shit? Don't you know where this kind of shit can lead'ju?"

Miguel stared at him for a moment, his lips trembling. "Yeah," he said, looking him up and down. "I figured I might become a cop."

The Latin Cop looked away as if he had been slapped. Then Cheese Face drew his gun and thrust it right in Miguel's face, pushing him back. Miguel froze, not even able to focus his eyes.

"Ah come on, man," the Latin Cop protested. "Put that away."

"Shut up," Cheese Face barked. He nailed Miguel with his ice-blue eyes. "Let me tell you something," he sneered. "You fuck with me and I'll blow your little street attitude all over the seat. Don't think I won't."

There was a pause in which the only sound was Miguel's swallowing.

"Ahh? You ain't spittle. You can't lick the shit of a good cop. You cun't ever be a cop. You say wha'chu said again. Go ahead. I dare you, you little fuck. What, you don't got much to say now, huh? You not so brave now, are you? Now you're all quiet. You keep it that way. Now you tell your little arachnid friend he better not be late next time or I'm personally gonna find him. You read my lips yet? Why don'chu nod like a good little boy?"

Miguel did not nod. Cheese Face thrust the cold steel up against his cheek harder.

"You better nod," the one behind the wheel said. His livid eyes floated in the rearview mirror.

Miguel's trembling was getting out of control, his anger making him twitch. "I heard'ju, man, get off . . ."

"Get off? Baby, you don't want me t' get off. I got strange ways of getting off. There are plenty of empty lots, you know. Just waiting for a stiff like you."

"Cheez!" the cop behind the wheel complained. "There's people walking by, man, wanna be seen doing that?"

Cheese Face didn't hear him. "You ain't nothing. You don't mean shit. I could take you out, mothafucka, ain't nobody gonna even miss you . . ." His eyes were like the heads on rivets. "Why don'chu sing me 'The Star-Spangled Banner.' "

"Cheezus!" The cop behind the wheel punched the dash. "Fuck this shit, Petey man. You didn't say anything about terrorizing some kid!"

"You shut the fuck up!" Cheese Face yelled, sighting down the barrel. "Now come on, Latino baby, give us your last name!"

"Torres," Miguel lied.

"Very good. And now how about your address?"

Miguel rattled off an address. The abandoned place on Wales.

"Is that for real? Ahh? You don't wanna lie to me, boy . . ."

Miguel had tears in his eyes, one hand slowly rising toward the gun. It was a reflex, something he couldn't help. He glared at the Latin Cop, who looked down as if he had lost something.

"Ah! Ah!" Cheese Face moved the gun slightly, but Miguel's hand was already on it. "Get off the gun!"

"Fucken shoot o' shut up!" Miguel said through clenched teeth.

The cop behind the wheel suddenly spun, reaching over with a disgusted grimace, pushing the gun away. "Get out," he told Miguel. "Just get the fuck out."

Miguel opened the door and tumbled to the sidewalk because his knees were all springy. He got up and wobbled, wiping blindly at his wet face, not even feeling the cold. He took about four steps, turned, and gave the cop car the finger as it silently flashed its red lights and coasted away up Fox Street.

He walked toward his car, glaring at anyone he saw on the street, thinking that Spider's stoolie should get to see what he had gone through. He dried his face and went over to his car, looking forward to a long, angry drive. The minute he saw his Baby he knew something was wrong. She was listing to one side. Sure enough, two of his tires had been slashed. How else were they gonna be sure I didn't go for a long drive with the money?

"Bastids."

Then he had to shut himself up in the car. Then the real tears came, along with a vicious rage that paralyzed him there for about an hour before he set himself to change the tires.

7

Cristalena worked on Sundays. He wanted to go see her but he couldn't. He was too upset. Worse than that, he needed to talk to somebody about what had happened, somebody he could trust. He wanted to run to her but knew he couldn't tell her a word. She would know something was up with him, and he'd have to bury himself with more lies. No dice, so he drove over to the Cuban sandwich shop to see Amelia. He had spent two hours taking care of his tires in the rain. When he came in through the door with its twittering string of bells, he was wet and exhausted and hadn't even eaten yet. Amelia was rushing from table to table, dropping off coffee, taking orders in her tiny flip pad, sending Miguel a loving wink as she balanced herself on one leg, leaning back to drop some dishes onto the counter. She looked so human standing there, so normal, not like the nocturnal creature he would drive to wienie roasts. He sat at a table right by the window so he could watch his Baby.

Amelia scooted over to him, hands on hips. "You look like shit." She brushed some wet hair from his face, stooped, landed a splotchy wet kiss on his cheek. Miguel wiped. It made her laugh. The place was pretty busy, what with the Perez Prado mambo blaring and the sounds of cups and saucers and the voices of old men sitting, spewing out cigarette smoke, dishes clattering, forks and spoons. The old man one table down from Miguel whacked his table and laughed. "Homenaje a Castro!" he yelled, ripples of laughter encouraging him, his eyes black marbles in tomato soup, dizzy spinning. "Le voy a dar un homenaje a Castro!" And with that he let out a long raspberry that inspired some applause.

Amelia sat across from Miguel, eyebrows knitted with concern. She noticed his eyes avoiding her, skipping around the room.

"Papi," she called out, "un san'wich de pernil y una Coca-Cola." Her father, a short pudgy man behind the counter, nodded and disappeared into the kitchen.

"So what happened?" she asked softly, leaning forward.

He shook his head and stared out at his Baby, then he took out a cigarette and lit it. "They slit the wheels on my car," he said, his hand trembling his voice trembling, and then it all started tumbling out, about the dead kid in the paper and Spider saying he trusted him and the ten grand and the cops. He had to stop when he got to the cops. Their faces kept coming back to him, rubbery and distorted. They made him want to kill someone, to rip a gun out from under his waistband and SHOOT just to see their faces their fucken faces contort collapse get chopped open by shells, splintering glass and shattering the blood-smeared dashboard. Then he could watch the big funeral on TV, with the fucken mayor standing there looking like an angry real estate broker amidst all those caskets draped flags solemn faces. The eager newscaster: "They died in the line of duty, trying to make life a little safer for all of us."

—"He was a good person, always helping out, helping people," says LILY-white neighbor from his LILY-white porch somewhere out on Long Island FAR from the action, maybe near a fucken beach. "He was devoted to helping kids." Pah pah pah, eat lead mothafucka, go play cops and robbers someplace else, this ain'cha turf. Occupation Army. Working-class scabs. Go shoot a black kid in the back, mothafucka.

No, he didn't want to get out because of what happened with the cops. They didn't scare him so much. With cops, that's just the way it was. But Spider scared him. Even Firebug scared him. It was the people he worked with that he couldn't trust, people who would do anything to get by, buy and sell anyone. Miguel was sick of being part of a machine that was eating up the city and spitting out the bones. Sick of the hollow-eyed kids clustered around corners showing off their .45s to impress the girls who stand nearby waiting to be impressed by maybe a shooting or at least some kinda gift, something to go with that diamond watch Orlando gave her last week BUT Orlando's a cheap mothafucka LOOKIT Jake, he gave me a diamond necklace an' tha' shit is DOPE. Words spilled out of Miguel's mouth like cannon fire; Amelia squinted at him like she wanted him to stop. When he stopped she looked relieved, but he was only catching his breath, his eyes wild dancing eight balls. Howabout Bozo? Thirteen-year-old AFRICAN AMERICAN calls Wales Avenue his turf; short, thin, always complaining because the big boys won't let him in all their reindeer games. Hangs with the tough posses, climbs fire escapes, sneaks through transoms; watches for cops, opens doors from the inside, sneaks them into schools. They give him candy. He smokes it up. One day Miguel saw it with his own eyes. That girl, reptile eyes, Veronica; everybody calls her Little Vicious. She was standing there looking at him with her legs all sparkling like she sprayed them, ass poking out of some striped miniskirt like she's already been through puberty and survived. Has she even had a period yet? Is she FUCKEN OLD ENOUGH? Who knows but she told Bozo she would fuck him if he could prove he was a man. Bozo bristled, he was like, WHA'CHU MEAN BITCH?? And everybody was laughing so she asked him if he had a gun, what kinda gun it was. He told her it was a .32—SHE SMIRKED and said a real man, well, he would have a .45. Bozo was stung burned fried frazzled sizzled boiled HATED the laughter of his elders all clustered around an old car drinking beer and doing NOTHING watching cars roll by in the fading sunlight. "So you gotta popgun, big deal," she says. "But'chu know how t' use it?"

"Bitch, I use my piece alla time." This gets howls from everybody EVEN Little Vicious laughs and clutches her quivering tummy what little there is of it showing between skirt and halter.

"The only way I fuck you is if I see you shoot somebody." She says it with a shrug as if dismissing him.

"I wun't kill f' no pussy," Bozo says, making everybody erupt some pounding car hoods some rolling against car chrome in spasms, pointing faces chinked up all in squiggles.

"So you don't gotta kill somebody," Little Vicious points out. "You can wound 'um. A real man he know when t' kill an' when not. Like Chuck Conners in *The Rifleman.*"

So everybody's head is nodding, going yeah, thass a good point, and Bozo looked at them for help but everybody just shrugged, the game was getting boring and so break off another beer bro'. Bozo walks up the street and this young guy comes out of the pizzeria wasn't nothing special about him just a young guy ALONE nibbling cheese dripping and quivering as he sucks on the long steaming strand. Then some smart aleck yells "HEY HERE COME SOMEBODY NOW, BOZO!" Was it Miguel? Was it him laughing and rolling on the hood of the car who watched as Bozo's predator eyes narrowed and focused on the young HERB? He gets three feet past Bozo before Bozo runs up to him and draws his piece. There's this collective GASP before the super-loud PAF! PAF! and the guy is spinning falling, hands racing for his thigh, pizza falling a sloppy bloody mess.

"Ohh shit!" Somebody half laughs and then they're all racing to pile into the car like college kids out to win a bet, leaving Bozo standing there looking stunned and HERB rolling around on the sidewalk with clenched teeth. Bozo makes for the car but gets a kick in the stomach, his popgun clattering to the sidewalk as he is pushed away, the same words in his ears he has heard before: "Outta here, SCRUB, you ain't big enough t' ride with us."

Amelia got up from the table, shaking her head. She brought him his sandwich and soda, placing it down like a mommy, passing a hand through his wet hair. Miguel stared at the sandwich like he'd had his guts taken out.

"We all got stories," she said. "I just hate hearing them. It's like listening to myself. Like I'm trying to . . ." She sat down again, leaning close, grasping his hands. "Like I'm trying not to see it. Like I'm trying to dance around it." She leaned back, sighed, and then she grinned. "You ever see me dance?" Something devilish twinkled in her eyes. He shook his head. "Well. You should see me dance to merengue."

In a flash her face changed, replaced by something solemn, the face in a car window at the funeral. "I was right about'chu," she said softly. "I knew you were too sensitive for this shit."

He took a bite from the sandwich, crumbs raining down on the table.

"I feel like I been insulted," he said with his mouth full.

She looked so dainty sitting there in a black skirt, black tights, and sneaks. She had on this black leotard top like dancers wear that gave her head and shoulders a slim girlish charm. Her neck looked longer because her hair was piled up on her head.

"You look like a giraffe," he told her.

"Well, nice to know you came all this way just to see me."

"Sure didn't come f' this food." He grimaced, chomping.

She grew serious. "Look. Spider's in a lotta trouble. He made himself a big man in this town, and now he has to start proving it. A lotta people gunning for him, Miguel. I'm sure you noticed how twitchy he is these days."

"Yeah, he's a little jumpy."

"His operation ballooned. He was just some two-bit street punk, a low-level thief who made some lucky connections. They trusted him. They gave him a railroad to run and he turned it into an airline. He ain't the top, he's only a middle manager. He runs it, keeps it going, forms mergers. Hires posses to do the dirty work. But the real brains, they scoop in the cash. Ten, twenty times what he makes. We don't even see those people. Spider ain't the top of the ladder. Just one of the hard-to-reach rungs."

Miguel made a face because she said "rungs."

"Who do you know that's made a life of this shit? Ahh? Anybody? Sure, a kid can make several thousand bucks a week, more even. So what? Don't he still live in the ghetto? What happens when he leaves the ghetto? Ain't he nothing once he steps out of this place? It's an addiction. You get money an' big chains an' guns an' cars but'chu can't get outta the ghetto, because the ghetto is where you matter. It's where the prestige and power is. You go out into the real world, that's someone else's turf. You can be a big man on Fox Street, but once you head downtown you're just another ugly spick kid."

Miguel was getting annoyed. It was like listening to himself talking. "Man, you think I don't know tha' shit?"

"It's a trap, Miguel. At least you can see it. Spider wants to become a drug lord, he'll do anything to get it, sell anyone, he'll even . . ."

"Yeah, I know."

"Time might be running out for him. It's all catching up, he can taste it coming. Thass why he's looking for a second, a lieutenant, somebody he can get to run the operation, to take the local risks, somebody he can trust. He wants to branch out on his own, start his own empire, so he don't work for nobody anymore. Thass why he's nervous. His boss could ice him. The competition could ice him. Distributors might not wanna risk upsetting his boss by dealing with him, so they might ice him. A posse could do it. He's arming up for civil war. He's gonna secede from the union. And all these kids he's using. It's funny when you think about it. They act like they got it made, but they live like rats in holes, scurrying from sunlight, still living in the same shit, with the rubble an' empty buildings an' all that fun South Bronx shit. Self-deception. We get some money an' it buys us VCRs an' stereos an' gold chains an' we drive through the streets shooting at each other like we're big bad successful men. But it's a trap. White people couldn't a' come up with a better way to screw up blacks an' Latinos."

Miguel leaned back, looking tired. He stubbed out his cigarette and grinned. "You sound like yuh runnin' f' office."

She grinned back. "Well, maybe I could, who knows? Who knows where I could end up?" Her lips quivered, grin fading as if she'd just received a bad news flash. "I think I already know," she whispered, petulantly tipping over the salt and pepper shakers. Miguel scooped out some ice from his soda cup and began chomping on it.

"What I don't get is how come you know so much about Spider."

She chewed on a lip, looking out the window. "Well, I know him. I know him pretty good."

She got up with a scrape of her chair, collecting plates from a table nearby, adding totals on her pad. Behind the counter, her father began fiddling with the dial on the small radio that hissed and sputtered before it filled the room with guarachas. Two men sat at the counter talking with him, their faces like road maps. She sat down again.

"Ohh, I get it," Miguel said. "It's 'cause a' the crack, right?" He lowered his voice. "You know 'im 'cause a' yuh bad habits."

"You don't know anything about it," she said stiffly, sitting up a little.

"The hell I don't. Listen, I met a whole lotta girls doin' crack. What they do t' get it, man, what it takes outta thum. Spider has a whole stable of 'um." He paused. "An' jus' now I'm startin'na wonder wha'chu been givin' away t' get it. Yeah, I really do."

He stared at her. She shook her head, cleared the table, dropping off stuff behind the counter, talking some to her father. The two men laughed as if there had been a joke. Then she returned, not sitting down. She wiped his table with a cloth.

"I get it now," he said, lighting another cigarette, irritated by her stern face. "You only know whass best f' me, right?"

"I don't wanna talk to you." Furiously she rearranged the salt and pepper shakers, wiping at the table again. "You confuse me. You make me feel sometimes like you really give a fuck about me. An' I really can't afford to think that."

"What the hell," he said, smirking. "We all make mistakes."

A grin trembled on her lips.

"Don't fight it," he said.

She sat down. "Miguel, you gotta quit. I know you want to. You ain't the type for this."

"You mean 'cause I'm sensitive?" He spit the words out like he was insulted.

"I mean because you're better than this. It's gonna be hard. Spider really likes you. He talks about'chu a lot. He wants to make you his second. But it's not because he loves you. It's because you're the only person right now in the organization that he can trust. He's gonna put more pressure on you."

"But if I'm so important, why he chump me out by throwin' me inna car fulla psycho cops, man?" There was anguish in his voice. Amelia whacked the table and leaned closer.

"Don'chu see that you're the only one he could trust with the money? He'd send in his own mother if he had to! I don't think he meant to freak you with that newspaper thing. He just got whacked out, desperate. He trusts you the most, but he still ain't sure. Like every great dictator. I tell you, he might put you in worse spots, Miguel. You just gotta quit."

"I didn't even know you knew Spider." He leaned closer. "So how come Firebug quit workin' f' Spider? Firebug's always real hazy about that. All he ever says is that he got a better offer."

She sighed, looking reluctant. "It was Spider who set him up with the better offer."

"Oh. So Firebug jus' dumped 'im?"

She sighed and all these words tumbled out: "Firebug was seeing me an' he was working for Spider an' one day he walked in on me an' Spider an' then, well, that broke us all up."

Miguel squinted at her. "What?"

"I'm saying that I was seeing Firebug an' I was seeing Spider an' one day he caught us together."

"You were playin' one helluva board game."

"Spider tried to make it up to Firebug, that's all. Him an' Firebug still talk, sometimes Spider'll do something for him. But they're not as tight like before." She shrugged. "An' thass because of me."

"Why does Firebug still see you?"

She rolled the salt shaker along the table. "Because I told him the only reason I was with Spider was to get crack. He didn't know I was a . . . Anyway, he didn't know back then."

"An' was that the real reason?" His eyes seemed to scorch her.

"Stop interrogating me!"

"Well was it?"

"What do you give a fuck for if I did or not?"

"You have a job! You don't need to work somebody t' get that!"

"Maybe I don't plan to spend my money on shit like that. Why should I pay anything if I can get it for free?"

"Maan, you call that free?" Miguel stubbed out his cigarette with a look of disgust. "Man. Whatta mess. So is that why you still see Spider? Don't lookit me like that, I know you still see 'im, I can tell by the way you talk."

"But thass so immature," she said weakly, tearing a napkin to pieces. "Do you think thass all there is to it? Sex? Did it ever occur to you that maybe Spider has other needs? I mean, yesterday night we spent three hours talking about Dickens."

"Ohh man!"

"Thass right. So he never got to college, so what? He still devoured that copy of *Oliver Twist* I gave him."

"You gave him that?"

"I gave him that. When I first met him, too. Before you even showed up. I told him he reminded me of it and he wanted to read it."

"So you'll be his sorta walkin' library, is that it? An' he pays you with—"

"I don't need to talk about this." She rose up. He grabbed her wrist.

"You playin' him an' Firebug!"

"I ain't playing nobody!" She lowered her voice, leaning closer. He looked betrayed, as if she had been playing him too. "Look, I told'ju where I'm at. You couldn't ever understand where I'm at. There aren't no rules in this game. You're looking at me like you're waiting to hear them. Thass why you should get out. Everybody here has an angle, a scam. I don't care wha'chu think. What, I look like Cinderella to you? So maybe I fucked Spider for crack. An' yes, I fuck Firebug too. Because he has a big dick. Okay? But I'm not in love with the fuck. There ain't nothing there to be in love with, or be loyal to. You'd need to turn him into a person for that. There ain't no such miracle. You think he's your friend?" There was pity in her eyes mixed with the harsh coldness in her voice. "You got a lot to learn."

"Great. An' whass yuh angle with me? Huh?"

Her face softened. "I'm in love with you."

"Oh shit, gimme a fucken break!"

"It's true Miguel, I'm in love with you. I've met a lot of guys, but you're the first one that—it's so ironic that you're younger an' everything because—fuck, you're just the closest thing to a young Marlon Brando I ever seen."

"Cut it out, Amelia. I already got a girl." He wasn't looking at her.

"Yeah, I know." She looked out the window, her arms crossed. "Whass her name again?" The mocking grin appeared.

"Cristalena."

"What?"

"I said Cristalena. Don't be makin' tha' face!"

"Sounds like some kinda dishwashing liquid."

"She's beautiful."

"Yeah. I bet. Straight, virginal, innocent, clean. Goes to church. Long hair. Doesn't know anything about all this shit, right?"

"Her parents are pentecostals . . ."

She choked back a laugh. "Yeah right, a little virgin, a device sent by heaven to cleanse your soul. Jesus, I'm disappointed. How predictable can you be? But if you weren't predictable, you wouldn't be a Latin guy, now would'ju? Marlon Brando looks or not. Have you ever seen *On the Waterfront*?"

"Nope." He spit an ice cube into his cup.

"You wanna come see it with me? It's playing this week at The Cinema Village."

"I don't think Cristalena would like that."

"She won't like that you're a runner, either. Face it, your thing with her ain't gonna last," she said with authority as if she had already checked the script. "She's not gonna understand about your life. You haven't told her anything at all?"

"No, no, no, not'chet." He flipped over his cup, ice clattering onto the table wetly.

"Mmm hmp." She nodded like a doctor making a diagnosis. "She ain't gonna understand, Miguel."

"Yes she will." He didn't sound so sure. "Anyway, I'm gonna get out." He sounded like he was giving in to something Amelia walked away from him, watching him tenderly as she took care of some departing customers and cleared their tables. She spoke with her father in crisp clear Spanish that surprised Miguel. She came back and sat at his table, with a cigarette between her lips.

"I'm on a break," she said, puffing, and then she took the cigarette and gently placed it between his lips. "You really gonna quit, honey?"

"Yeah man. I'm sicka this shit. I gotta think about where I'm gonna end up. I got eight thousand bucks."

"Did'ju change the hiding place?"

"Yeah man. Shit, what a nag you are!"

"Jus' wait 'til we married an' shit." It was her pretend street voice, thicker, her lips popping out. He laughed.

She kept mugging for him and he kept laughing, Amelia nudging him and bringing her face closer. "What? What is it? Whass so funny?" When he stopped laughing, his eyes lingered over her gratefully, and he wanted to kiss her and hug her and buy her a Jaguar XK-150 S.

"Ohh shit," he said, returning the cigarette to her lips. He sighed and the laughter was gone and something tender hovered between them. She was still in a kind of happy daze when she asked him if he had working papers.

"Nah." He shrugged.

"I could maybe find you some work. I mean, if you quit. You'll need to do something for money, you know. You could work here, I could talk to my father."

"Ohh man. Forget it."

"Just think about it."

"Miguel! You don't even have working papers! Where you gonna go?"

"I don't know, stop puttin' pressure on me!" He covered his face a moment like a little boy who had just been kicked by a bully.

"Sheez. There you go again."

"Well, maybe you should do somethin' f' yuhself before you go poking yuh nose in everybody's life. I mean, how come you got all the answers f' me, but not one f' you?"

"I have my answers," she said, her voice trembling. Her face darkened. "Jus' stop. Don't start confusin' me again." It was a little girl plea.

"Fine. Suit yuhself." He shrugged indifferently, looking out the window. He knew his distance bothered her. She got up from the table, pushing it at him.

"The food's on me," she said in her cold street voice. "Get outta here before my father starts to act weird. I'll see you later." She gave the table a quick wipe and disappeared behind the counter. He left and got in his car, turning the heater up full blast, waiting for his Baby to warm him. It bugged him that there was a side to her that he couldn't get to. He looked through the foggy window and spotted her, leaning against the storefront glass, staring at him.

8

Was he the enemy? He felt like it as he entered his building. Three of
the apartments on the first floor were empty, and one was a crack house.
He got nods from the battered fuzzy faces that lingered in the halls, the
junkies that waited for their fix from the sliding peephole in 3B. There
were still normal people: The frightened Mexican ladies with their thick
black hair scurrying down the stairs clutching their big-headed kids. They
always slam doors. A lady on his floor covered her door with posters of
saints. Some crackheads had pissed on it. He remembered seeing her the
day she tore them off, her sturdy furrowed face defiant. "You can't break
me," she told Miguel, as if it had been him all along. The Enemy. Maybe
he hadn't noticed it before, this state of war, not until Cristalena. She
made him feel like an insect playing at being human. From then on he
saw he was living on an anthill, his crib an ant hole, Firebug lying there
grinding his mandibles, funny sexy crack bitch licking up his thorax.

Firebug wasn't in. Miguel went straight to the refrigerator, grabbed
the half-empty carton of orange juice. He had his beeper out. It was off.
The minute he turned it on, it began to scream. Spider's code flashed.
"Urgent." Miguel turned it off, put it on the kitchen table and stared at
it. Then he went to the phone.

"Hello?"

It was Rosa's voice, sounding as if she had just recovered from a real
good joke, bits of laughter dripping off the edges.

"Hi. It's Miguel. Is Cristalena around?"

"She sure is. Hold on." He heard a vociferous I TOL'JU!! from Cristalena before she took the phone and said, "Hi, lover." Her voice caused tremors. He felt safe and scared.

"Hey Lena. Wha'chu doin' tonight."

She sighed into the phone. "Ohhhh you know, I'm so busy. Like I'm gonna have to check my schedule. Rosa dear, you han' me my schedule?" There was laughter, then a loud rustling of paper. "Uck, I'm jus' so busy tonight."

"Tough shit. I'm comin'na pick you up. Okay?"

"Mmmm. Lookit him take command. I like that in a penis."

"What?"

Howling girl laughter all around, with Rosa screaming, "Girl, you are in SIN!"

"I'm sorry," Cristalena said. "We're jus' actin' like little girls today. I'm always whack when I come outta work."

"Thass okay. Look, I really wanna see you, I need to real bad. Can we go out? We get some pasta up on Fordham, maybe catch a movie if it ain't too late? I know you got school tomorrow."

She sighed into the phone. "I'm yours, Miguel. Got'chu a special flavor today." She smacked her lips.

"Damn. I wonder what that means."

"You'll find out."

He had time to take a bath. It felt good to be with the kind of girl that you get on the phone with and then can't get off, saying goodbye over and over again and sighing and then talking about something else and then not being able to get off even after making all the smoochy kisses. The only thing was that she was living on another world, a nicely colored island with a Crayola crayon sky, and here he was storming her beach with his landing craft. The only thing was that no matter where he went with her, Spider and Firebug were there too, ugly gremlins chewing on his ankles, shooting him with rubber bands. He cursed.

He stepped into the tub, the hot water making him feel like he was suffocating. He soaped up; the water grew murky and foamy. His body was just starting to relax when the bathroom door swung open, making him hop up with a splash.

"Damn mothafucka!" he screamed.

"Hello there. Kemo sabe. Fellow artisan." Firebug leaned against the door, his puffy coat making him look like a dwarf. He had a long cigarette holder in his hand like one of those F. Scott Fitzgerald people.

"Close the fucken door!" Miguel yelled.

Firebug came in and shut the door.

"What the fuck you want? Can'chu see I'm takin' a bath?"

"Is tha' wha'chu was doin'? I thought'chu was jus' in here jerkin' off 'cause you like a lotta lubrication, so . . ."

"Firebug . . ."

"Calm down with the pato-phobia, pana. You know I ain't a' the tribe. Besides, I got a much bigger dick than you. I don't even got what they call . . . um . . . penis envy!"

"Only women get that, fuckhead." Miguel leaned back and shampooed his hair. "So where you been?"

"Oh me? Man, I tell you." He squatted down beside the tub. There was a joint in the cigarette holder. It had gone out but Firebug relit it, taking a long toke that filled the place with the aroma of good smoke. "I was up on Fifth Avenue today. One of the big buildings, man, you shoulda seen it. I was up inna suite. Floor-t'-ceilin' windows, man, you won't believe the view. I looked out, it was like, I could see all the fucken cars an' fucken little bug people crawlin' along, an' all thum buildings all shoved together an' lookin' like I could jus' reach out with a match an' light the whole shit, the whole fucken city burnin', all of it in flames, an' me standin' up there lookin' down on it like tha' guy Hitler in all yuh books, goin' 'Wow!' "

Miguel smirked. "I don't think Hitler ever went 'Wow' in his life."

"Well, maybe in German he said 'Wow.' "

"Nah man. Germans don't say that."

"Anyway, I was up there meetin' with some pretty important people. I'm takin' some big assignments, bro', movin' outta Little League into the majors." He passed Miguel the joint but Miguel thought better of it. Cristalena didn't even like cigarettes.

"So I met this guy called Donahue. White like a chalk. His thing is fires, bro', a real expert. He showed me all these high-time gels an' shit, jellies an' fuses an' shits like I don't even know about. Liquid explosives. Smoke pellets. I was droolin'." His eyes got glassy, as if he was looking at himself in a mirror. "I think he liked me. Yeah, he liked me. He saw I got real potential. They givin' me some real incentive." He looked at Miguel. "An advance like you won't believe."

He dug into his coat and handed Miguel a thick envelope. Miguel opened it without even drying his hands. Before he could even count it, Firebug began to giggle.

"Yo man, thass three thousand dollars."

"Get the fuck! For a torch? You got that much?"

"I got that plus a commission. It's like gettin' a promotion. I'm dealin' with the big boys now. You know what that mean? Big changes f' my life, f' you too if you stick around. But then, who knows about'chu? Who knows what team you playin' on?"

"Whass that mean?" Miguel had been immersing his head under the stream of water from the tap. He emerged dripping, eyes shut from the soap.

"Nothin'. Not a fucken thing. Okay? I'm tellin' you this money means a big change. Thass all I'm gonna say." Firebug got up, pausing to open the door a crack. "Hey, you know the phone's been ringin'?"

"Well what the fuck am I supposed t' do about it?" Miguel was splashing water all over himself, sitting up in the tub, soapy foam clinging to his pubic hairs, outline of his thigh muscles glistening. Firebug stood there by the open door. The phone was ringing all right.

"So wha'chu thinka my fire, bro'?"

Miguel turned off the water and stood up, grabbing a towel.

"Maan, I made some good smoke. Covered the sky, blotted it right out. The wind was right, the windows lit up nice, everything timed real good."

Miguel squinted. "You saw the wienie roast? You never go t' wienie roasts. I thought'chu—"

"Can you guess where I was at?" Firebug relit the joint and toked. "Nah."

"You can't even try?" Firebug's voice was abrasive.

"I don't know, man." Miguel was toweling off his muscular legs, stepping out of the tub onto the cold tile floor, goose bumps rising everywhere. "Damn, man, close tha' door!" The phone was still ringing.

Firebug gave the half-open door a shove. It bumped against the jamb with a hollow thud. "I was up on the el, man. I was up there, scopin' it all out, din't even pay fare!" His eyes narrowed. "Din'chu like my fire?"

Miguel exhaled as he wiped his shoulders with the towel. "Yeah, I liked it fine. It was a good one."

"Mothafucka," Firebug said with a hint of anger, eyes small and vindictive. "You din't even get out of yuh car." He stormed out of the bathroom.

Miguel tried to ignore it. He went into his room, slipped on some briefs and a pair of denim wrap pants when Firebug appeared.

"Yo man, it's Spider on the phone."

Miguel sighed, went over to his phone and picked it up, waiting for the other line to click. "Yo!" he yelled when he didn't hear it. "Hang up the other line!"

Spider's voice was calm; it sounded fragile and small. "Yo, whassup? What happened? I been tryin'na get'chu since one o'clock."

"My beeper's actin' funny, man."

"Din't I tell you to call me after the drop?"

"NO." Abrupt, loud. "You was too busy makin' newspaper deliveries an' shit."

There was a pause. "Oh. Well. Yeah, the drop went okay. I heard from my man on the force. You did good."

"Did'ja man on the force also tell you those bastids almost blew my goddamn head off jus' f' kicks?"

Spider exhaled. "I'm sorry about that, pana. There's always some danger, you know, cops are so unstable these days . . . But'chu know, on top a' all this shit thass been happenin' . . . um . . . I din't tell you but Rico's missin'."

"Rico?"

"Tall guy? Used to run the place on Brook? A good number, man. Dependable. I woulda sent him instead a' you, but it's hard, Miguel, you don't know how fucken hard it is t' find people I can trust."

"I know. Especially if they get they tires slashed."

"What?"

"Did'ju tell those apes you had eyeballin' me t' slash my tires?"

"Hol' up, hol' up, what?"

"They slashed my fucken cams, Spider. You told 'um to, right?"

There was a loud resonating beep. "Excuse me," the machine voice said. "Please deposit five cents for the next three minutes or your call will be . . ."

"Ahh shit, hol' up, man, I'm tryin'na find a goddamn nickel . . . there it go." There was a ding, then a sudden click.

"Hello? Listen man, I din't order nothin' like that." Spider's voice was starting to get rough.

"Oh yeah? Well, it happened. All by itself, right? Cost me a ton t' get my cams fixed, bro' . . ."

"You listen up t' me an' you listen good." Spider was breathing heavy now. "I had about all I'm gonna take from you two-bit putzes! You wanna go work f' Ace? You got any idea how my esteemed competition treats his boys? Maan, they do anything f' him, they scared a' tha' fucka. They know he'll eat 'um f' breakfast if they fuck up. An' here I am wif' you tellin' me off like I work f' you! I'm too fucken sweet t' be a crack lord. I treat you fucken brats like people, like my panas an' shit, an' what thanks do I get? Unreliable bastids! There are people I treat like shit. Damn straight. Some kids don't even see me, they see Mitch. You know Mitch, tha' one-eyed guy? You never hadda go through him. You been wif' me. I treat'chu like one a' my own, man. An' now you come wif' this shit like you gonna fire me o' somethin'!"

"Well, why you gotta tell me all this shit about trust an' friendship an' shit like that an' then stick a newspaper in my face like you really din't trust me? An' why these assholes hadda slash my tires? Don'chu think I know enough about this shit to know nothin' goes down on the street unless you say it's okay?" Miguel's voice trembled.

"Well you been actin' weird. Lookit what happened the other night with yuh run. I got people clamorin' f' yuh ass. I been protectin' you better than you know."

"Protectin' me?" Miguel was starting to yell. "I had a fucken .38 up my goddamn nose!"

Firebug entered the room, half a loaf of bread protruding from his mouth. He held a chunk of bread out to Miguel and stared.

"Look, pana . . ." Spider was trying to calm down. "I hadda do it. I din't have nobody else. You think I'm the top, but I ain't, man. There's somebody on toppa my head. It ain't always gonna be like that. Soon, soon pana. I'm gonna break outta this shit. You gotta try an' trus' me on this, bro'. I'll make it worth yuh while. Jus' try an' stick wif' me. I feel bad, you know? I mean, we friends . . ."

"Well maybe you got a conscience under all that stubble. That ain't my fault. Maybe you too sensitive f' this shit."

Spider sniggered. "Hmf. Now who that sound like?" he muttered to himself. "Yeah, okay," he said. "Maybe I do things a lo bruto sometimes, but these things gotta be done. You still a kid, Miguel. I wan'chu t' understand right now this thing, it's like a big corporation thing. Like

Exxon, Mobil Oil. You cross the corporation, thass it. Thass wha' happened t' Ricky. It was outta my hands. When I'm runnin' my own thing, then maybe I won't be so bruto, be so stupid, so fucken . . . scared. You think I like this shit?"

Miguel exhaled, feeling like Spider was being sincere. He glared at Firebug, who was munching and waving his lump of bread.

"Oh shit," Spider said in a different voice. "Tha' car looks real familiar . . ."

There was a funny sound, as if the receiver had struck something metallic; a black guy was going, "Yo, yo, yo, yo . . ."

"Spider, whassup? Hello?"

"Look, I can't be stayin' out here talkin'na you." Spider's voice sounded submerged. Miguel's mind suddenly filled with images of car windows rolling down, of 9mm gun barrels spitting out slugs.

"Get outta there, Spider," Miguel said, with a concern that surprised him. It made Spider chuckle.

"Still got a heart under all that ice, ahh?"

"Beep me, bro'. Get the fuck outta there."

There was the sound of shrieking car tires.

"Hello? Spider? HELLO? YO!"

The line went dead.

"Whassup?" Firebug asked, still chomping on bread.

Miguel hung up the phone, sitting on his mat pensively. "I think he's in trouble."

Firebug's face looked totally blank, eyes spaced before they focused on Miguel. "So where you goin'?" he asked, gesturing with his chin.

Miguel stared. "I said I think Spider's in trouble."

Firebug shrugged. "So what? Ain't he always in trouble? You forget I known him longer than you."

Miguel dropped it. He got up and finished dressing. He was going to meet Cristalena; to hell with it. Why should he worry? This guy tried to get him killed, sending him on an errand to go hobnob with a bunch of psycho cops. "Trust," he calls it. But Spider was really only looking out for himself. Amelia was right about him. Miguel wasn't scared of getting shot at; stuff like that always excited him, made him feel like he was in a movie when bullets were thumping into the trunk of his car. The excitement was no problem; it was just that WOMP FACTOR, that feeling of not knowing anybody you can really trust. All his posse friends were psychos, deranged misfits who were cruel for kicks. His "best friend" was a fire freak. The only girl he knew that he felt he could trust was Amelia, even though he wasn't sure about what she was doing. After his last talk with her, he saw something new about her, something manipulative and predatory. She was a player like everyone else, angling for a position. What was she after? It made him feel sick. The only normal human being he knew was Cristalena, and he was in love with her. But could he say he really trusted her if he couldn't tell her what was going on? Was it fear that kept him from owning up, or was it just a lack of faith? Driving over to Rosa's, he felt nervous; crazy anxious to see her, kiss her, hold her, while scared of what might come out. Absently he chain-smoked.

He double-parked across from Rosa's stoop, and waited. However much of a fuckhead Spider had been, Miguel was still worried about him; his beeper was clipped on his belt. He checked to make sure it was on. Still smoking, he started to get those violent images again when there was a soft tap on his window. He rolled it down, her smile getting bigger and bigger until the window was far down enough for her to throw her arms around him in a feverish hug.

> (And he used the hug to wrap his arms around her
> with a quick flick
> sending his flaming cigarette flying.)

"Mothafucka!" She was breathless. "I been waitin'." Close up, lips moistly brushing against his, her trembling coils of hair tickling his face, he felt the reality of her, something he could clutch and hold on to. (For how long?) He traced her lips with a finger and then kissed her softly, but she pulled back.

"Yuck. Cigarettes."

He laughed, fanning his mouth, shaking his head.

"You taste like an ashtray. Thass how you gonna greet me an' shit?"

"I forgot."

"You f'got? Nex' time, some Lavoris. Or breath mints." She was pressed up against his door as traffic flowed past, bathing her in headlights. Cars honked. In appreciation of her ass, he thought, which was poking up nicely.

"Damn man, you gonna invite me in, or jus' leave me freezin' to' death out here?"

He smiled warmly, taken in by her girlish abrasiveness. "Yes please, madam, come in and join me. I'll have the butler open the front door."

"Very well. Hmf. Treat me like a lady." She executed what looked like some kind of curtsey and scooted around the car. She was dressed way stupid. Black leggings, and that short leather coat, her ass looking all luscious. He opened the door for her. She jumped in, wrapping her arms around him. They kissed for a while, softly. She made pretty mmmmmm sounds. She seemed to shiver when they pulled back to look at each other, faces flushed with emotion. They both laughed softly, and then she shook this tiny package under his nose.

"Here," she said, sliding back. "Open it."

"Damn. Whass this?"

"It's a gift, stupid. Don't nobody ever give you nothing? Go ahead, open it. It ain't much. I jus' keep thinkin' about how you always so worried an' shit." She shrugged softly; her jacket crackled.

Miguel opened the box. It was a gold crucifix, plain and smooth and shiny on a thin gold chain.

"Ah shit." Light winked off of it as if it came with batteries.

"It's real gold," she whispered. "Fourteen karats." She shrugged. "It ain't so much. At least it won't rust."

"It's really great." He didn't know what to say. There was a funny silence, and then she jumped up and grabbed it off him.

"Here, I'll put it on." She undid the clasp and wrapped her arms around him. She smelled like strawberries.

"Mmmm. Strawberries," he said.

"Thass shampoo."

She tucked the cross in under his thin V-neck sweater, digging her hand in deep. Her hand was cold. He tried to pull the hand out, she tried to stick it as far as it would go, wrestling a little before she landed a series of soft kisses on his neck.

"Now you'll be safe, you shun't worry," she said, tenderly brushing hair from his eyes. "Everything's gonna be okay. Gah, but'chu know? I can lookit'chu like this an' tell tha'chore still worried about something."

"Yuh right." He felt ashamed.

"How come you worry so much?"

Now she did it. He pursed his lips and looked out at the busy street with its hurrying clusters of shadows scuttling along the edges of the tenements like roaches. He should fucken take her out, to movies and dinner and show her a good time. Then he should tell her. Could he do that? He looked down at his hands gripping the wheel.

"There's jus' a lotta shit goin' down." His voice was small; he ran out of words. She passed her hands through his hair.

"Shhh," she said soothingly. "It's all gonna be okay." He shut his eyes, everything around him dark and warm, a womblike safety.

They had Italian food on Fordham Road and caught a comedy that they both ignored. By then his cigarette breath had disappeared, thanks to pasta, popcorn, and a pack of breath mints she had bought him. Everything had been going fine, smooch heaven, lips so tender warm soft wet talking all intimate stuff, when she found the beeper. She held it up to his face while still kissing him. "You expectin' a call?" It was a funny voice, like she couldn't decide to be angry or to make a joke out of it.

"Yeah, I am," he said, after a pause, taking it and reclipping it.

After that, they snuggled and watched the movie. A heavy silence sank down on them. The quiet didn't end even after they got outside, walking to the car gobbling up the last few Raisinets. He made a few jokes, a few attempts at horseplay, but they all fell short. He barreled down streets, yearning for a cigarette as he hit Southern Boulevard, subway cars on the el twinkling, the streetlights scores of blinking moons.

"You're driving too fast," she said in a muffled voice, hidden by her scarf.

He shook his head, laughing with grief. "I can't drive, I can't smoke, can't carry a beeper . . ."

She was staring straight ahead, arms crossed as if she were cold. "I don't care about that," she said slowly. "I only wish you wouldn't hide things from me."

"I ain't hidden nothin'. I mean, what?" Something in him pulsed with a sick panic.

"It's not wha'chu say. It's wha'chu don't say. Sure I know kids are into thum beeper shits right now. You could've said a hundred things, an' I wouldn't have even thought about it. But'chu din't say anything. It's the way you didn't say anything. It's what scared me that first time, when you were talkin' about'chore friends."

He sighed, stroking the dash. A red light kept him rooted to the spot. "Look, I . . ." He pinched his eyes with his fingers and rubbed. No more words came out. A car honked behind him, and Miguel gratefully stepped on the gas.

"I wish you could be straight with me." Her words were almost lost as he gunned the engine. Then the beeper went off. Miguel scooped it off his belt while driving and checked the screen. Without even thinking, he pulled over to a phone and hopped out. "I'll be back," he said as he left her there.

It was Spider. There was no getting around it; Miguel had been worried about him. The minute his voice came over the line, Miguel exhaled as if he had been holding his breath.

"Compai'," Spider said. "Good t' hear yuh voice."

"Spider man, whassup? I heard all this shit an' then there wasn't nothin'. I thought they iced'ju."

"Me? They ain't made that gun yet, amigo, though I gotta admit, it was a good try. Listen, wha'chu doin' now? I kinda can't move. I wanted t' see if you could go check Spadgie's f' me. I mean t' see if Rico's been there. That is, if yuh still on the team wif' me."

Miguel exhaled, shooting a glance at the car. Cristalena was sitting there like a statue.

"Yeah, man." He sighed. "Whass this shit with Rico?"

Spider sighed, his voice concerned. "I don't know man, I sure hope that he din't play his cards wrong. Tha' boy was always gamblin'. He liked to play scams too much. In this business everybody be double-dealin' you alla time. Some people take it better than others, you know wham sayin'? I hope Rico ain't been . . . well, he's too smart f' that."

"I'll check Spadgie's. I'm on a date now, I'm takin' 'uh home."

"Good man. You know, findin' a good girl is always nice. I mean, good girls are hard t' find. A good straight girl can save a boy's soul. But unless you find Diane Keaton, you betta' stick t' crack babes an' putonas."

"Wha'chu mean?"

"You ever see the first *Godfather* movie?"

"Yeah, I saw it."

"Well, remember Al Pacino's wife? She was Diane Keaton, straight an' clean, not inta the crime family thing at all. An' at the end when they get married, she hasta stay out of it. When it came t' the man's business, she hadda stay out of it. She had no place."

Miguel felt a funny tremor in his stomach. "An' how do you know my girl is straight?"

Spider paused. There was too much confrontation in Miguel's voice. He repeated the question, only louder.

"Boy, I din't know you hadda temper on you. Remine me nah t' ever let'chu get a piece. I'm jus' rappin', pana, thass all. It jus' happened t' be on my mind."

"It wasn't Amelia, was it?"

Spider muttered, "Wow, man."

"What?"

"Hey, you know what high blood pressure is? You sure wound up these days. I don't know nothin', man, I'm jus' talkin' like t' give you some advice. The way you gussy yuhself up, how could I think you be hangin' with a putona? I seen yuh threads, man. Gone are the trappins of the posse boy. Now you be like this man, so who you gonna date? I'm tellin' you straight, right? Thass the fucken rock of it, bro'."

Miguel was taking his cigarettes out, fingers numb with cold. Then he remembered Cristalena, through the fogged-up window, sitting like a weeping saint figure, a dark silhouette of silent suffering. Diane Keaton?

"I gotta get," he said. He hung up the phone and got back into the car. Cristalena looked at him expectantly. Miguel inhaled, wishing he had some cigarette smoke.

"My friend was in some trouble tonight," he said. "I hadda make sure he was okay. I knew he'd try t' call me. So I had it on, thass all. Sometimes I don't even have it on me."

"This your friend the junkie?"

"What?"

"Is he the crackhead?"

"No. Yeah." Miguel tossed up his hands, like he was being drowned in questions before he could think up answers.

"An' you? Are you a crackhead?"

He looked at her, but her eyes didn't have that snotty sparkle of joking in them, that funky need of hers to mock. She was totally serious now, her face a little pained.

"No."

"You're not a drug addict?"

"Jesus, I feel like I'm bein' interviewed!"

"When was the last time you went on one?"

Miguel didn't say anything. He reached into his pocket and took out his cigarettes. He calmly lit one, then jerked the car into life.

"Less get'chu home," he said.

. . .

When he pulled up to her building, she sat there, not moving. There was a heaviness in the air that stunned them. They exchanged looks full of sadness, as if they had both lost something. She flipped the door handle with a funny thud but didn't push the door open. She looked at him, helpless.

"Listen," he said, but nothing came out. He rolled down his window and tossed the cigarette away. "Lemme getta breath mint."

She looked at him, then fumbled madly in her pockets for the roll, passing it to him desperately. He tore at the paper wrapping and popped one into his mouth.

"Jus' gimme a minute," he said, and then she laughed. She had tried to keep it in, but the laughter burst out of her. She looked at him as if she were annoyed with him for letting it happen.

"This is a serious moment," she scolded, the mocking sparkle in her eyes.

"I dint want it to end like this," he said honestly, sliding a little closer. He grabbed her hand and trapped it in both of his.

"Me neither."

"Cristalena," he whispered, touching her hair, "you gotta gimme some time. I would give anything in the world f' things t' be okay."

She leaned against him. "I don't know," she said. "Something inside me keeps sayin', 'Run, run.' But I can't. I never been through anything like this."

"It's called fate."

"Nah. I've always been scared of things I don't know enough about."

"Cristalena," he whispered into her ear, "I'm crazy mad about'chu."

She checked his eyes to see what was in there; then she kissed him. When she finally scooted out of the car and up the stoop, he pulled the cross out from under his sweater. He squeezed it between his fingers and softly chanted her name.

9

Rico? Who the fuck was Rico?? Miguel didn't know and almost didn't care. There were bigger things to think about. Cristalena. The need to tell her everything was growing stronger, the moment approaching like an execution. He came so close this time! Still, their need for each other seemed to override it. He was almost convinced that if he told her, she would understand, would help him break free. She wouldn't leave him.

She was an actress, too. She kept him from her parents. She lied all the time, storming her house like an unrepentant sinner. Her mother would sit in the kitchen and wait for her, every time, as if she didn't believe her stories.

"She calls Rosa's," Cristalena told him, "an' asks to speak t' me. Rosa tells her I'm in the bathroom. Or else I went downstairs. Sometimes my aunt answers. My aunt is cool, she covers f' me."

"What if yuh mother shows up there t' check on you?" Miguel had asked.

"My aunt will stall. Me an' Rosa, we'll sneak out a window, shimmy down a rope, hide inna closet, wea' disguises . . . this is war, Miguel, WAR. An' when I fight a war, I fight t' win."

She fought her war with clothes, with designer pantyhose, with her stack of racy catalogues, her newly won right to come and go without too many explanations. (That meant only saying, "I'm goin' t' Rosa's.") She was dying to leave, to be on her own. She talked about it, but always ended it with "But I can't; I'm a good girl." Sometimes she'd be in Miguel's arms and they'd be sitting there staring up at the big round moon shining into the car and she would sigh and say, "I'm such a good girl. I'm sick of being such a good little girl." He would promise to help her, making lewd suggestions. She was full of hunger. It was in her desperate kisses, the way she clutched at him, her hands roving possessively, staking out claims. Just thinking about it made him feel a happy tension. He wanted to be alone with her, too. Her birthday. "The present."

"You know what I want," she says, her hands sliding up his thighs.

YEAH YEAH Miguel wanted her, too, but first he had to tell her, didn't he? Could he bring her to his crib without telling her? Trailing that problem like a rattling caboose was the need to tell Spider he was quitting. He was almost sure of it now. The fringe benefits he had associated with so much success now reeked of defeat, a sick pretend game, a "self-deception"—Amelia's words. She had come closer than anyone in the biz, had looked inside of him and seen stuff worth redeeming. It was her determination to make him quit that rattled his insides, her words jumping in his head like Bouncing Bettys. Was she telling Spider about him, about Cristalena? He didn't want to think she was giving Spider information to hurt him. He couldn't believe that. He had to trust someone wholeheartedly to survive right now. She was that person. She wouldn't sell him out to Spider.

Spadgie's was a tiny bar just off Longwood Avenue. It looked like a condemned storefront, planks of wood everywhere, but through the corrugated tin door was a party. A red-eyed junkie in a ratty brown coat played doorman, standing outside like a homeless guy. Inside there were wall-to-wall posse boys in their colors of the week, shaking their heads and twitching their necks to blaring house music that throbbed from a monster sound system buried deep inside, past the surreal black lights by the door. There were smaller constellations of blinking red and blue lights throbbing along the graffiti-splattered walls. Girls were everywhere, here laughing and clutching a shoulder, an arm, a waist, over there gyrating in clingy bright colors or baggy clothes that dwarfed the girl bodies. Crack pipes flashed like the sudden glimmer of fireflies on an empty lot at night. Miguel walked through it as if hallucinating. He didn't know this guy Rico, but he knew Spadgie, and Spadgie would know where Rico was. He was a stooped midget with a knowing Indian face and a wicked hoarse laugh that Miguel could make out over the noise. He was trying to follow it through the forest of faces. He worked his way around a pool table. A girl named Wanda grabbed his arm, her wet cold liquor lips were sliding over his, her tongue trying to poke past his teeth. He had fucked her once, or twice, he couldn't remember. Her smile was all teeth, her eyes chinked up. She thrust a crack pipe at him. "Ahh, um, later, later." He threaded past her. Gloria? Hoh fuck, there was Gloria, her red hair tumbling down her back like a flaming river of fire. Her tiny eyes spotted him and gleamed with malicious glee. She said something to him as he passed, her smile cherubic while her eyes blazed with crazy mad fever. Tried to become his woman, wondered why he hadn't tagged her with some jewelry. Hadn't they fucked four times already? But he told her he wasn't looking for a woman, a steady, A WIFE, whatever she called it. She was begging to be tagged. (A cow asking to be branded. Ho ho ho, want some steak boys?) NOW as he passed by her she held up her wrist TRIUMPHANTLY showing off a sparkling diamond bracelet with some guy's name dangling from it in tiny glittering letters. She tickled it with her fingers. Miguel squinted but couldn't make out the name. "See wha'chu missin'? It coulda been you." And he smiled and waved and wanted to get the fuck out of there because maybe she wanted to make a little power-trip display—she was with these three gorillas tall and thick on parole from THE ZOO, arms down to their ankles, eyes born glaring. All she had to do was turn to the man who owned her: "Tha' guy, thass him, the one I tol'ju about. He tried t' do it t' me, papi." And bullets would start flying, tattooing walls and bodies. Miguel had seen that shit scores of times. He was glad to get away, to spot Spadgie in a corner surrounded by three guys and two girls with a big brown German shepherd that kept sniffing up this girl's dress making her go WHOOOP! and giggle while the dog's tail wagged like he had found a relative. "Spadgie, Spadgie," Miguel said, tugging on his paisley shirt, its colors seeming to vibrate.

Spadgie looked at him. "Miguel, right? The one with the beautiful car." He started singing. "My Babeee does the hanky-panky. So how's Spider? He ain't been by. I get the feelin' maybe he's getting uppity."

"He's been throwin' his own parties," Miguel replied, leaning closer because of the loud everything all around. "I'm really lookin' f' Rico. You seen him?"

Spadgie's face hesitated, as if caught between expressions. Then he slapped on a grin that looked like a last resort. "No idea, really," and then he turned to a tall guy beside him, a black guy holding a fat jay wearing a redyellowgreen leather fez. They both laughed as if Miguel weren't there. Miguel was never very good at taking hints. He tugged on Spadgie's shirt again.

"When was the last time you saw 'im here?"

Spadgie frowned. "Shit. Yuh a real Eliot Ness, man." He rolled his eyes, put a pinkie to his chin. "Let me thinkie-winkie. Last time I saw him was Wednesday. Was that Wednesday? Hard t' tell sometimes. He was with this bitch called Rosie, drank my wine, dug my earth, a real bitch. Actually he was quite a bastid himself." His eyes glowered for a second. "You know, I do hate people who come in here acting as if they own the place. Like sometimes people have to learn a little respect." His eyes became jovial again. "Is that enough information, officer?"

What a fucken pato, Miguel thought. He hadn't noticed it before, but then Spadgie's had never been his kind of place. If he had stopped by, it was usually because he couldn't find no pussy on Tinton and he was on the rove. He was glad to turn away, glad he was forgotten the moment he turned his back. Just as he was making his escape this tall dark and homely got in his way, with Gloria on his shoulder like a parrot.

"Yo bro', you disrespeck my girl?" The guy reeked of armpit and beer.

Miguel patted the ape on the shoulder and laughed. "You fucken lucky guy, yessir," he said, walking past him.

"Yo bro', I din't dismiss you yet."

Miguel was lighting a cigarette. He took his two puffs and grinned at him and grinned at Gloria and then he flicked the cigarette right into the guy's face.

"HEY!"

Miguel was too fast for the guy. He was in his car and revving up way before the ape found the door.

Down Longwood he drove, dark streets like empty stages, dimly lit and waiting for the actors. The wind whipped winos around corners, hunched and tripping, coats flapping. Over off Kelly Street sat a long black limo, six doors, blackened windows. A visiting dignitary on the quiet lonely street. Miguel was sick of this beaten landscape, sick of thinking about all the money he had and how he still couldn't change it. "Self-deception." That Amelia, she talked some fine shit sometimes. What was it she was telling Spider? He didn't want to think about it. Wasn't it enough to just think about her? Why did he have to come home and hear her with Firebug, crying with desperate pleasure? Why did it unnerve him? The house music wasn't loud enough to drown out her love crooning. He was touched that she was in love with him, or at least that she said it. Her feelings for him seemed genuine. He knew she was a big player rolling for some kind of high stakes, but with him she had been straight from the beginning. She didn't want to hide anything from him, and got scared of him when he probed. She was the only real person there.

Then there was Cristalena. Dreaming of her was a calming soul trip that involved more than just his dick. She was changing him, making him softer, more tender. He had never touched a girl the way he touched her. He knew it was love. He was going to send her flowers. Tomorrow. Send them to her cousin's. And there was that diamond bracelet he had, that stunning glittering nine-hundred-dollar bracelet he had bought about five months ago, as a sign of affection for a girl named Patti. He had been trying to show off or tag her or something, he couldn't even remember feeling goofy about her, just that she was black and had juicy tits. (The thought of that made him laugh now as he sat in the tubful of steaming water, smoking a roach and letting his mind roam.) The reason he still had the bracelet was because before he gave it to her, he showed Spider. Spider scooped it up and looked at him like he was crazy.

"You look here, you fuckhead. You a young tenda' thing an' all. I appreciate yuh bein' so head over heels an' all, but'chu go home an' you put this shit away, because I know this Patti an' she ain't worth this. Tha' girl see more traffic than the Holland Tunnel. So you put tha' shit away an' save it f' some real girl someday." And that's what he did. The real girl was here. It was going to shock the shit out of her! He laughed, then frowned, because he knew he would have to tell her by then. Wouldn't he? How else would he explain being able to afford it? And once she knew where it came from, would she accept it?

Ugh. It made his stomach twitch. He got out of the tub, his sinewy body dripping water. He tied a towel around his waist and walked out, getting goose bumps as he thumped along with bare squiggly wet feet. There was a full-length mirror near the fake petunias, another free find on an empty lot, the edges stained with paint. He removed the towel, stared at his body, took in its lines and rough edges, the soft bumpy muscles, his stomach flat and well defined. (Two hundred sit-ups a day.) His arms were good and firm, molded. (He has weights.) His legs could be a lot better. He was thinking he should get one of those indoor bikes when outside there was the sudden popping of guns, minute flashes against the windows. Miguel smiled, lighting a cigarette. He put on the towel again and went over to peek, but there was nothing down there but some puffs of smoke and a cop car making a hasty U-turn. He sat down by his bookcase, flipping through some paperbacks in his bookcase, trying to see if he could dig up anything on that guy Sartre, when he felt the soft foot tread out in the hall by his door. Had they stopped fucking? The music had still been playing when he came out. All he knew was that he couldn't hear her; that was all that mattered. She was by the door, squinting at his lamplight, wearing a big striped shirt and maybe nothing else. She crossed her arms and crossed her ankles and grinned at him as she leaned.

"Oh, look. He's reading." She giggled.

"I was tryin'na find somethin' on tha' guy Sartre."

She sat on his mat, drawing her knees up. She smiled when she noticed him trying to peek between her legs to see if there was anything. She tilted her legs open a little, just a little.

(She didn't have anything on.)

"Hey," he said. "Don'chu ever thinka what might happen if Firebug came in an' saw you here with me?"

She smiled as if he was flirting with her. "He won't wake up. I fuck him into total unconsciousness." Her eyes got trancelike. "Besides, I like my private time with you. I slip Mickeys in his rum whiskey."

He laughed, leaning against the wall, watching her. She laughed too, and he realized they were both drifting in a light buzz. They were far apart but he felt as if he were only an inch from her face, could almost feel the hair as it slid over her eyes in soft waves. Chin in hand, feet close together, there was something coy and flirty about her. It made him laugh again. "You seem pretty stoned," he said, and laughed.

"Yeah well, you too. I was thinkin' about'chu today. Over an' over, I kept wondering where you were."

"Well, I wish I was with my girl tonight."

She was still smiling with those sleepy eyes, as if she hadn't heard him. "You know, I could use some smoke myself."

He grinned and sat beside her, grabbing his bag of smoke and rolling a jay.

"So what's your girlfriend do?"

"My girlfriend?"

"Yeah . . ." Her eyelids fluttered drunkenly, sweetly as she leaned her head against his shoulder.

"She's in high school."

She bumped him with her chin. "So that's it, school? What else? She a dancer? Does she dance? Walk around in leotards all the time?"

"Are you okay?"

"Yes."

"No, I mean because thass a weird question. Maybe I should check yuh temperature." He put a hand up against her forehead.

"That's not where you should check my temperature."

"Oh no? Where then?"

"Mmm. Gimme your hand."

"Nah. Man, leggo, you gonna spill the smoke!" He put the bag away and licked the joint shut.

"I did some dance when I was in school."

"Yeah? You got a dancer's body." He lit the jay.

"That mean I got little tits?"

"No. You got fly tits." He passed her the joint.

She toked, staring at him as if sizing him up. "So this girl, she just gonna go to high school all her life? She dying to be someone's wife? Sounds like one of my sisters an' shit."

"She wants to be a dress designer. Thass what she said. She works at this store on Third Avenue called Butterfly's."

"She works there?"

"Yeah."

She toked some and handed the joint back. There was such a look of tenderness on her face as she stared at him that he had to ask what was up.

"Do you know smoke makes me real horny?"

He shook his head. "You gotta cut that out. I mean, I like you too, but I got a girlfriend."

"Oh yeah." She pouted mockingly. "What a loyal little husband'ju are."

"Besides, Firebug is my friend."

She choked on a laugh. "Gah! What a baby you are! You really think he's your friend, huh? An' how long you think you're gonna be friends when he finds out you're quitting the biz? You think you'll still be living here with 'im?"

He shrugged. "I don't know."

"Well, I know." She sighed, lying on his mat, stretching out. "Are you still gonna quit, or was that all talk?"

"Yeah I'm gonna quit. I jus' gotta tell Spider."

"When you gonna do it?"

"Soon. That reminds me. You been talkin'na Spider about me, haven't chu?"

She sighed and pressed her temples with her fingers. "I have to talk to him about'chu. You jus' come up. I don't know how. He was wonderin' how come you actin' so funny. So I told 'im why. I told him about your girl. I gotta seem to give him information, you know, if I'm gonna get anything out of him I can use. Don'chu ever watch spy movies? How about Graham Greene? Ain'chu read any Graham Greene?"

"No."

"I'm playin' 'im so I can get what I need. Right?" She stroked his chin. Something about what she said made him move away slightly. She was a little stung. "Look, I talked to my father about'chu maybe workin' at the restaurant."

"No way man, thass out."

"You gotta get started some place, Miguel! You don't even got no workin' papers!"

"Yeah? An' how much he gonna pay me?"

"It ain't that much. Four, five bucks an hour. So what? You think you gonna move on to a career that pays twenty-eight K?"

Miguel laughed, rolling down onto the mat beside her. "Yuh jokin'."

"No I ain't. Come clean, bro'. What do you think is gonna happen when you tell your Latino Barbie Doll that'chu were a runner? Think she'll just get over it an' settle down to live off your riches? Get real, man. Wha'chu got? Eight thousand you said, right? You got eight thousand? Man, that ain't shit. That won't last you a month. You know what rent is?"

"Workin' f' yuh pop ain't gonna pay nobody's rent. You know that, too."

"Yeah, but if your girl sees you got a job, she'll know you're tryin'na go straight. An' that's a start."

Miguel nodded, knowing she had a point. He looked at her a little resentfully.

"An' you?" he cried. "What about'chu? You gonna tell me all this shit so I get my life straight, so I leave behind all this crack world shit, ditch my old life, an' yet you expect me t' go work at yuh father's place, with you, a fucken crackhead?" He got up and paced, adjusting his towel. "Why don'chu give up tha' shit?"

She sat up, digging around in his things until she found his pack of cigarettes. She lit one and slid over to the wall, pulling her shirt over her thighs with a grin. "Don't bring that up," she said, with a toss of her head.

"Fuck that. Why don'chu go back t' school?"

"You're not gonna get me t' talk about my life. You couldn't understand my life."

"The life of a crackhead. Big fucken deal. I know enough crackheads. They all end up the same way. You think you so slick, but'chu playin' with fire. You ain't so tough. I noticed tha' shit."

She laughed and shook her head. "You're being a pest."

"I'm jus' payin' you back f' buggin' me." He came over and sat beside her, rearranging his towel. "I was jus' thinkin' about this today, about how you always see all this shit about me, an' I think maybe you'd be good at all this psychotherapy shit."

"Yeah"—she smiled proudly—"I sorta got'chu figured out pretty good, huh?"

"An' all that stuff about self-deception. I was lookin' around t' see if I had anything on that guy Sartre but I don't."

"I can lend'ju a book on 'im." There was a funny pause, Amelia leaning her chin on her knees, watching him adoringly.

"Stop tha' shit," he said.

"Why do you always ask about me? You're the only person I know that asks about me. It sorta makes me think you soft on me."

He shrugged. "Well, I love you." He said it like it should've been obvious. Then he got up and went to the window, to look down on the streets, to get his thoughts in gear. She quietly reached over and pulled his towel off with a delighted shriek. "Oooh yeah, lookit thum nice buns." He spun around, reached for the towel, and fell beside her on the bed. A girlish playfulness possessed her, and they wrestled like two little kids on the mat, rolling kicking pulling until she had him on his back. He stopped moving. Her eyes twinkled with a lustful joy that sent an electric thrill through him.

"Man, you got such a nice body."

"Yuhs is nice too." His hands were on her smooth, arched back, sliding down the curve. She brushed her lips against his, her moist tongue probing lightly. That's when he rolled her over, patted her flank, grabbed his towel, and got up to tie it on. He had his back to her. He cursed and tossed down the towel, digging in a drawer for a pair of black bikini underwear and then running shorts.

"You don't care about me," she whispered resentfully.

"I do," he half yelled, turning to look at her all crumpled up in the corner. "I jus' don't think we should fuck."

"I'm saying tha'chore like every guy I ever known in my life. Doesn't care about what I need."

"Wha'chu need is t' get the fuck outta this street-scene shit. You don't even need it. I don't know why you playin' with it but you should get the fuck out an' get'cha life straight."

His words tumbled out with such authority that she didn't say anything, looking at him as if he had grown ten years older in a flash.

"Besides," he went on, pacing, "is that wha'chu need? A good fuck? Is that as deep as it is f' you? Din'chu jus' get fucked? Fucken guy is still sleepin' in the next room."

"I don't need a good fuck," she said in a burst. "I need love, real love. Like in the song by Jody Watley." Her voice got soft. "You're wrong to think so much about Firebug. He wouldn't think twice about'cha feelings."

"You want I should be like him?"

"I want you should follow your heart. There's nothing between him an' me."

"Right. Is that why him an' Spider split? 'Cause he don't care that he found'ju fucken Spider f' crack?"

"Jesus Christ!"

"Well thass what it was, wasn't it?" He lit a cigarette, then decided he didn't want one and tossed it down, stomping on it with his bare foot. He searched for his bag of smoke. "Shit," he mumbled as he opened the bag and laid out some choice buds on a book. "You use him. You use Firebug for his dick. You use Spider f' his crack. An' all the time, you usin' yuhself. Throwin' yuhself away."

There was a deep rage in his eyes, an ugly anger that shocked her as she sat in the corner.

"Don'chu fucken see? I got sicka people like you, it's everything I know. Everybody's fucken everybody up the ass, behind each other's back. Used t' fuck girls so doped up, couldn't tell a dick from a whip. You could do anything to 'um. It makes me fucken sick. I don't know where I got the feelin', but I think there's more to it than this shit, a buncha people runnin' around thinkin' they got it made. An' you already know this ain't shit." He glared at her. "If you think different, then maybe you should go back to school, man.

"The way you talk, it reminds me of my mother. I can still see huh, puttin' on huh putona clothes t' go out t' some social club an' let the drunks play with huh titties. Like she was teachin' my father a lesson. You think I wanted t' see that?" He was still glaring at her. "To see thum fight out their war? T' hear stuff about yuh mother on the street, an' know it was true? I got in fights 'cause a' huh. I got laughed at. Then I jus' said fuck it. She wanna do that? Fine. Fuck it. You know how they say, never say YUH MOTHA to a Puerto Rican, how if you do he'll kill you? Well, not me. You could joke about huh an' I would join in, add a few good ones." He was rolling the jay now, licking it shut. "Yuh so smart. Mmf. Yuh jus' like all the rest of 'um."

She sounded wounded when she spoke. "You know something? You're a lot more of a man than I thought. Sixteen, but able to hurt women as well as any adult man. Congratulations."

He lit the joint. "Love. You know less about it than me. Shit."

"How the fuck would'ju know? Jus' because you found some virginal little doll you can lead by the collar? Some wordless angel with half a brain but a tight pussy? What's her grade point average then?"

"Yo." Her voice was getting hysterical, so he fought to stay calm. "Don't be dissin' my girl, you don't even know huh."

"I know her, believe me."

"You don't even know yuhself. All that big talk, like you got plans. Sartre an' suicide an' self-deception. It's all a dodge. You jus' don't like yuhself. How could'ju expect anybody's gonna fall in love wit'chu when you hate yuhself so much?"

He was toking on the joint, his voice calmer, the smoke starting to mellow him out. He slid back on the mat to where she sat, and he handed her the jay. She was looking at him as if she were stunned and mystified, a smile wiggling on her lips.

"I'm pretty impressed," she said, toking.

"I thought'chu would be mad."

"I love you, remember? How could I be mad at'chu?" She leaned against him, her head falling onto his shoulder. "I just don't wan'chu to see me like you see all those other people. I don't wanna be that. It's just, when you're surrounded by them, sometimes you become like them."

"Yuh above this shit, man. You should give this shit up."

"Well you should too."

There was a silence, and they couldn't look at each other. She nudged him with the joint. "So when are you gonna tell Spider?"

"Soon."

"An' what about your girl? When are you gonna tell her?"

"Soon, too."

"You really love that girl, huh?"

"Yeah. I do."

"You think she'll still love you after you tell her?"

He didn't say anything. She was caressing his face when the phone rang, making them both jump a little. Miguel crawled over to where it sat on the bureau.

"Yup."

"This is Spider. I thought'chu were gonna call me?"

"Spider!" Miguel laughed, exchanging funny glances with Amelia. "What a nice surprise, bro'. Yo, I forgot to call. I got tied up an' shit."

Spider didn't sound like he was in a jovial mood. "Look, I don't wanna hear no excuses. Did'ju go t' Spadgie's, or was that too much t' ask?"

"Yo bro', I don't think this snottiness is called for."

Amelia dove, trying to stifle her laughter, which erupted anyway in mad peals.

"Who's that?" Spider asked quickly.

"Nah man, thass some sea gulls. Here, I'm closin' the window." He motioned to Amelia to chill out.

"Look," Spider rasped into the phone, "did'ju find Rico?

"Nah I din't. I talked t' Spadgie. You know, I din't have no idea tha' guy was such a pato, bro', he—"

"What did he say about Rico?"

"He didn't say anythin'. It was the way he said it though, Spider. Acted real funny, like he knew somethin' but wasn't gonna say. Said I was some Eliot Ness. A real asshole. Lotsa snide laughs."

"Thanks a whole fuck of a lot."

The line went dead. Miguel looked at Amelia, who was getting up with difficulty.

"I think he's mad." They both laughed, nearly collapsing on each other. Amelia headed for the door.

"Well," she said, "since you ain't horny an' I am, I'm gonna go see if I can revive Firebug an' 'cause him to please me. But'chu, you wear fucken earplugs. I'm gonna be singing my songs of love. I plan to make you hear what you're missing." She slid along the wall, grinning, disappearing around the bend.

10

He was putting everything off.

That's why he still hadn't told Cristalena that he was a runner, or that he was quitting. He was trying to cheat it, courting ideas of maybe not telling her at all, especially if he found a job and could look legit. After all, the important thing was that he quit, right? So that mucky Monday morning with the rain and sleet he sent her flowers, a dozen red roses on long stems, like guys do in the movies. Couldn't find the words, felt mushy and goofy. Finally: "Love you forever, Miguel." Sounded formal and stuffy, but "Crazy mad about you" sounded corny in a new way.

Then he was putting off telling Spider. He felt good and then felt sick about the way he had pissed him off on the phone like that. The impulse to make it up was too strong in him, which was why when he spoke to Spider that morning he was sweet and apologetic.

"Sorry about yesterday, bro'. I was womp on some good smoke."

Spider shrugged it off reluctantly, his tone stoic. Things weren't going too well right now. Rico was missing, and Spider was grieving like an old lover.

"I think they iced him," he said at one point.

"Who's they?"

But Spider wouldn't talk. In the street-level war game of the crack trade, "they" can change from one week to the next. This week it'll be a local posse, trying to make points with someone. Next week it'll be a rival crack lord, upset over some turf infraction. Sometimes it's someone in your own organization who sells out for an extra gram, a new position, a better corner, who provides THE ENEMY with info that leads to that corpse in a plastic bag in an empty lot on Leggett Avenue. Sometimes the head man gets too chummy with the new boy and the old boys get jealous. Actually there are so many more reasons for murdering someone than not that it's a miracle that bodies don't have to be pushed off lots by bulldozers like in all those classic black-and-whites of the forties. Miguel could shrug it off. The first thing he had learned was that nobody really mattered. He wouldn't miss Sammy or Jimmy or Careta or any of those fractured faces he had shared laughs with, and they wouldn't miss him. Even Jokey's Flyboys kept changing, since every other week he had to bash one's head open. The so-called sense of criminal camaraderie was bullshit. Even the oldest posses broke up over a piece of pussy, a pretended slight, a prank, and then posse brothers would be busting caps at each other on the street at four in the morning. It wasn't about tribes or clans or brotherhood; money was all that mattered.

Miguel had never trusted anybody. Before he met Firebug, he was out on the streets making chump change dealing smoke, enough to keep him in clothes. He saw people who trusted each other get arrested, ratted on, finked, fucked over. Only a sucker trusts anyone. That was how he got on. A woman on the Lower East Side named Vilma let him stay at her house if he would fuck her. (There were other girls, or people he would pay off with weed.) Everything was bought and paid for. There was always a deal. Nobody was just "nice." No favors out of the blue, and if someone was good to you for no reason, you watched him. It wasn't until Firebug came along that something human woke up in him—the need, the ability to trust. "Come live with me," he said, offering, "I'll get'chu work." He trusted Firebug, and when he met Spider, he trusted him, too; somehow Miguel lost a little bit of that street attitude that kept him insulated.

"Don't trust Firebug too much," Spider had told him early on, and so Miguel shifted more trust to Spider, who took good care of him, opened up the world. All along, Miguel was looking for someone to trust in, and Spider was there to give him everything in record time. Miguel reminded himself of that now as he drove over to Franco's in the wet sogginess, windshield dotted with clinging raindrops. He was telling himself he was quitting, he was through with it, a new man now, while at the same time he drove there to start another day of drops.

Spider was sitting on a milk crate in the back room when he got there. His face looked worn, his stubble now a black beard.

"Man oh man," he said, looking Miguel up and down. "Check the threads. My gentleman runner. You been readin' *YM?*"

Miguel shrugged. He was dressed in brown baggy slacks, a paisley print shirt with a thin black tie, and a big brown Swiss Army coat. His hair was slicked back from his face.

"Whass this about, m'man? You were a regulation beat boy once."

Miguel laughed. "I don't know. This is more like how I feel."

Combat boots, floral jacquard sweaters, black factory shoes, pleated pants, cowboy shirts. Since meeting Cristalena he had become a real fashion head. He'd blown at least a grand on clothes already, maybe a little more.

Miguel just wanted to jet with his stuff, but Spider seemed to be hesitating, rubbing his beard, his eyes glassy and staring into space. Miguel knew where the stuff was usually kept for him to pick up, but whenever Spider was there, Miguel would wait for him to give it to him. It was a sign of respect, so he waited, standing by the door of the stockroom as if not wanting to come in any further. Outside, a fat man sliced cheese for a customer and blathered in Spanish about religion.

"Umm, you know, if I can't get Rico later," Spider said hesitantly, "I might have to ask you if maybe you'll do another special job."

Miguel lit a cigarette with a suave mannerism that had been well rehearsed. He was hesitating now, realizing he had made a mistake in not telling Spider earlier that he was quitting. Spider was upping the ante, depending on him even more, which meant Miguel would have to stick his neck out farther.

"You hear me, bro'? I said I got another special job."

"I don't know," Miguel said through the smoke, which seemed to give him courage.

"You don't know?"

"No, I don't know."

"NO, YOU DON'T KNOW? WHASS THAT FUCKEN MEAN?"

The scream caught him off guard, but Miguel made up for it. "WHA'-CHU THINK IT MEANS? IT MEANS WHAT I SAID!!"

Spider got up, kicking the crate away, storming right up to Miguel like he was going to bop him.

"So now you a big man, ah? Gonna gimme the orders, tell me what t' do? Maan, I bought'chu those clothes, mothafucka. I bought'chu tha' car. You wun't be shit if it wasn't f' me. How could'ju f'get that, m'man?

Huh? Get'chaself some new threads an' you think you own the joint, ah?"
He was talking right into Miguel's face. Miguel pushed him back.

"I dress the way I want," he said, "an' I ain't no jerk, you hear me?
All the time I do wha'chu say. You tell me go out on my run, I do that.
I done my job, I earned this money, all this shit! I din't suck nobody's
cock for it! I worked hard an' I did it 'cause I trusted'ju! I fucken
trusted'ju! More than anybody, more than Firebug even! You were my
friend, you sonofabitch! An' you tellin' me you trust me, you trust me,
shovin' a newspaper in my face an' runnin' off 'cause you ain't got the guts
t' face me an' be honest about'cha doubts. An' then slashin' my tires, you
fucken . . ." It was all coming back to him in ugly flashes. At that moment,
a tall Dominican with orange tea skin and short curly hair appeared at the
stockroom doorway.

"Mira, chill," he said to Spider with a grin. "This a family bodega,
right Spider?"

Spider laughed. "Yeah. This homeboy ain't had his Wheaties." They
both laughed, the Dominican clapping his hands as though Spider was a
great comedian. Miguel stood there simmering. He hated them, all of
them, all the crackheaded junkies and the pop-eyed addicts and the spicks
who looked honest and weren't, like this fucken Dominican rat carving
cheese for the lady diatribing about how the church has let down the
masses while his store is a front for a drug op. The guy laughed, wide smile
dotted with gold teeth. Miguel turned away, stamping out his cigarette,
facing the wall like it was his future. He waited until the Dominican was
gone before he spoke.

"It don't matter what the fuck I say," he half whispered, as if talking
to himself.

"Thass fucken right," Spider said with contempt. A silence ensued,
filled only with the bored prattle of men drinking beer outside in the
bodega, of the cash register dinging and snapping shut, of the front door
squeaking on its hinges. A year seemed to pass while Miguel stared at the
wall. He was mustering up the courage to quit when Spider touched him
on the shoulder. Miguel turned, and there he was, looking short and
pensive, eyes glassy as he smoked his cigarette down to a stub. He picked
up the crate and sat on it again, reaching over into a box to bring out
Miguel's packages. They went into a mangy old briefcase that Spider kept
there. As Miguel made his runs, the packages disappeared, the briefcase
filled with dollar bills, crumpled into rolls, banded together in clumps,

rubber-banded into wads. It was a good operation. No enforcers, no roughhouse. The money was always there, no fighting, no bickering. It was all on trust. Spider had a unique setup, all right. No wonder so many people wanted him iced. His thing was like a family affair. His word was enough. Miguel thought it was ironic that Spider had distrusted the one person he needed to trust the most.

"You gonna do yuh run?" Spider asked quietly, the briefcase open in his lap.

Miguel stared at him. "Yeah," he shrugged. The last time.

Spider held up one of the packages. "Well. You see this one? This is f' Ritchie. It's the last one. Give it t' him last. It's important. Okay?" Miguel nodded, hands in pockets. Spider seemed to linger for a moment, the package dangling over the briefcase as if he were trying to decide about something. Then he looked at Miguel and dropped it into the briefcase and shut it.

"Baby, baby, baby," Spider said wearily, "where did our love go?" He leaned back against the boxes. Miguel came closer and took the briefcase. He felt like he was moving in slow motion.

"Yuh the one that did it," Miguel said.

"You ridin' a fine white horse," Spider said as he watched Miguel head for the exit. "Make sure you don't fall off." Spider chuckled.

Miguel was thinking about how he was going to do it. He thought about how Spider might get vindictive and send a posse after him. Would Spider try to ice him? He couldn't answer that, and it depressed him. He didn't even want to begin thinking about what would happen once he made his move. That would be skipping too far ahead.

He roared down the glistening wet streets. Up Leggett Avenue, he stopped off at Beck, where Domino sat on the stoop of a beaten blue building. Miguel parked the car in front, stashing the briefcase under his seat before joining Domino on the stoop. Sitting there, he noticed that the large porticoes on either side of the stoop had been freshly painted.

Domino was staring at his Baby. "Man," he said. "That is one bad-ass machine."

"Thass right. An' it's mines, all mines. Ain't nobody gonna take tha' Baby away from me."

Domino looked at him. "Fine. Look, you wanna share a roach?"

They went into the vestibule, out of the drizzle, and over to a frosted window from which Miguel could still keep an eye on his Baby. There

Domino opened his packages while Miguel lit the jay. Satisfied, he slipped Miguel two wads of bills paper-clipped together. Miguel didn't even need to count it. Trust.

"Mmm. You know this place sucks, bro'. You tell Spider. I ain't seen 'im in too long, man, he don't stop by here f' nothin', man, like this operation gonna run itself. He better start givin' his DO some QT or he gonna find it sliced an' diced."

"What the hell that mean."

"We got trouble here. This damn building . . ." Domino stopped talking as the clumpclumpclump of a fat lady coming down the stairs interrupted. She looked big and hostile as she passed, glaring at Miguel, who indifferently leaned against a glazed window and toked.

"That one," Domino said, pointing at her as she disappeared out the vestibule door. "She's one a' thum. Fucken tenant organizers. Nasty bigmouth bitch. They been cleanin' up the building. See the fresh paint? Then my two boys got evicted. Now I got jus' one crib in 2C, an' you gotta tell Spider, man, we gonna lose this op if he don't do somethin'. You know what these nuts been doin' at night, man? Durin' my rush hour? A buncha thum come down so they can watch whass goin' down. Don't lookit me like that, I ain't bullshittin', bro'. My boys threaten 'um, but they come back, they work in shifts. It's gonna come down t' some icin' soon, unless Spider be makin' a move. Yo bro', le' me some smoke, bee."

Miguel handed him the roach as he sucked in some air. He could smell the fresh paint, could see the people were turning it around. "Maybe next week," he said, stifling a laugh, "they'll get Jesse Jackson t' come down an' make a speech."

"Boooolshit, bro'. We gonna have t' do somethin' serious here, man. It's already affectin' the customers, they complainin' about it. It's like they feel they be gettin' some heat. Two nights ago, they called the cops, man. In the middle a' my rush. You know I pay my man on the force, bro', but'chu know, they report a robbery, they call 'um in on a wife-husband thing, the cops come. An' then they be hangin' all over the halls an' shit, an' damn, there went my rush, down the fucken toilet. My tin shield, he said that they cun't help comin' t' answer these calls. He said these tenant organizers, they was smart, that they know if they make a drug-bust call, they won't get no cops t' come. But if they put in a call on 911, they gotta come. So they call, two, three times a night when they wanna bug me. Robbery, marital dispute, man with gun, this kinda shit." Domino sucked in the last of the roach and tossed it down with disgust. "I tell you, Spider gotta do somethin'. About all my tin shield could do was gimme some names an' shit. So I know who it is makin' the calls. I don't got no numbers. These people smart, they make calls from pay phones!"

Miguel was trying not to listen, getting into the buzz as it descended on him, reaching into an inner pocket for his aviator shades.

"You tell Spider," Domino said, poking him. "You tell 'im we need some work here 'cause I'm startin'na lose money. Maybe we can get some torch action goin'."

Miguel looked at him. "Torch? Who he gonna get t' do that?"

Domino shrugged as if it were obvious. "Firebug. Who else?"

"I thought him an' Firebug din't work together no more."

Domino sat on the rocky window ledge beside him. "Bro', they still do business. You know Spider shot him upstairs, got 'im some big contracts, but'chu know, thass 'cause he was tryin'na make it up t' him."

"For what happened with Amelia?"

Domino nodded. "Yeah, right. I seen you drivin' around in yuh car with huh. How close you are? You fuck huh?"

"Nah man, we friends."

Domino slid closer, his voice a low rumble. "Firebug found 'um in bed together. Spider was fucken huh doggie style. When Firebug saw it, he whipped off his belt. He swung tha' shit, it had this heavy buckle? His name in gold. He swung it at Spider but he ducked. He got Amelia. Thwack! She still gotta have the mark on huh back. Six stitches." He had taken out another joint and was lighting it. "You seen it, right? The mark?"

"Yeah, sure," he lied.

"How you seen it if you ain't fucked huh?"

"She walks around half naked when she's at the house," Miguel said smoothly.

"Yeah. Tha' bitch. I believe that. Seems like tha' bitch always playin' somebody. She was doin' Firebug, right? An' she was also doin' Spider f' some free crack."

"Why's she doin' Firebug?"

"Fuck if I know."

Miguel started to laugh. Domino asked him why, but Miguel didn't say anything about Amelia's words reverberating in his head: "I like his dick."

"See, Spider felt bad about what happened, they both did. I think they both saw Amelia f' what she was, some kinda scummy skeez. So Firebug ends up gettin' helped by Spider, who felt guilty enough t' set him up with some big-time arson dudes. Thea's this guy called Toasty? He's another fire freak, works over on Grand Concourse. He was tight with Spider, so Spider set Firebug up with 'im. Now Firebug's gettin' a lotta work, an' he still fucks Amelia. An' Spider, well, he's still friends with Firebug, an' I think he still fucken Amelia. She mus' be a fucken bitch in bed t' keep 'um wrapped around huh pussy like that."

Hearing Domino talk that way about Amelia suddenly started to bother him. He headed back toward the stoop, Domino hopping along beside him.

"Tha' girl man, she don't love nobody. She's got this whack attitude. She uses people. I tried t' do huh, bro', I tried. Fucken bitch man, she touched me up, she did like this." He passed his hand over his crotch and squeezed. "Then she say sorry man, you ain't big enough. Fucken bitch."

Miguel laughed, getting into his car. "You know," he said, turning on the engine, "I wun't be braggin' about tha' story."

"Right?" Domino laughed with him. They slapped hands, and then Miguel drove away. "Don't forget t' tell Spider!" he heard Domino yell after him.

Smoke made him drive slowly. He cruised along toward Petey's spot on 156th Street near Kelly. Petey, leaning against a post, looked pissed off. He walked over to Miguel's window.

"Maan, you playin' with fire, you keep comin' late, bro'. I swear t' God." His lower lip quivered as if he were going to cry.

"What is this faggit shit?" Miguel yelled. "Where's Spider's Washingtons?" He pounded the wheel. "Come on! I ain't got all day!"

Petey stared at him as if fascinated. He passed him the bundles of money and then waited for his packages.

"Well?" he screamed. "Come on!"

"DON'T SCREAM AT ME! YOU SEE I'M BUSY, RIGHT?" Miguel dug through the briefcase, picking out Petey's stuff. He handed him the packages with a rude thrust. "You should shut up with tha' bossy shit. It ain't even yuh rush."

Petey stared at him. "Spider's right about'chu," he said. "You sure outta control all right." There was a touch of sadness in his voice that made Miguel look at him a moment. Then he stepped on the gas and sped away from him. He made his next two stops without the attitude. Sometimes smoke made him get crazy, right? Made him get nasty. He knew he didn't have that much power as a runner. His only strength lay in being tight with Spider. Spider made things easier for him, spoiled him. Miguel was a privileged child. People on the street knew it. He should be nicer. They hated him as it was. Instantly, he started thinking about that shit he had pulled on Ritchie, who was his last stop. What made him run off like that while they were under fire? Wasn't that fucked up? Did Spider really have a point about him after all?

He crawled up Dawson, looking around for Ritchie. The posse spotted him first. Six of the biggest black-coated boys ran over, surrounding his car. Two of them had sticks.

"What the fuck?" Miguel yelled, honking.

"The window, the window, roll it down!" one of them screamed, his face distorted by glass and vapor. Then Ritchie popped up, pulling on Miguel's door, beating on it. "Unlock it! Unlock it!" Miguel had hardly lifted the button before he was pulled out of the car, yanked up and across it, thrown first against the hood with a hollow thump. Then somebody hit him with a stick while he struggled to get loose of all those hands. He felt a sting in his left ear but didn't really feel the blow, just heard the thwack. The second time, third time, his skin felt like it would crack open. He covered his face, grasped at a stick, a flash of clenched teeth real close before a punch blinded him. He rolled down, got kicked trampled fell, rolled from kicks to his sides and face. His hair was being pulled. He swung with his fists and hit empty air and jacket zippers, looked up and caught the image of a huge fist coming. The smack blackened everything. He could have sworn he saw Saturn with the rings all twirling by, stars blinking, his rocket spitting out twin spumes of flame. He fell backward, was dragged along the pavement tearing at his hands like shark teeth. Then they pulled him up. His legs had no power, his arms like a rag doll's. He was surrounded by twisted jeering faces. Four guys were holding him. He tried to twitch free. Ritchie stepped right up to him.

"Who the fuck you think you are, runnin' out on me an' my boys, mothafucka?"

"Benny got shot 'cause a' you!" one of the guys holding him yelled into his throbbing pulsing ear.

"No way!" Miguel yelled, blood dribbling from a torn lip.

"You didn't come on time, an' then you almost get my boys shot.

Din't Spider tell you t' be here before twelve?" Ritchie's voice was a hoarse whisper. His eyes looked wet, the color gone from his face.

"It wasn't my fault!" Miguel yelled. Somebody kicked him in the leg.

"Get off 'im! You hold 'im, hold 'im. There ain't gonna be no nex time, Miguel, I swea' man, I don't care if you Spider's girlfriend! Nex time this happen, I'm gonna fucken ice you!" He drew a pistol.

"Oh shit," Miguel said, his knees buckling. The fuck's gonna kill me! He looked around, but the streets were empty, cloudy skies indifferent. The figures he spotted across the street walked under the spidery tree branches as if coming across a marital spat they didn't want to get involved in. They were gonna do him, they were gonna do him, and there's nobody to even . . . he fought the urge to scream.

"Nex time, my brother," Ritchie said, his voice trembling. A tear popped out of one eye, or was it sleet that was still falling? He brought the gun close to Miguel's face. Miguel stood still, lips trembling. He was shitting himself he was so scared but he didn't want to show it. He clenched his teeth and closed his eyes, but Ritchie didn't shoot him. When he opened them to look, Ritchie bopped him with a right that sent him tumbling against the car. Hands were still holding him. Ritchie connected again. When Miguel fell to the wet street, clutching his head, Ritchie kicked him, making him curl up. Then Ritchie stepped back and reappeared holding a broomstick, tapping the street with it like a stickball batter preparing to roof one. "Get up," he said. By now the six boys had spread out, covering the street. When a car approached, two of them gently slid Miguel out of the way. When the car passed they pulled Miguel up on his feet. He was still teetering when Ritchie came at him with the stick. He hit Miguel in the ribs, making him suck in air. There was another blow, and then Miguel grabbed hold of the stick. Ritchie tugged and pulled, but Miguel wouldn't let go. One of the others kicked him in the side, forcing him to fall with a flash of pain, but he was still holding the stick. He came up on one knee and with one giant heave had the stick. He slumped there on the wet street, coat muddied and stained. He held the stick, eyes stinging as if there were salt in them.

"Yo," one of the guys said, "Ritchie man, take my stick, you guys can duel it out wif' sticks!"

"Shut up."

Miguel glared back like a cornered rat, lifting himself up with the stick. His legs felt wobbly, blood streaming into his face from the cut on his forehead. He probed at it with his fingers and touched a welt that sent a shiver of pain through him like an electric shock. Ritchie walked right up to him.

"You tell Spider we're even now." He nodded to his boys. One of them grabbed Miguel. He tried to pull away but the guy was gently escorting him back to his car, almost supporting him with his weight. Sitting back behind the wheel, Miguel felt his emotions well up, his face contorted with the effort to hold it back. Ritchie stood by the door, vapor pouring from his mouth.

"So, Miguel," he said, looking up and down the street. "We got any stuff today?"

Miguel's hands stung from minute scrapes and cuts that burned every time he flexed his fingers. He went to the briefcase and gave Ritchie his two packages.

"You tell Spider I said thanks. You make sure an' thank 'im." Miguel stared. Ritchie had opened one of the packages and was holding it upside down. It was open, but nothing was coming out of it. He held the empty package out to Miguel, who took it with trembling fingers. Ritchie had opened the other one. It was empty too, nothing but newspaper inside.

"What the fuck," Miguel whispered, desperately pulling out the crumpled paper. He looked in the empty briefcase and even under the seats with growing panic.

"Stupid, there was never anythin' in there," Ritchie said. The hurt appeared on Miguel's face. Ritchie quickly handed him his three wads of money and walked away, the rest of the posse falling in behind him. He waited for them to vanish before he turned the rearview mirror on his face, saw the blood, the damage, and started to cry. He pounded the wheel until it honked, checked the empty packages, and stepped on the gas, sending it down the street like a bullet. On Fox Street, he jumped the sidewalk, plowing through the tall grass on the empty lot, coming to a stop in front of an old couch. He jumped out of the car and screamed. He ripped the beeper off his belt and tore and clutched and pulled at it before he sent it flying off into the sky.

He sat on the hard dirty ground crumpled up against the car. So it was Spider that did it to him, Spider! Spider who set him up for a beating! "You ain't no better than us." Eat shit, mothafucka, with yuh fancy clothes an' the mousse in yuh hair an' tha' goddamn car. This beating comes straight from the Man, who made it clear you need some discipline.

Miguel inspected the empty packages again, as if through some miracle he had missed something.

He got back into his car, his face throbbing, his sides aching. Was there anything broken inside? He couldn't tell, but he figured he'd be in more pain if there were. He drove off the lot, up Fox the wrong way so he could park on Prospect. The house was empty. Firebug found him in the bathtub when he came in, lying perfectly still in the steamy murkiness, body covered with bruises.

"Shit," Firebug said, chomping on a slice that oozed cheese over the tip. "What the fuck?"

Miguel's eyes opened slowly. He gave Firebug a tired look and shut his eyes again.

"What happened, bro'? Somebody teach you a lesson?"

Miguel's eyes snapped open. He dabbed his forehead with a fat sponge. He winced, sucking in air.

"Maybe you know more about it than I do." He wiped at his thighs with the sponge, the effort making him groan.

Firebug came closer, holding out the slice. "Now what kinda thing is that to fucken say?"

Miguel didn't answer him. Firebug shrugged, kneeling by the tub.

"Hey man, I got another commission," he said excitedly. "It's not so big-time, but'chu know, steady work in a day an' age like this, it feels good. I can laugh at all thum clowns over on thum lines f' unemployment!" The laughter rolled out from him in happy ripples. He leaned forward to look at Miguel's head. "Coño, what a tajo, man, they clipped'ju good on the head." He took a big bite off his slice, a thick thread of cheese making him lean forward as it stretched like elastic. "So who fucked'ju up?"

Miguel stared. Firebug's face carried the curiosity one shows for a baseball game score or the description of a good play. Amelia was right about him. The guy just didn't have feelings. Miguel decided not to go into details.

"Ritchie an' his boys," he said, the gruffness of his voice surprising him. "He din't like the way I made my delivery Friday night."

Firebug nodded absently, popping the last of the pizza crust into his mouth. "So you comin' t' my wienie roast Wednesday?"

"Wednesday?"

"Yeah, I tol'ju, weren't'chu listening'? Damn bro', wha'chu on? No wonda' you got the shit kicked outta you. I said I got me this commission, it's a rush, an' I'm thinkin' I can do it Wednesday. It's nah really a big place. An' it don't gotta be a big torch, jus' cause a lotta damage. Whass yuh schedule like Wednesday, think you can be there?"

"Why don'chu ask me Wednesday?" Miguel wanted him to go away. He dabbed his wound again and winced.

"Maan, I can see you in a lousy mood again. Like, take the rag out already, bro'." Firebug got up and stomped off.

"An' close the fucken door!"

Firebug returned, mugged, and slammed the door shut.

When Miguel came out, he went straight to his room, very slowly. Everything on his body ached. He had a large black bruise shaped like Africa on his left side. His head throbbed, and every tiny movement of his mouth stung. He turned off his lights and lay in the semi-darkness, listening to Firebug's box playing softly in his room. Spider's money was stacked up beside him on the mat. If he wanted it, he'd have to come and get it. Miguel was angry enough to burn it. He wouldn't be making any deliveries for a while, that was for sure. Every blink set off fireworks behind his eyelids.

He saw his mother, clearer than he had seen her for a long time, wearing a gray pantsuit and matching vest. Her face didn't show the marks of pain or age or the results of his father's fists. Her skin was clear and pure, like the plastic on a mannequin. Her long fingernails clacked against the rim of a champagne glass. Beside her, a husky man with a freshly shaven face poured his beer into a tall glass.

"It's just that I worry about you, Miguelito," she said in a singsong. "I mean when you are gone for so long. I don't know where you are, you come and go, you don't even call." She looked to the man beside her for help. He took her small hand in one of his huge hairy ones. Almost a paw. Fingers as thick as sausages.

"What she's trying to say," Nelo continued in a smooth voice, "is that we have made some plans. And we want to know if you wish to be included in them. Because your behavior, well . . . it's understandable to us. Considering what you went through at the hands of that man—"

"My father," Miguel corrected him, lighting his cigarette.

"Yes, your father." Miguel using English did not force Nelo to join him. He was sticking to a stiff, formal Spanish that sounded alien, barely used. "Anyway, it's understandable why you do these things. We've discussed it at length."

"Well thank you, doctor."

"Miguel." His mother's voice pleaded.

"It's all right. Look, what I'm saying . . . what we're saying is that it's understandable, but not acceptable. It's time to put the past behind us. Your behavior, well, it's a reaction to the past. It's time to bury it, and to start anew. Your mother has suffered a lot. Doesn't she deserve a new life?"

Miguel looked from one to the other. "Whass this about?" They had invited him to a fancy Mexican restaurant on 23rd Street, with cactuses and drapes and a serenading trio. Except for his shirt, Miguel was wearing the baggiest clothes he could find, his sneakers the grimiest pair he owned.

"Your mother and I have decided to live together."

Miguel glared at his mother. "But'chu still married!"

"He's not coming back," she said sternly, as if reprimanding him.

"How do you know? Can'chu even get a divorce first? Jesus!"

"He abandoned us. What am I supposed to do, spend the rest of my life tracking him down so I can divorce him? I can get one later. But I want to do it this way first."

"Man, yuh playin' with fire! Suppose he comes back an' finds this clown in bed wit'chu? You think he's gonna be polite about it?" Miguel didn't look at Nelo. He had turned his chair slightly so he could face her only.

"We're not planning on staying in that apartment," she said, looking past him through the clean glass, into the street. "I'm going to move. I mean we are. To Nelo's apartment. He has a gorgeous four-room place in Soundview."

"Oh nifty."

"You can have your own room," Nelo said, taking a drink of beer, foam on his lips. "No more sleeping on a sofa bed."

"Did'ju tell Diana?"

The image of his sister, playing like an old newsreel, seemed to suspend one memory with another. She's twenty now. Has two kids, looks thirty. Hair matted down on her head, the little that flows onto her shoulders lifeless. Miguel could see her walking down Hunts Point, dragging the two-year-old by the hand. The little girl has a long droopy face but big goofy eyes real close together. She keeps wanting to stop because

at her age the world is an amazing place to be checked out CLOSE UP.
Diana always yanks on her hand viciously, all angry words and spit flying.
The little girl gets pulled again, falls with a loud smack. Her siren cry is
just starting to get off the ground when Diana spins, forcing her to her
feet, straightening her clothes with bitter yanks and pulls. "Din't I tell you
t' shut up an' move? Like how many times I gotta tell you that you fucken
stupid li'l bitch, don'chu lis'sen'na me? Shut up. Look, I said shut up!"
The first slap sounds like a pistol shot. The second is more like an angry
drubbing, as if trying to erase the tiny face.

"Yes," Miguel's mother said, cutting in on the stock footage, "I told
her. And she was very understanding about it." Her voice built up momentum. "Why can't you be that way? Why must you be so impossible?
You do what you want, you come and go as you please, you don't care
how worried I am about where you are, and then when you do show up,
all you make are demands. Hasn't my life been nothing but one long series
of demands? Don't I deserve to be happy?" Her voice was getting hysterical now and the white couple at the next table, pink-skinned and white-
haired, cast quick glances in their direction.

"Of course you do," Nelo said, holding her hand, patting it like a
gerbil. He looked at Miguel hopefully. "How about it, chief?"

The waiter arrived then, unleashing a torrent of steaming hot dishes,
of yellow rice melted cheese and beans tacos burritos.

"You don't gotta worry about me," he said, not looking at anyone.
"I'm gonna be okay." He dropped his cigarette into his burrito. It fizzled,
drowned.

"Just like your father," she spit out venomously. "You want to ruin
my life."

"No, I don't," he said, getting up. "I want to leave you to it. When
you gonna move?"

"Next week we start. Friday." Nelo's voice was stern and cold.

Miguel stared at him, surprised at the determination on his face.

"I'll get my stuff out by then." Miguel murmured a quick goodbye,
and that was that. The last time he saw her was that Wednesday, when
he picked up his stuff with the help of a friend, a pothead named Quique,
a partner in his weed network. She was pretty distant, seemed to accept
it fine that she'd never see him again. It was like a soap opera. Boom. He
walked the streets, crawling from crib to crib. Boom. Then he ran into
Firebug. Boom. Spider. The images burned him, exploded in flashy colors

like burning rockets. Ritchie, overturning the empty packages. To show him he had been set up, duped. Ritchie had betrayed Spider. Sure, Ritchie seemed to be saying, I asked him if I could beat'chu up. But he said yes. Holding up the package: "You ain't protected anymore, sucka. You jus' like us now. Better remember that."

There was a lot of phone ringing. Evidently, nothing for him. Miguel could hear Firebug chattering away. Invitations for the upcoming wienie roast. Business details, money, in hushed tones. Then Miguel heard: "Nah, he's okay, he's sleepin'." A pause. "Nah, not too bad. Lip looks like a life raft, though."

Miguel's eyes were open wide as he leaned forward, straining to listen. He thought of picking up his extension, but decided not to try it. The call ended and Firebug went back to his sing-along with LL Cool J. He appeared at the door, a short bulky silhouette in his coat.

"Yo man, you need anythin'?" He yelled, as if Miguel were lying across town.

"Nah."

Firebug came in, lowering his voice. "Listen, um . . . Spider's gonna be at Mongo's, man. I jus' wanted t' ask you if maybe you want I should take his receipts f' you. You don't look like you be seein' him soon."

Miguel sat up a little more to look at him. "You gonna see him?"

"Nah man, but I know he's gonna be there. An' I gotta be there."

"Why don't he come an' get 'um?"

"Yo bro', you forget tha'chu the one supposed t' bring 'um t' him?"

"I know that, but I kinda got beat up."

"Well, I know that shit!" Firebug was losing his patience, gesturing angrily. "Thass why I'm offerin' t' help, like yuh friend an' shit!"

Miguel fell back against his pillows. He felt drained, weary. He could see what was happening. He grinned bitterly. Pain shot through him from his swollen lip.

"Why ain'chu called Spider, anyway?" Firebug asked suspiciously. It was too much for Miguel to get into it. Besides, he no longer trusted Firebug. He grabbed the bundles of money and handed them to him without another word.

"All right," Firebug said. He left and came back with a brown bag that he threw the bundles into. Then he stepped out of the room, turning off his box. Miguel listened to Firebug's boots clumping off into the hall. The front door shut with its usual clatter.

Miguel turned on the lamp, slid the phone closer, and dialed.

"Cristalena," he said simply into the phone. Rosa didn't understand him, his voice so hoarse and broken. He tried clearing his throat but it only made things worse.

"Damn, you sound like shit," Rosa said, with a warm familiarity. "I'll get huh." There were other voices and the sound of records. Milli Vanilli?

"Lover!" Cristalena's voice sent tremors through him, as always. "I don't believe you!"

"Cristalena," he sighed with relief, rubbing his tired eyes.

"Listen, I'm at my cousin's, she got some of huh obnoxious friends here. You comin'? Oh please say you comin' because I felt it was like really so important f' me to be able to thank you in person f' thum beautiful flowers! I never got no flowers like that in my life! I jus' gotta see you, do some of that serious hugging action."

"Oh Lena, I jus' wanted to let'chu know—"

"Uhhh I love when you call me that."

"What?"

"When you call me Lena. I love it, Miguel. I love you. Do you hear?" She screamed it into the phone again. "Less get down already, okay?"

"Damn."

"Less you an' me jus' go someplace where we can be alone, okay? I mean it. Do you have candles? What am I saying, shit! My ma has candles, whole boxes of 'um. But nah, we can't use 'um for um . . . I mean they religious candles, you know . . ." There was a sudden burst of laughing and giggling on the other end. Miguel could hear Rosa yelling GRAB THE PHONE! There were mad scuffling sounds, Cristalena screaming as hands wrestled with the phone. A strange husky girl voice suddenly said, " 'Ey boy, she wants t' fuck you!"

"Get off." Cristalena's voice interrupted with a half-laugh.

"Yo, she's tight, she's a virgin!" another voice yelled. Cristalena was yelling GET OUT GET OUT! and trying to muffle the mouthpiece. Miguel managed a smile, despite the sting. He was thinking, anyway. The diversion bought him some time. He couldn't have paid to have it done any better.

He hadn't thought about calling her. It had been a reflex, a need, and he had obeyed the urge without thinking. Now he was trying to figure out what to say to her. It was good he got her the flowers. That way, he didn't have to see her right away, could stay away for a few days or a week until his face got back to normal. (How long would that take?) Or no, maybe it was stupid that he sent the flowers because now she was all hyped up, dying to see him, ready to cross streams, ford rivers, climb mountains. For a brief moment, he fantasized about telling her, just telling her he had got the shit kicked out of him, inviting her over, sitting her down beside him and telling her everything. And what would happen? She'd stare at his beaten face, recoiling from the RATHOLE he lives in and WOOPS there's Firebug with baggy filthy clothes junkie eyes dirty fingernails and this girl by the hand, NO not AMELIA, she could sometimes pass muster when she wasn't dressed like some PUTONA in all that lace and tight spandex. NO; IT'S SPIDER. FIREBUG WALKS IN WITH SPIDER, WHO CAME BY TO CHECK ON HIM AFTER THEY . . .

"There, I locked 'um out," she said in an intimate whisper, as if she was inside his head. "Ohh Miguel, I really loved the flowers, that was so sweet. It musta cost a bitch!"

"Long-stem roses . . ."

"Excuse me, BEAUTIFUL RED LONG-STEM roses, Miguel. I felt like I was in a movie or something. Should've seen Rosie, she was really playin' it out, you know, like I got somethin', but she wouldn't say what, until finally I almost strangled her. I got 'um here, my aunt found 'um a pretty vase. They make the whole living room smell real sweet." She sighed. "I miss you."

"I do too." His sigh was longer than hers, sadder.

"Miguel, whass wrong? Your voice sounds funny."

"Yeah well, I gotta tell you. I sorta got bad news. I'm really sick." He swallowed. "I got a real bad flu. You hear my voice? I got strep throat. Thass real contagious. I can't even move I'm so weak, I'm in bed . . ."

"Are you at your place?"

"Yeah. I mean nah, I'm not at my crib. I'm at my mother's house. She jus' moved in with this man, his name is Nelo. He . . . they been tryin'na get me t' join 'um, I even got my own room. I feel weird here but I cun't stay at my crib. I'm too sick an' Firebug's never around."

She sighed. "Where are you at?"

"My ma is out on Elder Avenue."

"Listen, I could come over on the train. Miguel, I can cook you something. Make you some tea. You need oranges, a lotta oranges, an' chicken soup."

"Baby, I can't let'chu come up here. You'll catch it. My ma I don't care too much about." He whispered this part as if she might be near. It scared and depressed him, how easy it was to lie. "This is killer shit. I'm bein' taken care of, don't worry."

"But I wanna see you! Can't I jus' pass by? Maybe they can cover you in a glass bubble."

"No baby. I love you. When you see me, I want it t' be right."

"Pssh. Get real."

"I don't wan'chu gettin' sick."

"I love you, too. I'm seein' you tomorrow. Gimme the address, quick."

"No."

"Whass your last name again? Maybe your ma's number is listed."

"Stop that, Cristalena."

"Now you sound like my father."

"I din't mean it to come out like that. Can'chu hear my voice? See how fucked up I am? I don't wan'chu anywhere near it. Jus' gimme a few days' rest, thass all." The words came out all wrong, and the long pause that followed hurt him.

"You want a rest from me?"

Oh man, her voice was trembling. It was going to come out of him, it was going to spill out. He wanted to see her, he wanted to touch her and feel her, all that bullshit, like on soap operas.

"I wanna see you, Lena," he said desperately, his voice shaking. "This whole week has been so . . . I mean that everything jus' sucks. I jus' wanna hide an' . . ." He gasped for air, felt like the walls were closing in on him. "I'm with you an' I see you an' I feel like I'm floatin', like my whole life is good an' it means something an' I don't have to worry, I found something real. An' then we say goodbye an' yuh not there an' I have to live my life an' it gets so fucken hard to take this shit . . . Like I jus' wanna be a normal kid. Like I'm sicka this already an' I jus' wanna be a normal kid an' not live in this dump an' . . ."

He stopped it, stopped it before it was over for both of them.

"Baby," she whispered. "Can you feel it? I'm stroking your face."

He sighed, leaning back, a hundred pains assaulting him. "Oh damn, why did I have t' meet'chu now when my life is so fucked up?" The first real glimmers of his frustration were starting to slip out. It felt good to say it, to let it out. It made him feel honest.

"Miguel, listen. I don't care wha'chu are. I love you already. I'm glad I know you. It don't matter when. Just that I do."

"You don't even know me." A kind of panic.

"I know enough t' really love you."

"But I could be a murderer. For all you know."

"Really?" Mock admiration, and then a soft laugh. "So could I then."

"No you cun't."

"Yes I could. You act all the time like WILL YOU GET THE FUCK OUTTA HERE AN' GIMME SOME FUCKEN PRIVACY??"

A door slammed.

Her voice again, tender and soft. "You act like I'm so perfect. My parents thought I was going to be perfect. I was their little child of Christ. They wanted me to be a holy child, something clean and exemplary. But I guess I had other ideas. I just wanna be normal. I wanted to always be normal, to go out an' dance an' hear music an' go to movies. Wear sexy clothes. Try to grow into a normal lady, not some ugly plain deformed Christian woman in a white dress, with hairy legs."

"I never knew you were a Christian when you were in school. You used to dress real dope, those tight blue pants an' shit?"

She laughed softly. "You noticed."

"Nicest booty in the school. Used t' bug me I cun't get'chu. Then that Raul guy happened."

"He was my first boyfriend. You know, it took me a long time to get up to pants. Pentecostals think pants are sinful on women, they put bad ideas in men's heads. First I had to fight with my mother about lipstick and earrings and pantyhose. Pantyhose, man. That was a big fight. A pious God-fearing woman's legs are supposed to be bare. When I won the fight for pantyhose, then I crawled over to pants." She sniffled, and for a moment Miguel thought she was crying. "I used to go to Rosa's house in the mornings and after school, to change. I had a friend named Dolores, I used to change at her house, too. I was wearing pants at school for half a year before somebody spotted me on the street an' ratted on me to my mother. She exploded when I got home in my usual safe unsinful skirt, saying I was the devil's daughter, that I had deceived my parents, all this guilt-trip stuff. I tried not to fight with her, because I knew I had to be what I wanted to be, regardless of what she said. I don't know where I got it, this need to be myself no matter what. But I stood up to her. We still fight about shit, but usually I jus' lie an' lie. If she knew about'chu, I think she'd probably kill me. Her an' my father both. So I'm still underground. I feel like I'm living a double life."

Me too, Miguel wanted to tell her. ME TOO! His heart was thumping in his ears. "It seems to be workin' okay," he said lamely.

"Yeah, I got this whole system. But damn, I'm sick of it. I wanna jus' break out, come clean an' be straight an' lay it all on the table. I jus' can't yet. I don't know why. I wish I could jus' get outta here."

"You'll get out." He was immersed in her words, lost in her ability to be straight. She said things he felt he should've said, words that seemed to come out of him. She was a mirror image, a girl with a mind and a life and her own battle for independence, her own turf war. He admired her, at the same time oppressed by his own cowardice.

"I wish we could jus' get in my car an' drive the fuck outta this town." From the heart.

She sighed. "This ain't no movie, lover."

"Then you know already that however much it fucken hurts, the time ain't right. Tha'chu gotta bide yuh time an' play it slow 'til the moment comes when you can come clean an' make a break." He exhaled, feeling he was really saying it for himself.

"But sometimes you can wait too long."

Fuck!

"Like telling me I gotta wait to see you," she continued. "What if I don't see you tomorrow? An' the day after, you die?"

"Oh Lena, come on, man."

"You kiddin'? In the nice neighborhood we live in? All those crack shits shooting up the streets? How about that little kid friend of yours who shoved his nine in my face?"

Jimmy. Able to smash vestibule windows with a single brick. Boasts of having fucked thirteen women, all older than him (it ain't hard to be older than him, he's fourteen), BUT word has it that the only girl fucked him was Little Vicious. He let her shoot his gun from the hip. She got real horny after that.

Miguel laughed. "So you could come here tomorrow an' get shot on the way. How do you think I would feel?"

She breathed into the phone with frustration. "Ohh Miguel! Let me see you tomorrow, please. I'll wear a veil like an Arab girl. I'll do a striptease."

"You mean a belly dance?"

"Yeah, I'll do that. I swear."

"You ain't doin' no belly dance, girl. You be sure t' catch my cold then, 'cause if I look, I gotta touch."

They both laughed, a great sense of relief flooding them both.

"You could put one a' thum rubies in yuh belly button," he added.

"Then you'll have to take it out with your teeth."

"Bet," he said, thinking he was lucky to still have teeth.

"So I'm seeing you tomorrow, right?"

Miguel paused.

"No, man. Womp."

"Miguel!"

"Gimme a chance t' get better, okay?"

"But'chu gave me those goddamn flowers, an' I gotta thank you!"

"But'chu did thank me already on the phone!"

"But I gotta thank you in person!"

"So you gave me that cross. I got it on. I gotta thank you, too."

"Look. I'm tryin'na be mature about this. But I can't help thinking maybe you got some woman over there tha'chu gotta give equal time to."

"There cun't ever be another girl. It's jus' you, Lena. You the real Marilyn. You think I'd blow all that money on roses if I was playin' you?"

"How much was it?"

"Oh no, you don't. Mind yuh own business."

"Maan. Hold on. I gotta talk to my girlfriend." Cristalena covered the mouthpiece. He heard little snatches of talk that made it clear he was being discussed. When she came on again, she was laughing softly.

"My girlfriend wants to know if you have a brother."

"Nah. I got a junkie roommate, though."

"No."

"How about Jimmy with the nine?"

"Look," she said authoritatively, "I'm gonna call you tomorrow, okay?"

"Okay. Only I broke my beeper and . . ." Something else suddenly occurred to him. "Ah fuck! My ma don't have a phone yet, the phone company screwed up."

Something got tense in her voice. "Well, what are you calling on?"

"Womp. I'm at my friend Julio's. He lives three blocks from my ma's."

"If you're so sick, how come you're at his house an' not at your ma's?"

"I crawled over here t' call you, stupid."

It made so much sense to him that he started laughing, which really made his lip bug out with pain. The cracks seemed to open up and burn and scald. He could taste blood flowing into his mouth. "Ouch. Ah shit."

"Miguel, I'm fucking depressed."

"Don't be. I'm gonna call you tomorrow if I gotta crawl back and forth all day. You know I'll call you, don'chu? So don't worry, I'm okay. You gotta have a little faith in me, you know?"

She sighed. "Okay. You win."

"I love you, Cristalena." When he got off the phone, he felt scared of everything. There was no way his face would heal by her birthday. No matter how much he tried to put it off, he already knew that it was going to happen this week. There was just no escaping it.

After that he lay in bed with the covers up to his chin, reading Dickens and refusing to answer the phone, which rang several times before midnight. He didn't go near it, because he knew it could be Spider OR it could be Cristalena, calling to check on him, her fear irritating him because it was well deserved. He decided it was just Spider; maybe it was better not to know.

Sometime after midnight, Firebug returned with Amelia. They were both flying. Firebug was yelling and screaming about how he was going to buy a color TV for his room. They appeared together at his door, Firebug flicking on the lamp.

"Rise an' shine, beauty boy."

Amelia's eyes, crazed with rocks as they were, still showed a sign of something. Concern? Fear? Hatred? Anger? Miguel couldn't tell.

"What happened?" she headed straight for him.

"I tol'ju he got beat up. Some fight wif' one a' thum posses." Firebug turned to him, pointing a finger like a schoolteacher. "You better cut tha' shit out or Spider's gonna can yuh ass."

Miguel didn't say anything. He squinted from the light. Firebug looked at him and at Amelia as though he were enjoying the show. "Don't he look better like that? It's like the beatin' gave his face some characta."

"Get out," Miguel said to the two of them, turning toward the wall. "An' put the fucken light out."

"What a crab. Fuck."

"Are you okay?" Amelia asked. Firebug pulled her out of the room, turning off the light.

"Sure he is. Wha'chu think? He's a man, ain't he? A little beatin' ain't gonna kill him. He knows he's still in the bess business in the world."

That night there were no sounds of frantic sex. The silence was broken occasionally by a muffled gasp or a quivering sigh that was more like the hiss of air brakes. Miguel couldn't sleep. Everything on him hurt too much, making him think that maybe there was something wrong inside. He kept getting the urge to piss, only to stand over the toilet for a stinging drip, drip. He accepted the pain as proof he was still alive. Even the cigarette he was smoking hurt, the taste acrid and foul. In the dark he sat up slowly and went over to sit by the window, which he opened after a lot of groaning. Cold, biting wind seemed to soothe his face like a block of ice. When he started to tremble, he figured this was the best way to catch a cold. He was weighing the benefits of having one when he felt someone in the room with him. Amelia's thin curvy shape appeared at the door, moving slowly toward him like a mirage. The light that spilled through the window framed her, spotlighting her like the statue of an olive Amazonian, her dark nipples round and pointed.

"I hope Firebug comes in," he said. "It would serve you right."

She was standing there in the splash of streetlight, almost defiantly, as if daring him to look. Not a stitch on the bitch. He took in her fine tits, her well-muscled curves, the soft slope of her tummy leading down to that dark tangle of bush.

"He won't be coming in," she said in a husky whisper. "You ever take Seconal? I turned him on to it. He'll sleep real good." Her face softened. "Are you okay? What happened?"

When he told her, he expected her to be shocked. He had saved the empty-bags thing for the punch line. Amelia came over to where he was on the mat and sat, half covering herself with the comforter. He leaned against the cold wall, puffing on his cigarette, waiting for her reaction.

"He was disciplining you," she said, her eyes pensive.

"What?"

"He wanted to remind'ju that'cha didn't know your place. He was just slapping you back down into place." She snatched his cigarette and puffed on it.

She wasn't looking at him. It really irritated him. "What, did he tell you that? Did'ju know about this?"

She looked at him and shrugged. "No. I didn't. He didn't tell me all of it."

"Well jus' what did he tell you?"

"He told me people complained about'chu and that he was going to teach you a lesson, that's all. It was bugging him a little. But who knows? It's hard to say with him. He's like Firebug. They're both insects. Man, how could he do that?"

"You mean you don't know?" Miguel asked bitterly. "The nex' time you fuck 'im, why don'chu bring it up?"

Outside, a tractor-trailer braked with a loud moan. The streets sounded wet, tires sizzling, raindrops thumping against the window. Somewhere, a baby cried itself awake. He listened to the muffled sound waver and fall in pitch, like a faraway siren. Then he realized that Amelia was crying, her body shaking, hands covering her face. She crept closer.

"Hold me, Miguel." Her fingers clutched tentatively at his arm. "Please hold me." Her hand scraped against him like the paw of a dog trying to open a door.

He pulled her close. She was shivering, her skin soft and cool. Her face was wet against his neck, his shoulder, his cheek, her fingers tracing his lips.

"Ahh man, lookit what they did . . ."

"Shh. It's okay. I'm sorry I said what I said. Forget about it."

"You care about me, Miguel. Say it."

"Okay okay, I care about'chu. Now stop crying like that."

It wasn't like she was loud. It was just the way she trembled and gasped for breath that scared him. "I just needed to hear it once," she said, wiping her face with his comforter.

"Don't get boogies on my sheet."

She laughed suddenly, her eyes grateful. "So are you gonna quit now?"

He nodded. "You don't think I'm gonna take this shit, do you?"

"I need another cigarette," she said. "I'm giving you this one back."

"But I don't want it back. It ain't hardly a stub."

She held it out to him.

"Naah man, I don't want it . . ." He shuffled around for the pack. He offered her a fresh cigarette but she was still smoking the stub and looking up at the ceiling.

"I knew it was a girl. The minute you stopped picking up pussy an' competing in Firebug's fuckfests, I knew. Did'ju tell this girl Rutabaga about . . ."

"Cristalena."

"Now you tell me what kinda fucking name that is!"

"It's a magic name."

"An' whass this? Some fairy tale?"

"Thass right. A South Bronx fairy tale. Sex, drugs, money, vice, an' loud hip-hop music."

"Well great. Have you told this magic chava about all this?"

Miguel got up. He shut the window, a sudden pain shooting up his back. He sat beside her and lit the cigarette he had fished out for her.

"You haven't told her." Amelia tossed her flaming stub into a glass ashtray.

"Nah."

"How you gonna explain this beating?"

"She wanted to see me tonight. I told huh I had a cold."

She shook her head. "That ain't the way. I tell you, if you don't tell her quick, she might never understand. Why you wanna hook up with a girl that won't understand?"

He shrugged, not wanting to look at her. "I don't know. She's just like everything I ever wanted in a girl."

"Yeah, like how?"

"She's smart, she's pretty. She got respect f' huhself, an' she makes me wanna respect myself. She's funny, makes me laugh. When I'm around huh I always wanna give huh something." He absently fingered the gold cross around his neck. "She gave me this cross."

Amelia sighed and rolled her eyes. "You think you're quitting for yourself, or for her?"

"I don't care. Why you gotta ask so many goddamn questions?"

"Because I care, you little fuck. I have for a long time. I wanted to get to you a long time ago, and I couldn't. I don't know why, but'chu know? That's been my story. I can attract any guy when I really don't want him. But a guy I really want, I never get him. Not even once." Her eyes were glassy and far. "You got any smoke?"

"Yeah." He searched around on the floor and found the bag. He was going to roll a joint, but she suggested using Firebug's bong. She got up to get it, sauntered in and out with hardly a sound, like a dark thin ghost.

"He's out like a light. I gave him enough of that shit to keep him out for a week."

"Get the fuck."

"Yeah." She laughed while he cleaned the pipe and packed it with smoke.

"What made'ju wanna do that."

"I planned to sleep with you."

He laughed and said NAH MAN PLEASE, laughing and leaning against the wall, grasping his stomach because the laughter grew painful. "Amelia man, you know that can't happen."

She was wearing a grin, slick and knowing. "I didn't say fuck. I said sleep. I want to sleep with you."

"Yuh a weird person. Nah, don't laugh. See my face? I'm serious. I really think yuh great, but'cha fucken weird."

"You don't understand. See, I've never slept with anyone I loved before." Her voice shrunk a little, her eyes glassy. "I been with a lotta men. But I can't say sleeping with them was good. It was just sex. I guess because I couldn't find someone I loved, I just focused on the sex."

"You mean like with Firebug?"

"Yeah. You know, he's the most dead person I ever met in my life. Always talks about himself, no one else. Every time you see him, he's got something to say about himself. Even when he comes out of the bathroom, it's 'Maan, you should see the fucken brick I jus' laid.' Him and his ego. He can't love."

"But he's still with you. He caught you with Spider and look what it did to him. Don'chu think maybe you helped make him that way? You betrayed him, right? So did Spider. Maybe before that he was different."

"Before that he was the same. He used to see me an' he had three other girls. Do you remember Donna? That bleached blonde with the big tits? She was one. He would fuck me and he would fuck them. I was a possession. He knew I was older, used to try to taunt me by saying, 'Oh you know Donna? She's twelve.' Like I was this old lady dying for his cock. He used to ask me if I wanted to go three-way. He wasn't hurt by what I did. He was just mad that I showed him he didn't really matter to me, and that I would even use Spider to make my point. He really only kept me around after all that shit because I still fuck him better than anyone. I don't care how young or how big their tits are. He knows it. I made him, showed him things he had never heard of. I just take what I want. You know me." She grinned tiredly, swiping the cigarette from his lips gently for a few quick puffs. "He helped me get cold. When I saw he only wanted me around because I was this older woman who could really fuck him, I learned to use that. He's the one got me into crack. I had only done it once or twice with a few friends at school, a real casual thing, but Firebug said he could get me lots of it and used to do it with me. But he didn't care about whether I had a hit or not. He used to joke about it. 'Well you so bad off,' he would say, 'why don'cha go to my friend Frankie? He'll give you some rocks for a real good blow." Ha ha ha. So I went to Spider, his best friend. Is that bong ready yet?"

"Yeah." He was looking for the lighter.

"Spider was real reluctant at first. But'chu see? I got my way with him in the end. I get my way with everybody that I don't love." She stared at him a moment. "I'm good when I'm vindictive."

She snickered. He held the bong out to her. "It needs water."

She got up and walked off into the bathroom. In a quick instant, he spotted a scar, thought he spotted it maybe, a dark frown like the jagged line a little kid draws in a circle to make a sad face. She came back and sat beside him, snatching the lighter. The bong made gurgling chortling sounds, the pipe lighting up brightly before she covered it with her thumb to keep from wasting smoke. She shut her eyes. Her voice sounded huskier.

"The first guy I fell in love with was named Alejandro. He was big on Latin culture. Always talking about Betances, Albizu Campos, nationalism. We took statistics together. He was so interesting, he opened up my mind. I started to learn things about Latino culture, stuff I never even thought about. I started learning on my own, and we started getting into fights about things. He didn't like I had different opinions about things, and that I could argue about them. One night after fucking, we got into a big fight, and it all came out of him, about how fucked up women are and how he didn't want to end up with a woman who didn't know her place. He felt that the problem with women today was that they don't have discipline and don't know what to do with themselves, the world offers them too much, so they're always flying around trying to find themselves in careers and school and books. He said he didn't want a woman like that. He wanted a woman who could devote herself to a man, kids, family. He said a man strives, a woman maintains. Most Latino guys I've met have that same attitude buried deep down inside. It's like they already resent you. Can you be supportive? Can you cook? Can we fuck anytime I want? Downhill from there on." She passed him the bong. "Every guy I been with since has read me some riot act about how I didn't know shit about being a woman, like if I was born damaged and was doing it wrong."

"That why you left college? 'Cause a' guys?"

"I guess so. Ain't that stupid? I wanted to be so independent, but here I am waiting for some man to make me feel better about myself. I think my last boyfriend was right about me. He told me I had no discipline and no clear direction. An' what did I do? I end up dropping out. Losing interest. All because some guy says I'm a piece a' shit."

"Maybe you been tryin'na prove yuh a piece a' shit."

She frowned, then laughed at him. "How old are you?" Her eyes looked sleepy, her face buzzed, softly sensual.

"Sixteen and a half."

"I'm five years older than you. I bet'chu see me like yuh goddamn mother."

"Nah. Not huh. I love you." He took a hit off the bong.

"Shit. The way you say that, so simple. With a shrug. People lose that when they grow older. It's like you learn to be dishonest, to talk around things."

"But I already do that," he admitted with a shrug. "I gotta do that with Cristalena. It's womp."

"Do you treat her like your little girl? Hide things from her? Think you want to spare her? Protect her? Ahh, I can tell from the way your eyes are crossing that this is what's happening! You feel dirtier than her, she's so pure and holy! Something for you to aspire to. And you're scared to tell her because you'll lose her!"

"You gonna ruin this smoke f' me?"

"How can you love somebody tha'chu gotta lie to all the time? Man, you can't even be yourself!"

"Well I'm gonna tell huh, you can rest assured on that shit. 'Cause I asked myself that already. I gotta tell huh. Lyin' jus' makes me feel worse."

"More unworthy of her."

"Yeah."

"Keeps you being strangers."

"Yeah."

She stared at him. "You think I'm pretty?"

"Yeah. Yuh body is dope."

"I like being with you so much. I figured maybe I could find a way to get you to fall in love with me, but once I realized how much I love you, then I knew I would never get'chu."

He sighed, feeling the buzz descend on him. "I cun't fall in love with you. Firebug's still there, like a friend, right? Regardless of what it really is. I cun't do anything 'til it's over between you an' him. Then there's all that other shit: yuh life." He made a face.

"What."

"Yuh life. When I first met'chu, I jus' thought'chu was some skeez. Slidin' around, smokin' that shit, fucken like some animal with Firebug.

I thought'chu was shit. When I heard'ju was in college, I felt mad. I felt like you had no right to be scrapin' around in the streets like you were. I mean, college? You don't belong here. There was no way I could get to college an' there you were, an' what were you doin'? Hangin' out with these loser brats, playin' posse tramp, fucken Firebug even though you hate 'im, smokin' crack 'cause a' Sartre o' something. I mean, I just thought'chu were sick. But you know, at the same time I felt like I wanted t' talk t' you. An' the more we talked, the more I got to like you an' think you were both cool an' stupid f' smokin' that shit." He grabbed her hand. Her eyes closed; the eyelashes looked wet. "When you gonna quit this shit?"

"I love you." A tear tumbled down her cheek.

"You gotta stop with this shit. Gotta stop usin' people an' bein' used. This Spider thing. It's disgusting, man, why you wanna do that to yuhself? I think maybe yuh worth more than that. I think you should stop seein' Firebug. An' stop givin' it to Spider. Just blow all this shit off."

"Yeah," she said, wiping her face with the comforter again. "I think you're right. I ain't getting anything out of this. Except bitterness."

"You talked to me about it, when I didn't have nobody to talk to. Now I'm returning the favor."

There was a long pause. She came closer, with tiny little jumps, until they were hugging close. She brought her face right up to his, and stroked his face, and then he pulled back a little.

"Sleep with me, Miguel."

"I can't."

"All you gotta do is lie down, like if I'm not even here. An' I can sneak in an' lie beside'ju. Come on, I ain't gonna attack you." She laughed. "I ain't no rapist."

"I don't know, I . . ."

"When Firebug falls asleep, I'm alone. Every time it's like that. I always thought when you slept with someone, that you'd feel all safe an' warm an' shit. But nah, I don't get that, an' that's because I haven't slept with someone I'm truly in love with. Do I gotta get all psychological about it? Come on. Don't be like that. I only wanna sleep beside a warm, caring human being an' not some living corpse. How about it?"

"Okay," he said.

They got into bed. She helped him, asking what parts of him hurt. She tended to him like a nurse, checking all his wounds. They didn't have anything in that apartment, not even some Blistex or iodine or alcohol. She swore to get some stuff in the morning. He lay down with his back to her. She nestled up close, tugging on the waistband of his running shorts.

"We gotta both be naked," she said.

"Don't push it, girl."

"You be fair." She had already pulled them off anyway and he was too weak to resist. She then stripped off his underwear, her warm body pulsating against him. Her arms came around him, his broad soft shoulders a kind of pillow.

"This is nice," she said. When he didn't say anything, she said, "Thank you."

"Oh, cut that out." He wouldn't turn around. If he did, he knew they would intertwine legs or worse, she might give him her back, with that soft tender booty in his crotch, and then:

he imagined her hands sliding down to his cock now stirring

her breath hot against his ear

she was holding it in her hand as it got bigger and throbbed

and she was going mmmmmmm nice and he could feel

he could feel the softness of her breasts as they pressed against him

and if there wasn't a Cristalena, he would

fuck her

It was new for him to abstain from something so close at hand, new to be faithful and giving in this way. It was unselfish. It made him proud. Lying there with his back to her, he realized she was being unselfish, too, that she hadn't really done anything to put him on the spot. He turned toward her slowly and instantly she snuggled close, her head on his shoulder, her warm leg close but no threat. Just the feeling of her made him hard. She knew it. He knew she knew. When she looked at him, she seemed ready to laugh and cry.

"You should see your face," she whispered tenderly.

"I don't wanna hurt'chu," he said.

"Look," she said, "if you want I'll go back to sleep with the corpse. I didn't . . . I mean, I would never wanna put'chu in a position where . . . I wouldn't want . . ."

He laughed, his stomach twitching. "Oh shit," he cried, delighted that she was fumbling for words. She made a move as if to go, her face a little confused, but he held her down and put his arm around her.

"We'll sleep like this," he said, giving her a kiss on the neck.

"Okay," she said, her voice shaking. She leaned up and gave him a warm kiss on the mouth, a lingering peck, slow and careful, her leg brushing against him in a kind of slow taunt. Then she quickly settled in beside him, his arm holding her close. They both seemed to lie awake for a while, but finally Amelia fell asleep, her curled hand lying on his chest. Miguel didn't dare move. He felt a little tense. He lay there thinking about how after all the fucking he had done, he had never slept beside someone he really loved who really loved him. It was a funny feeling, and he found himself relaxing and hoping that it would be this warm and cozy when he lay beside Cristalena.

12

When Miguel woke up, Amelia was kneeling over him. Dressed in a baggy dress with huge white buttons, she looked like a coffee-skinned Alice in Wonderland. She squeezed something out of a tube and applied it to his lip. She dabbed boric water on his cuts and on the ugly gash on his forehead. "Shit, you hardly even washed these," she scolded like an old cranky nurse. "You know what an infection is?"

"Shut up, leave me alone."

And she did, disappearing out the door with a swish. Was Firebug still asleep? The goddamn phone was ringing. He checked the clock. Nine? No fucken way. The phone was inches away. Too far. He rolled over, fell into strange dreams. More bells ringing. Cristalena was in the hallway at school in her tight blue slacks. He was laying the rap on her and had just gotten a hand on her booty when she pushed him away. "No," she said, her face strangely cold and pinched.

"What the fuck," he said. "After all we been through?"

Suddenly Raul stepped out of a doorway, swinging a huge knife. Miguel spent the rest of the dream running from him and looking for Cristalena. He slid in and out of other dreams, all of them vague except for this search for Cristalena, and Raul reappearing with the knife. Miguel ran and ran until the bells started ringing again.

The phone. Afternoon. Sunlight blasting in through the windows. Was Firebug still asleep, or had he left? He tried raising himself a little as the ringing went on, pains shooting up his sides. Could it be Cristalena? Wouldn't she be in school?

He picked it up. "Hello."

"Damn but'chu sound like shit." It was Spider. A tremor of revulsion made Miguel's stomach twitch.

"Ah shit, wha'chu want?" The words tumbled out naturally. He didn't try to stop them. He had a definite need to inflict.

"Yo, whassup? This is Spider. Remember me? Yuh boss?"

"You ain't my nothing. Don't even talk t' me. You gotta lotta fucken nerve."

"Wha'chu talkin' about?"

"You know what I'm talkin' about. Fuckhead."

"Would'ju mind talkin' some English?"

"All right then. In English: I quit. Fuck you. I'm outta this shit."

"Yo, yo. Calm down. Whass this about?"

"It's about me gettin' set up by my boss, my pana, my friend. Thass what. The guy thass supposed t' take care a' me. The guy I trust, right? Who's always talkin'na me about trust?"

Spider sighed into the phone. "You, you just, I mean, you ain't makin' no sense." He sounded lost.

"I'm not, ah? Well. Le' me ask you. Did'ju know Ritchie beat the fucken shit outta me?"

Spider sighed. "Yeah. I got word about it. Thass why I called, you know, t' see how you was doin'. I been on the run, pana, I haven't even been exertin' the kinda control I really need to have. I been too busy runnin' around. I gotta tell you I was a little steamed about it, pana, but at the same time, I gotta lay down some fundamentals a' the game on you: First, you fucked up so bad on yuh run Friday. You really fucked up. People coulda been iced, lucky it din't go down like that. But'chu know, if one a' Ritchie's boys got hurt, I cun't a' saved' ju no matter what. There just ain't no gettin' away with tha' kinda shit, man, you gotta be responsible in this business or else somebody's gonna take you out." Spider's voice got louder, angrier. "An' all 'cause you was out jolly ridin', cruisin' Tinton. Couldn't'chu've done yuh work first?"

"Couldn't'chu've talked t' me about it? Did'ju have t' set me up like that?"

There was a silence.

"Hol' up, hol' up. Wha'chu talkin' about now? Ritchie was bound t' get'chu. I cun't stop it."

"You coulda warned me."

"Ritchie's a good kid, real reliable, but he's got a wild side. He was super pissed. Bad enough some kids out on the street think you gettin' preferential treatment. What he tol' me about'chu din't make me feel so good eitha. I cun't protect'ju, bro'. Not this time. You gotta be adult enough to realize tha'chu goofed, but tha' now you can still step up to the plate an' bat f' the team."

"You set me up, you fuck." The words almost choked Miguel, who was having trouble breathing right. "Din't say a word, din't explain or warn me. Nothin'. You give me a delivery f' him when he din't even have one comin'. Sonofabitch . . ."

"Now where'dju get somethin' like that? Why you gotta try t' get outta takin' responsibility f' yuh own shit? The reason you got beat up was 'cause you fucked up . . ."

"Nah. The reason I got beat up was 'cause you wanted me t' get beat up. 'Cause I was ridin' high on my horse, remember? The reason I got beat up was 'cause you set me up, mothafucka."

"Thass not true!" Spider screamed.

"Yeah? I got the fucken empty bags t' prove it, asshole!"

"You wasn't supposed t' be lookin' in no goddamn bags!"

"I din't look. I trusted'ju. Ritchie. He showed me."

"That mothafucka," Spider muttered under his breath.

"How's it feel to get set up? Huh? Do you like it? I quit, man. I'm through."

"You can't do that, Miguel. Calm down, yuh talkin' stupid."

"I'm talkin' straight. I'm talkin' the straightest piece a' the rock I ever talked. I'm talkin' Prudential, bro'."

"You got any idea how much you fucken owe me?" Spider's voice was high-pitched and desperate. "Now you fucken calm down. Thass it, we gotta calm down, we all real emotional right now. I think you could use a rest now anyway, don'chu? A kinda vacation. Jus' so you get back on yuh feet."

Miguel sighed. There was a sadness in him that he couldn't explain. There was greasy gunk on his lips and his mouth was full of rancid sourness. He worked his way over to the window, opened it, and took a spit into the fresh biting coldness. The wind set fire to his lips; the gash on his forehead burned.

"Spiderman, you let me down," he said in a hoarse groan. "I can't trust'ju no more. There's jus' no way."

"Whoah man, you jus' got this all wrong. You actin' like some emotional putz. You gotta put it in perspective, see what happened, an' learn from it."

"I did learn from it. I thought we were friends. I thought I could trust'ju. I don't wanna be involved with anybody I can't trust. Thass womp."

"But I tol'ju already," Spider said, his voice sounding electronic and strange. "Business is business. Don'chu forget that. There can be times when I can't help you. This was one a' thum times. Sometimes there's a price to pay. I know it's a hard world, bro'. But come on, you can't be that stupid. This ain't in yuh interest. You can't jus' throw it away. Now you know better, thass all. Part a' the education a' Miguel. I got big plans f' us, pana."

"I don't think we got anything t' talk about," Miguel said dejectedly.

"But there is, pana, there is. The police found Rico."

There was a sudden silence.

"Yeah," Spider said, "he's dead. Found 'im in a garbage bag. Okay? Who says we ain't playin' with high stakes?"

"Yuh the one playing with high stakes," Miguel said calmly, "not me."

Spider let out a weird high-pitched cackle that scared Miguel. He had never heard it before.

"No no no, my friend, it ain't that easy. Not that easy, pana. You wanna get to that place where I can't help you, fine."

"I think I already got there, judin' by whass been happenin'. You taught me a lesson all right. I learned that I wanna have a life, I wanna make some kinda future f' myself. This is all shit."

"This shit got'chu a license, an' a car, an' a life," Spider barked. "It keeps you in clothes an' money. You ain't nothing' without it. It is yuh life. There ain't no place else t' go. An' when you go, you get t' find out, well, the Lord giveth an' the Lord taketh away."

Miguel leaned back with the phone in his hand, staring at it, trying to decide whether or not he was going to hang up. Spider's voice was still buzzing like an insect. Why should he listen? What could Spider possibly say that would change his mind? There was no point in listening, but he put the receiver to his ear.

"I'm givin' you a couple days off. Jus' so you can get over this shit. I'm runnin' an army here, not some nursery. You gotta have a certain amount of discipline. You gonna sit there an' tell me you weren't outta line, tha'chu weren't fucked up doin' wha'chu did? Maybe you need to grow up, to realize tha'chu pay a price sometimes. So stop with this whinin' an' shit, man. You had it comin'."

"Two days ain't gonna change my mind, Spider." Miguel's tired voice sounded final.

"But'chu—" Spider paused. "I'm comin'na see you," he said quickly.

"No Spider, I ain't—"

There was a click.

"Hello? Spider?"

A weird sense of panic flooded Miguel. He got up, feeling like an old man with creaking bones; with sore legs and aching chest he shuffled over to the bathroom. He checked on Firebug, who was still lying in bed under tossed sheets, arms and legs at odd angles as if he had just lost a wrestling match. It made Miguel grin. He should be real careful from now on if Amelia offered him any drinks.

He took a dunk in the tub, the hot water calming him. He didn't like what he saw in the mirror. His lip was swollen, his face discolored. There was that gash on his forehead. His whole face looked ashy gray and all stretched out of shape. He resented not being able to see Cristalena right now, when he needed her. He knew it was his fault.

"I'm just gonna tell 'uh," he said to himself, the rising steam making him sleepy. But he knew it was talk. He threw on some clothes; now he was on the run. He'd already told Spider he was quitting; why did he have to see him? What was the point? Was he so fucking important? Didn't he have other people? Why did he have to chase him down like an old lover? He tried putting off the darker thoughts, ones that told him Spider wasn't about to let him defect. Such things are bad for business. This is war, and defectors get shot.

He took down the fake petunias. What was he thinking of? He removed the backing as though he were planning to take all his money with him. He could tell it was all there, untouched. He retaped it. Maybe Amelia was right; his money should be in a bank somewhere.

He put the fake petunias back up on the wall, then went into his room to get his wallet and keys. He was lacing his white hi-tops when he noticed Firebug standing by his door in huge polka-dot boxers, rubbing hie eyes like a little kid. Miguel stared at him, as if he were hallucinating.

"Firebug," he said because he was startled. The guy was like a cat. Not even a sound.

"Whey you goin'?" Firebug asked, still rubbing his eyes.

"Out, I don't know, I don't wanna be in here," Miguel said as he laced up. He decided not to say anything about Spider. It was funny the way that Spider was always mentioning Firebug—"Firebug tells me you been gettin' all gloomy"—as if wanting to show there was always a connection there, while Firebug never mentioned talking to Spider or even seeing him. It made Miguel suspicious about both of them. He could expect anything from them. Miguel felt they were tighter than anyone knew, that theirs was a SOUL thing. Miguel had become some kind of tool to them.

He stared at Firebug, who leaned against the bureau, his groggy face pulled out of shape by sleep.

"You look like yuh inna rush," he said in a posthypnotic drawl that included a long yawn.

"Yeah. I wanna get on my feet as soon as possible."

Firebug nodded. "Yo man, you wanna do me a favor?"

Miguel looked at him and grinned. "No, but what is it?"

"Aw right. Thass cool."

"I'm joking."

"Be like that. Thass cool."

"Just a joke, stupid."

"It's nah like I give a fuck or anythin'."

"Come on, man."

"Well, I was thinking' of buyin' a TV, bro'. Like we should have one. Don'chu think? Like I don't know why we ain't got one before. I thought'-chu could maybe drive me over t' the Save Mart an' we could pick one up. I jus' really wanna get one."

Miguel stared at him, rising up from the mat. "Are you serious? You were the guy always tellin' me we shun't get shit like that, makes us get too attached."

"Well . . ."

"That we should not have a lotta shit like that because people in our kinda work, we gotta be ready to be on the move."

"Yeah well, thass true, a good point."

"To be ready to move at a moment's notice, without a lotta baggage."

"Yeah. Like we could get a portable. No big-screen shit, who needs that? Maybe when we move t' Long Island. But now? One a' those little things. Like the one Amelia has in huh house. A thirteen-inch, man. Color. They havin' this sale, bro'." Firebug looked up at the ceiling. "Maybe a VCR, too."

"What?"

"For the future, I mean. Loosen up, bro'. You sound like my father."

Miguel laughed, feeling a strange happiness. Firebug's oddball humor was in effect, always a good sign. Already his eyes were twinkling with that wild brew of childlike maliciousness. The grin meant it was open season. Miguel hadn't seen that in a long time. Something about it happening now made Miguel feel grateful. Maybe this was Firebug's way of being intimate, of hanging with his buddy who had just gotten the shit kicked out of him.

"Okay my brother," Miguel said. "Get some clothes on."

"I think I look pretty dope like this." He stood straight up, pulling on his boxers.

"You might be cold, though."

"I'll throw on a coat. Maybe I can be like a flasher an' shit."

"Get some fucken clothes on, bro'. I wanna get the fuck already." Because Spider might be on the way, maybe riding down Prospect Avenue right this second, in that dark blue Torino that guy Victor was always driving him around in. (Spider doesn't drive. "Only people who lack real power in life drive," he says on the cassette about his life. "Real men walk. Or are driven.") Victor was this husky guy with greasy black hair. Wanted to look like a big mafioso, had a gun in a holster, saw *The Godfather* twenty-two times already. Might be downstairs already, the sound track blaring from the car's tape deck! No way, Miguel was out of there. He followed Firebug into his room.

" 'Ey man, how about I wait f' you down in the car? I gotta warm it up, it's been havin' some problems."

Firebug spun around, his eyes hurt. "Ahh man, don't be like that."

"What? I'll wait f' you."

Firebug's voice was mournful. "You gonna be like that wif' me?"

"Firebug. Cut tha' shit. I'm gonna wait f' you."

"Nah man. You gonna cut out."

"I ain't man, stop it!"

"Then why can'chu jus' chill?"

"I tol'ju, stoop, I gotta warm up the fucken car. Now grow up an' put some goddamn clothes on. I'll be waitin' downstairs."

Firebug scowled. "I'll be there fast, you know. Like right behind'ju. No reason t' get like that, bro'."

"Ay ay ay." Miguel left, shivering when he hit the street. He checked everywhere for Victor's car, feeling safe in his Baby as the engine hummed warmly. He was starting to get tense when Firebug showed up; his blue parka dwarfed him. His scruffy face was hidden under the furry hood.

"So you waited," he said, shutting the door with a slam. He searched in a pocket and took out a large spliff. "I can't believe it."

"Man, what makes you say shit like that?" Miguel shifted gear. The car jerked forward eagerly.

"It ain't nothin', right? I mean we go back far. It's just that YO, CHECK OUT THA' BITCH SHE GOT THUM HOT TIGHT PANTS ON, LOOKIT THA' SHIT! SHE GOT THUM DAY-GLO LEG WARMERS AN' SHIT YO! LOOKIT THA' CULO, BRO', JUS' LOOKIT! I DON'T BELIEVE . . ." He rolled down the window frantically. "MIRA MIRA!! 'EYY! QUE BUENA TU ESTA, CARAJO!!"

Miguel laughed as they drove past a curvy girl who stared back as if mystified, coils of hair blowing over her face.

"Damn, you saw tha' shit? How is that possible, how they do tha' shit? Dress sexy in the summer, an' the winter too? Like I saw this girl the other day bro', you'd think they wun't be wearin' no skirts 'cause a' the cold an' shit, but nah, I know this girl, she got this thermal pantyhose an' it don't even look thick. This other girl I know, she says spandex is warm, can wear it like long johns."

Miguel shook his head. "Who's that? Amelia?"

Firebug looked at him. "Nah bro'." He had the spliff on his lips like he was sucking on it. There was something weird about his eyes, like he was appraising Miguel, so Miguel said, "What?"

"Nothin'. Jus' lookin'. You don't look so beat up now."

"Ohh, you noticed I got beat up, huh?"

"Yeah, well. There's a little bit a' the orange color about'cha face. But you look okay."

"Not bad for a guy with so many friends, huh?" It came out funny. Firebug was still staring at him.

"It's the business, bro'." He shrugged. "Ain'chu ever worked in a place where you hated yuh boss? Sometimes tha' shit happens. What can you do? You can quit an' be broke. Or you can take it, keep rockin', an' have some money."

"Yeah, right. Look man, I don't mind gettin' beat up on occasion. Maybe thass something we all need, but I hate dishonesty. I hate people lyin' an' settin' me up like that. If yuh friends do it, then you got nobody. Then you gotta start thinkin' about who yuh friends are."

Firebug nodded, flicking his lighter. "Thass a good speech." The thick pungent smoke from the spliff filled the car in no time as Firebug took long leisurely tokes and sat back. The tires seemed to sizzle on the wet street as the windshield got foggy. "Yuh problem is tha'chu don't trust nobody, bro'."

"I trust everybody," Miguel shot back. "Thass what my problem has been. I'm gettin' smarta now. I mean, I've trusted'ju an' then I noticed you were goin' through my money."

"Ah man, thass bullshit!"

"So I hadda change where I keep my money now."

"Yeah, I noticed that," Firebug muttered, making Miguel laugh. Firebug grinned sloppily and passed him the spliff. Miguel slowed the car and took a hit. It was strong shit; Miguel could feel his brow grow hot and when he breathed out smoke it was thick and tasty.

"Goddamn," he said.

"So listen t' me," Firebug said slowly, pulling down his hood. "I gotta ax you somethin'."

"Okay."

"It's about Amelia."

Miguel took another hit and passed the spliff back. "Shoot."

"You know she's in love wif' you?"

Miguel shot him a quick glance. The look Firebug gave him made him laugh. "Fuck," he said, "what makes you say that?"

Firebug shrugged, sucking on the spliff. "It's true. She loves you. She pretty much told me."

"Did she now." Miguel was trying to act like it was all news to him, but his chuckling seemed a little forced.

"Oh yeah. But'chu know, it don't mean shit t' me. I jus' wanted t' warn you about huh."

"Warn me?"

"Oh yeah. She uses people. Not only is she a crackhead, but she's a fucken putona. Sleeps around t' get crack. I learned that about huh a long time ago. Thass why you see how loose we are with each other."

"But how come you still with huh?"

"I don't know." Firebug shrugged, his eyes distant. He slid down deeper into his seat. "She's a great fuck. She's older. I learn a lot from huh. But I wun' say we steady o' nothin'."

Firebug was casting sideways glances at him as if trying to check out Miguel's reaction.

"I mean tha'chu should be careful an' all, not 'cause a' me o' nothin'. I jus' mean—"

"I don't like Amelia, Firebug," Miguel said sharply, feeling irritated. "I got my own chava, bro'."

"Yeah, right, I heard about that. She calls the house. What kinda girl is she? Maybe you should bring huh t' one of our fuckathons." He snickered encouragingly.

"She ain't the type."

"Ahh. She a straight girl?"

"She's a nice girl," Miguel corrected him.

"Tha' explains it."

"Explains what?"

"The new threads." There seemed to be more, but Firebug wasn't talking. He was looking out his window, wiping the fog away with his hand.

"You gonna tell Spider?"

Firebug spun to face him. "Whass tha' shit?"

"I said, you gonna tell Spider? I mean about my girl. I mean maybe he put'chu up t' this."

Firebug leaned toward him, pointing a finger in his face.

"Yo! Check it out. Spider don't put me up t' nothin'. I'm a freelance, you got tha' shit? I don't got nothin' t' do with tha' shit between you an' him."

"Spider's always tellin' me you said this an' that about me, like about my bein' down, outta sorts, about us bein' back at school . . ."

"That was from way back. I don't talk t' him."

"You weren't on the phone with him yesterday night?"

"No." Firebug wasn't looking at him. "We don't talk."

"An' why's that?"

"We drifted apart, bro'. Differences of opinion an' shit, but I still recommended you t' him 'cause I knew he could start'ju out like he did me."

"Ain't it true you ain't so tight with him because he fucked Amelia? Ain't that why you ain't so tight no more?"

There was a pause, and Miguel enjoyed it.

"Who tol'ju that?"

"I got ears out jus' like you."

"Thass a fucked-up thing to say, bro'." His voice sounded a little hurt.

Miguel knew how good Firebug was at turning on that fractured voice at will. "We had a fight, yeah."

"About Amelia."

Firebug shrugged, looking out the window like he was thinking of jumping. He in no way wanted to talk about it. Miguel laughed.

"Shit," Firebug thundered. "Why you laughin'?"

"'Cause a' you. Jus' lookit'chu, bro', yuh actions speak a thousand words. We supposed t' be tight friends, pana, an' there you are gettin' all fucked over talkin' about'cha past. Here I am gettin' the scoop from other people. I guess we ain't so tight, huh?"

"You insult me, pana," Firebug said tersely.

"You an' Spider are fucken the same girl," Miguel said authoritatively. "Why don'chu jus' admit it?"

Firebug whacked the dash with his fist. "You really piss me off! Like you can jus' take a person's life an' rewrite it. I heard'ju was doin' Spider's life story, but this is cold. You startin'na believe yuh own fantasies, bro'." Firebug fell back in his seat, grabbing his head and muttering.

"Calm down, goddamn. You wanted Newmark and Lewis?"

"Nah man. Fucken Save Mart."

Miguel parked the car on Alexander Avenue. They walked from there in the cold drizzle to Third Avenue.

"So you heard this shit from Amelia? She the one tol'ju tha' shit? Because you know, if she did, like, she's jus' tryin'na use you, bro', tryin'na make huhself some kinda victim. She always do that. You can't trust huh."

"It wasn't huh," Miguel said, enjoying the disappointment on Firebug's face. They walked up 149th Street, Firebug putting up his hood.

"I was wrong when I said you an' Spider ain't tight no more," Miguel went on. "I meant to say that I know this much: that Amelia hurt'chu at first with what she did, that it surprised you and hurt you even more that Spider had done it, but'chu got over it. You know the kinda girl Amelia is. You treat huh accordingly. An' Spider, he's been makin' it up. You guys are more in touch now than before. Ain't that right? Because Amelia corrupted huhself."

"Thass a real purty story," Firebug muttered, shuffling along with hollow clumps.

"Spider an' Amelia dicked'ju. Spider felt bad an' tried t' make it up. Amelia din't. She din't care one way o' the other, she was only gettin' back at'chu anyway 'cause you were always fucken other bitches. So you still fuck each other but it don't mean nothin'." Miguel jangled the keys in his pocket. "What a waste a' good human sweat."

"You think you know everythin'?" Firebug suddenly yelled.

"Nah. Nah, not even close. But I got this story pretty good, I think. Too bad we ain't the kinda friends we could talk about it."

"I'll tell you the kinda friend I am," Firebug said as they approached the store through the thick crowds. "I'm enough of a friend t' tell you tha'chu fucken up royal if you get jaíton with Spider, man. Spider is the bes' fucken guy t' work for in the whole city, man. You ain't gonna find nobody like him. Other dealers used t' laugh at him, man, they said he could never pull it all together his way. But'chu know what? He's done it, man, he proved it. I can't see you workin' f' nobody else if you drop Spider. You drop Spider, wha'chu gonna do? Work f' tha' crazy fucka, Ace? Tha' guy terrorizes his young. You don't know what dealin' is, you jus' got no idea, bro'. You cun't say even half the things you've said t' Spider an' still be breathin'. You complain about a little beatin'? Man, I know a guy, they chopped his pinky off. An' tha' was jus' 'cause he was late once. I'm tellin' you bro', you don't even know.

"Spider is the best, man. You can't go anywhere on the streets an' find somebody like him. Thass why I still stick by him. I know enough t' appreciate it."

Miguel didn't say anything. He knew if he got on this topic, maybe things would come out that he didn't want Firebug to know. He knew Firebug would tell Spider.

They walked past stores with piles of sneakers, bag of tube socks, soldiers that crawled along the sidewalk and fired their M-16s. People bustled by, mouths trailing vapor, faces flushed and bitten by cold. A black guy in a red jacket bobbed from foot to foot holding out subway tokens in his thickly gloved hands.

The store was warm and not too crowded. The television sets were lined up along the walls, screens bursting with colors. Firebug was looking at a big 27-inch with remote, but Miguel talked him out of it. "After all," he said, "what if we gotta make a sudden move?"

"Mothafucka." They both laughed, spending time weaving back and forth between sets, irritating the fat Boricua in the suit and tie who was trying to figure out if they were serious about buying something or if they were just two junkies wasting his time. Finally Firebug settled on a small 13-inch with a sharp picture. They walked it back to the car while Firebug harangued Miguel on the importance of paying with cash. "By the way," he said as they approached the car, "what did'ju do wif' yuh money?"

Miguel looked at him and laughed, almost falling with the TV on the wet icy street.

"Nah man, it ain't like that. I jus' wanna make sure you take good care a' yuh investments an' shit."

Miguel kept laughing. He opened the trunk but Firebug didn't want the TV in there, so Miguel shut it and put the TV in the back seat. In the car, Firebug took out his spliff and relit it.

"I put it in the bank," Miguel said, recovering from the laughter. "My money's in the bank."

"Wha'chu got? Passbook savings?"

"Yeah."

"Too bad. Can't get a fucken bank card. Gotta wait 'til yuh eighteen."

"It's okay."

Firebug passed him the spliff. "Why din'chu get Spider t' open an account f' you? He did it f' me. I got a fucken bank card an' everythin'. Fucken bank even offered me a credit card! I cun't believe tha' shit. But credit cards are poison, man. Highway robbery. Make a poor man think he got more than he got. Ends up payin' for it the rest a' his life."

Miguel sucked in some smoke with little sips of air in between.

"So what bank?" Firebug asked.

Miguel looked at him. "Mine'ja fucken bees wax. Pana."

Firebug laughed. "Okay. Be like that."

"If Spider opened yuh account, that means he has access to it, 'cause it's really his account. He could make withdrawals. He could close it if he wanted to."

"Yeah sure, but why would he do that?" Firebug struggled with the teeny roach, trying not to burn his fingers. Miguel had a clamp in the glove compartment. He took it out and handed it to him.

"Well, suppose you fucked up. He could take all yuh money."

"I'm not gonna fuck up."

"Shit," Miguel said as it hit him. "You tellin' me you ain't close with the guy an' he still controls yuh bank account? How can you not be tight?"

Firebug took out another spliff and lit it with a motion.

"You know everythin', right? But check it out. He has access to my account, like you say. But the same week it went down with him an' me an' Amelia, he put eight grand in my account."

Miguel sucked on the new joint. "Damn."

"You see what he's like. He got feelings, bro'. You should be straight wif' 'im."

"I ain't the one not bein' straight."

Firebug shrugged it off. Miguel started to drive, but slowly because he was starting to feel real fucked up. To make matters worse, Firebug turned on the radio full blast and was playing drums on the dash.

"Cut tha' shit out!" Miguel screamed. "I can't drive!"

"So pull over, like they say on TV. How about into that lot?"

They were one block short of St. Anne's Avenue. There was an empty lot there full of overgrown weeds and crunchy brown grass and the shattered remnants of a shack. Miguel turned sharply and jumped up the sidewalk with a violent bump that sent Firebug bouncing against the top, the door, the dash. Miguel drove into the tall grass with a loud crunch. They lay there laughing and looking at each other. Miguel couldn't explain it; it was as if he hadn't seen Firebug for a long time and wanted to welcome him back. As the laughs died down, he said, "Damn man. When was the last time we really hung out?"

Firebug played with the cord on his parka. "Fuck. A while, bro'." He gave Miguel a funny look. "But'chu been actin' so strange. Maybe it's tha' girl. Takes a girl t' take it outta yuh."

"Whass tha' mean?"

"It jus' means that everybody looks f' stuff, like dreams an' shit. Me, I already know where I'm goin'. I know this is my life an' my wurl'. This is all I'm gonna be. What, you think I'll be able t' torch some buildings, make some money, then go work f' Merrill Lynch? I mean, I got dreams, but I ain't crazy."

"This ain't gonna be goin' on f'ever," Miguel said.

"So what? The animal adapts, bro', the animal adapts. Don'chu ever see no Wild Kingdom? The weak ones die, bro'. If you can't roll wif' the new thing, you out, you get snuffed, you don't make money. Take me: sometimes I have this nightmare where all the buildings in the world, they been burned down, an' there ain't no longa this need f' my services. What am I gonna do? Well, maybe then there'll be a market f' people who wanna blow up subway trains. All I gotta do is get hip t' it, learn the craft. But thass jus' a nightmare I have like when I have too much chili an' shit. I'm pretty adult. I know people gonna be burnin' buildings f' a long time. You should see these people I meet, man. Professionals. They wear suits, they drive big cars. They use special powders an' jellies an' they make a real livin'. So you see, my life, bro', it's jus' beginnin'."

"Great. I'm happy f' you," Miguel said bitterly. "But what about when yuh twenty-one? Ah? Or maybe thirty? How about when yuh older an' maybe got a wife o' some kids? You see yuhself livin' like this?"

"Naah man, I see myself livin' like these pros in they suits, rentin' suites at the Waldorf, drivin' Jaguars an' doin' coke an' fucken blond ladies."

Miguel laughed. "But'chu ain't white! You think you gonna have everything these white guys have? They gonna use you, bro'. You only gonna go so high before they go snip-snip."

"Man, you missin' the point! You tell me one sixteen-and-a-half-year-old kid you know who's livin' better than me right now! I mean like a normal straight kid. No way, right? How about'chu, don'chu got it made, wif' yuh own money an' yuh own li'l love buggy?" He pulled on Miguel's coat sleeve. "You don't think you got it made, mister six thousand dollars in my drawstring bag?"

"You asshole!"

"Well? How can you want anythin' better than this? Maan, think, bro'! Use yuh head, yuh supposed t' have a good one! Spider was always sayin' about how you got all these brains. Where are they? 'Cause you can't even see it when it's right under yuh nose. Wha'chu want, t' be back wif' yuh folks?"

"No. I don't want that. I just can't trust anybody. Why should I tell you anything?"

"Well, welcome t' the wurl', putz. You ain't supposed t' trust anybody. In a' wurl' of business, you never trust anybody. How you gonna live better than this? Huh? Don't be scowlin'!! Tell me." Firebug grabbed Miguel by the coat and shook him. "How you gonna live better than this? Lookit this car. Lookit yuh threads! Lookit this roach! Don'chu see this is the sweetest fucken thing t' ever happen to teenagers since fucken masturbation?"

Firebug went back to his corner, exhaling with disgust and looking out his window. Miguel clutched the wheel and stared into the tall grass and the chain-link fence and the dimly lit windows with their crisscross gates.

"Why are you doin' this?" Miguel passed a hand through his hair, snarling as dozens of white dandruff flakes fluttered down.

"I'm yuh friend, right?"

Miguel stared at him.

"I'm tryin'na make yuh see some things. You got beat up. It happens. I been beat up too. But don't go all apeshit. Thinka wha'chu got t' lose."

"Is this Spider talkin'?"

There was a pause. They weren't looking at each other.

"It's jus' yuh friend, man," Firebug said in a low voice.

Miguel lit a cigarette. By now the buzz had floated down out of him and off into nowhere, and he felt disenchanted and vacant. Outside it slowly got darker, a gloomy purple descending on the car as it stood in the empty lot. There were traffic sounds and jittery kid laughter and the scraping of pots, pans, and dish rattles from one of the windows.

"Spider's a real vindictive bastid," Firebug said in that same low voice.

"Did'ju talk t' him? I mean recently?"

"Nah bro'. Chill."

Miguel was clutching the steering wheel like he was going to rip it right off the dash.

"What did he tell you? Did he put'chu up t' this?"

"No man. I tol'ju, I'm strictly free-lance. I don't work f' him. Now you gotta cut this shit out 'cause I'm startin' t' get insulted an' shit."

"I don't butter yuh bread," Miguel said in a low rumble. "I don't have yuh account in my hands like he does."

"Well, maybe I do favors f' him, but I don't really know, man, I'm not into whassup between you an' him."

"You talk pretty funny f' a guy who don't know whassup."

"It don't take much t' see whass happenin'. You been through the shit, right? So maybe I feel a little guilty about it. After all, I was the one hooked'ju up with Spider. I don't know shit about all of it, I jus' know once we used t' have laughs! We used t' tear up the fucken city, bro'! Quemando tela, brodel! We spent weeks drunk stoned womped an' tryin'na crawl up the fucken stairs. If we had branded all thum bitches we fucked we'd have a bigger herd than the Cartwrights an' shit! Yo, we used t' party up."

Miguel tried to suppress his smile.

"You act like people can't see this shit on you, the way you changed. Now you all glum an' shit. An' you don't hang much, none a' yuh boys see you. All thum guys, Sammy an' Jimmy an' Careta be axin' me whassup wif' you, how come you been dissin' everybody, like lookit'cha threads, like you better than thum now. I told 'um nah, it wasn't like that. But'chu know, people been noticin'. It don't got nothin' t' do wif' how much I got from Spider."

Miguel wanted to trust Firebug; he came close to letting everything spill out. But something held him back. "Then why you gotta talk about Spider bein' vindictive?"

" 'Cause you actin' funny. Like maybe you wanna quit."

Miguel leaned back in his chair, feeling like he had been set up again. "Ahhh shit."

"Do you?"

"Nah man. What make you say a stupid fucken thing like that?"

"I jus' tol'ju what made me say a stupid fucken thing like that."

"When was the last time you saw Spider?"

The question caught Firebug off guard. He stammered, then he punched the dashboard.

"Coño meng! Wha'chu gotta ax me tha' for! I already tol'ju I ain't got nothin' t' do wif' him!"

"Then tell me the last time you saw him!"

"I ain't gonna fight wif' you, bro'. If you can't see I'm tryin'na help you, like a friend"—here he fractured his voice a little—"then fine, man, be like that." The effect was almost comical. Miguel got real pissed off now. Firebug was trying to snow him. He pressed his head with his hands. He had to get out of this shit. But was he going from the frying pan into the fire? He could see himself deserting his gangster life, throwing himself at Cristalena's feet, and having the uppity bitch reject him. "No," she said in the film clip. "No way I'm gonna throw in with a lying drug-dealing motherfucka."

He stared at Firebug, feeling fatalistic. "I ain't leavin'," he said calmly. "I jus' don't like gettin' my ass kicked an' I don't like gettin' set up. Maybe the business was one way back when you worked with Spider. It's a new way now." He quickly told Firebug about how Spider set him up without even a hint of what was waiting for him. Then he scooped the two empty packages out from under his seat and tossed them in Firebug's lap.

"No shit!" Firebug seemed impressed, turning the packages over and over, a couple of fingers in his mouth. He seemed speechless. Miguel was forced to goad him. "Well? Wha'chu thinka that?"

"Purty open-an'-shut," Firebug said, handing the packages back. His face showed his reluctance to commit himself.

"I knew I could count on you," Miguel muttered with contempt. He turned the key. He stepped on the gas again and again, making the car exhale angrily.

"Business is business," Firebug said with a shrug, his voice obscured by the car's pulsing drone.

"What about friendship?" Miguel felt like some wimp.

"Spider's still yuh friend, bro'. You got the wrong attitude. Talk t' him about it, man. Jus' tell 'im how you feel. You can't go out an' fight 'im, you gotta talk t' him. Just think about it some. I'm sure he's givin' you some time off, right? Take a few days, bro'. Relax. Fuck some girls. Smoke some ses. I'm sure in a couple a' days you'll see that maybe you acted fucked up, an' tha' maybe you deserved a beatin'."

Miguel's eyes narrowed. He suddenly shifted the car and reversed out of the lot with a lunge and a bump against the sidewalk as he pivoted. He checked the traffic flow, watching the lemon-drop headlights approach in pairs. He gunned the engine and swerved into traffic, tires squealing. With a heave the car surged forward, Firebug rolling back into the seat. The car was like an extension of Miguel's arms legs fingers, smooth yet with a resistant torque that made him want to speed up. He pressed down on the pedal. Streetlamps sped by, flashing. The tenements on both sides were hazy blurs. A swerve and squeal and he had passed another car, another bus with crazed brake-light flashes like splotchy bloodstains.

"Damn man, slow down," Firebug said.

Miguel couldn't believe the guy. His loyalty to Spider irritated him. In a mad fit, his voice spiraling upward, he blathered out the story of his adventure with the cops. The rubbery faces, the gleaming muzzle so cold against his cheek, and then his cams getting slashed.

"Now you gonna tell me that guy trusts me," he screamed, "when he goes an' slashes my fucken tires??"

Firebug looked worried. He nibbled on a thumb, popped a gumball, offered Miguel one. Miguel tossed it into his mouth. It was a mistake. The minute the sour flavor exploded in his mouth, slivers of intense pain filled his head. He rolled down his window and frantically spit it out while Firebug watched him in amazement.

"Maybe cherry ain'cha flavor? I got apple if you . . ."

"Nah man, it hurts." Amelia was right about Firebug, sitting there looking out the window all vacant-faced and glassy-eyed. Fucken guy was hollow.

"He slashed my fucken tires," Miguel said, still pushing for a response.

"Maybe it wasn't him who ordered it. Coulda jus' been one a' the guys on the street was supposed t' watch you, an' he figured that was a short-cut."

"Ahh come on, man." Miguel scowled and the pain this caused made him wince. He was giving up. He slowed down the car as they hit Prospect Avenue, looking for a good space.

"Look," Firebug said in a sudden burst, "you jus' puttin' yuhself through the shit f' nothin'. I say you should f'get it. Thinka all the money you got. Thinka the doors gonna open for ya. Jus' think about that."

"What doors?" Miguel couldn't disguise the scorn. It stunned Firebug, who gave him a serious look. It was like the face on an officer about to scold a private for leaving his shirt unbuttoned.

"Yuh talkin' like a real idiot, man. You should appreciate shit a little more. In business there are good days an' bad. Look, le' me invite'chu to a wienie roast. Tomorrow. During the day, not a night one. Ain't that keen? I don't know if Amelia can get off, but if she can, you mind bringin' huh?"

Miguel was parking the car—backing up, crawling forward, until the trunk of the Ford Escort ahead gleamed with his headlights. He turned the key and the churning stopped.

"414 Leggett," Firebug said, opening his door. "It's nah too big a joint, but it'll make some nice flames. I'm nah supposed t' torch the whole shit, jus' one side of it." He was outside now, stretching. "It should be a good way t' show off my new skills, my control."

Miguel's head was a mess of tangled thoughts. He got out of the car. Firebug had the TV.

"So, you gonna be there, o' what?" He stared at Miguel across the car top, which glistened with drizzle.

"Yeah," Miguel said, even though he had no intention of going. To him it was over. At least he'd be able to talk to Amelia about it. What was it she told Firebug? That she was in love? Miguel couldn't bring it up with Firebug, he might think something was up. Why did Firebug tell him? It still bugged him. That shit about being concerned just didn't wash.

He came around the car. Firebug was waiting to cross the street with him, but as a bus droned by with a swish, Miguel leaned back against his car.

"You go up," he said. "I gotta do some shit."

"But don'chu wanna check out the new tube, bro'?" He shook the TV box.

"Later."

Firebug shrugged. He didn't say another word as he hobbled off across the street with his package, his new toy. Miguel felt sad as Firebug disappeared into the vestibule, the ugly steel door closing behind him with a clank. It was a pretty final sound. Things just couldn't ever be the same again, no matter what he did. He was stuck. He couldn't go back even if he wanted to.

He walked to the corner, gathering up his long Marine coat, doing up the buttons and neck flap. He walked over to the phone and shoved in a coin with cold fingers. His heavy sigh steamed up the phone's silver tummy, reflecting part of his brooding bruised face. He looked away.

"Hello?" Crisp clear female voice. Music in the background. Milli Vanilli? Ahh shit.

"Can I speak to Cristalena?"

"Oh hi Miguel. Yeah, hold on." Rosa's voice was smiling to him now, he could hear the lips crackling wetly, the familiarity warmed him.

The phone carried vibrations from the stereo, pulsating rhythms and those fake Milli Vanilli voices. Sounds of girl talk, girl laughs, words skittering out quickly. There was something about the way some Latin girls say s: Not a whistle, more like a kazoo sound. The rhythmic clapping convinced him they were dancing, probably teaching each other routines. A kind of girl clinic. Basic training. Later, a symposium on lipstick shades. Pantyhose: to gleam or not to gleam? How to run in high heels and not look stupid.

"Hello?"

It was Cristalena, sounding breathless. It made his heart twitch. A crazy nervousness took over.

"It's me, Miguel." He sounded sadder than he had wanted to.

"Baby baby baby," she whispered, "how are you feeling? Damn, I wanted to call you but you said . . . I mean, I din't wan'chu to think I was . . ."

"Thass okay. I miss you."

"Me too. You know, I was gonna bug you about maybe seein' you tonight. It's not like I'm tryin'na push anything, you know. But I got a lotta love backed up. I should leave it t' you, right?" There was a hungry earnestness in her voice, like she was already snuggled up beside him and talking into his ear. "Listen, hold on, I wanna change phones."

There was music and yelling and then her yell OKAY I GOT IT! Then Cristalena's soft breathing.

"Wow. Now we sound alone," he said.

"Yeah. Just how I want it. So how are you feeling?"

"Okay. I was wonderin' if maybe I could see you tonight."

Cristalena screamed with delight. She must've jumped; the phone was rattling and banging. "Damn, you mean it? This is dope!"

" 'Dope'?" He had never heard her talk like that.

"Yo bro'," she snapped in a nasal voice, "long time I don't flesh it up with my piece, know wham sayin'?"

He laughed. "Oh shit. Please no. I hear tha' shit all day."

"Miguel! We got a lotta catchin' up to do."

"I thought maybe we could go do some Italian food. I can pick you up." His voice was filled with dread and fear and heavy weights. She sensed it.

"Miguel, you don't sound so good. Whass wrong?"

"Nothing. Just got a lotta shit on my mind." He sighed. There was no way out. "But I still wanna see you."

"You over your cold?"

"Yeah." He sighed with disgust.

"Man, I don't know, honey. You sound real funny."

"Well, I missed'ju. Wha'chu expect? I'm supposed to be happy when you ain't around? Man, I just feel like . . . like I wish I had told . . ." His fingers accidentally hit the keypad and a clump of beeps sounded. "Sorry . . . I just know if I had handled things different maybe all a' this might notta been necessary."

"Mmmm. You say the sweetest fucken things. Makes me wanna mmmmmm all over you."

"Well why don'chu?"

"I gotta warn you though. We girls been dancin' over here. Doing these deep pelvic gyrations an' shit? I'm horny as they come right now. You know what I kept thinking of while I was doing it?" Her voice was a breathless whisper that excited him. "Tha'chu an' me, we were fucken."

She laughed, and then he laughed, tension melting away from him. He felt grateful, even though he was still weighed down by what he had to do. "Ahh damn, I miss you. I hope you still wanna be with me."

"I do," she said, as if making a vow.

"From here t' eternity."

"An' thass jus' for starters," she said. "Thum flowers you gave me are still lookin' dope. My aunt put 'um inna vase an' they still there in the livin' room. Hey! You'll see them when you come to my party, right?"

"Sure."

"You comin', right?"

"Yup."

"Ohh Miguel, fucken guy make me so anxious like I'm pressed up against the bureau, like I'm gonna hump it."

Miguel burst into laughter and then he couldn't stop. Cristalena pretended she couldn't figure out why he was laughing so hard.

"But I jus' thinka you," she added in a throaty whisper, "an' it's like the river starts runnin'!!"

"Ohhh shit!" Miguel couldn't stop laughing.

"You think I'm nasty, right?"

"Yeah," he said, trying to calm down. "An' I hope you always stay that way."

"So when can you be here?"

"How about ten minutes? I'll meet'chu downstairs."

She pouted and whined about him not wanting to come up to meet her friends and how she was going to either drag him up or else drag her friends down to the stoop, they'd all be lined up waiting to spy him but he told her please no so seriously that she gave it up. "I guess they'll see you at the party," she said, but he made her swear three times because Cristalena was probably not above bending the rules and then these girls would be hanging from windows or across the street or some shit like that. He sent her a string of kisses to make her feel better, and then he walked toward his car, slowly, as if heading for his execution, like Robert Vaughn in *The Bridge at Remagen*, where he plays this German major who's supposed to blow this bridge up. He tries to hold it and the Yankees take it, so the Germans arrest him and line him up against a post. Miguel saw himself against that post now in his stained, tattered, torn uniform, an SS officer in his crisp black uniform offering him a cigarette. He accepted, remembering how much she always hated cigarettes. He looked up at the sky and heard the rumble of planes flying above the cottony blanket of sky. The SS guy was looking up with him. He looked something like Firebug, didn't he?

"Those planes," Miguel said. "Theirs or ours?"

The SS guy looked grave. "Those are enemy planes, sir."

Miguel stared blankly ahead. "But who is the enemy?"

Then they shot him.

. . .

He was fighting the urge to smoke as he waited for her to come down, suspicious of every glance every girl shot him on the street, as if maybe it was one of her friends sneaking a peek. Every time the vestibule door opened, he tensed up.

It shouldn't be a problem. He was going to look right at her and tell her. "I got beat up." That's easy, right? And from there on it should be a piece of cake, coasting downhill all the way, into tales of mayhem, mad sex, drug money, and the fast life. He was going to wait for that part, wait until they were in the restaurant.

Movement on the stoop? Some fat woman with two tiny kids bundled up in puffy coats: tiny bouncing barrels. He was exhaling with relief when he spotted Cristalena and then his breath reversed and he felt like he was underwater. She looked pretty in that short leather jacket she wore with the long colorful silk scarf. Her hair was tied back from her face in a long ponytail. She looked like a little ballerina. She spotted his car and raced down the steps in her knee-high suede boots; his heart was pounding. Wasn't she dressed up real dope? She rapped on the window, pulled on the door handle, rapped louder, stamped the glass with her palm, making desperate noises like she was freezing to death. He flipped open the lock. A burst of cold air swept her into his arms. She hugged him hard and pulled back to look at him. Her face changed in a flash.

"What happened?" Her hands swept over his bruised face slowly, her fingers lightly touching his lips.

"I din't tell you," he said, sheepishly grinning. "I got beat up."

"You got beat up?" Her eyes narrowed. "When? How?"

Ah shit.

She leaned closer, sweeping away the hair that covered the scab on his forehead. "Shit. Lookit that. Are you okay? Who did this? Did'ju go see a doctor?"

"Yeah yeah, don't worry. Nothing's broken. I just got into this fight. Some people I know. I guess I wun't call thum friends, right?"

"But why'd you get beat up?"

"It was like an argument. Kinda long story."

She looked at him a moment with dark eyes. Was there an argument going on inside of her? Miguel could almost hear the voices. She slumped a little, her hands caressing his hair. "Why din'chu tell me?"

"I din't wanna worry you."

"Is this why you wun't see me?"

"Yes."

"You lied to me about havin' a cold." Her eyes grew bitter, wrathful, resentful. Miguel could see it. He didn't care; he was on the verge of telling her everything, once and for all. If she couldn't accept it, to hell with it.

"There's a lotta shit I gotta tell you," he said, rubbing the steering wheel, not looking at her. She had her hands in her lap. "I knew something was up," she said, almost to herself.

There was a sudden pounding on Miguel's window that made them both jump. Miguel knew who it was the minute he caught a glimpse of that ugly, dirty brown coat.

"Spider!" He said it like it was some kind of curse.

"Miguel, yo, open up, we gotta talk!" Spider's voice came through the shut window. "Yo! Open up!"

"Spider, I can't talk now!" Miguel yelled, pounding the wheel. "This just ain't the time!"

Spider peered into the car, cupping his hands around his eyes.

"The woman can wait," he suddenly snarled in a voice Miguel had never heard him use. "We gotta talk business, an' I mean now, pana, right this second. I got Victor waitin' in the car, so hustle."

Miguel didn't look at Cristalena. He stared through the windshield at Spider as he leaned against the hood and lit a cigarette. Spider motioned impatiently.

"I'll be back," he said, but Cristalena wasn't looking at him. It was all going to happen, now. What was it that Amelia had said about timing?

Miguel stepped out and slammed the door, leaving Cristalena sitting inside like a porcelain doll. Spider was smoking his cigarette, his eyes scanning the streets, the sky, the streetlamp directly above.

"You been worryin' me, pana," Spider said.

"Worryin' YOU?" Miguel was already yelling, and trying to stop his arms from twitching. "Why should I be worryin' you? Was I worryin' you very much when you threw me in a car fulla psycho cops? Was I worryin' you when you sent me over t' Richie so he could beat the fuck outta me?"

"Yo, chill."

"Nah. I'll tell you when I had'ju worried. When I had'ja cop money, thass when you were worried. So worried tha'chu slashed my fucken cams!!"

"I said chill."

"CHILL? HOW THE FUCK I'M GONNA CHILL?? I TOL'JU I DIN'T WANNA TALK NOW, BUT NAH, IT DON'T MATTER WHAT I WANT O' THINK O' FEEL, ONLY WHA'CHU WANT! HOW THE FUCK DID'JU KNOW I WAS HERE, YOU GOT'CHA OWN CIA O' SOME SHIT?"

"I tol'ju I was comin' over," Spider said forcefully, glaring at him. "I din't tell you t' go runnin' off wid' nobody. Victor an' I happened t' spot you makin' yuh move. So here I am. Come to visit my sick friend, an' what do I get? I tol'ju we was gonna talk. So now we gonna talk."

"Like you gotta have everything yuh way, right? Like yuh big shot mothafucken ass gotta come in here an' get in my way, right? Yuh a real fucken creep, man. You set me up twice. Twice! An' you call me a friend. You gotta be crazy." Miguel came closer to him, still yelling. "You wanna talk about that?"

"You stop yellin' an' try an' listen."

"Listen'na what? More bullshit? Yeah, I trust'ju, I trust'ju, don't worry, an' lookit wha'chu do. Mothafucka. You the one got me beat up! Ain'chu even gonna try t' deny it?"

"No, I ain't gonna deny it! I'm gonna tell you t' stop bein' such a fucken pussy an' face certain facts! You had this beatin' comin', man. You just gotta realize that. There was no way out. You screwed up. I tol'ju there were gonna be times when I cun't save you from shit. Thass why you gotta keep yuh nose clean. There are rules, you fuck. The world is fulla thum an' you can't escape 'um, they down here too. You think you gonna live yuh life without 'um? You guys with brains are all alike, man. People told me I'd be crazy t' trust'ju!"

"BUT YOU DIN'T, YOU ASSHOLE!"

"You shut up!" Spider poked him in the chest, his eyes burning. "All this week you been givin' me the attitude, blowin' me off, actin' like you was yuh own man! Well I got news. You work f' me!"

"Not no more."

"Bullshit, pana."

"Nah, no bullshit bro'. I quit."

"Pana, thass bullshit . . ."

"I QUIT!!"

"You fucken SHUT UP WITH THAT SHIT!" Spider screamed, wagging his finger in Miguel's face. "YOU AIN'T GONNA TALK T' ME THAT WAY!"

"Fuck you!"

"Fuck me? A thousand bucks bonus I gave you this week, mothafucka! Fuck me? You gotta lotta nerve bitin' my hand like that! You fucken piece a' shit! Standin' there in those threads I bought'chu, ridin' inna car I got'chu, with the FUCKEN GODDAMN LICENSE I FUCKEN GOT'CHUUUUU!"

Miguel pushed him back because Spider charged him, wanted to walk right through him, eyes large and rabid. He lunged, screaming into Miguel's face. "YUH A PIECE A' SHIT, A NOTHIN' T' BE TALKIN'NA ME LIKE THAT! MAAAN, YOU AIN'T EVEN BOOGIES OUTTA MY NOSE!!" He spun and walked away from Miguel, turning to pound on the car hood with resounding thumps. "Maan, you got me maaad now." He paced, then stopped, glaring. "You think you made now, you gonna run out on Spider?"

"I ain't runnin' out on you. I trusted'ju," Miguel said calmly, already feeling spent. A light drizzle was falling on them, a ticklish mist. He looked into the car and there was Cristalena's dark, troubled silhouette. "I jus' feel like it ain't worth it anymore. I don't trust'ju." The regret was genuine. It softened Spider's face a little. "I thought'chu was really my pana. But'chu jus' lookin' out f' yuhself, Spider. Everything you do is to save yuh ass, an' you'll give anybody up f' that. I can't work f' you, f' anybody like that. I'm sicka bein' surrounded by people I gotta be watchin' alla time. There's more to it all than jus' this shit."

Spider tossed his cigarette away, orange sparks flaring for an instant as it skidded across the street. "But I been offerin' you my number two, bro'. Can'chu see that? So maybe I fucked up, but—"

"Nah, you din't fuck up, thass just it. You did wha'chu had t' do t' save yuh ass. Where does that stop? Maybe next week I get another gun shoved up my nose or maybe another beatin'. Where am I gonna end up so you can stay on top? You think all that money's worth it? Maan, I'll give you the damn bonus back, fuck it."

There was such a defeated resignation in Miguel's voice that Spider didn't say anything. He sagged against the car.

"Yuh pissin' on me," he said. "After all I done, yuh pissin' on me."

"I'm not pissin' on you. I'm jus' savin' myself. Before I get eaten up."

Spider scowled but Miguel was already heading for the car door. He had had enough talk. It had probably done more damage than good. He looked at Spider and thought of Cristalena sitting in the car hearing all of this. "You fucked me," he said wearily. He was opening the door when he felt Spider's hand on his arm.

"We gotta talk more about this shit," he said.

"Not now."

"I'm gonna be in touch. Whassup wit'cha beeper?"

"I trashed it."

"Fuck."

"I'll talk later." He was opening the door again when Spider suddenly grabbed him by his coat lapels and pressed him close, eyes seething, breath sour and hot.

"I'm the one in charge, you got that?" It was a hoarse whisper. Miguel sagged, his eyes indifferent. It was the same kind of feeling he used to get when Mr. Fisher used to interrogate him and Firebug in the detention room, the same tired indifference as Mr. Fisher slapped them around a bit to teach them "respect."

"You gonna beat me up now?"

"I'm sayin' have some fucken respect."

Miguel exhaled impatiently, rolling his eyes. Spider stood holding him like that for a moment, just staring. Then he loosened his grip. Miguel was straightening his coat when the window rolled down and Cristalena's worried face appeared.

"Miguel," she said, looking at him, and then at Spider. "You okay?"

Spider suddenly laughed, pointing at her and laughing, tiny cackling ripples. "You sure got'cha hands full there, pana," he said derisively. He patted Miguel on the back and walked off. "We'll talk later," he said, as if they had just had a friendly chat about sports.

"Check." Miguel stared at the slick street as Spider slinked off with that streetwise limp. Victor's car was double-parked down the block. Miguel waited for his car to pass by them before he got back into the car, his hands cold and trembling. Cristalena had slid back to her spot and was sitting there with her hands in her jacket pockets, staring straight through the windshield.

"Who is he?" she asked, not moving.

Miguel rubbed his forehead and started fumbling for a cigarette.

"He's a guy I work for," Miguel finally said, breaking the silence.

"Doing what."

Miguel traced the speedometer with a finger. He felt like he was back in the detention room in junior high, a guidance counselor grilling him while he poked holes in the gym mats lining the walls. "Why did you do it?" The voice was ingrained in his memory. His answer was a shrug, the same shrug he gave Cristalena now. The cigarette dangled from his lips, unlit.

Her voice sounded like it was coming from the bottom of a well. "Miguel, what are you into?"

"I was gonna tell you."

"Really? I wanna fucken believe that." Her voice shook with anger. "So you been lyin'na me. Like all this time." She looked away, her arms crossed. She shut her eyes tight.

"It wasn't lying. I jus' cun't tell you right away. I was ashamed. I been up an' down with this shit, tryin'na think what to do. I decided to get out of it. Din'chu see me arguin' with the guy?"

"I just thought all this time you were being straight with me. I really thought'chu was so straight! An' you turn out to be like all these people, all these . , ."

"I'm not like these people, Cristalena."

"No?" Her face was contorted. "Jus' wha'chu been doin'? Hustling crack? Is that it? Are you some crack dealer? I don't care about it, I just gotta know. If you don't wanna be with me, fine, but'chu tell me whassup."

"But I do wanna be with you. Thass why it was so hard."

"But how could'ju just lie to me? All this time?"

"What, you thought I would tell you right off? Like you would've understood, would've kept seeing me?" The anguish crept into his voice. He ripped the unlit cigarette from his lips.

"You could've tried! You could've trusted me!"

"Oh yeah? An' if I had tol'ju about it right from the beginning, would'ju have kept seein' me?"

She paused for a moment, clutching her head like it would explode. "I don't know, thass an unfair question, you should've trusted me!"

"Well, I'm trustin' you now."

"You should've trusted me then, now's too late. You lied, you led me along. It's not like you told me at all." She was gasping as if the air was running out. "I don't understand this. Things are supposed to be simple. My God, you're seventeen!" She covered her face.

"I was gonna tell you. I was jus' startin' to!" He smacked the steering wheel. His voice was cracking, everything in him brittle, flaking, crumbling. "Man, I was gonna tell you!" He had waited too long. Amelia's words about timing haunted him. He felt the heavy burning in his eyes.

Miguel opened his door and lunged as though his head were on fire. He grabbed hold of the chain-link fence that surrounded the empty schoolyard. He walked right into it and gripped the cold yielding links, pulling and pulling until the rattling chiming links bit into his fingers. Why couldn't he scream? He pressed his face against the cold metal as the rain started to come down. At first the large drops tapped him gently; then they beat against him as if trying to drive him off the street. Through the misty downpour that shrouded the street, he saw her run, away from him, her arms swinging desperately as if she were fighting restraints. She didn't even look at him until she had crossed the street and was on her stoop. She stared at him a moment, shaking her head as he took three steps toward her; then she disappeared into the building.

13

He had to be a man about it. He wasn't going to run after her like one of those HONKY putzes on TV, violins building to a passionate crescendo as he screamed out her name. He could've run into the vestibule and rung all the bells until somebody came down or buzzed him in, but he didn't. After she ran off, SHE ran off. That was that. Not the kind of loving support he had expected or needed. It made him think she really didn't love him after all. Maybe he had invented her like a dream, an excuse to get out of the business that was starting to make him sick already. Sure, there had been tears in her eyes, but maybe she was just crying for herself. He had come up short of being her dream date.

"When you love, you suffer," his mother told him one night after his father had decked her because the beans were runny. She used to come into his room and sit there by his bed and cry. Maybe that was why his father was always storming in there and ripping things off his shelves. "But I'll get back at him," she would always mutter, wiping the tears. Miguel didn't want to get drafted into their war. He hated both sides. He would lock himself in his room and stare down at the pretty church yard across the street. He thought he could escape with books but his father kept busting his door open and throwing them out. Miguel would have to sneak out and rescue them from the garbage. Dickens. Tolstoy. Twain. The more his father hated them, the more he read them. If he ever saved up three dollars, he would blow it on a book. He had a box of them under his bed. It was too much to be around all the tension in the house. He started hanging out on the street. By the time he got to junior high, he was a bopping street punk with enough attitude to pull fly chavas and survive the necessary street brawls.

He was falling away from school. He had girls and friends and Firebug and plenty of kicks, but school didn't interest him. He was halfway through seventh grade when his English teacher gave the class the assignment that at first excited him and later disgusted him: write about your father. What does he do? What kind of person? Why do you admire him? At least one page, front and back. Miguel had locked his door and sat on the floor in his room for hours. He could hear his father and mother yelling at each other, the points snapping on his pencils as he pressed the words harder and harder into the paper.

> My father was a Marine. He was very tough and is always showing pictures of himself in his uniform. He used to box. He was muscular. Now he looks like a sack of shit. He has a big tummy and his arms all flabby and they quiver. All he knows how to do is punch things. He was a postman. Then they fired him and he became this construction guy. But not construction like you think with yellow helmets up on girders making bricks. He broke rocks with a big hammer and tossed them into dumpsters.
>
> My father is always angry. When he gets home he sits in front of the TV and drinks a beer until Mom serves the food. If the food is okay he won't yell. If it isn't, he yells. Then they both fight. Mom screams and breaks dishes. He watches for a while, then he gets up and belts her. Then Mom comes to my room. "I'm gonna get him," she says, sitting by the window.
>
> My father is a fucking chump. He made $132 last week. A friend of mines and me got us into business selling something. We made $400. So what do I need HIM for?

Miguel filled three pages. He went to school the next day but he didn't hand in the assignment. The teacher gave him a zero. In the schoolyard with Firebug during lunch he took the papers out and scrunched them into a ball.

"Yo Firebug," he said. "Light this, man."

Firebug took his can of lighter fluid right out without a word, just a funny happy gleam in his eye. There was nothing like a small fire to take the boredom right out of things. In a second the ball of flame had fallen and rolled into the dust, quivering as the flames consumed it. Tiny wisps of ash floated up. Miguel watched, chomping on a plastic straw, not saying anything. Then he walked off the schoolyard.

"Yo Miguel, whassup?" Firebug had asked. Miguel waved him off. He was through with it. He would not return to school again. He spent a whole year bumming from friends, crashing in strange places, selling weed with pals to make his bread. Nothing was permanent. Friends came and went with the weather. Quick deals, a chump hustle, a box of stolen phones that he sold for $60. Then the weed was gone. His connection dried up; so did his money. He slept on the subway, on a bench in St. Mary's. Sometimes girls helped him but he didn't have money, so they avoided him. He walked around a lot, up and down 149th Street, looking for familiar faces and maybe a drink or a free toke or some kind of chump hustle to get into. The streets opened up to him like a whale mouth. He made friends, had adventures, found ways to fight the boredom with his cluster of rat-eyed Latin Bowery Boys. Girls liked him. Sometimes all he had to do was sit next to them. They liked him when he was disgusting and filthy and a criminal, and he acted it up. He had his look, his top sneaks, and his D.A. combed up good, a cigarette always dangling from his lips. He wasn't a fighter, but a lover. He got beaten up a few times, but that was part of being a man. It wasn't winning that made you strong, it was having the cojones to stand your ground. That was what manhood meant to him. Standing ground. Regardless of what you lost.

He never noticed when his father left because he was hardly ever home anymore. He had friends. He had places to crash: Donna's on Tinton or Mikey's on Jackson. When Miguel bothered to stop by the apartment, he found his mother looking better and better every time, with sunny smiles and youthful eyes, black and blue marks fading.

"So where is he?" Miguel asked. Four months, and no sign of the fuck.

"Gone," she said, looking grateful. "Gone gone gone. As if God has answered my prayers. Now I can have a life."

He resented that. "We should call the cops," he said.

"No, no," she said, because she didn't want to know where he was, didn't want him found. She already had Nelo.

He crashed at Mikey's, started dealing smoke. It wasn't a bad life, but he needed to make more money. Girls were more demanding and didn't waste time with chumps who didn't have cash or wheels. He had to start making bucks if he hoped to get laid. That's just the way it was.

One day he spotted Firebug, a year older and grungier. Firebug opened up a new world for Miguel—he brought Spidertown with him.

"Spider really likes you," Firebug told him one night. "I mean, he took you ridin' in his car, din't he? Showed'ju his empire? You think he did that wif' me? Fuck no. Wif' me it was, 'Here, stand onna corner an' pass these out.' I didn't get no guided tour." He started at Miguel as they sat in his room. "Maybe he wanna dick you or somethin'."

"Shut up with that shit."

Spider gave him driving lessons in a pretty Firebird. They were informal sessions, just to check on what he was picking up from Kenneth in the Buick Skylark. Spider gave him the road test, presented him with the license. The memory of that made him feel guilty now, and more guilt followed when he thought of the night Spider gave him the Impala. Hadn't been much to look at back then, but Miguel had transformed it, made it his own. That was what Spider had given him.

How could he have turned on Spider, treated him like that, after all they'd been through together? Who knows what the guy was thinking now? Miguel was getting desperate thoughts about it, convinced he had been hasty. What was it he was taking a stand against, anyway? Was he even sure? He had been so happy before. He felt angry that things had changed, angry that it could now never go back to being the way it had been. Maybe that happiness had come from ignorance. He knew too much now. He couldn't look at Spider the same way anymore, or Firebug, his two must trusted chums. Now everybody in his life was shot full of holes, even Cristalena. Nothing gleamed; everything was rusted and stained.

He wanted to be alone, but knew he couldn't survive that way. He felt as if other people had created his life, had made it all possible for him, and that maybe he still needed people to help him get the fuck out. He had thought he was independent, but that was a lie: It was all pretend freedom. A self-swindle. It looked like the high life, but it was life on borrowed time. Spider's troops didn't have to think about tomorrow; for them, now was enough, and if NOW looked good then that was life, even if later in the evening they'd get a blow job followed by a hail of bullets in a crumbling vestibule.

Miguel sat there in his Baby long after Cristalena had left, rain drumming against the car, creating glowing orange blobs on the windshield. He had been stupid to cry like that. Women hate a man who cries, who loses control. They want to ride on a boat with a strong rudder. His father had told him that. Could the bastid be right? Cristalena had darted right out of there: She didn't even think of comforting him, of trying to stick with him. The damned bitch just took off. Did she expect him to chase her down? Why do girls always expect to be chased? They like the guy to dash himself against the rocks, to climb mountains and scream for her to let down her hair so the dumb fuck can climb up her tower. Nice to know there are callers. Nothing better for the ego.

Miguel drove under the Westchester el, crossing Hunts Point, heading up toward Elder Avenue. It was a sick instinct. He hadn't even really thought about it; he was like those damned fish that swim upstream before they die. Was that what he was doing?

He had been to the apartment on Elder Avenue only once. His mother looked ten years younger in jeans and flats like a teenager, her hair piled up on her head. Driving now through the rain, he found it hard to figure out why he had showed up that time. Maybe he had been curious or a little jealous of her new life, her happy smiles and her newfound youth. It was as though she had thrown off the past completely, as if none of that had ever happened. Had Miguel also been discarded? He had thought so, had maybe gone over to check. He remembered the living room with its huge stereo system/TV combo, the elegant lamps with their carved elephant bases (Nelo had gotten them from Turkey), shiny new linoleum, everything smelling of fresh paint. She'd offered him a tall glass of beer as if he were a guest. And there was Nelo, still the squat little frog prince, one kiss and POOF, he was some fucking man of the house complete with monogrammed slippers, a satin housecoat with Oriental scribbles, and a pipe, a fucking pipe, like the guy wanted to be David Niven. The hand was still doughy when Miguel shook it, weak and spineless. Was Nelo some kind of pimp? No, an exporter of shit like those funky Turkish lamps, the shades covered with writhing pythons and dangling tassels. The apartment had a wall lined with shelves, the kind Miguel would've liked for his books; here there were porcelain mermaids with clocks in their tummies and wide-eyed saints clutching staffs, and one guy with wings who had a squirming red demon under his sandals. Was this for real? There was even a dish with Elvis Presley on it.

"Isn't this a nice place?" his mother had asked him, walking him into the bathroom so he could see the bright blue and white tiles and the pebbled glass sliding doors. Miguel drank the beer down in record time and asked for another. She dragged him into the kitchen to show off the dishwasher. "And you," she had asked, "how are you doing?"

She took his tales of self-emancipation seriously, not really probing into the realities, not asking well, what kind of work is it? Who do you live with? Is it a nice place, can I come visit? She saw the money in his wallet; he had bothered to show her a row of twenties. She didn't probe because she was grateful that he was on his own and out of her hair. This was HER time and she didn't need anything to stand in her way. Wasn't it a little late now for her to turn into his mother? She seemed relieved when he turned down her offer to come live with them. Sure she cried a little, but that was probably a tiny chunk of guilt. She was glad to be free of her past, and like it or not, Miguel was part of that. This was her second chance. Even Miguel's sister Diana knew it. She seemed to be worse off than Miguel right now, stuck with two brats and a useless husband, but she had already checked her mother's bare cupboards. "Listen," Diana told him over the phone, "in this family there's one thing I learned a long time ago, an' thass that the kids are on their own. You carve out your life, Miguel, don't even think about it. Thass what she's doing, right?" Diana's voice quivered with emotion. She took a moment to yell at her brats, who were crying in the background as if they hadn't been fed in years. "But thass cool, let huh fuck us. Oh man Miguel, we really came out fucked, din't we?" Miguel had to laugh as the babies cried louder in unison like a Greek chorus in mourning.

Last visit, his mother had walked him into a large room at the back of the apartment, down a long hall covered with wood-grain paneling. "This," she said like a tour guide, "was going to be your room." If you had decided to accept, her eyes seemed to continue, but since you didn't . . . It was a big room. She added, "You know it'll always be here." With friendliness. Hadn't they always been friends?

Later, he had spent a few minutes sitting by Nelo in the living room, watching a videocassette on the projection TV. Miguel downed his third beer. His mother was in the kitchen frying chicken and inviting him to stay for dinner.

"You know," Nelo said, leaning back, looking like a fat Dominican goblin, "I think this is a wonderful thing that you visited. I think maybe the one thing your mother needs now to complete her life is her son, to come back. Maybe you could think about that, and drop by more often."

Oh yeah, right. "Daddy." Nice TV. Looks like shit. I won't be stayin', "Mom." Gotta go. Yeah, I love you too. Keep in fucken touch.

Now, months later, he was double-parked a block away from where she was building HER life.

He told himself he was quitting this Spider shit, that he was doing it for himself, not Cristalena; she didn't have anything to do with it. If he left Spider, he would have to leave Firebug. He wouldn't be hanging with him or any of his posse pals. Once he kissed Spider off, that whole world was closed to him. He would be a nonperson. They might even come after him, who knows? He sat there in the car, rain still beating a martial tattoo that matched the scrape-squeak of his windshield wipers. He'd have to stay somewhere. Could he really live with his mother again, and that man? Being around them made him want to break glass and destroy furniture, as if the spirit of his father possessed him.

He hopped out of the car, over to the phone, and dialed the number. "Hello?" It was Nelo's wheezy voice, an ugly, alien sound; Miguel hung up.

A bus madly honked as Miguel U-turned under the el and sped back to his home grounds. All of it a blur. Dancing black girls writhing under the twinkling neon of a pizzeria. A guy and girl hugging on a stoop. A little kid being pulled along by his mother, emptying his water pistol at Miguel's car. The screams of an old woman and her two daughters coming out of church pressing down their skirts as their umbrella gets snatched by wind and turned inside out.

When Miguel got home, he found Firebug in bed with a girl, his rolling giggles mingling with her sharp cackle. Miguel couldn't say why, but he was relieved when he looked in and saw it wasn't Amelia, just some bleached blonde, skin like hot chocolate, her ass thrusting and twisting, Firebug still giggling insanely until he spotted Miguel by the door.

"Yo!" he yelled happily. "The wienie roast is tomorrow at two!"

The girl didn't even look at him. The new TV was sitting on a blue milk crate, pictures flashing with no sound.

"You want I should pick Amelia up?" He thought this would get some kind of response from Firebug, but all it got was a shrug. He put a huge spliff to his lips.

"Whatever," he said, and then he started giggling again, his eyes popping as he stared at the girl wriggling on top of him.

14

He spent most of the night reading *Christiane F*, falling into heroin dreams where Spider was holding him down, injecting him. In one, he found Cristalena. He was with her only long enough to tell her he was as clean as they come, but she unrolled his sleeves and revealed his scarred-up battleground arms. Then she ran, reappearing in the next batch of dreams. It was eleven in the morning when Firebug woke him by jumping up and down on the mat.

"Yo," he said as Miguel squinted into the daylight, "I'm gonna step. Don't f'get the wienie roast, okay? You got it on yuh calendar, ride?" He squatted down. "Listen, um, you don't gotta bother axin' Amelia t' hang wif' me at the bar after. You know, today's a workday f' the poor girl. Don't wanna tax huh, get huh in the shits with huh daddy. Ride?"

"Well, you want I should pick her up or not?" Miguel was shading his eyes and rising up slowly, feeling irritated.

"'Sup t' you, bro'. I hear you like havin' huh in yuh car."

"What the fuck that means?"

"It don't mean nothin'."

"Don't fuck with me, man, it's too early. My body feels like shit. I cun't even eat yesterday. Whass all this shit about me an' Amelia?"

"I thought'chu could tell me, bro'. The other night she tells me she don't wanna see me so much."

Miguel got up, his limbs aching. His lips were all crunchy and there was blood on his teeth. He went into the bathroom, hating the look of himself in the mirror. "Thass got nothin' t' do with me. What did'ju do t' huh?"

"I din't do shit," Firebug said, appearing at the bathroom door as Miguel rinsed his face. "She jus' tol' me she's sicka sleepin' wif' a corpse."

Miguel had a coughing fit, spitting up toothpaste.

"Yeah. I know. I had the same reaction, bro'." Firebug patted him on the back. "But'chu know, she's old an' shit. She's all crackheaded. Maybe you can talk to huh about it."

Miguel looked at him, drying his face very carefully with a towel. His face was all valleys gullies bumps and ridges, and they all ached. "Look man," he said, "we're friends, huh an' me. Thass all. I got my own girl problems right now."

Firebug stared at him. Miguel walked past, heading for his room. On the way he spotted that fat blond girl lingering in the living room. She had the kind of vacant face that only showed emotion while being fucked. The thought made him laugh.

"So you'll be there, right?" Firebug followed him into his room.

"Yeah. No sweat." He fought the laughter.

"Whass so funny?"

"Nothin', man. That bimbo." He came close and whispered. "Where you got the bitch?" It was like the old days.

"They were havin' a fire sale," Firebug said, clapping, the two of them twitching with laugh spasms. He headed for the door and paused just outside the room to give Miguel another long, searching look. "Later, right?"

"Yeah man, you bet."

And then he was gone and Miguel was sitting there on the mat, feeling alone and lost with a dull ache in his chest. He was thinking of calling his mother. He couldn't do anything but stare at the windows.

He got dressed and went out into the cold gray drizzle. He was wearing his new flyer's coat and felt pretty suave despite his rubber-raft lip and his aching chest. He went to Hunts Point and wandered into Kiddie City, where he saw Cristalena around every bend. He saw her playing with the video games, checking out the board games, giving the stuffed animals trial hugs. He grabbed the sad ones, the puffy ones, the fat ones, until he came to the bear, the one she had talked about. He was sure it was the one, its large dark browns looking pensive, the tummy soft and fat, perfect for sleeping with. He checked the tag. THIRTY DOLLARS? Fucken bitch. She could hurt him like that, and there he was buying her shit. He stood there a long time with the bear, even walked it around the store, clutching it close like a baby. Finally he walked it over to the cashier.

Then he sat his boxed bear on the front seat beside him and went for a drive. The weather was perfect for it, clouds never ending. An endless drizzle clung to the air like fog. He drove up to Third Avenue for a slice, sitting and munching with the boxed bear in the car. "She won't wan'-chu," he told it. "She'll tell us both to get lost."

Driving back, he turned up Wales Avenue, parking by the big church with its gloomy chain-link fence topped by coiled spirals of barbed wire. Behind the gates, he knew, was a pretty garden, a brick walk flanked by rows of bright flowers and trees that led to the tall wooden doors of the church. He used to stare at it a lot from his room window across the street while his parents argued. He always could hear them screaming and yelling but it seemed to be happening on another planet far away. His mind used to wander through that garden as if exploring a new world born from a collision of stars.

The private house where he used to live was still there across from the church, empty windows gaping, an ugly burnt-out hulk. Like an old garish hooker wearing too much eyeliner, it called to him. "Come back." His old window was shattered and blackened. No matter where he turned there was an old empty building waiting for him, an ugly fragment of past, an old dead life. Seventeen almost, but he felt like he was already fifty, looking back on a long, cluttered road. How would he ever be a kid? He was trying to make big decisions about life and about love, whatever the fuck THAT was. He had been wary of fetters, had encouraged looseness in all his relationships until he'd met Cristalena. She ratified a belief dormant in him that there was more to life, that maybe he had to think about doing something besides staying in his rat hole, part of the pack. He didn't know why he was different, but early on he had seen the decay in Jimmy's face, the death dancing in Jokey's eyes, the emptiness of the street joy the crazed gun thrills the pop of the NINES, the splintering glass raining down singing like pretty wind chimes, the ineffectual cop cars cruising by all of it, a nowhere land, a nothing experience. Miguel could rattle off names of a few kids he had known by face by name but not much else, kids that were walking tall, rocking hard, like you couldn't even look at them a certain way without them popping a scene on you. Each one ended up sliced and splintered and bitten by shells and who knew why? Miguel remembered cop lights swirling like disco strobes as he and his buddies craned and pushed and shoved to see who it was who'd got it.

"Oh, thass Michael."

"Holy fuck, they got Rolando."

"Uch. Lookit how they shot up Shorty."

"Oh shit! I tole Joey nah t' go in there tonight! Fuck, lookit how they iced his ass!"

Even Spider had to be careful and on the run. Spider was no show-off. Some guys made their drops from the back seats of limos; Spider stayed small. He spun his web and ran there and here in scummy clothes with bloodshot eyeballs. When he rode the subway business types and blond women in pretty office wear would move away from him. There was a distinct Spider aroma: sweat piss armpit dirty sneakers.

"This is the American dream," Spider was always telling him. "We livin' it, bro'. We climbin' the ladder, man." But Spider was wrong. Miguel was the one with the American dream, of making it to the top honestly and cleanly. It was a stupid dream and he had no reason to even hope for it. Inside he felt like the American dream was a lie. No spick kid was going to make it that way.

He drove away feeling emptier than his old vacant building. He checked his watch and then cruised over to Kelly Street, coasting by the Cuban sandwich joint. He didn't spot Amelia. He had a feeling she wouldn't be going anyway. If she had really told Firebug to get fucked, why would she want to go check out his handiwork? Miguel didn't even know why he was going to the roast. He approached the burning building, fire trucks scattered across his path like children's toys, when he noticed that the building was the same one he had stopped in to chat with Domino.

Firebug's groupies were across the street by one of the engines. He leaned against his car and lit a cigarette. The small building stood with one side of its face in flames, tongues of fire flicking up defiantly through the rolling black smoke and the stabbing beams of water. Miguel recognized a fat woman across from him in a tattered housedress and thong sandals, one of which had ripped and dangled and dragged as she marched up and down the street screaming and crying. Her words were not words but howls, her fists beating her chest. Miguel focused on Domino, his green beret over his head of stiff frizz, laughing and getting poked by a girl named Stephanie, who was trying to get him to stop. Miguel looked back at the woman. "That one," Domino had said to him that day she passed them on the stairs, glaring. "She's one a' them. Fucken tenant organizers." It made Miguel think of what the Nazis used to do when someone got out of hand. Now she was hanging from a lamppost with a sign around her neck: I DARED DEFY THE GREATER GERMAN REICH. Scratch that. Spider. I DARED DEFY SPIDER. I'm hanging from a lamppost. Me. Soon.

Miguel stood there smoking and grunting and nodding to himself with the grim satisfaction that comes when your suspicions are proved correct. This fire proved that Firebug was still palling with Spider, still working with him, and still lying to Miguel about it. Why? After he had seemed so chummy and all, and Miguel pressing him on Spider, and Firebug denying everything, still inviting him to this torch as if Miguel wouldn't ever know. What did it mean? Was this some kind of warning, or was Miguel just being paranoid? He looked over at Firebug's groupies, the smug jeers and leering monkey faces with none of the lyric cynicism and intelligence of an Amelia. He missed her. It was weird.

He got into his car and drove away, not sure where he was going, until he found himself parked outside the Cuban sandwich place. He sat there a minute, finishing his cigarette, then locked up the car and went in, the jangling bells on the door ringing on in his head long after the door had closed behind him. Inside it was warm with the smell of hot coffee and fried pork. The old man behind the counter nodded, like he knew him. Miguel asked for Amelia. The old man passed a cup of coffee to another old man, whose hands resembled an ancient yellowed map complete with valleys, streams, arteries.

"En el baño," the old man said, motioning absently for Miguel to sit and wait with an arm motion that said, "Over there, though—not here." So Miguel took a small table by the window so he could watch his car. He felt her beside him before he caught her reflection in the mirror.

"How now brown cow," she said, stopping to kiss him on the cheek. His chair moaned as he twisted it around to look at her. She was smiling, her hair up on her head, her slender neck and girlish shoulders exposed. She had on a pink hairy sweater that seemed to grip her arms to her sides.

"What good is that?" he asked, stabbing her bare voice box with a finger. "You ain't hardly covered. Thass some useless sweater."

"I got a scarf."

"Oh."

"I told my father I'd be taking time off today. I knew you were coming. Can we talk?"

"Thass why I'm here."

"Wait f' me."

She went to her father and blathered some, then went into the back and returned wearing her big blue coat, a thick scarf, and a large wool ski cap with a red ball dangling from it. Miguel started laughing.

"Come on," she said, whacking him as they walked out. She was carrying some books and looked like a student. He paused, thinking they were heading for his car, but she took him up the block to a steel door that led to the back of the big building there on the corner. They went down some rattling steps, then past a row of garbage cans into a long stone hallway that smelled like ammonia. There under a yellow light bulb was a door; she unlocked it with her keys.

"Well? Come on." She pulled him inside into a dark corridor full of boiler fumes, a furnace door glowing with flames, heavy warmth circulating everywhere. She opened another door and they entered an apartment.

"Maaan," he said, impressed.

The first room was large, a kind of living room with a couch and TV, flowers, and some funny paintings of dark semi-naked people in colorful clothes. Beside that was a bedroom with a large bed, another tiny TV, and a stereo. Flowers sat everywhere, in pots on shelves, hanging from the ceiling, on top of tables. The kitchen was like a big utility room with a huge sink, a stone floor, and a large wooden table. The stove was stuck in the corner. It looked old and didn't seem to fit right. The bathroom was a tiny room with a sparkling new toilet, a pretty tub surrounded by black and yellow tiles.

"I just started to put them on," she said shyly proudly, "but I don't think I'll finish. I'm planning to move."

"You really live in here?"

"Uh-huh." She seemed pleased with herself.

"How come?"

"My father is the super. We have this big apartment just down the hall there. There's a door leading into the yard where their place is. But I don't feel comfortable living with them. So I scouted out this place one day and asked my father if I could make something out of all these rooms. He said sure, what did he know? Maybe he thought I was going to put in a sewing room or something! Instead I built my own apartment. Put the tub in, hooked up the pipes, I even brought that stove down."

"Damn."

"Yeah. My pop didn't like it, you know, says women ain't supposed to be doing shit like that. But I did it. And I put in all these doors, see? So I have privacy like I couldn't ever have living over there with them. I locked this place up. He can get into the boiler room fine, but this section's locked off. There are three doors, and each one has a different-sounding bell, so I can tell which door it is."

Miguel leaned against one of the stone walls, the meager lighting in this hall between rooms making everything seem dusty. "Maan. You got thum brains."

She smiled, then dragged him into the bedroom. She threw off her coat, twirled off the scarf, sat on the bed to undo her sneakers. She told him to come in and sit down because he was lingering by the doorway. He couldn't shake the feeling that maybe someone was coming. Everything seemed so open and yet so isolated.

"Don'chu feel scared in here? I mean, what if some guy comes in here?"

"There ain't no way."

"But'chu takin' off yuh clothes. What if somebody—"

She laughed, pulled him over to the bed, took off his coat and his scarf. She pushed him against the headboard. She had slipped her jeans off, was wearing a pair of neon-colored bicycle pants.

"Would'ju relax a little? I got a jay in the ashtray."

"Look, I din't come here t' get stoned, Amelia. There's some serious shit goin' down here. I need t' talk to you. It's pretty serious."

She smiled tenderly, mussing up his hair as she knelt beside him on the bed. "Miguel," she whispered, her eyes closing slowly, as if she were making a wish. When they opened, she seemed to be dreaming.

"Tell me you don't need a hug," she whispered, her hands softly caressing his face.

"Nah, man."

"What?" A whisper, a slight smile, tender, questioning a child.

"I said nah, I don't need a hug."

"You don't gotta play that with me, Miguel. There should be one place you can go." She paused, her fingertips tracing his lips. "They look better," she said.

"Thank you." Self-conscious, losing control, no place to be distant. He was on her turf. Home-field advantage.

"Did she hurt'chu?" Her voice was soft and calming.

His voice rose with suspicion. "How did'ju know about that?"

Mentor figure

"I talked to Spider." Straight up, no lies, no evasions, her eyes solidly on his, searching him out. "He told me what he did, how he cornered you. All he had to say was that she was there, and I knew." A whisper, a warm breeze: "I'm sorry, Miguel."

He leaned back, unable to speak.

"Had you gotten to tell her before Spider showed up?"

He swallowed hard. "No."

She shook her head. "Ts. Ohh Miguel."

"I was gonna tell huh," he said desperately, her hands pulling on him, drawing him closer. "I was jus' gonna start when he showed up." Then he was in her arms, buried against her shoulder. There was warmth, a scent of Chanel and something girlish.

"I don't wanna cry," he said in a trembling voice.

"You're only sixteen and a half," she said, her hands massaging the back of his head. "Cry."

It was a blur, his crying, just like when you go to a hospital to get stitches. At first there's this fear, and then the blank-faced doctor comes in and sticks you with anesthetic and then asks does it hurt? The pain has you screaming and writhing and crying and afterward you hit this calm sea where everything is rolling; you feel like you had gone through something like death and survived it, so the little shame that you feel for screaming behind the pleated curtain in the emergency room doesn't even matter anymore, you've gone so far beyond it your eyes don't even see the same anymore. That's how it felt to cry and sob and give it all up the way a little kid does. He lay there on the bed looking up at the ceiling painted bright blue and spotted with adhesive stars and planets. She had taken off his sweater and unbuttoned his shirt. Now she lit a joint. Her sweater was off. She had on a strapless bra that looked like part of it had been slit, the tops of her tits threatening to spill over. It was bright white against her hot cocoa skin. She handed the joint to him after taking the first toke, filling the room with scent. It was very strong smoke. After two long tokes, Miguel was feeling really buzzed.

"Damn," he said.

"Listen." She was sitting on the bed across from him. The bed was up against the wall and she leaned against it, her legs tucked up, as if she didn't want to get too close YET and threaten him. Miguel strained to hear.

"What?"

"Do you hear anything?"

"Nah." He listened.

"No cars, no traffic, no dudes on the street." Her voice was soft and a little hoarse. It seemed to be inside his head. "That's why I like it here."

"But don'chu feel like yuh alone?"

Suddenly his words sounded stupid. He laughed. She did too, taking the joint from him.

"Yeah I feel alone here! Everybody should have a place like that. Your room is like that too, don'chu know that? Your books, records. It's like your own private sanctum." She toked. "You're only the second person that's ever been in here with me."

"Firebug."

She frowned and nodded.

"But nobody else? How about the gang? The ol' Firebug posse? How about Spider?" She shook her head to all of them, very hard when he said Spider, and he laughed and came closer and stopped her head from shaking with his hands.

"No way." She was shaking her head still, but slower. "Firebug was here only one time. But he's a corpse. I never wanted him back in here. He wasn't worth it. After he left there was a smell in here. Lasted for weeks, I couldn't get it out." Her head stopped shaking. "You know, you're the first real person I've had in here with me."

He was still holding her face, trying to free her hair from its clip so it could tumble down. She looked at him with a faraway smile. "Hey," she said. "You're touching me."

He nodded and grinned. "Yeah." After crying like that, his face looked younger, the eyes a little swollen, the way a baby's eyes get just after it wakes up from a long sleep. "So what happened between you an' Firebug? He tol' me some strange shit." He leaned back, not touching her after he spread out her hair onto her shoulders. She pouted for a moment, giving it up with a shrug and a sigh.

"I told him he made me sick. I told him that he didn't care about me, that I was tired of him and that I didn't want him to fuck me anymore."

"Did'ju tell him you were in love with me?"

She laughed, covering her mouth. "No. See, we were yelling, and I told him he'd never be half the person you are. So he said oh yeah, now I see, you been screwin' him! And I said nah, I haven't, I tried but he wouldn't, he's too good a friend to do that to you."

Miguel laughed. "You told him that?"

"Yeah, yeah, I told him he didn't deserve a friend like you."

"He don't deserve you neitha."

"That's sweet, Miguel."

"Don't be gettin' all goofy."

"Then I saw Spider. He was upset. He had spoken to you. He told me you were quitting and he wanted to know from me if I thought'chu were serious. I told him yeah. He got all disturbed, started talking about how you're playing with fire, how he's gonna have to do something about it." She leaned forward, grabbing both his hands like she was going to tell his fortune. "When he told me about your girl being there and all, I figured you might lose her. I figured she wouldn't understand and then you'd be hurt and angry and you might start thinking that you were crazy to think about leaving the business. You'd think about all the stuff he's done for you and then you'd never leave." She squeezed his hands. "I think you should quit, Miguel. I think you should get your shit out of that dump and just jet. Don't stay with Firebug anymore. Get out of there. Him and Spider, you can't trust them."

He stared at her. Trust? And how much did he trust her? He felt guilty for wondering what her angle was. She hadn't asked him for anything. YET.

"Spider's changed, Miguel. It's been happening over the past couple of months. I don't know what it is. Maybe he's not as powerful as he wants to be. Maybe he's already got too much power. You know what they say about absolute power? It absolutely fucks people up. Spider's getting trigger happy. He's making his move now, and don't be surprised if a lot of people get iced."

"You really think so? Spider?"

"Yeah. I know he's breaking away from his boss. Do you think there's a kind way to do that? Who knows if he's planning to make off with money or something? That's one thing he don't talk to anybody about. I don't know a single person who knows him who has any idea how much money he's got. But if he's making his move for independence he's gotta be pretty well set up." She sighed. "Get your money and your car and get the fuck outta there. Don't leave an address. Just go. You and that damned car."

"Excuse me?"

"You can spot the shit a mile away! Even if you moved into Ace's turf.

They could still spot'chu an' hit you! Even some of their people might know the car! You should dump it for a while, park it in a garage. That big one on Third Avenue."

"Are you serious?"

"You can move in with me," she said quickly. "I don't mean here. I'm moving out of here soon." She smiled sadly. "See, I'm planning to go back to school next semester. I'm quitting this shit too, Miguel."

He wanted to hug her. "Well thass dope."

She grinned at him. "Dope, is it? I guess so. But it's all your fault, Miguel. I met you and everything changed. You said things to me that nobody's ever bothered to say." She seemed to bite down on her words, looking down at her hands. "So, what about this girl? What did she do after?"

"You mean after Spider?"

"Yup."

"She ran away, jus' got up an' ran outta the car, she wun't even listen, jus' ran."

"Did'ju go after her?"

"No."

"Why not?"

"Wha'chu mean why not? Don't I get t' have some fucken dignity, too? I gotta throw myself down an' beg on toppa everythin' else? I blew all this money on the bitch. Flowers, food, all this shit. I even got huh a fucken bear. An' she leaves me crying t' go runnin' outta the car like that. Man, I was cryin' an' shit, I was messed up, an' she jus' ran off."

"I tol'ju that would happen."

"You did not."

"Did too did too. I said she wouldn't understand and would probably go running right outta the car the minute you told her. My words exactly."

Miguel smirked, lips quivering with his attempt to kill the smile. "You liar."

"I ain't no liar. I tol'ju. You gonna need some pretty special woman to deal with you, Miguel. Not some teeny girl thing with her head in the clouds looking for Mr. Perfect. You're a complex guy. You need a woman, Miguel, not a girl. Somebody older. A woman, a real woman."

"Ohh bullshit."

"Don't be so hasty. Maybe you need time to think about it." She paused, then kicked at him with her foot. The toenails were painted a light tan. "So, is that enough time?"

"Amelia . . ."

"You really love this girl?"

He shrugged. "Yeah."

"You don't know that. You don't even know what love is."

"You think you know?"

"I think you gotta be older to be in love, in real love. When you're young it's just the idea of being in love."

"Thass goofy."

"Yeah? Well, if you were really in love you would've gone after her instead of letting her run off. Love's a responsibility, you know. You don't have time to be standing there thinking about your honor or dignity. How dignified do you look when you're fucking? Huh?"

"I look crazy dignified!"

"Get real. Sometimes a girl's gotta be chased. Sometimes she'll run on purpose. If you don't come, she's going to know you don't love her, and maybe later when you do show up it'll be too late."

"Well she wasn't there f' me!! Wasn't I cryin'? Why cun't she be there like I'm supposed t' be there f' huh?"

"You're both too young. She has expectations of you already and you just shattered them. And you, you're in dreamland, I told you that, to expect her to be understanding and forgiving and so goddamn mature. What you want is natural, but you're way mature for your age. Maybe she isn't. Why do you think she ran off? Her senses got all overloaded."

"Shit." Miguel shook his head. "So what makes you such an expert?"

"I know men," she said, bursting into laughter. Miguel leaned back against one of the pillows, watching her hair toss this way and that, her hands raking at it. She was really pretty like that. A girl who feels pretty has a tendency to reach for her hair. Why? He watched. It was written on his face. She stopped laughing and crept over to him, her eyes probing him.

"Miguel," she said softly. She kissed him, brushing her lips against his ever so softly. Careful of his wound. He let it happen, didn't pull away, closed his eyes to lose himself in the sensation of her so close so near. Was it the joint? It was her, he couldn't fight her. He fell backward into a springy sea of pillow. She slid over on top of him, warm. His hands relished the feel of her, the soft skin, the legs, muscles taut yet giving softly, so smoothly and without a crinkle were her curves constructed.

They began to fuck, desperately, as if some inner need compelled them. Bodies speaking in tongues. "We have to stop," Miguel whispered several times breathlessly. "Yes," she said, like a prayer, a chant. After it was over, they lay beside each other, limbs all springy, eyes dizzy stoned. She radiated, prettier than before, softer, something he had never seen before. It made him sad. She lay close beside him, intertwined, her hands softly dreamily caressing him. Then she started to cry quietly, her tears warm on his chest.

"But it's always like that," she said.

"We shunta done this," Miguel said, playing with her hair.

"Don't say that."

"I'm sorry."

"That's one of the worst things you can say to a woman after making love. 'We shunta done this.' 'I'm sorry' doesn't rate too highly either." She dried her face with a hand, still lying against him.

"An' whass the best thing?"

She sighed. "I ain't never gonna hear it." She looked at him. "You should say you love me and you can't live without me and that now you'll be able to get your shit together."

"I can't say that stuff."

"I know you don't love me."

"I do love you. Not like that, though. Thass why I said I'm sorry. The fucken was great. It was beyond anythin' an' I know thass 'cause you ain't some slabba meat t' me. There's more to it with us. But like, I gotta check out this thing with Cristalena." He paused, his voice filled with a commanding energy. "Lookit that. I jus' say huh name an' I feel this thud in my chest. Like maybe I let huh down."

"She let'chu down first."

She was protecting him. He smiled.

"I trust you," he said, softly, tenderly, tipping her face up to his. It was the closest to I LOVE YOU she was going to get. Her lips trembled. There was a soft kiss. They settled into a long, sleepy silence, snuggled up against each other, until she finally asked him, "So what are you gonna do now?"

He sighed. She got up reluctantly, stretching like a long thin cat, all naked, curvy, and elastic. It made Miguel want to fuck her again. She had a crazy pretty body, he even liked the hair on her legs, but he knew he didn't love her like that, not like Cristalena. He felt grateful and wanted to do things for her, to stay friends forever, to always hear her words, feel her eyes on him, hear her funny laughter. He stared at her admiringly. She looked over. "Stop looking at me. I said, wha'chu gonna do now?"

she asked, stamping her foot with playful annoyance as she slipped on her panties.

"I'm gonna quit."

"And what about your little girl?"

"I don't know yet," he said.

"Well I know. I know you better get your shit together with her. You better go out and find her and put it to her and see if she's serious with you or not. Put the case to her, because if she loves you, then she owes you a little understanding. Can you do that, can you find that out?" There was anger in her tone. It was almost a reprimand.

"Sure."

"If you have to go over to her house, you do it. If you love her, I don't think you have a choice. You gotta put yourself out, at risk. Love means being vulnerable, don'chu know that? Fuck that shit about being safe. In love you're always out on a limb. You chase her down and find out. You can't be so proud like that and be in love. You sure ain't gonna get her back by fucking me, that's for sure. Don't laugh. Are you serious about going straight?" She was tying back her hair, large barrette between her teeth. "Because I am. I'm through with Firebug and I'm through with this crack shit. It might be hard but there ain't no way I'm going to be through with it if I keep hanging around on the scene." She sat beside him, holding his hand. "You've really helped me see things, Miguel. I know that sounds crazy but you really . . ." She wanted to say more, he could tell, but then she got up and faced the wall, her head bowed. Her shoulders shook a little. Miguel felt like he should get up and hold her, but he couldn't because it would lead to other stuff that she wanted and needed and he was confused enough sitting there. She turned, wiping her face; she looked small and young and scared.

"If you wanna work at my pop's place, just let me know. I'm sure I can swing it for you, but'chu gotta let me know soon. You're gonna need a job, you know." Her cracked voice made him sad.

"What about you?"

"What about me? I'm going straight. I don't need this shit anymore, Miguel, I've had it. I'm going back to school."

He nodded, confused at her anger. "But thass good. Why you so mad?"

She sat on the edge of the bed and stared at him, her hands wrestling with each other in her lap.

"I saw her," she said.

"Saw who?"

"I know why you like her."

"Saw who, Amelia?" He moved closer to her, grabbed her hands. "Hey, whassup?"

She got up off the bed. "Please don't touch me right now."

"I'm sorry."

"I was in that store, surrounded by all those gaudy clothes, trying to look like I was interested in something."

"Cristalena?" He got up, approached Amelia's back. "You saw her?"

"Sure I did." She looked at him with an arrogant glimmer.

"When did you see her? Why?"

Miguel was staring at her, his face unreadable. She touched his cheek. "Don't be like that. I only wanted to look at her. I didn't do anything. At first I thought it was this short-haired girl that was helping me. I was blathering about skirts and sizes and shit like that, and then I heard this lady call for Cristalena. And when she stepped out I swear I heard violins and birds chirping, it was like that movie, *Tess*. You ever see *Tess*?"

"Nah."

"You want to go with me? It's playing this week at The Cinema Village."

He smirked. Her smile trembled.

"She's really pretty, a living doll." Her voice broke. "A little Latin angel cakes."

Miguel took her in his arms. She resisted a little but he forced her, and she fell against him for a little while. He petted her hair. He lifted her face up to his.

"I love you, man," he said.

"Miguel, make sure she loves you. Make sure she's worthy of you. Because if she's not, hey, don't laugh!" She pushed him away and turned to the wall again.

"I'm only laughin' 'cause you already know if it weren't for Cristalena I might feel different."

She peered over her shoulder at him. It made him laugh.

"Yeah?"

"Yeah, man. But it ain't like that. I know what went down with us. But'chure my only friend, yuh the only person I trust."

She nodded and sat on the bed a moment, staring at him. Then she got up, still putting on clothes.

"You might not see me for a while," she said. "I'm not gonna be out on the scene anymore. But'chu know where I live. I'm giving you my number." She seemed nervous and fumbled for paper, scribbling on a small pad and handing him the pastel blue note. "I mean, if you want." Her eyes were shy and looked away from him as he took the paper. With an unlit cigarette dangling from his lips, he stooped over to the bureau and grabbed the pad, scribbling his mother's address and phone number. It was a hunch that he would end up there. He hadn't yet made up his mind but it seemed the safest bet. He gave her the slip, and there was a pause. It was like a goodbye at the airport. Any minute now her flight would be announced.

"You let me know if you move," he said.

"Okay."

She smiled warmly, heading for the doorway as if she were going to lead him out of the room, but he grabbed her and turned her toward him and then he gave her a loud smooch and a big hug. With a flick he lit his cigarette and took a puff. He dried her face with his hand, then he took his cigarette and placed it on her lips.

"Okay," she said. "Me too."

"So take me outta here."

She wiped her eyes and, grabbing his hand, led him out.

15

In the morning he was groggy and unshaven. Only sixteen and a half and he looked like that? It was unbelievable. He shaved. Started at fifteen. His father had laughed at him. "Some Latino you are," he said with derision. "What's a man without a mustache?" Miguel liked looking young. All his friends kept their baby fuzz, thought it made them look sophisticated. Miguel was in no rush to look old. After a shave, he felt fresh, newly born. Rejuvenated.

There had been no Firebug. Evidently he had partied somewhere else, had found some new place to crash. Miguel hung in his room watching some Victoria Principal movie where she played a woman with enormous breasts. It seemed Victoria Principal was always playing a woman with enormous breasts. Miguel smoked Firebug's smoke, leafed through his porno magazines, jerked off, didn't clean the sheet. The crime shows on TV bored him. Watching people get drilled like that just didn't excite him anymore. He was living it. Only fools in the suburbs dug that.

The shave didn't hide the tired eyes, the bruised lip. He threw on some clothes and drove out to Alexander's, where he bought some more clothes. Shirts, slacks, shoes. After that he zipped away, passing Butterfly's. Everything felt empty without her.

Then he went to see Careta on Southern Boulevard, a skinny eighteen-year-old kid with a face like a bumpy moonscape. He had six young girls working for him and had a pretty good smoke hustle going. How he got the girls to hook for him was a mystery, but they did it happily, earning him the bucks so that he could set himself up. This was a real apartment: furniture, drapes, color TV, stereo, all the comforts of home WITH NO

PARENTS. Miguel lived in awe of it. Stepping in again now, Miguel felt that this was the way he wanted to live. How would he be able to pull it off?

Careta was wearing red shorts and an old wrinkled tee. His eyes looked tired. He shuffled around barefoot, offering Miguel a drink from a carton of orange juice.

"So what can I do f' you?" Careta's voice was friendly but sleepy.

"I don't know, I jus' thought I'd maybe stop by an' say hi," Miguel said sluggishly, a little confused. Were all his posse pals going to diss him once word got out? He knew they would all forget him. He didn't mean shit to any of them.

Careta might be different. He knew Spider and a lot of the posse kids but he didn't work for any of them. He dealt in weed and flesh. That was it. He'd had a few run-ins with the local dealers but he didn't deal crack, he wouldn't go near the stuff, so they left him alone. He was an independent. Back before Miguel had gotten in with Spider, he had been introduced to Careta by one of his partners in his smoke operation. A supplier had gotten busted, and Careta promised to fill the void. They did good business, but it wasn't until Miguel quit the weed business and got in with Spider that they became friends, hanging out and talking and sharing a toke on occasion. Miguel grew to like him, his keen mind, his quiet ways, his sharp jokes. He did his thing quietly, without a lot of noise.

"Careta bro', I wanted to ask you if I could score some smoke, I mean like a big haul 'cause I might be jettin'."

Careta rubbed an eye and looked at him as if waking up for the first time. "Jettin'? Wha'chu mean jettin'?"

Miguel sighed. "I mean that I outta smoke but thinkin' I wanna get enough t' maybe deal some."

Careta grinned. "You goin' into business again, bro'?"

"Yeah, maybe."

"There ain't nothin' like bein' on yuh own, is there?"

"Nah. I'm startin' t' learn that."

"Spider been gettin' you down?"

There was a gentleness to Careta's voice that made Miguel want to spill everything. The guy had never foxed him or double-dealt him. Miguel took the juice carton from him and took a sip, preparing to let it all out. Careta, sensing this, sat on top of a small table by the kitchen doorway.

"I'm quittin'," Miguel said.

Careta stared at him like it had scooted right by him. "What?"

"I said I'm quittin'."

"Spider? You gonna walk out on Spider?"

"Yeah, I'm gettin' the fuck out."

"Man oh man. You sure he won't kill you?"

Miguel half laughed, but when he saw Careta's face remain grim, he shrugged.

"Look," Careta said, "you gotta think about this. Spider's goin' through a bad time right now. There's this other crack king. His name is Ace. Big black guy. I saw him at a party. You know he was in 'Nam? Fucken guy. He's a mover. He's pushin' in all over the place. Spider has his hands full with him. The worse thing is that when I first met Spider an' all, I saw that he was runnin' a different kinda op, you know? Not like the others. He had a more humane kinda approach. Thass why when you tol' me you was workin' with him, I felt good, ya know? But now he's changed, man. I heard some nasty shit. They killed some kid out here f' tryin'na swipe some cop money."

Miguel nodded grimly. "Yup."

"That ain't all. This posse out from Dawson, they went to this party out near 152nd an' they crashed it. Shots everywhere. Spider's gettin' crazy, man, he's encouragin' that shit with the posses. Now that brings 'um comin' over here, turf for turf, bro'. If his posses gonna disrespect the other posses, they gonna start ridin' by bustin' caps. Know wham sayin'?"

"Yeah."

"Lots more shootin'." He reached over into an ashtray and took out a fat joint. He lit it and toked. "An' you know they got tha' guy Rico, right?"

"Yeah, I heard about that, too."

Careta exhaled, passing Miguel the joint. "Looks to me like there's another organization within the organization. Sound crazy? It's true, bro'. Looks like Rico got in on it, then decided like he was gonna rat to Spider. So they fixed his ass."

Miguel thought about that strange night he went to Spadgie's, the looks he got when he asked about Rico. It made him shake his head to think about how many eyes you need out on the street if you want to avoid a knife in the back.

"Spadgie's," Miguel said absently. This made Careta snap his fingers and point at him.

"Yeah. Exactly. I think something's gonna go down over there soon, man. Something big, an' it's gonna be Spider that pulls it."

"You mean like a hit?"

"Yeah bro', a master ice. Maybe a whole posse. Lotta people gonna get iced there. You ever see tha' movie about the Valentine's Day massacre?"

"You can't be serious." Miguel passed the joint back and sucked in some air.

"I'm sayin' there's a double organization at Spadgie's. I'm sayin' there's a whole group of snakes in there playing Spider dirty. I'm sayin' Rico was in on it, and Rico was maybe workin' like some undercover sting, you know? An' they killed him. Now you know Spider's gonna clean house. He's changed, man. He's makin' his own power play. An' he's spillin' blood."

Miguel sighed. "So whass all that gotta do with me quittin'?"

Careta leaned forward, his voice a husky whisper. "If you duck out now people might think you in on some a' this shit. Who's t' know? Maybe yuh in with Spadgie's gang after all. If something big goes down like I think it is, an' you duck out, who knows what the boys on the street gonna think? Forget Spider. A lotta thum kids don't like you too much, know wham sayin'? Think you got it easy, like maybe you let Spider dick you."

Miguel's eyes opened wide. "No way, man." They both laughed a little.

"What I'm sayin' is that maybe those little fucks on the street gonna think you cut a deal, maybe you set Spider up an' are makin' yuh escape. So they shoot'cha car up."

"But thass not true, I jus' wanna get out already. I'm sicka this shit, man."

"You should wait, bro'."

"I can't wait." Miguel, exasperated, handed him the orange juice carton. "Every day that passes I get in deeper."

"Sure you do. Thass because Spider needs you. He ain't gonna let'chu go, man."

"He's gonna have to."

Careta gave him a sympathetic look. "You ain't no good, bro'. You keep thinkin' about climbin' out. Don'chu? Don'chu think about leadin' some kinda straight, happy life? Money without the risks, the shooting,

the cops, the bullshit? All this GI combat shit? But'chu bein' stupid, bro'.
Can'chu see that f' people like us there ain't no other way f' us t' get
money? Even if we can only hold it f' a day, if only f' two days, or an hour,
before we get the bullets. Whass it matter how you get it, if you get it?"

"Life's better than this," Miguel said hesitantly.

"Ohhh yeah! Like you really believe that. An' tell me, who's it better
for? Mr. White Man? Maybe some suck-ass spick? So what? You wanna
do it all their way so you can still end up livin' in a place like this, bein'
such a decent human being? An' why you wanna even be a decent human
being when you livin' in a place like this? You wanna work forty hours
a week, come home, look out'cha window at all this misery an' shit, pay
yuh bills an' still be broke? Rats wakin' you in the mornin', gotta chase
roaches away jus' so you can eat'cha food, an' you wanna talk about
becomin' some hardworkin' jerk?"

The anger in Careta's voice struck Miguel like a fist.

"You wanna go join the human race, right? Start at the bottom? Go
back to school, right? Wha'chu gonna do, go live with yuh folks? You still
got folks, right?"

"Yeah."

"Damn, an' you wanna go back t' that? How can you give up yuh
freedom? It don't make sense."

"It makes sense all right. This ain't freedom. I'm just as chained down,
ain't I? Who knows, Spider might not let me go. So what? You think that
would stop me? I gotta get out. I'm sicka this shitty life. Maybe all these
people can fool themselves into thinkin' they doin' good. I can't. Lookit
these streets, man. We live like animals. There's gotta be somethin'
better. An' I think I'm gonna go lookin' for it."

Careta smirked. "There's a better way all right. Welfare."

"Get fucked. Thass a disease, man, like takin' from Spider."

"But thass what it is, bro'. Look around'ju. Sometimes I think Spider's
right. The parents here, they fucked up. Now the kids are gettin' smart.
They makin' they own way, gettin' they own money, carving out they own
life. Because they look, man, an' they say fuck tha' shit, I ain't gonna end
up like my parents. They chumps. It's like a whole generation sayin', 'Fuck
you, you lost the game already, now I'm takin' care a' number one.' I'm
tellin' you, man, there ain't nothin' out there f' you."

"You can believe that if you want, Careta. Not me."

"Wha'chu gonna do, then, get a job?" Careta sounded hatefully sarcastic. Miguel didn't say anything. Careta got up, draining the carton of juice. He threw himself down on the sofa.

"Look man," he said calmly, "I'm really not the man t' talk to. I'm in it no matter what. This is it f' me. There ain't no place I can go runnin'. I guess if you got choices, then maybe you think like that. I don't. But I'm yuh friend, man. I don't wan'chu should get yuh ass shot up. You should be real careful 'bout how you do it. Don't rush it. Did'ju tell Spider?"

"Yeah."

Careta reached under the sofa and took out a cigar box. Inside was a large plastic bag full of weed. "So how much do you want?"

Miguel sat beside him, taking out his wallet. He had spent about five hundred on clothes. Now he laid out another five. Careta checked out the bills, then went into the bedroom. He came back with a bag. "You'll like this one. Good stuff, a good count if you wanna sell some."

Miguel opened the bag and checked the bouquet and texture. "What, no rug fibers?" This was a long-standing joke with them from the days when he and his partner Robert would get together with Careta and gab about how to add all kinds of shit to make the smoke go farther. Careta laughed as he put the cigar box away.

"So what did'ju tell Spider?"

"I told him I was leavin' an' he said we gotta talk more. He's givin' me a few days to think about it."

"Good. Take those few days, bro'. Maybe you should wait."

Miguel nodded. He pocketed the smoke and got up, extending his hand. Careta took it, held it for a moment, a real concern in his eyes that disturbed Miguel.

"Be careful, bro'."

"You spookin' me out here."

Careta laughed. "I don't mean to. It's just this is a shitty business." He walked him to the door. "It's why I stay on my own as much as I can, you know wham sayin'? The best thing is not to depend on anybody." He opened the door. "Don't worry, bro'. This is all between us."

Miguel turned to look at him. He was thinking about the miles this guy must've traveled, the age in his eyes, the money, the scams, the apartment he had furnished. A whole adult life in only seventeen years. And he did it alone. It was almost inspiring.

Miguel headed down the stairs. Careta held up a hand and crossed his fingers.

From there Miguel drove uptown to see his mother. He had thought about putting it off, but something told him he might as well find out what her attitude would be right now. If she wasn't into it, he'd have to find another place to go. Where? He'd lost touch with the old friends he used to crash with, and his posse pals were out. His mother was the best bet. He didn't like to think about it that way because it meant that he might have to work to make it happen, maybe do some acting, lie, say some of the right things—even befriend Nelo. His stomach rumbled.

The street was quiet and gray. A parking space awaited him by a bodega with a large red-and-yellow awning. The train roared by above, the cars blurry blue blocks. He got out of the car and walked over to a phone. It only rang once.

"Hello?" His mother's voice was still a stranger's to him.

"This is Miguel."

"Miguel, hi!" A burst of air struck the phone. "This is Catarina." Oh yes, as if he had never met her before, a formal introduction. Two new friends. She has a new apartment, a new man, a new life. So now she's not "mother." Catarina. The voice of a teenager, bubbling with delight. "How nice of you to call."

"Yeah. Listen, can I come see you now? I'm down the street." Miguel had felt the urge to say "So how are you? How are things?" Like a pen pal opening a letter, but he couldn't play the game. He went straight to it, and she noticed.

"Sure," she said, a little deflated. "I'm here. Come right on up."

The building was clean, the vestibule door glass clear, almost invisible. Inside, no stench of piss or shit, no rotted plaster dangling. He scooted up the slick, freshly mopped stairs. She was waiting for him at the door. When he stood in front of her she seemed unsure of what to do. She held out her hand stiffly, then gave him an awkward hug. She led him inside as if about to give him another tour.

"Nelo doesn't come until six or so," she said as if he had come to see him. "Will you stay for dinner?"

"Nah, I can't. I just stopped by to talk to you."

She stared at him a moment, and Miguel felt like he had made a mistake. Was that fear in her eyes? Could she sense a threat to her new life approaching? She was still his mother; didn't she have an obligation to help him? Wasn't it her duty? He was about to lay it all on her when she spun into the kitchen.

"Something to drink? How about some orange juice?"

"Sure." He sat down at the kitchen table. It was covered with a brown cloth that had embroidered patterns that reminded him of Careta's living-room couch. Careta would never let him stay. The guy was a businessman. He wouldn't endanger himself. He already felt Miguel was walking on eggs as it was. He wouldn't put himself and his business at risk. He needed his ties, his connections. Miguel was touched by his concern but not carried away with thoughts of brother love. He could trust Careta because he was on the outside of the Spider thing, but he lived by the rules of the trade like everybody else. If Miguel were excommunicated, Careta would probably turn his back on him if he saw him on the street. One of those things. Miguel could picture him turning, shrugging helplessly.

The juice was cold and it had pulp. He chewed, he swallowed, he stared at Catarina standing there in black slacks and a checkerboard blouse. She had rolled up the sleeves as if getting ready to duke it out with him.

"So what's the matter?" This she asked in English, always a bad sign. English made her voice sound testy and severe, hinting at an oncoming barrage of churning, scathing Spanish if the answer didn't please her. He took out a cigarette and lit it, finding it hard to look into her probing eyes. It wasn't fear; more like contempt, and he wanted to hide it from her, hide the resentment he felt at having to return and ask.

"I jus' remember you sayin' that if I ever needed a place to stay, that I could come here." He stared at her then, trying to see the changes on her face, but there was nothing. She just leaned forward a little.

"Miguel, did something happen to you? You look tired. You're not in any trouble, are you?"

"No. I jus' have to move. I don't wanna stay where I am. It's a lousy place an' I have to get away from my roommate." He grabbed a paper towel that was on the table and started tearing it into strips. "I don't see it bein' like a big permanent thing," he added.

"Why not?"

Oh shit. Wrong tack. "I don't know, I'm jus' not thinkin' long term right now."

"Okay." She reached out and patted one of his hands. "You can have that room I told you about. Only I'll need some time to talk to Nelo . . . you know, maybe you should talk to him, too." She squeezed his hand. "Miguel, I know this is all really hard for you, I understand that, but if you could just be nice to him. If you could just stop treating him like he's the enemy. The man saved my life, he gave me a new lease on life . . ."

"I don't wanna hear this." He was holding his cigarette, looking for a place to dump the long smoldering ash. She reached over to a drawer behind her and plopped a huge glass ashtray on the table.

"But I think you have to understand it, to accept it, before you can come here and be part of . . . well, it'll be like being a family again."

Miguel groaned and covered his face. He couldn't help it.

"Miguel, you'll have to respect him, treat him like the man of the house, because he'll be your father technically, don't you know that?"

"You din't even marry him!" Miguel's face twisted with derision. "You din't even get a divorce!"

"That doesn't matter. What matters is the heart, how a person feels. I think Nelo will be a much better father than your own real father. He's proven to be a better man by far."

"I'm happy f' you," Miguel said, "but I ain't lookin' f' no father."

"You should be happy. Don't you see that this is our opportunity to do the family over? To really have a family this time, not what we had before."

"I said I'm happy f' you already."

"Why must you be so contemptuous? Why can't you answer me in Spanish?"

Miguel exhaled, leaning back in his chair like a kid about to be lectured.

"You walk in here and you expect to be welcomed with open arms. As if you have so much to offer us! All you want to do is shoot everything down. Don't we deserve a chance? If you plan to come here and live your life like some adult, forget it." She was on a roll now, steam engine cranking out power, eyes blazing as she stood to hurl words at him from a greater height. "You're sixteen and a half years old! I don't care what kind of life you've been living out there. I'm not blind, I know what kids do these days. But if you come to stay here, play time is over. You're going back to school, you're going to live the life of a regular sixteen-year-old kid! Because that's what you are! I don't know who told you you could live your life like an adult! That will have to change here. We demand respect, and if you can't give us that, then I guess what I'm saying is that you can't live here. I got rid of your father. I don't expect him to come back in a photocopy version. That part of my life is over, over, over."

He stared at her, contempt in his eyes.

"I'm not my father," he said in a calm steady voice, hands buried deep in his Marine coat pockets. "I'm not even you." And a small grin appeared because nothing that she said really mattered to him. She was outside of him. All that he cared about was whether he could stay there or not. If he couldn't, he'd leave, just like he'd done once before when staying home was no longer safe. He had nothing to lose. All he needed was a little time, a week or two, maybe a month if he could bear it. Then he could poof. Amelia could help him find a place. He sighed, trying to keep it all in perspective. Staying at his mother's would be the easiest and cheapest way. He could blow it all if he kept acting contemptuous, so he shrugged and rubbed his eyes as if he were sleepy.

"I'll be quiet as a mouse," he said. "I mean, don'chu think I thought about all this shit? Would I even be here askin' you if I din't think I could make some changes? You keep talkin' about me givin' you an' Nelo a break. Why don'chu gimme one?"

She sighed, crossing her arms and leaning against the sink. Her face softened.

"You're not like your father at all," she said. She nodded. "You're right."

"I mean, I think it'll be hard f' everybody. But I'm willing to give it a shot."

"Bien. Will you talk to Nelo?"

"Yes. I mean, si."

She laughed at that, came closer, caressed his hair in a sloppy way as if scared of getting too mushy. He got up and then she seemed dainty, standing by the window with the gleaming blinds.

"It will be good to be a family again." She hugged him, for a long moment clinging to him silently. Then something girlish came back, and she led him into "his" room again, home to some boxes and an old bureau that sat by the windows. It was pretty nice, almost as large as his old room, and it had a locking door. He could almost imagine the domestic scene if he moved in. Catarina would be in the kitchen cooking, Nelo would sit in front of the TV with his paper, while Miguel would be in his room with the door, locked, stereo blaring. Right by the open window, sucking smoke from a bong.

"So when do you think you'll be moving in?" she asked as they stood in the cool hallway.

"I don't know," he shrugged. "Soon."

"You'll talk to Nelo?"

"Sure."

"Bien." She offered her cheek and Miguel planted a kiss on it. "Hasta ahorita." And he zoomed down the stairs, an old Latin saying ringing in his head: "De Guatemala a Guatepeor"—roughly, "from the frying pan into the fire." Miguel was going back to everyone that hadn't wanted him, every place that had set him loose. In his car now, he drove "home" to prepare to storm Cristalena's beaches.

16

He would need fresh threads for this. He was clean-shaven, bathed; his hair was moussed. It took a long time to pick out the right combination, but when he felt he had it, he went over and modeled the look for Firebug, who was lying on the floor in his room watching his new TV. Firebug looked at him, then got up and threw himself against the wall, legs spread out, hands up high.

"What the fuck?" Miguel asked.

"You look like one a' thum narcs, man."

"Ah come on. Bullshit. I look fresh."

"You gonna frisk me now, or do I gotta wait 'til we get to the station house?"

"Ha ha. Fuck you."

Man, he even put on a tie, a long black skinny one. He felt like he was going to an interview. He jumped into his Baby, cradling the bear in its box, which sat beside him all the way. He was trying to remember her schedule. She worked three days a week from three-thirty to six-thirty, and alternate Saturdays. What day was this? Was she working? He parked on Westchester. He walked from there, up barren gray streets, streetlamps painting the sidewalks a murky bronze. His hands were cold from carrying the box. He stood outside the boutique, peered in and saw her in a big black coat talking with the cashier. He shuddered. It was the same kind of shudder he got whenever people were shooting at his car. He leaned against a parked car and waited, out of sight of the storefront so he couldn't be spotted. An ambush, he thought to himself, grinning. He was trying to calm himself but he was tense enough just trying to keep from lighting a cigarette. The sky turned dark when she came out. He had been staring up at the deep purple blanket with tiny freckles of stars and wisps of cloud hovering. Then it all went black.

The moment he saw her he knew he could never walk by her and not say hello, that he could never walk past her or pretend he didn't know her. It was beyond him why, but they had shared something, a kind of secret. He couldn't face seeing her and not saying something. She was almost a whole world to him, a country that had offered asylum.

When she saw him, Miguel spotted the flash of denial, as if she were trying to wish him away with her eyes. She looked away from him in that very split second, as if she would walk right past him and leave him there. Could she do that, walk right by as if he were some stranger? Because he couldn't do that to her.

She did it to him.

She walked, then stopped, but she didn't turn. Then she kept walking a little faster as if more determined. Something in him buckled. He stood rooted to the spot. Then he heard Amelia's words: "Sometimes a girl has to be chased."

His legs were like lead at first, then he ran to her, saw her long hair coming closer, twitching, twirling shiny streams wriggling, her bright red wool cap jiggling as she outpaced him.

"Cristalena," he said, gasping. "Yo, wait up."

She kept walking. He caught up to her at the corner. She crossed her arms and didn't look at him. He stood beside her, holding the box, looking at her as if she was crazy. Cars sped and their lights spun crazy flashes all around them. Suddenly she was off, all engines GO, her hair quivering like liquid. HOH SHIT, THE BITCH WAS RUNNING! She was trying to catch the bus that was greedily gobbling up passengers at an angle across the street. He ran too, every inch of his body reminding him he had just had the shit kicked out of him; but the anger racing through him gave him speed. He overtook her and spun around to face her. She sidestepped him, her shoulder jutting out like she would ram him aside. He body-checked her like a good hockey player. She recoiled and let out a funny squeak sound. Her eyes sizzled viciously when her bus hissed a quick goodbye.

"Fuck! I missed my bus." She looked past him with a weary anguish.

"Damn man, you crushed my goddamn box . . ." You goddamn bitch, you fucken dirty cunt, who you think you are runnin' off like that? But all that came out was an astonished "Hey man, whass with you?"

She didn't answer him. She walked over to the bus stop and leaned against the bus-shelter glass. She was looking up at the sky. "I don't believe you," she said.

"You don't believe me? Thass funny." He tried to keep his voice calm. "I thought we were gonna run the fucken marathon."

"I don't wanna talk to you."

"Fine. Don't. I'll do the talkin'. Can I drop you? My car is over there." He gestured down Westchester.

He had wrapped the damned box with the shiny silver paper and a white ribbon with a bow. And the bitch, she just banged into it, scrunched it like that. A corner of it was all crinkled, and a piece was torn off.

"No, thank you."

"Please, Lena."

"No."

"Man, how can you be so cold? I really din't mean that much after all, did I?"

"You lied!"

"But I din't mean to," he said wearily, wanting to touch her. She flinched. "Look, I'll drive you. We gotta talk. An' if you never wanna see me again, fine. But we gotta talk."

She didn't say anything, stepping out to the curb to see if a bus was coming. There was no bus.

"Where's your car?"

He led her to it, thinking that he had scored his first victory, but he was depressed. He knew that she was in control. Her face looked so cold and distant that it scared him, scared him even more to think that she mattered so much to him that he was going to do this, go down on his knees. He had never needed a woman like this before, and when he looked at her face, he had to wonder if she really needed him at all. Shit. Maybe he had seen too much in her. Maybe Amelia was right after all, and he had already failed Cristalena's KNIGHT IN SHINING ARMOR test.

He unlocked her door first. By the time he came around the car she was already sitting there like the jury. He put the box between them and felt a sudden sadness that all the warmth between them had been yanked away. He stared at the wheel. She looked straight ahead, her hands in her lap. She was waiting. A speeding subway train startled them as it roared out of its tunnel like a metal earthworm. It woke her out of her trance.

"Well? You gonna drive?"

The voice chilled him. "We should talk some first."

"You said you'd drive me."

"I will. But how we gonna talk an' drive? Be reasonable. Jesus."

"Maybe I should just take the bus."

"What, you gonna run out on me again?"

Her eyes were big and round as she slowly spit out every word.

"Maybe I don't wanna hear wha'chu got to say."

"The girl never wants t' listen."

"Get the expert."

"Yuh makin' me a expert right now."

"Well wha'chu wanna fucken say?"

He stared at her. She had her arms crossed, coat wrapped tightly shut, her eyes boring holes through the windshield. He took too long staring at her.

"Wha'chu wanna say!" she snapped.

"Well, just I love you. Just I'm sorry about how it went down. I didn't mean t' hurt'chu. I shoulda been stronga an' tol'ju earlier."

She sighed and closed her eyes. "An' how do I know you ain't just lying to me again?"

"Well, because I got'chu this here bear an' he's sittin' between us an' I wun't lie in fronta him because I wanted, see"—he leaned a little closer as he spoke—"I wanted t' get'chu this bear so you could always hold 'im an' think good things about me. An' so I cun't lie in fronta him an' to you because then you'll hate me like now an' I can't take this, this is really hard, I ain't never been in nothin' like this, at least not somebody I cared enough to say all this shit to but . . . the bear, you know, if you don't take him then fuck, he'll be all I have left about us if you go." He paused because her face softened a little, even though she still wasn't looking at him. "That, an' the cross you gave me."

The words tumbled out with such stumbling sincerity that she looked at him, the ice in her eyes melting. He saw some warmth in there for him, but it was more like pity. He grasped at it.

"Please," he said as he passed the box to her. "Take it, Lena. Please. At least open him."

She pulled at the ribbon. "Nice ribbon," she said, her eyes darting around.

"You know, the guy himself is a little insecure."

She squinted at him. "Who?"

"The bear, the bear! I had a pizza with him. We sat and talked about it. An' you know, after I told him all the scoop, he really din't think you'd keep him."

She smiled politely but didn't say anything, her hands ripping at the paper. The bear's furry head showed. She pulled him out slowly as Miguel grabbed the box and tossed it into the back seat. It was a fat bear, arms open to her. She caressed its face a little, made it hop a little on her lap. She let out a sudden giggle that startled him.

"What?"

She looked at the bear and brought its nose up to her nose. Then she was trembling, her shoulders shaking as she began to cry. With a choked sob she brought the bear closer until she had buried her face in it. He wanted to touch her, one hand hovering close to her hair, until he was softly petting her shoulder.

"I'm sorry," he said, shaking his head. "I'm sorry I'm sorry I'm sorry. But I still love you."

She fell against him, still clutching the bear, letting him hold her and caress her hair.

"I can't love you," she said. "I can't."

"Why?"

"Because I don't like you as a person anymore. You can't be a person and do that. You can't. It's impossible."

"But I do that an' I am a person. I've always been a person."

"No," she said, trying to stop crying, her breaths coming in choppy spurts.

"Yes. Lena, I was a runner. I run around town makin' deliveries."

"Shut up. You ain't no postman. Stop tryin'na play it down." Her voice was mournful, not angry. "I thought'chu came to rescue me. An' now I see the kinda person you are."

"Me? Rescue you? Jeez." He swept his hair back with a hand. "Thass real funny, you know? 'Cause here I was thinkin' you were gonna rescue me."

She leaned back into the seat, her eyes shimmering like the surface of a crystal clear pond.

"You can say I'm not a person, but I know I'm a person. I don't think maybe I ever got a good shot, man. But'chu know? When I looked around me an' saw what this crazy place was doin' to people, it hurt me. I cun't always see it, Lena. I think you helped me. You don't even know. At first I sorta suspected it, like I was blind to everythin' around me. But somethin' bugged me about it, all the time. I started thinkin' like there was somethin' better than all this shit. I don't know, maybe it was the books or TV. I used to look at it an' I never felt like any of it was mine, you know, like all those smilin' faces an' lawyers on TV an' shit? An' people livin' in big houses on pretty blocks an' tree-lined streets. I din't belong to it, or anythin', I was just floatin'. An' then you came along an' then I felt like there was somethin' better f' me, maybe even somethin' waitin' out there f' me, all this time. Then I started to see that I am a person, I got dreams an' hopes. I can't say right off that I know where I'm goin', but I know where I don't wanna be, where I don't wanna end up. I saw enough of that. Thass why I quit. I was startin' to feel like somethin' was wrong with it all, but then when I met'chu, it really made sense. Then I knew I hadda stop lookin' f' the easy way out. 'Cause it's easy to let yuhself go, easy to break the rules. Harder to try an' make somethin' of yuhself." He stroked the steering wheel, words piling up. Now that he could tell her, he wanted to let it all spill out.

"I quit. You don't have to believe me, 'cause I really feel like I din't do it f' you. I hadda think a while about it, but I realized that I'm doin' if f' myself, 'cause yes, I'm a person. I wanna grow into one real bad."

He took one of her chilly hands from out of her lap and pressed it between his. "I think, I don't know, like I went crazy, like somethin' happened, like I hit my head on a rock. But since I met'chu I feel like I can't make it without'chu. I wan'chu around all the time." He said it with a childish wonder that touched her. A sob came to her throat like a cough.

"Me too," she said. "I'm fightin' it."

"Don't, man. Come on. Don't be like that."

She interlaced fingers with him. His face changed color for a second with a mixture of relief and the urge to cry.

"Me too," he said, grinning and squeezing her fingers. "I'm fightin' it."

"Don't man," she said. "Come on. Don't be like that."

"Can I kiss you now?"

She paused, her lips trembling. "Yes."

When he kissed her there was a long, shared sigh. They both trembled; it was heaven, reacquaintance, joyful return to a trusted flavor. Her hand in his, warm but frightened; tentatively interlacing fingers. Her eyes looked at him as if checking to see if he was still there, if the devotion was still in his eyes, as if she expected him to disappear or change shape at any moment.

He drove her up to Fordham Road. They stopped off at a phone so she could call Rosa. She returned to the car, shaking her head.

"Rosa says I'm crazy," she told him, slamming the door shut.

"How come?"

"She's not happy I'm seeing you now."

"An' why's that?"

Cristalena shrugged. "I don't know, I guess it was my telling her you're a junkie."

He slowed to a stop at a red light and stared at her, his foot pumping the brake. "Thass wha'chu think I am?"

She looked embarrassed, tossing off her wool cap and mussing her hair as if trying to hide under it. "No," she said in a small voice. "I was just mad."

They went to the Italian restaurant and had lasagna. In the candlelight Miguel told her all about Firebug and Spider and the cops and the kind of work he did. He cut a lot of corners, but even with editing, it affected her. She stopped eating.

"Whassup?" He felt happy to finally be able to come clean about it, but he felt her withdraw. He held her hand and squeezed it because he felt like he was losing her.

"Nothing." She seemed distracted, eyes glassy with candlelight. "I'm just scared." She gave him a helpless look but there was love glowing in her eyes. It warmed him.

"Maybe I should leave you," she said like a woman trying on coats in a department store. "That way, if you get killed, I won't know about it."

"But won'chu miss me?"

She looked at the stuffed bear, which sat in its own chair beside them. Miguel had tied a napkin around its neck like a bib.

"I have Emilio now," she said.

"Emilio?"

"Yeah, his name is Emilio. I'm gonna get him a bandanna so he can be an Emilio, tie it around his head." There was a funny sparkle in her eyes, the first sign that her goofy sense of humor was slowly coming back. She suddenly grabbed a napkin and thrust it into the candle flame. "Hey hey, guess who this is, guess who I am." She took the flaming napkin and brought it close to her face like she would kiss it. Miguel laughed so hard that bits of food flew out of his mouth.

It was like that from then on. There'd be some serious talk, like when they were in the car snuggling and waiting for the heater to kick in, and he told her, "Please don't ever run away from me. I want we should always talk. We should be able to talk. It hurt me to see you go like that."

"I'm jus' a little kid," she said back quietly. "I was freaked out. Too much at once. I wasn't thinking of you. I guess I just gotta grow up."

Then they'd be kissing softly, and the car got hotter; she started to emit tiny squeals. They bought yogurt cones, even though it was cold. She pressed hers against one of his cheeks.

"What the fuck?"

She laughed and liked how he looked so much that she stamped his other cheek.

He wiped it off. "Cut tha' shit out!" He socked her in the face with his a little too hard, then felt guilty and started to lick it off her face. There was more kissing; the cones melted all over sticky hands and faces. He ran into a fast-food joint and swiped some little handy wipes that made them smell all lemony.

In one of those little stores run by Asians, full of earrings watches glow-in-the-dark Virgin Marys Chinese slippers whales that spout water and soldiers that crawl and shoot, Cristalena picked out a pair of earrings that dangled down in long pretty strips of cheap emerald stones. He got them for her along with a black bandanna for Emilio.

They saw the Spanish movie *Camila*. It seemed to tell them that love was dangerous. They clutched each other and fed each other popcorn in the half-empty theater where there was no one to complain when she straddled him with her legs and began giving him long fiery kisses that made him forget about fake petunias and psycho cops and Spider. He pulled her shoes and socks off. The soles of her feet were feathery soft. He had never felt anything like them. The socks were short lacy things. He held them up to look; they were like something made for a little doll. "How the fuck you get these on?" While they smooched, Emilio sat in his seat, locking dope in his bandanna, holding the popcorn.

Her mouth was salty, her eyes sleepy as she leaned against him. "So," she said, "would'ju say we made up okay?"

"Yeah, I would."

"Good. So you givin' me my present?" And she ground her pelvis into his hard-on like she would pare it down.

"Uhhh . . ."

"You know what I want, right?"

"You asked for it, you got it."

She kissed him deep and long. The reward.

"Can we go to your place?"

Miguel cringed visibly. "You wanna go there? I don't think thass a good idea."

"Why?"

" 'Cause thass a parta my life I wanna put behind me."

"Then we can kiss it goodbye."

He gave up because of her intense look, the one that told him maybe she'd start doubting him again.

In the car she got pensive. "Do you have a piece?"

For a moment he looked at her as if he was sitting there with one of those crack tramps.

"Nah."

"I thought all you drug dealers had guns."

"I'm not a drug dealer. I'm a runner."

"I don't see the difference."

"Whass with you now? I thought'chu were over this."

"I don't know. It just looks like you got off so easy."

He zoomed down Southern Boulevard, his voice rising. "How can you say that? With me crackin' up an' you runnin' off like you did, I don't know, man, you got off pretty easy yuhself."

"Excuse me?"

"Uch don't say it like that, you remind me of those fucken guidance counselors at school. They were always sayin' that shit. I mean, din'chu apologize before? Din't I? Din't we both come clean? Maybe you don't know it, but'chu a lot more like me."

"Not even close," she said, her eyes alarmed. "You act like I lead some double life."

"You gonna tell me you don't lie to yuh parents an' use yuh cousin like a front so you can go an' do wha'chu want? Tell me you ain't livin' a double life!"

"Don't yell at me."

"I'm not yellin'! But why you wanna make me out t' be some criminal an' then act like yuh so pure? You ain't so straight, either."

"Well I don't deal no crack!"

"Yeah, right. You don't. But maybe everybody does a little somethin' thass crooked. I don't know anybody who ain't a little crooked, not even you."

"But'chu know all these crack dealers an' posse boys an' fucking arsonist junkies . . ." Her voice shook, her hands wrestling with each other.

"An' a spoiled brat!" he yelled. "Wha'chu so proud of anyway, huh? Tha'chu fool yuh parents so you can wear some pantyhose? Is that all? That makes you better than me?"

His car tires squealed as he swerved past a bus.

"Don'chu think tha'chu actin' like Little Miss Purity alla time is gonna hurt me? Don'chu even care you might hurt me? Maybe I'm wrong, maybe you don't love me . . ."

He stopped the car. They were a block from her house.

"But I do love you," she said quietly, hands in her lap. She was looking at him with wide-eyed wonder. It was almost like she was scared of him. His anger melted away. He felt like he had molested her.

"Sorry," he said.

"No," she replied, moving Emilio so she could slide closer. "You're right. I'm sorry. I just get all panicky."

He put his arm around her and drew her closer, kissing her hair.

"I'm insecure. Thass the word right there. I just feel so fucken dirty alla time now, filthy dirty an' stinkin'. An' you'll say things an' I know it's not'cha fault, but I can't help feelin' like you always gonna think I'm shit . . ."

She whispered, "I don't think you're shit." Touching his face. It was nice to be touched the way she touched him. She was suddenly in his lap again, kissing and pressing against him, her hair covering him.

"Hey," he said, as if he wasn't able to put it all away, "would'ju have accepted the stuff you know about me if I had tol'ju at our first date? Would'ju have even seen me again?"

She had her arms around his neck and was staring at his lips. She didn't say anything for a moment, her lips moving silently as if she were chewing over a thought. Then she just smirked, shifting position a little so she could be even closer to him.

"I would rather kiss you than answer a question like that."

"How can you say that?" he asked, and then he was muffled by her kisses. His hands slipped under her sweater and blouse to run up her soft, warm back.

"You think I would kiss you like this an' be all over you an' shit if I didn't love you? Can'chu see it? Why do you gotta ask so many questions? Can you tell I wan'chu? You think I do this with anybody else? Okay, fine. Maybe if when I met'chu at first, an' you had told me, maybe yeah, I woulda not wanted to see you. 'Cause I find out everything I can about a guy I like that first date. I ask, I probe. I like the way he smiles." She traced the outline of his mouth. "He's so cute, the way he talks, the way his eyes jiggle around, and the way he makes me laugh. I feel comfortable with him. But what's under all that? Does he just wanna make me? Am I like a person to him? Whass he into? You lied to me, Miguel, an' you must never do that again. It really hurts to get lied to."

"I know. I'm sorry."

"But I gotta be adult about this. 'Cause I know if I had heard that right then an' there, I would've said well too bad, he's cute an' all but he's in some sick shit an' I don't wanna deal with it. I guess I had to be honest an' admit it. I guess you were right not to tell me. Now it's too late. I like you too much. I feel all committed. You lied but I understand why. An' I really wanna keep believin' you. But if you lie to me again . . ."

"Nah, I won't." He kissed her frantically. "I always wanted t' tell you. It always bothered me."

They hugged for a long time, and then she had to go. A passing car had honked and Cristalena jumped, bonking her head against the car top.

"Relax," he had said. "We got tinted windows." But she couldn't stay. She was still scared. It made him feel that maybe she was ashamed of him. There wasn't a reason for him to believe that, but he did. That new word: insecure. Outside she walked away and he could tell she didn't want to turn around and look at him, but she did it, twice, quick little turns. She blew him little kisses, and he felt love and pangs of something that frightened him. Amelia was right about them. They were both too young. Everything was too crazy, too intense. Was it like that with older folks? (Like when you're TWENTY?) Was he ready for all this? It didn't matter, did it? The changes were coming, no matter what he did. Sixteen years old. He was already staring at the lines on his hands. The first change came when he got upstairs and found Firebug rolling under the thick comforter with someone. Hip-hop blaring from his box, Miguel followed the girl-laughter to Firebug's room and peeked in, hoping it wasn't Amelia. When he looked into the room, they both looked up at him, Firebug's head poking out from under the comforter like a delighted baby romping.

"Yomo!" he yelled happily. "My man wif' the frown!"

The girl was dark-skinned with hazel eyes and bleached-blond hair. She was laughing insanely, her eyes fuzzed out, shrugging the comforter off her shoulder as if she wanted Miguel to see her tits.

" 'Ey pana," Firebug called out when Miguel left the door and headed for his own room. "Yo yo! This is my new steady. Huh name is Angela."

Miguel walked back to the door and waved.

"So wha'chu thinka my little wienie roast? Did'ju like it?" Firebug was trying to rise up but the girl was on top of him laughing, struggling to retain a handhold. He toppled her. She rolled off, trying to disentangle herself from the comforter.

"I thought it was efficiently done," Miguel said. "Especially striking was the way you were able to limit your fire to only one side of the building."

Firebug looked up at the ceiling as if searching for the narrator. They both laughed. Firebug came over to him, eyes gleaming with a funny intimacy, the girl on the bed forgotten. "You noticed that. This guy I met, that white guy? He taught me some real shit, bro'. Anyway, that ain't nothin' compared t' this big one. I tol'ju about it, right?"

"Yeah, yeah. Thass this week?"

"Nex' Tuesday." Firebug picked up his bong and took a hit. Smoke poured out of his nose, two blue rivulets. "So you think you be there?"

"Yeah man." Miguel turned to head for his room. Firebug followed him.

"So hey, you feel like gettin' a piece, man? We can play fuck Olympics. See who's louder, like before."

Miguel stood there by the car seat, thinking about Amelia. It was true, she was through with the place, with Firebug, maybe even crack. She wouldn't be showing her face in this dump anymore. Why was he still there? He suddenly felt a surge of pride, as if his baby sister had graduated or something.

"We'll see," Miguel said doubtfully. He was unable to shake him. "The night is still young." He grinned and headed for his room. He was almost there when he heard Firebug's bare feet stampeding after him. "Here," Firebug said, handing him the bong, "this'll get'cha inna mood."

Miguel took the bong but looked at him as if he doubted it would work. He stood there waiting for Miguel to light up.

"So thass yuh new steady?" Miguel whispered. "I mean, really?"

Firebug shrugged. "Maybe not. You know, I'm thinkin' this last relationship taught me a lot about stuff. Now maybe I jus' wanna hang loose. Why get tied down? So I guess maybe I shunta used that word."

"You mean 'steady'?"

"Yeah. Yomo, you got a steady now, right? That girl you always with."

Miguel stared at him. How did he know that?

"I mean the one that always calls." Firebug corrected himself hurriedly.

"I don't know wha'chu mean," Miguel said.

"Ahh, come on man, you gonna be like that wif' me?"

Miguel walked away from him with the bong. There was no way he could trust Firebug anymore. He saw Spider behind it. Firebug gave up and went back to his room.

Miguel shut his door. He turned on his stereo to drown out the sounds from Firebug's room. Motley Crue. He remembered the time Amelia had come in and gone through his records; he didn't have that many, but they were all rock.

"How'dju get into this stuff?" she had asked. "I don't know many Latino dudes into metal."

He had shrugged, watching her squatting there in nothing but a huge T-shirt. "I don't know. When I was little my cousin used to come over to my house. He was into the Beatles an' shit. He lent me some records. An' I got into guitars. I like guitars, real loud. The louder the better." He remembered playing Motley Crue for her, and getting mad when she collapsed to the floor in a laughing fit.

"You got no taste," he snapped, offended.

"Of course I don't. I'm with Firebug, remember?"

He missed her. He knew he liked her, liked her a whole lot. He had never admired a woman before. He missed having her around, even hearing her fuck, and then getting that late-night visit from her after Firebug had fallen into the land of the dead. He felt nostalgic about her, but he was glad she wasn't there, fucking Firebug. Maybe he wouldn't be able to respect her if she was doing that after all that she'd said, after everything he knew about her. It would be like asking her to respect him if he chose to keep working for Spider. After a point, you break with the past. That's that. Otherwise you never change.

. . .

Around midnight, the phone rang. He pounced, knowing Cristalena had mentioned calling him later. She had seemed determined, her brow all knitted up like she had made a big decision. "Yeah?" It was his secret voice, ready to hear secrets. There were traffic sounds.

"Hello?"

"Miguel." Cristalena's voice sounded strange, all fractured.

"Lena, whassup, what happened?"

"Lena," she said, sighing. "I love when you call me that."

"Lena Lena Lena. Tell me whassup."

She sniffled. "It was horrible. Just crying and cursing and then my father wanted to hit me. He's not the hitting kind, Miguel, he was so gone. Miguel, they called me a tramp!"

"But why? What did'ju do?"

"I told them about'chu, Miguel."

"What?"

"I said I told them about'chu."

"But why?"

"Because you were right. Because I decided after wha'chu said that I was gonna face it. No more masquerade. I told them I ain't no Christian, that I'm gonna live my life no matter what they say. My father said he was gonna tie me to the bed like some goat to keep me from falling into sin! That's when I left." Her voice broke. "Miguel, I feel really fucked up."

"Where are you? I'm comin' t' get'chu."

"Corner of Concord on 149th. Miguel, wait! I wanna ask you something."

"Shoot."

"Can I stay with you tonight?"

A whole series of tremors flooded through him, chills and funny whooshings in his ears, as if he had seen a ghost.

"You stay put an' be careful," he said. "I'll be right there."

He threw some clothes on and raced down to find Cristalena standing by the phone booth, clutching her arms as if she were freezing. They fell into each other's arms.

"I didn't think I could do it, Miguel, just stand up to them like I did. I stood up for myself." Her eyes were shining like gemstones. "It's all because of you."

Then she started crying. It was like a water-main break; Miguel had it all over his hands and on his Marine coat. "Damn," he said, running out of tissues. He held her trembling body close as she rocked from sobbing, her baby squeals rupturing his heart.

"Stop, baby please, it's gonna be okay . . ."

"They said I'm a cheap putona!"

"Yuh no putona. Yuh my girl. Come on."

"How can I ever go back there?"

"Shhh. Come on. Less get off this fucken street."

On the dark street there was nothing but creeping shadows and black figures and cars that seemed to move closer only when you weren't looking. A large Buick suddenly tore around a corner and soared down the avenue, its insides dark with bouncing figures that yelled like Indians on the warpath. He pulled her closer, made her really step. He knew that on these streets young kids with guns used people on the sidewalks for target practice.

By the time he got her up the stairs she was a little calmer, her face wet and hushed. She was in no mood to take in the line of junkies on the second floor waiting for their fix. Up on the fourth floor there was hip-hop blaring through an open apartment door while three boys in baseball caps and black coats traded pipes. Miguel looked at her but Cristalena didn't seem to even see it. She was in some kind of shock. He dried her face with his sleeve and pulled her into the apartment. She brought him close and they kissed, her lips salty and warm.

"Miguel," she whispered.

"Lena," he whispered back, and it felt perfect. "We gonna be all right. I mean if we get past this part."

She laughed a little, then leaned against him, her eyes starting to take it all in as he walked her into the apartment. They walked past the silent kitchen and walked through the living room and there was Firebug's door wide open, bursting with frantic flickerings from the TV set. Miguel had wanted to maybe sneak her by but Cristalena was drawn to it because of the music and the lights and the grunting, giggling gasps. They both ended up right by the door, looking in. They saw Angela on top of Firebug; the comforter wasn't covering enough of her. She stopped in mid-thrust and turned to look, her face just as curious as Cristalena's.

"Whoah whoah, who's that girl?" Firebug screamed, his face delirious. His face lit up and Miguel knew it was because he thought Miguel had run out to find "a bitch."

"All right, pana!" Firebug yelled. "Party down! You found a real good one!"

"Firebug," Miguel said, holding up a hand and shaking his head, "this is my girl, Cristalena."

Firebug squinted at the sound of the name. "Ohh, man." He was looking her up and down. "How dee, gorgeous. This is my bitch, Angela."

Angela nodded politely with a little giggle. She shrugged and thrust with her hips, making Firebug laugh. Cristalena sniffled and waved. A very nasal "Hi" was all she managed.

"She's gonna crash," Miguel said, amazed at how well Cristalena seemed to be taking it.

"Join the party, man."

"Naah, no partyin'," Miguel said quickly, yanking Cristalena away by the hand. He brought her into his room and shut the door but the music throbbed in anyway, the floor vibrating. At least they couldn't hear the fucking, although every now and then some kind of victory whoop would resonate. Miguel sighed and grabbed her by the shoulders.

"Are you okay?"

She was looking at him as if he had saved her from something. He had never seen such adoration on a face before, and it was all directed at him. It made him pulse with some kind of electric energy. That's why he kissed her. She hadn't even noticed the room. He had expected her to say something but she couldn't take her eyes off him. Something ignited between them; and he realized why she was there. She hadn't come to talk about what had happened or where she had ended up. She wasn't even going to think about it. He knew it in the way she clutched him, the way her lips pressed against his, the way she pressed him so close he thought his neck would snap. It erased all of Miguel's doubts. She had already decided about everything. For Miguel, the suspense was over. Cristalena was calling his bluff.

They both fell on the mat. She was on top, kissing him, eyes wet with tears. He kept trying to wipe them; she would laugh and shake hair from her face, and it would come tumbling down again in lovely dark swirls. They were holding hands and staring deeply, he was tracing her mouth with his fingers—all that mushy shit that he used to see in movies and think: yeah, right—only now it was really happening and he was completely carried away by the emotion. It was a soul thing, not like fucking anymore, but something closer, more precious, leagues above anything Firebug could ever understand. A corpse, Amelia called him. Now he realized why she had cried, what she was missing from her sex life. It made him feel happy and sad at the same time.

The music from Firebug's room continued pumping. It made her laugh as she sat up to undo her blouse buttons. "You do this to that kind of music?"

"I used to," he said. "You don't like it?" He was just lying there looking at her as if he was dreaming with his eyes open.

She made a face. "I think the music should be mushier. Maybe like classical music or Lionel Ritchie or something."

"Lionel Ritchie?" He grimaced and was about to crack a joke when she peeled off the blouse and stared at him defiantly, as if waiting a long time for this.

"Wow," he said. "Nice bra." It was gold and shimmery. She smiled—silent, catlike, pleased. He slid his hands over her waist, so soft like baby skin. He drew her down for a few soft kisses that turned wild. "Yuh gorgeous," he couldn't help saying, struggling with those damned bra clasps. She laughed, squirmed free, grinding down on him smugly. She pulled on his shirt. He unbuttoned it and then she took over, drawing it off him with relish. It flew across the room like a kite. She pulled off the T-shirt, too. ZOOM. She fell against him, the fresh, cool feel of skin on skin delicious.

He descended into the deep recesses of her neck where it was scented sweetly and so warm. He dropped kisses all the way to the tip of her bra, even gave the lace a lick. She seemed to be dancing on top of him and then that pleated skirt was off, dangling from her hands like a prized pelt, joining his shirt at the other end of the room. Her next kiss was deep and savage and left him breathless. He slipped his hand underneath her black tights.

"Okay big man," she said, sliding a hand down to his crotch. "Time to take these off."

"Nah, you gotta take those pantyhoses off first," he said drunkenly. "We won't be even if I take off my pants."

She was squeezing his cock. "Ahh, come on. You don't wanna leave 'um on."

"Damn."

"Come on," she purred, and the button on his jeans went POP. The zipper slid right down and she had her hand right on him. "Mmmmm," she said, kissing him. "It's like a joystick."

"Uggg ahhh you gonna break it you keep doin' like that."

She laughed and kept on.

"This has to come off," he said, lowering the bra straps. She reached back, popping the bra right off with an arrogant smirk. And there they were. Not too big, not too small, just right.

"Damn, yuh gorgeous," he whispered reverently, sitting up so he could press his face into her breasts. She stroked his hair and then pulled on it as his tongue teased and nibbled at her nipples.

"That did it," she said, jumping back and pulling the pants right off him. She looked at him lying there at her feet, her eyes ravenous and tender. She leaned against the bureau to peel off her tights. Then she stood there in her blue lace panties, playing with the waistband. "Should I? Wha'chu think?"

Miguel let out a loud pleading sound like a dog begging for scraps. She laughed, dancing a little to the booming music.

"Oh man," he said, watching her hips sway. "Don't do this t' me."

"Take it off then."

He sat up and stripped off his underwear and then he stood up to come over to where she was and he could see the utter amazement on her face, the way she looked at him: his rippled flat stomach muscles, his muscular arms, his chest hairless and boyish and shaped like a Greek statue she might've seen in a textbook. She touched him slowly, amazed at how soft he was, something boyish and tender and hard and manlike all at once. He could see it on her face, and it affected him. It was beyond the high of a good joint. It was beyond any woman touching him, even Amelia, whose raw emotion had taught him what good sex was. Cristalena's fingertips explored him softly. No matter how she touched him, her hands always slid down to his cock.

"Wow," she whispered, touching, squeezing. "It's so hard."

He picked her up, light as a feather, her hair spilling everywhere as he kissed her. In one motion he put her down on the mat and pulled off her panties. She twisted her waist and lifted her legs and when he touched her pussy she sucked in air, her entire body contracting, her hair shivering all over her in curly ripples.

He paused to look at her. "Damn. I love you, Lena."

"I love you, too, Miguel." They rolled over and over in a hug, her eyes stoned and delirious, her voice suddenly husky with passion. "So you gonna fuck me or talk me t' death?"

"Jesus."

"Hey, I know what I want." She had his cock again. She rolled over on top of him pressing her lips against his, her tongue teasing, her hand rocking him. And she put him inside and their bodies gasped flexed twisted, joined. The flood of warmth and pleasure flowing through them seemed to blot out everything except for the music from the next room, which got louder and louder. Firebug's box was blaring:

> Pussy me up
> every day every night
> pussy me up
> jungle fever nice and tight
> pussy me up . . .

17

He watched Cristalena sleep beside him, her mouth curled with contentment against his chest. He couldn't resist touching her. He hadn't known that he could be so tender. The streets hadn't taken that away from him.

They lay there all night, floating, whispering, half dozing in the musky warmth. He was still inside her. She liked to keep him there, and when he slipped out with a wet slap, they laughed. The soft touching and smooching stirred him back to life. He tried going slow but she liked it fast, so he lay back and let her ride him with her hair swinging down over his face in ticklish squiggles. She trembled and twitched and collapsed against him. He loved to make her come. He was trying to keep track of all the times she had come but she told him that was silly. He knew it wasn't all about that, but when she came, he felt it deep inside, crashing waves of joy that made him feel like he was really giving something of himself to her. When she was grasping and reaching he pushed for her. It was like a team event, both of them together, both of them winning.

"You're the sweetest lover in the world," she whispered breathlessly into his ear with a string of kisses attached. "I can't believe how this feels."

"Me either. Whatta crazy dope bitch."

This made her laugh. He could feel her laughter inside. She dismounted and said it was his turn. She damn near tore his cock off; when he came, he exploded eight different ways and yelled like he was being murdered. The music from Firebug's room stopped. Cristalena collapsed in a mad giggling fit.

Night. Warmth. Arms and legs intertwined. Soft words. Fingers tracing fingers.

"Does it bother you I'm not a virgin?" she asked.

"Nope."

"I only had one guy before you."

"Was that Raul?"

They burst into laughter.

Hugging close under a dark warm tent of comforter. Deep kissing. Hands clasped. Not even aware of minutes or hours, or Spider or crack vials. Cristalena asked him about all of it. Miguel felt his soul grow lighter as he let it all flow out of him. It was only when she got real quiet that he realized he might've said too much at once about women and parties. He drew her close.

"Listen," he said. "I hadda lotta women an' shit but not one even comes close to you, Lena. You put 'um all away. This ain't like nothin' I ever felt. You gotta be the sweetest lover in the world."

She had his cock in her hand again, just looking at him and smiling. "Yes," she said, as he got harder. Again and again they dove into each other. The sun lit up the windows shyly, as if afraid to interrupt.

"Are you gonna be in trouble?" he asked softly.

"No. It's beautiful."

"I don't wan'chu to get in trouble." He was thinking of her parents. She snuggled against him.

"I don't care what happens," she replied dreamily.

Sunlight filled the room. They were fitted together like spoons. Miguel had a glazed, faraway look on his face.

"Miguel?" Cristalena pressed her chin into his neck, making him laugh. He cradled her face and thought about how nothing could ever be the same again. Could he be just another ordinary kid after all this? He thought about Careta and how the guy had managed to pull it off, a boy who lived like a man, by his own rules.

"If I could pull it off," he said, pulling her close, "would'ju live with me?"

She smiled slowly, still looking stoned. "Ohhh Miguel, I would love to, but I don't think we got the money to—"

"Shh. Don't worry about that. I got me about eight thousand dollars." He grinned, mugged for her. "Don't look like that. I'm serious. I got it all saved up." In the fake petunias, outside. He wanted to show her but it felt too good to get up. "I'm thinkin' we can use the money t' get started, get a place an' hold us over 'til we can start workin'."

"But we'll never make enough to support ourselves, Miguel. I gotta finish school an' I make shit at the boutique. We're both way under age. How we gonna get good jobs?"

"We got eight thousand dollars! We can live off that for a while."

"I know. But you're gonna quit the business, right? So we won't have that kinda money comin' in no more, right?"

He nodded reluctantly, biting on his thumb pensively.

"Right?"

"Yeah, right."

"So the money will only go so far. If we get a place, we gotta pay maybe three months' rent, security. Let's say we find a place for four hundred dollars a month. That's twelve hundred right there. Then we need furniture. You got furniture? You wanna live like this?"

Ohh, man. Miguel shook his head. She was just getting started. She was so rational. Goddamn.

"We should jus' take the risk," he said.

"I don't think so."

"But thass the way I live my life, Cristalena." There was something coarse in their voices, as if they were entering a new phase full of adult tension and fear. "I don't really wanna wait t' be with you."

She smiled sweetly and touched his chin but there was something in her face that made him realize that she was way older than him in spirit, that she had a powerful mind that was used to organizing life into well-behaved clusters. She wasn't some pretty little ditz. She made him feel young and stupid and maybe a little crazy. He was used to just jumping in and not thinking about what came next; she was cautious, her every move part of a well-thought-out plan.

"I take risks, too," she said in a patient voice that somehow implored him. "This thing with my parents? What was that? I did it. It was an impulse, sure, a crazy one, but I did it because after you said all that shit about me leading a double life, I got to see tha'chu were right and that I hadda stop it. I took a chance. Hey, I know they're mad at me, but I know my parents. They'll still put up with me, no matter how sinful they think I am. I'm ready for whatever happens. If I knew they were gonna throw me out, then, Miguel, I would tell you to find us a place. But it isn't like that, Miguel. I can stay with them. I don't want to, but I can. It's the cheapest way for us, don'chu see? It might get hard for me, but this is the only way I can teach 'um I'm gonna live my life. My staying all night like this should show 'um."

Miguel felt a funny pang inside as though her staying with him had nothing to do with him, was only meant to get back at her parents. She sensed his thoughts and softly kissed him.

"I wanna live with you, too," she whispered, as if she would cry. "I just don't think we can do it."

"We can do it," he said.

They slept, and when they woke again in the strong bright sunlight, Cristalena pinched him. Hard. He sat up.

"What the fuck?"

"Just checkin' to' see if I was dreamin'."

"Why the fuck don'chu pinch yuhself?"

She grinned. "I gotta put my mark on you. You're my man now. You belong to me. I gotta brand you like they do cattle."

He whapped her on the ass, then he chomped down on one of her buns. She squirmed and let out a scream.

"There," he said, sitting up proudly. "Now you got my brand on yuh ass."

The phone rang.

They both looked at each other like they were wanted criminals. It rang four times before Miguel picked it up.

It was Spider. His voice sounded tired and hoarse, and maybe even a little broken. "Don't hang up. It's me, Spider."

"Spider," Miguel said, looking at Cristalena.

"Yeah. Listen, are you okay? You sound funny."

"Nah. I mean yeah, I'm okay."

There was an uneasy pause. "So. You been gettin' yuh rest?"

"Um . . . yeah."

"Good. Good. Look I jus' wanted to tell you somethin'."

Miguel was puzzled by Spider's voice. Where was he coming from now? Miguel felt suspicious but at the same time he felt something inside of him melt a little.

"But I'm only gonna say it once, so you gotta listen an' catch it the first time. I ain't inta doin' this shit, but sometimes you gotta. You gotta do things sometimes that are more important than business. Anyway, I been under alotta pressure lately an' I know I ain't been myself. But ah . . . so have you had time to think about things?"

Miguel tensed up. "Spider, I—"

"Nah I ain't sayin' you should tell me yuh decision yet. I jus' am like, you know, askin' . . . There's all this shit happened an' you know the story, it jus' goes on . . . but nah man, maybe we meet in a coupla days, okay? So we can talk?"

Miguel didn't know what to say. Cristalena came over and lay against his chest.

"Anyway I jus' wanted t' say I'm sorry. I jus' got crazy. Things got outta control. But I'm gonna keep it togetha. 'Sides, I really wan'chu t' write my life story."

Miguel fought the smile. "I was gonna write it anyway."

There was an awkward pause.

"Well. Get'cha rest. I'll give you a call in a couple days."

"Okay."

"Catch you later."

Miguel hung up and sat there staring into space, with Cristalena lying against him. His mind was all screwed up. It would've been better if Spider had called and screamed at him and threatened him. That, he could've dealt with. It would've been sign of Spider's descent, of his cold unfeeling selfishness. Instead he sounded like the old Spider, a little too frail, a little too human.

"Miguel?"

He wasn't even conscious of her for a second as she pumped his hand.

"Miguel? What's wrong?" She gently pulled his face closer and stared into his eyes as if searching for the answer.

"Gah you know, you so pretty alla time."

"Miguel." She stroked his face.

"That was Spider," he said. "He sounded crazy strange. Like all sad an' hurt. I thought he woulda screamed at me o' somethin', but instead he was all quiet. Like maybe he had thought about things."

Cristalena's eyes narrowed. "Maybe it's a trick."

Miguel didn't seem to hear her. "He seemed like the old Spider, like when we used to hang . . . you know, he's really a much deeper person than most."

Cristalena bit her lip. It made Miguel stop talking. Up to now they had been locked away in his room as if it were their whole world, and nothing existed outside of it, nothing else to keep them apart. The world had intruded. She had never heard him talk nicely about Spider. Now she saw Miguel's eyes light up with an emotional nostalgia that scared her.

"Are you still gonna quit?" Her voice was small, almost as if she didn't want to be heard asking. He took her hands and squeezed them and sighed.

"Yeah, sure." He drew her to him. "It's just I can't believe it, that maybe the old Spider is back, that maybe he'll be understanding about all this."

She drew him close, clinging desperately. The deep kisses she gave him erased Spider. They fell into bed, and then he was writhing under her twitching hair. She came again, her body wracked with spasms, her nails tearing into his arms. She started to cry, hugging him tightly.

"Ahh man why you cryin'?"

"Ohhh gah I love you so much Miguel . . ."

"Yeah me too but why you blubberin'?"

"Ohh gah I love you . . ."

"Yuh gettin' my neck all wet, yuch . . ."

He showed her the fake petunias, tearing open the back so he could give her half the money. He wanted her to take it home and stash it. She refused at first, but he made her see that she was the only person in the world he trusted. "It's our future money," he said, "for us to get started with." This made her cry a little, but there was a new strength in her eyes when she took the envelope. "You can count on me," she told him.

They bathed together in the tiny tub. Firebug and his new woman had fled and they had the place all to themselves. Miguel joked and felt free of guilt, no longer having to hold anything back from her; but Cristalena seemed real pensive. It started to bother him. He kept blowing foamy soap bubbles at her.

"So whassup?" he finally asked.

"We'll need jobs," she said. "Great to talk about our future life, but we need jobs, Miguel, real jobs."

"I know." He sponged her back, sighing. "You gotta stop bringin' this stuff up, Lena. I mean, I know all that shit. I'm tryin'na do my best. I can only go piece by piece. At least we got this money. It's not a whole fucken life, but it's a start, right?"

"What a way to start," she mumbled.

He dropped the sponge into the water. She turned quickly to look at him, leaning against his chest.

"I'm sorry," she said. "I'm just scared."

He wanted to say, "Me too." Instead he hugged her. He had to be strong enough for both of them.

She cut school that day. They got dressed and watched Firebug's TV and went over to a pizzeria and sat around in the cold drizzle at St. Mary's Park, watching little kids in fat bulky coats dive down slides and grapple with monkey bars.

"You really gonna quit?" she asked him, her mittened hand squeezing his.

"Yeah. I got it all planned. There's no turnin' back now." But his voice sounded reluctant.

18

After he dropped Cristalena off at Butterfly's he went to work. It felt like a drastic step, but he felt desperate. He had to start taking steps. It was important to show Cristalena. It was important to show himself.

Was he really breaking with that whole world? Because if he was, it meant saying goodbye to Firebug. He would have to make a reality out of all those visions of leaving. He was setting it all up even as crackheads nodded to him and dealers grinned and fired their fingers at him like pistols and Jimmy chased him for a block to tell him about Little Vicious, his dirty hands gripping Miguel's door.

"I made huh, bro', I made huh! I knew I would get that bitch! Me, I did it! Me!"

"High five," Miguel said, and they slapped a high one, two high ones, right through the window, Jimmy leaping into the air, his sneakers stamping.

"I knew I would make huh!"

"Did'ju have t' shoot anybody?"

"Naah, bro'. I jus' let huh shoot it an' shit. Now she can't get enough!"

Miguel looked at him a moment, the tiny runt with the eyes gleaming and the face all radiant with joy. He had never seen that on Jimmy's battered face. It made Miguel pat him on the head. It was the happiest he had ever seen the brat.

"You cookin', bro'."

Jimmy leaped into the air. "Word up! Yo, there's Manny. I'm gonna go spread the dope. You be aroun' later on Tinton?"

"Nah, I gotta do some shit."

"Yeah? Like what?"

Like have dinner with his mother and Nelo. Why did they pick the same Mexican restaurant they had met in last time? It seemed stupid to him, but maybe Nelo just liked the place. Miguel was dressed twenty times nicer, with black slacks and shiny squeakers and a shiny pompadour and a clean well-pressed white striped shirt, skinny black tie, a four-hundred-dollar gold Rolex. Catarina was very impressed and kept grabbing his hand all through dinner. She was surprised he had set it up so fast.

"You know," she said, everybody digging through the nachos, "I really didn't think you would go through with this."

Miguel, crunching on a mouthful of chips, wiped at the elastic strand of cheese dangling from his lips. "How you mean?"

"I just didn't think you were serious."

He looked at both of them as they sat side to side across from him, fingers interlocked. Nelo looked at peace with the whole world, his head thrown back, a roll of fat hanging over his stiff shirt collar.

"So ahh . . . what kind of work was it you were doing?" Nelo sat up as if getting ready for the real part of the interview. Catarina pressed his hand, a worried look on her face.

"We kind of agreed not to discuss this with him, didn't we?" She lowered her voice as if Miguel wouldn't be able to hear her. Miguel watched them, still crunching on scores of chips.

"Yes, I know," Nelo said carefully, "but I believe it's important if we are to know him as a son. For example, uh, Miguel? Are you in any trouble with the police?"

"Nup." Miguel stuffed another gooey mixture of chips and cheese and beans into his mouth.

"Were you dealing drugs?"

Nelo nailed him with a look that made Miguel laugh. It was like a cop look or a guidance-counselor look or the kind of face the prosecuting attorney wears in the last minutes of a crime drama when he has the criminal on the stand. Miguel shrugged, took a sip of soda, wiped his lips, and looked at Catarina, who seemed nervous.

"I did small-time shit," Miguel said, turning to Nelo. "Some smoke. Stuff like that. Chump shit. I'm sicka that."

Nelo nodded. "So you've been living your own life, right? Doing what you want, when you want."

Miguel stared, crunching slowly. It suddenly occurred to him: What if the bastid says no? A strange warmth crept up to his face. He could smell it coming, the whole big fucking point. It was going to be the same shit from last time . . .

"I mean that you did whatever you wanted without the slightest bit of concern as to how your behavior might affect others. Isn't that true?"

Miguel shoveled some dinky shredded salad stuff into his mouth. "Mmmmf."

"You know that if you came to live with your mother and me, you'd have to follow certain rules."

"Mmmmf."

"You'd have to live your life like a normal sixteen-and-a-half-year-old kid. Your old life will effectively be over, almost as if you had woken up from some fantasy. Now comes the reality. And do you know what that reality is?"

He downed the last three chips with a chunk of cheese.

"The reality is that you'll be part of a family, that you are a child and we are the adults. And that all this life you were living, well, that has to be completely over."

"Mmwango moba."

"Excuse me?"

Miguel swallowed. "I said I want it to be over, thass why I'm here. I'm here t' change everything, t' get normal. Can we get more chips, man?"

The dinner dragged on slowly. Catarina cracked jokes in staccato Spanish about people he didn't know, Nelo's laughter bellowing out so loud that scores of white people turned to look. Catarina pressed for more assurances that everything would be okay with Miguel.

"You know, Nelo—well, I—don't expect you to call him your father right away," she said, grabbing hold of Miguel's hand, "but I do hope you'll be able to respect him as the head of the house."

"Yes. Can we get some more soda?"

He felt proud of himself as he drove home. He felt like maybe he had been a little bit of a whore, but it had to be done. So what if he had to take some shit for a while? The important thing was that he was getting out. He could worry about all those little details later. The fact was that he wasn't planning to stay with Catarina and Nelo for too long. His mind was set on living Careta's kind of life, on his own, and with Cristalena. So maybe Cristalena didn't see it; maybe she was chicken or she just wasn't aware, but Miguel knew they could be on their own, and he was going to do everything with that one goal in mind: to live with her. Period. He hadn't told her about his step tonight; now he could call her and let her in on it. It was, in his mind, the first step toward his liberation.

It was dark by the time he hit Prospect and started scouting around for parking. He was standing behind a double-parked truck when he noticed a couple of beat boys that looked real familiar. They passed his car, then turned and disappeared behind the truck. An alarm went off in his head as it occurred to him what a sitting target he was in his Baby. All these kids out on the street knew his car by sight. Who knows what would've happened if Miguel weren't so tight with Spider? He started to think about it and then it hit him that he and Spider weren't so tight right now. He started to back up the car when someone leaned against his door and tapped against the window.

It was Ritchie, his pale face looking weary, nose pink from cold. Miguel stared at him through the beads of drizzle on the window, wondering what to do. Was he going to get another beating? Ritchie motioned for him to roll down his window.

"Whassup?" Miguel asked.

Ritchie squatted down by the door, chapped lips grim. He sniffed at the air.

"There's this lady over on Avenue St. John, bro'," he said. "Makes the best fucken empanadas you ever ate. You eat tha' shit?"

"Empanadas? Nah. Not much."

"I thought'chu was Boricua, bro'."

"I am, I jus' wasn't into tha' shit too much."

"Well, it just so happens I got'chu one. Willyboy." He gestured over his shoulder. A shorter kid stepped forward, holding a brown bag, a kid who looked just like Ritchie, with the same close-cropped hair under a black cap. He took out an empanada wrapped in a crackling napkin and without a word handed it through the window to Miguel, who almost dropped it. He looked at Ritchie helplessly. "Good, right?" Ritchie munched loudly, and flakes of crust fluttered down from his lips.

Miguel took a bite. The crunchy yellow crust gave way with a crackle. The steaming meat inside almost scalded his tongue. "Damn," he said, holding his mouth open.

Ritchie popped open a tall can of beer and passed it to Miguel, who accepted it gratefully.

"You know," Ritchie said, looking around, "it's pretty cold out here. Like you think maybe I could sit in yuh car?"

Miguel shrugged, wondering what was up. Already he had noticed members of Ritchie's posse appearing around the car in groups of two and three. Two leaned against the hood. Willyboy and another kid stood by a brick wall staring at him with their hands in their pockets, and there were three across the street with the bored, disinterested faces soldiers wear on post. Miguel opened the door for Ritchie and he got in.

"Yeah," he said with a sigh, "I figured'jude have the heata on."

Miguel didn't say anything. He was munching desperately on his empanada.

"Man, lookit'chu eat. Like ain'chu eaten inna while?"

It wasn't hunger that was making him eat. He took a long drink from the beer can and passed it over.

"So whass this about?" Miguel said, voice choked by beer. "Do I maybe got another beatin' comin' up?"

Ritchie stared at him. His eyes were unreadable.

"I heard'ju quittin'," he said.

Miguel stared at him. "Where'dju hear that?"

Ritchie shrugged, passing the beer back. "What, you think I'm new around here o' somethin'? Maan, me an' Spider, we go far back. I don't gotta wait in line t' get no scoop."

"I wun'ta thought that," Miguel said. He was starting to feel nervous; his hands stroked the steering wheel. He was watching the posse kids, who seemed uninterested in what was happening in the car. "Af'ta all, yuh the one that let me in on Spider settin' me up." He looked at Ritchie, who laughed and crumpled against the door.

"Wow man!" he cried. "Thass a snap! It's true about'chu, bro'. You got thum brains. But I don't know if you use 'um too much."

"Oh yeah?" Miguel was taking out a cigarette.

"Yeah. It true you leavin' o' ain't it?"

Miguel shrugged. "Which answer will get me beaten up?"

Ritchie laughed again. There was something so good-natured in the laughter that Miguel started to laugh too, almost as if there was some kind of joke going on. Miguel looked around as if trying to spot a candid camera or something.

" 'Ey man, whass this shit about?" He lit his cigarette. "It's not every day I find'ju an' yuh boys casin' out my car, waitin' f' me."

"Well, I jus' thought I'd bring you an empanada, bro'. I wanna get this straight wit'chu 'cause I heard what I heard, an' then I thought like you were the only person I could talk to right now. Thass pretty straight, right? You got the shit kicked outta you. I din't wanna do it. You screwed up, though. We hadda do somethin'. So I went to Spider an' he said yeah, he thought'chu was all outta hand. Then he started goin' on about'chu, all this shit. An' it occurred to me like hey man, here I am with my posse, doin' this bastid's dirty work. Like he cun't care if some a' our guys got hit that night o' maybe any night. All he cares about is his own ass. I was mad at him. I felt like you was his sweet boy, but once he tol' me all tha' shit, well . . ." He paused, his fingers pulling on the tangle of Christmas lights under the dash. "I just felt like we had somethin' in common."

Miguel puffed on his cigarette, still not getting it.

"So I did it, I kicked yuh ass, right? But my boys, we were real soft on you, bro', you gotta believe that. We didn't break yuh bones, right? We were easy on yuh face 'cause we all felt it was already fucken ugly enough, why ruin you f' life?"

"Thass real funny."

"Well, don't get snotty. Like gimme a cigarette an' shit."

Miguel passed him the pack. He didn't know Ritchie that well. They had met a few times at parties or hung on the street on occasion, shared a few words, but no big laughs. Ritchie was a pale serious kid who only seemed to laugh with a select few; everybody else got that hard look, as if he was constantly reappraising you. His posse was one of Spider's first, one of the earliest groups of kids that he put to work. The posse had changed since then, the older kids had moved on, it seemed, and now Ritchie was surrounded by tiny kids in big black coats with stern, strict faces. They seemed to scowl and scorn everything around them, their eyes full of mockery except for when they looked at Ritchie: him they worshipped and adored. Miguel had always felt uncomfortable around them. He always had the strange sense that they were laughing at him. Now Ritchie was sitting in his car, talking and laughing as though they were old friends. Maybe the beating had brought them together?

"So what is it'chu want, bro'?" Miguel finally asked, but in such a low voice that Ritchie didn't seem to hear him. He rolled down his window and whistled.

"Yo Joyboy!"

A short little black dude appeared by the window, handing Ritchie a beeper and slapping hands with a laugh. Then he walked off across the street, taking the posse with him. The kid had on a green beret with two tiny medals on it and some beads.

"Hey," Miguel said, "what is that kid? Some kinda Guardian Angel?"

Ritchie looked at him. "Nah. He's my second louie."

Miguel watched them walk down Prospect like some shadow army.

"You know," Ritchie said, "I would really like t' go f' a drive. Like away from here? Might not be too cool to be seen wit'chu, know wham sayin'?"

Miguel shook his head, but he turned on the car with a whoosh.

"I mean, I know about'chu. Who knows who else knows about'chu? Who knows what's been said about'chu out here?"

"Well, what have you heard?" Miguel did a U-turn and headed up Southern Boulevard.

"We gotta take this story one step at a time, bro'. You can't rush it. Can't sell this wine before its time. Less jus' say Spider already spread the word about'chu."

"But whass that mean?"

"It means he's gonna cut'chu off, man. It means he's gonna put a fucken stop t' you, bro'. How stupid you gotta be?" Ritchie's voice rose, his eyes smoking. "I mean, you tellin' me you still trust this fuck? Look, man, my advice t' you is get ridda this car. Ain't a posse on the boulevard don't know yuh car. An' once Spider puts out the word, every little fuck with a piece'll be lookin' to' make himself some points by icin' you."

His words landed like a bomb. After the explosion there was just a deathly quiet, the engine throbbing softly. Miguel had parked by an empty lot on St. Anne's Avenue by the park. Rows of torn benches and trees holding up shriveled arms.

"Tell me, bro'," Ritchie went on softly, sinking down into his seat. "You still trust Spider?"

"Nah." Miguel was thinking about the phone call, about how Spider had sounded so much like the old friend he had always trusted. He was confused.

"I knew Spider was gettin' screwy 'cause a' Pacheco. You ever meet Pacheco?"

"Nah."

"Pacheco was around before you showed up. He was this amazin' car thief, man. He got into some trouble with Careta one time, an' Spider helped 'um out. They went into hidin' f' a while, an' then Spider wanted t' put 'um both t' work. Well you know Careta, that guy don't work f' nobody, but Pacheco, he was cool, he started workin' f' Spider, even though Pacheco had this thing about drugs. He hates 'um. I think his sister was a junkie. So even though he gets in tight with Spider, he quit. Him an' Spider had this screamin' match right on Southern Boulevard, an' then Pacheco quit. Told him t' stick it all up his ass."

Miguel was getting nervous again. He rolled down his window to let in a little air, drizzle splashing against his face. "So?"

"So Pacheco's dead. One a' thum new posses man, they found him on the street an' they took 'im for a ride. An' now they in tight with Spider. That was the first news I heard about Spider that was womp." Ritchie suddenly leaned closer, grabbing hold of Miguel's coat. "Now what makes you think that Spider won't do you the same way? Maan, he knew you less time than he knew Pacheco."

Miguel gently pulled off his hands. "When did this shit go down?"

"Uh." He shrugged. "Maybe five, six months ago. You had just come in. Man, I tell you, Spider is in this f' himself. You know Ricky?"

Miguel squinted. "He's the kid got iced 'cause he was gonna run off with the drug money, right?"

"Yup. You made his drop. After he got it." Ritchie leaned back, his eyes glassy as he stared through the windshield. "Did'ju know him though?"

"Nah."

"We iced 'im," he muttered. He turned to look at Miguel with those dark gleaming eyes. "We iced the fucka." And his face twitched with something that Miguel felt was regret.

"Shit."

"We did Spider's dirty work. I shunta gone in on it. It was my mistake. But he fucked us. He set us up, man, made it look like we had somethin' t' prove, like we weren't high enough in the ratings, you know? I shunta fallen f' that shit. All f' one an' one f' all, right? But after we did it Spider turned on us. He handed one a' my boys to the cops." Ritchie stared at Miguel with a real hurt twitching on his face.

"No way," Miguel whispered.

"Yeah, way. He was my friend, man. My longtime ol' buddy. Spanish Fly. He was my pana. Spider squealed on 'im. At first he told us it would be cool, no problem, but then somethin' happened with the cops, like they

wanted somebody. You know, community leaders o' some shit, the cops
wanted somethin' t' give people to show they doin' the job. So they put
the bite on 'im. You know, like, hand over somebody we can prosecute
or we start puttin' pressure on yuh street trade. Spider din't want that,
no sir, it ain't like he's on his own. We all know he has a boss, too. So
he gave 'um Spanish Fly. Squealed. I went runnin' t' him when the cops
grabbed 'im. Where'd they even get an idea that it was us, man? It was
Spider. When I talked t' him, he gave me all this shit about bein' under
the gun an' pressure an' jus' wait until he gets his own thing goin' an'
meanwhile my pana is sittin' at Rikers. He tol' me he was gonna get
Spanish Fly out, that it was jus' politics kinda thing, but the Bronx DA
smelled somethin' fishy an' started huntin' around for a posse." Ritchie
paused to swallow. "So they killed 'im."

"They killed who?"

"Spanish Fly. They killed him. The cops. Spider. Thum. All thum
bastids. They killed him. Like Spanish Fly was gonna talk. Like he could
ever betray thum."

The anger seethed in Ritchie's eyes. Miguel leaned across and opened
the glove compartment, pulling out his fat plastic bag of weed. He
pinched some out and cleaned it on a crumpled paper bag, not knowing
what to say. Ritchie watched him, nibbling on fingers, something Miguel
had never seen him do.

"Then he told me that it was screwed up an' it wasn't his fault, that
the cops coulda clamped down on all the posses an' so people above him
had made the choice. He said he had overreacted about Ricky an' that
he was sorry about the whole thing."

They both looked out at the dark empty park, the soft rain that fell
whipping up a misty fog that hung three feet off the ground. Miguel rolled
a joint, but his stomach was churning, the air heavy with emotion. He lit
it and took a toke. Maybe the smoke was a bad idea. He paused in
mid-toke.

"So you think Spider had him killed?" His voice sounded hollow and
strange.

"I don't care. It's all Spider's fault. To me, he killed him. An' things
ain't been the same with us since."

"I don't think I can smoke," Miguel said, handing Ritchie the joint.
He grabbed it but he was too busy talking to toke on it.

"It's like, jus' when you think you found somethin' really good, like really real, somethin' comes along to remind'ju you just a little sucka ain't worth a piece a shit . . ."

Ritchie's voice broke, and Miguel didn't want to look over there. He heard the funny breathing, then heard the brittle plea: "Yo, light this?" Miguel looked at him, at the wet face, the glittering eyes. Miguel reached into his pocket and took out a packet of tissues and tossed it on his lap as if it had happened by mistake. Ritchie grabbed the tissues and covered his face for a moment.

"He was like my brother," Ritchie said.

"Don't worry about it."

"He was older, man. He taught me a lot. He told me doin' this was gonna be a mistake. He was older."

"Calm down, bro'."

"He used t' take orders from me, even though he was older! Everything was easier with him around. Now, it's like . . ." Ritchie seemed to collect himself suddenly, and stopped talking. He blew his nose and sent the ball of tissue flying into the dark. Miguel relit the joint and passed it to him.

"Spider murdered 'im," Ritchie said in a thick, strange voice. "He murdered 'im, an' believe me, I'm gonna pay 'im back. Thass why when I heard about'chu leavin', I hadda look you up."

"Man, who tol'ju I was leavin'?"

"Spider."

"You talked to him?"

"Yeah. What, thass a surprise? I talked to him las' night. You were mentioned, but it wasn't all about'chu, see? It was mostly about Spadgie's."

"Spadgie's?"

"Yeah." Ritchie passed him the joint, sinking into his seat and exhaling as if trying to calm down. His eyes looked a little less edgy now. He seemed to be talking and dreaming at the same time. "This Rico thing. You know they killed 'im. Spadgie's been runnin' his own op right under Spider's nose. He's been playin' with the competition. Rico was in on it, but Rico squealed to Spider. He was too tight with the man t' sell 'im out. I don't know how much Spadgie knew about it. Maybe Rico threatened him, who knows? Anyway, Rico got fucked real good. This pissed Spider off: He's a gone fuck now. You should see his eyes light up when he talks about Spadgie's. An' thass where it's gonna go down, bro'. I'm talkin' a massacre like they ain't seen outside of a mafia movie."

"Serious?"

"Yeah bro', an' this weekend, too. I know 'cause Spider wanted me an' the boys t' be in on it. But I said nah. That an' the other thing has him pissed off at me."

"What other thing?"

"Well. You told 'im I let'chu in on bein' set up."

Miguel took a long heavy toke and closed his eyes. "Man, I wish I was away from this shit already."

There was a moment of calm quiet. A bus hissed as it sped by on splashing tires. A man and a woman lazily scraped along the iron fence by the park, kissing and laughing and holding hands, turning round and round as if to see themselves from different angles. The sheer delight of their being together made Miguel think of Cristalena. But Ritchie's sudden words brought him right out of the dream.

"Help me set 'im up, Miguel."

Miguel sat up, staring at him. "You crazy?"

"But he still wants to talk to you! He told me he's gonna set up a pow-wow an' set'chu straight."

"Is that what he said?"

"All you gotta do is tell me when an' where. Thass all, bro'. You don't even gotta show up."

Miguel's lips trembled angrily. Was this really happening? What kind of a crazy place was this? He pounded the wheel, startling Ritchie, who gave a small jump.

"I wun't do that t' him, man. I wun't do that t' nobody. I ain't down with that shit. No fucken way."

"He set'chu up! He set me up! He murdered my pana!"

"Man, are you crazy? You think yuh jus' gonna walk in there an' jus' kill 'im? You an' yuh dinky little posse?"

"Yo. That ain't nice."

"I mean where the fuck you gonna hide!"

"I got eight thousand dollars. Between all of us, we got about sixty grand."

Miguel looked at him, realizing now how foolish he must've sounded in front of Cristalena. It immediately depressed him. He was just a kid. So was Ritchie, even though the guy was two years older. They were unformed, unfinished.

"Why don'chu jus' set 'im up yuhself?" Miguel asked wearily.

"He might not trust me now."

"Well, how the fuck he's gonna trust me? I'm the one thass leavin', remember?"

"Yeah, but he wun't expect'ju to do somethin' like that. He knows you ain't down with this shit. You ain't the kind, right? An' thass exactly what would make it sweeta. Jus' thinka his surprise, bro', when he's comin' over t' lay it all down on you an' instead he ends up with a chestful a—"

"Stop it, man, just chill."

"He wun't suspect'ju, man. He thinks yuh too fucken straight. Thass what he told me about'chu, tha'chu too fucken straight. He thinks thass a waste of a good young mind."

"I don't give a fuck about that, man. I just want out. An' if I see him this weekend I'll tell 'im that. I don't need to set 'im up."

Ritchie's face contorted, hands gripping the dash like he was trying to rip it off the car. "Don'chu see that Spider don't care about'chu? What, you think you gonna sit with him an' have a nice chat? The dude has changed, bro'. I got no fucken doubt in my mind that he'd set'chu up."

"Set me up? But din't he do that already?"

"I don't mean for a beatin', stupid. I'm talkin' about him settin' you up, like he ain't gonna trust'ju so much anymore." He made a machine gun noise with his mouth.

Miguel could see it. If Spider wanted him, it would be real easy. All he'd have to do is call him and tell him to meet him someplace. Miguel would drive over and wait in his car and then the boys would come over and ripple his car with machine-gun fire.

"I don't doubt it for a minute," Ritchie added, as if viewing the same footage of Miguel's murder currently playing in his head. "Even if you went back to him, I don't think he'll trust'ju."

"But I ain't goin' back."

"Not even t' help me set 'im up?"

"No."

"Yuh a fucken putz, man."

"Maan, I can't even believe you got the cojones to think you can just walk in an' ice Spider. I jus' don't believe that."

"Nobody said it hadda be my boys t' do the hit. Did I say that? Who's gonna even know it was us? Somebody else can go in an' do it."

"Like who?"

"Like maybe Ace." Ritchie leaned forward, lowering his voice. "Thass fucken who."

"Oh no. Not that. You can't be serious, bro'. I don't hardly even know you an' already I feel bad f' you. Din't Spider ice him?"

"Nah bro'. Guy's made a' rubber."

Ace. The fabled opposition. A huge black Vietnam veteran, built big and sturdy like a comic book villain. Every kid on the street had an Ace story. Miguel's favorite was told to him by a brat who saw him take three machine-gun bursts on a warm summer night. They heard his laughter up and down the street. His black Mercedes was dotted with holes, and Ace's chest was streaming with blood. Still, he laughed. "I saw worse than that in 'Nam! You can't stop Ace of Spades! Ace got the bug spray, Spider!" Miguel looked at Ritchie like he was nuts.

"Man," he whispered, "do you know wha'chu gettin' into?"

"I'm jus' switchin' bosses, you know. Makin' a career move. Once it goes down, we'll be in good shape with the man."

"But how can you trust that guy?" Miguel's voice got high-pitched. "He's probably ten times worse than Spider!"

"That mighta been true once, but not anymore. Besides, this really ain't a question a' trust. This is business."

Miguel stared, feeling defeated. It was that word again, and the way Ritchie used it. Just like Spider.

"Spider's taught'chu real good," Miguel said with some contempt as he started the car. He felt like he wanted to puke. The joint hadn't done a thing for him. He swerved the car out of its parking and dove into traffic, making a whining U-turn.

"So you won't help?"

"Nup."

Ritchie didn't say anything as Miguel drove him to Dawson Street, his turf. He only asked if he could keep the fat roach that was left from their little smoke. Miguel shrugged. He stopped the car on the corner of Dawson and Leggett, and there was that Ritchie clone, Willyboy, holding a beer, leaning against a wall with the kid in the beret.

"I don't want anythin' to' do with this shit," Miguel said, letting it all come flying out. "No career moves, no business. I just want the fuck out. An' I'm gettin' out, no matter what Spider says. He can't keep me here an' if he don't know that, tough shit. My mind is made up."

Ritchie leaned over, tugging on his coat. "Then you better get smart, bro'. You better dump this car someplace. If you tell Spider yuh out, he may do a job on you. An' thass it, this car won't get'chu far enough. It'll be open season. Get the fuck outta that apartment, too. You know somethin'? Maybe you shun't even meet Spider. You should fucken clea' the fuck out, bro'. Don't lookit me like that!" There was a sudden rage on Ritchie's face that made Miguel feel weird. "Jus' get'chaself the fuck out. You'll be stupida than you look if you plan t' have a nice chat with Spider about it."

Miguel removed Ritchie's hands from his coat again. He wanted to tell him about the phone call he got from Spider, to tell him how different he sounded; but he couldn't. It occurred to him that maybe Ritchie wouldn't understand it, that maybe his relationship with Spider wasn't as close. Or was Miguel just being wishful?

Ritchie slid away, opened the door, and threw Miguel a kiss that resounded. "Have a nice life," he said, and he slammed the door.

Miguel stepped on the gas, roaring past all of them with a gust of dirt. Now he was thinking paranoid thoughts about Spider. Maybe Ritchie was right, maybe he shouldn't even think of showing up to any meeting. Maybe Miguel should just do a fade-out. Or maybe it was just Ritchie trying to twist him up so he would set Spider up. Goddamn, but it's tough when you can't trust anybody but have to believe someone in order to make a decision.

Spider's call had confused him, made him feel almost guilty. Hadn't Spider apologized? Didn't he sound like shit? How could Miguel help thinking that maybe the bonds of their friendship mattered more to Spider than he had originally thought? Maybe it had even surprised Spider. He was full of dark thoughts. If Spider wanted him, why would he bother setting him up? One phone call, and he could have some junkie walk up to Miguel's apartment door and blast him.

Miguel parked his car across the street from his house so he could see it from his window. The junkies in the hall depressed him. A woman on the third floor was screaming at them, pushing her children inside with her thick arms. "Don'chu come nea' my fucken kids again!" she yelled in a hoarse husky street voice. "I'll kill you, I swear! You come nea' thum again with tha' shit an' I'll kill you!!"

"But I was only showin' 'im my pipe," the junkie bellowed back in a voice just as coarse, sandpaper face dotted with strawberry-colored patches.

When Miguel got inside the apartment, everything was dark, except for a few candles glowing. The wind moaned through the shattered glass in the window. Firebug was sitting on the floor right under the fake petunias, his face half lost in the dark. He didn't turn toward Miguel but only nodded absently, legs spread out wide with a bottle of brown stuff in between.

"Pana," he said. "Hel'mano."

"Firebug," Miguel said wearily, leaning against the wall. The darkness, the candles, all brought back a feeling of intimacy that he hadn't felt in a while. "Firebug Firebug Firebug . . ."

"Come, hel'mano," Firebug said, holding the bottle up to him. "Come an' join me."

Miguel squatted down on the floor and took the bottle. The warm rum stung and sent tremors through him. He sat, tossing off his coat, locking his hands around his knees and rocking. He was just settling into the dark calm, ocean waves softly crashing, when Firebug spoke in a voice that Miguel didn't recognize.

"Spider called," he said.

Miguel stopped rocking.

"Spider?"

"Yeah." It was like a croak. "What happened t' yuh beeper?"

"Din't I tell you I threw the fucka out?" Miguel instantly realized he hadn't.

"Nope. You sure din't tell me that." Firebug sighed tiredly. His face was slowly becoming more visible as Miguel's eyes grew accustomed to the dark.

"Spider an' me, we been through a lot," Firebug said heavily. "We went through the shit. He fucked me over, I fucked him over, an' we was still in business. I can't explain tha' shit. But he's done a lot f' me. I owe him. I know thass hard t' get, but I owe him. Owe him everythin'." He gestured for the bottle. Miguel crept a little closer and passed it to him, trying to see more of his face.

"The Amelia thing," he continued, "jus' happened. I think it was Amelia's fault more than any of us. She jus' wanted t' play us. She was foxin' us out from the start, tryin'na scope out what she could get. An' she went f' all of it, bro'. Thass why I always blamed huh more than Spider. I can't blame him. An' he made it up t' me. She din't. She din't care. She was out f' huhself."

"But everybody is," Miguel said hollowly.

Firebug shifted his weight, sliding closer. "I never had no reason t' give a fuck. I only know I take what I can, when an opportunity comes, grab it. All the time, man, no matter who gets burned." He emitted a sad chuckle. "Ha. Who gets burned. Thass a good one." His voice sounded fractured. There was too much emotion in it. It made Miguel's face grow warm.

"It's an instinct," Firebug went on. "I live that way, thass all. I cun't stop if I tried. Do you understand? I can't even help it. I try bein' friends wif' people, but'chu can't have friends. Not in this life, bro'. Times are too hard. I think you know that already."

"Yeah," Miguel said. There was a strange silence. Miguel sensed that Firebug was apologizing. His face started to burn. He took another slug just to try to hide it.

"Forget it, man," Miguel said. As if forgiving him.

"Naah, I mean it. Thass the way I am. I do what I gotta do t' get ahead. Maybe someday I can stop tha' shit. Not'chet. Not'chet." There was regret in his voice. He stared at Miguel and shook his head, grinning tiredly as he swiped the bottle and took a drink. "Not'chet."

Miguel got up, all wobbly because of the rum. He stripped off his sweater and lit a cigarette, pacing in the darkness. His booted steps thumped like heartbeats.

"So what did Spider say?" he asked after a deep breath.

Firebug shook the bottle at him. "You know I got another fucken wienie roast?" His yell was weird, not jubilant, more like he had stepped on one of the candles with his bare feet. "I do, I do. Wha'chu doin' tomorrow? You gonna be here?"

There was a desperation in his voice that worried Miguel. He stepped closer, squinting into his face, half covered by a hand that seemed to grip on to an eyebrow.

"Firebug, what the fuck is up?"

"Gimme a cigarette is whassup," he said, snatching the one from his lips with a quick motion. Miguel fished for a fresh one. "I'm axin' if you comin' t' the goddamn wienie roast tomorrow." The hostile bark put Miguel on his guard. He resumed his pacing.

"Where is it gonna be?"

"What the fuck should I tell you for if you ain't gonna show up anyway? Jus' tell me if you gonna be here tomorrow."

Miguel shrugged. There was Cristalena's birthday party tomorrow. That was still on, wasn't it? He thought of how she had looked as they had left the apartment, passing all those junkies and crackheads.

"I'm not gonna be around," he told Firebug.

"Yeah well," Firebug said roughly, "good f' you then."

"What the fuck is up wit'chu?" Miguel thundered, sensing the bitterness.

"Din'chu even thinka the spot you'd put me in if you quit?" Firebug yelled, waving the bottle. "I'm the one got'chu in, remember? You ever thinka what I gotta do t' make it up?"

Silence fell like a black curtain. Miguel stood by the window where the gusts of cold wind hit him in throbbing drafts. Was that guilt he was feeling, a sense of shame? What made him feel more ashamed, standing in front of Cristalena, or Firebug? Even Ritchie seemed stunned that he wanted to leave the world behind. He wasn't making sense to any of them. It was as though he had been fooling himself all along. He had always been outside. He stood there, hoping the cold wind would bring sensation back to his rum-numbed body.

Firebug got up with some effort. He laughed a little as he half slid, holding the bottle out to Miguel.

"Nah," Miguel said.

Firebug let the bottle hang in the air a moment before he retracted the offer and took another drink. "Oh well," he said sadly. "No more parties f' this place." He sat on the car seat with a creak.

"So what did Spider say?" Miguel asked again, feeling as if he were totally alone in the room. Firebug rubbed his eyes and sighed.

"He said he wants to meet'chu day after tomorrow. To talk. One las' time. Some drinks, some laughs." There was a strange irony in his voice as if he were an old man who saw through everything. He pulled his legs up and tucked them under himself as if trying to take up as little space as possible.

"Where?"

Firebug looked at him as if he were looking at a dead man. Something came over his eyes that made Miguel stop pacing.

"Where, Firebug?"

It was a knowing half-whisper: "Spadgie's."

Miguel didn't move. The name was sinking in slowly. "Spadgie's? He said Spadgie's?"

"Yeah," Firebug said, snapping out of some trance. He rubbed his face. "Spadgie's. He said ten o'clock. The last meeting. Yuh last chance."

"But why at Spadgie's? We supposed t' have it out at Spadgie's?" His voice was getting hysterical.

"You ain't gonna have it out. You gonna meet f' the last time, right? He said you should meet him right at the bar." His eyes flashed a challenge. "He ain't stupid, you know. He knows you gonna quit anyway."

Miguel was trying to think but it was hard. His mind was bursting with images, of him going to Spadgie's, of Spadgie's big rubbery face laughing, folding, shattering as 9mm slugs tore into it, the walls splitting in chunks, glass breaking, women screaming, people running, machine-gun fire raking the bar, splashing liquor, splashing blood. Miguel felt the bullets entering him, not pain at first but a dull splatter and a spinning, a dizzy turmoil with legs folding under him, and then he was falling backward, chest exploding with a gruesome splash that blinded him.

He took such a long puff on his cigarette that he began to cough, his throat burning.

Firebug got up and vanished into his room for a moment. Miguel could only wonder about how much the guy knew about what was going down. There were too many questions burning in his gut, and the frustrating thing was that he couldn't ask them. If he let Firebug know he might know something, Firebug might tell Spider, right? So he bit his lip until it bled.

Firebug came back carrying a wrinkled brown bag. He gave it to Miguel.

"I got'chu somethin'," he said, coughing a little.

The gesture caught Miguel by surprise. "Wha'chu talkin' about?"

"It's nothin'. My way of sayin' hey."

"Hay?"

"Hey." Firebug laughed a little and the room seemed to get a little warmer. Miguel slid down to the floor in a squat. Firebug joined him.

Miguel opened the bag. There was a small .32 revolver inside that felt like a toy. A handful of gold-tipped bullets clattered onto the floor like marbles.

"Yuh kiddin', right?"

"Nah I ain't kiddin'. You might be in some trouble. Better tha'chu got a little somethin' to . . ." There was a pause. Firebug wiped his hands on his pants vigorously like there was blood on them. "Jus' watch yuh back, thass all. Ahh shit." He got up, then held out his hand clumsily. Miguel, still squatting, took it. Firebug grasped it firmly and held on.

"We go back," he said, and then something failed him. He quickly let go of Miguel's hand, picked up a shoulder bag that Miguel hadn't seen over by the kitchen door and headed down the hallway. "Jus' you watch yuh back," he muttered tersely. The door opened and flashed with light and then it slammed. Firebug was gone.

Miguel didn't move. It was goodbye. He knew it. He'd never see Firebug again. Miguel wasn't on the team anymore. He had ceased to exist. Miguel had worried about how he would leave Firebug, and here was Firebug leaving him. Somehow he had expected all this, but he hadn't expected the hurt that came crashing down. The liquor made it easier to cry a little, sitting there on the floor with all that loneliness washing over him in crashing waves. He was trying to restrain himself because he was a man.

But
he broke
like a sixteen-and-a-half-year-old kid.

19

Firebug's stuff was gone. Miguel went into his room and looked around: Even the TV had disappeared. The guy had cleared out like Miguel had some disease. At first he felt abandoned and scared, as if he had been set up; maybe soon they'd be knocking on his door to take him out. Then he thought about how Spider was meeting him day after tomorrow at Spadgie's, and he relaxed, thinking either that Spider wasn't going to kill him but talk to him, or else that Spider wasn't going to kill him right now but rather wait until Spadgie's. Either way, he was safe until then, right?

He tried to get in touch with Spider. He tried all his numbers. He left messages on two machines. He went down to the bodega and asked Franco, who only shrugged for a while at all his questions before leading him over to the cold cuts slicer.

"Spider is underground," he whispered. "There's too much goin' down. Ace is really gunnin' f' him. The other night they hit Mexican House." That was one of the party pads on Tinton Avenue run by an ugly Mexican named Mamita.

"Serious? I din't hear about it."

Franco scowled, the arrogant Spanish making Miguel feel as though he were being scolded. "Well, how do you expect to hear anything when you are causing so many problems? People don't even know if it's worth coming near you. Yes, it was Mexican House, a drive-by at three in the morning. They missed Spider by a matter of minutes. Obviously somebody in the organization is trying awful hard to set him up." He stared at Miguel with coal-black eyes.

"I don't even know where he is anymore," Miguel said, sensing Franco was making a nasty foray.

"Well, good for him."

Miguel left feeling ultra-paranoid. He started to notice that some of the kids out on the street looked at him funny, that clusters of kids pointed at his car. Now he was really wondering what Spider might've told people. Judging from the way Franco was talking, it must be pretty bad. It was still hard for him to believe that Spider could've changed that much, that Spider might've set him up. Those images of him lying on the floor at India House, Spider pouring words into the tape recorder, kept coming back to him. They were friends, weren't they? Hadn't there been something special between them? Fuck. He had been wrong about Firebug. Why not Spider? The thought made little tense springs twitch in his stomach.

The looks he got while driving down the streets (WAS HE IMAGINING THEM?) made him start thinking about what he was going to do about his car. If this weird shit was going down all around him, it would pay to be as inconspicuous as possible. The car was his own personal tag. They could spot him coming a mile away. Could he get another car? It would mean hiding his Baby, but he was sure he didn't want to part with it. He thought of parking it in that big garage on Third Avenue, but he felt like he was abandoning his best friend. The car had become an extension of his arms and legs. It was like parting with his dick.

Six months he had lived in this car, dreaming and driving, relishing the freedom and power it gave him, the girls it brought him, the stares when his magenta dream pranced down the street, so seductive and sleek. He had created HER. He had repainted the dull worn skin, reupholstered her insides in shiny new leather, dropped in a dope stereo system with the bass that goes BOOM. All the posse boys had that ugly black tinted glass; Miguel's were tenderly smoked like expensive shades. That's because he wanted to be seen when he was up on that throne. Now he was going to lose all that prestige and power and maybe some of that slick street respect, all in one go.

Ritchie had told him to dump it; he could never do that. There had to be a way to save the car. He started thinking about Careta, who he knew was in with this car-theft ring that operated in the area. They would steal cars, repaint, refurbish, and crack new cylinders for them. Then they would sell them to posses from a garage on Bruckner Boulevard that doubled as a muffler repair shop. If Careta could help him get a new car, Miguel might be able to "store" his Baby someplace safe until he could have it again. But even now, as he scoured the streets looking for Careta, he had another troubling thought. He was, after all, just a sixteen-and-a-half-year-old kid. Once he went to live with Catarina and Nelo, he wouldn't be driving a car. Spider had made that possible, right? Without Spider, there couldn't be a car, at least not for another two years, until he was legal. The thought depressed him so much he double-parked outside a candy store on Southern Boulevard and had a cigarette. Try as he might, he couldn't think his way out of it. He was going to lose the car. It was a part of his street life. It wouldn't survive the transition. Who could he trust? No one. Could he leave the car with someone? No. Who could he even talk to about it?

He fired up the car and drove away from Southern Boulevard, up 149th. The nighttime streets were empty and dark, with only a few clusters of dealers hanging out by one of the bodegas near Prospect Avenue. He jumped out of the car and went right to the phone.

"Hello?" The voice on the other end was groggy and slow.

"Amelia? It's me, Miguel."

There was a long yawn. "Miguel, it's almost three in the morning." She didn't seem mad, just a little surprised. "Anything wrong?"

"I really need to talk to you. To talk to someone. I know it's late but if you could—"

"You know the address. Pop on up."

He drove over, parked the car on a pitch-black Kelly Street. The two nearest streetlamps had gone out, or else been broken by a few dark shadows that leaned against the drab row of fences. It took Miguel a while before he found the stairs leading down to the basement.

She came to the door wrapped in a terry-cloth bathrobe. Most of the lights were off. She took his hand and led him through the dark boiler room with its fiery red flames showing through the boiler hatch like clenched teeth. Soon he was back in that bedroom, surrounded by glowing candles. The walls looked orange. She kissed him wetly on the cheek and offered him a glass of very cold orange juice before she slipped back under the thick comforter and stared at him as he stood by the doorway.

"You look totally lost," she said, rolling herself into a ball under the blankets and laughing. "It's so cute. A little boy in a huge coat looking totally lost."

"You shut up with that." He sat on the bed beside her.

"I thought'chu were Spider," she said softly, suddenly grabbing his hand and pulling it under the warm blanket. "I got a bad feeling about him."

"Wha'chu mean?"

"I mean that he's real ticked off at me. I told him I was quittin' this shit. Don't ask me why it should matter a fuck to him what I do, 'cause I don't know! But he got mad an' said I wasn't gonna be playin' him for no sucker. An' then he said it was all your fault."

"My fault?"

She sat up to look at him. "Yeah. Now I'm scared he'll come over here."

"He been here before?"

"No. But I tol'ju that Firebug was. He could get the info from him." She was caressing his hand gently with the tips of her fingers. "Ohhh Miguel," she whispered, touching his face, her eyes glimmering with candles. "You're so pretty. Such a pretty boy. Why don'chu take off all that shit an' get all snuggly with me?"

He got up rudely from the bed, shutting his coat with a motion, as if he were freezing.

"I din't come here f' that. I came here t' ask you f' help." He poured it out, about Spider's call and how sorry he sounded and how confused he was, and then the stuff about Spadgie's and what was going to go down there. And then he threw in the part about meeting Spider there Sunday night. All of it came out while he paced. He finally sat beside her again. "I don't know what to do."

"Yes, you do," she whispered. "Just get out. Fuck meeting with him. Get out. Don't even try to meet with him."

"But maybe if I meet with him we can come to some agreement, you know? End this in a cool way. He might even be able to help me with my car."

"Forget it, Miguel." She grabbed his hand again and squeezed it hard. "You stop this shit. You stop this about Spider. The old Spider is gone. This is a new Spider, you hear?" Her voice grew angrier. "Don't be walking around with these foolish dreams in your head about ending this amicably. Spider just ain't the type. You burned him. I know you don't believe it but'chu did. Hell, even I did that. And I'm a little scared of him, of what he might do. Don'chu see he thinks he can do anything?"

"You don't gotta yell at me." He snatched his hand away.

"I'm not yelling. I just wan'chu t' stop looking for excuses not to do the right thing. What you should do is just get the fuck out already."

He hadn't even told her about Firebug. Once he told her, she got even more hysterical, jumping up out of the bed and pushing him up against the wall.

"Don'chu see what that means? You gotta get out of there, Miguel! Don't waste any time. Who knows what went down with them? They're like evil twins. Get'cha money an' get the hell out of there."

She moved away from him, going over to the bureau for a cigarette.

"And you," he said, because he wanted to burn her, "what about'-chu?"

She stared at him but her eyes seemed to see right through him.

"I don't happen to have eight thousand dollars saved up," she said, arms crossed, flicking ash off her cigarette with a thumbnail. There was something in the air of the room, musty and suffocating. Tension. Anger.

"What about my car?" His question sounded stupid. It made him seem indifferent to her problems, only concerned with himself. He cursed under his breath.

"What about it? Do you have a place you can keep it for two years until you can get a real license?"

"No. I thought'chu could help me with that."

She gave him a look of contempt, the look one gives a spoiled brat. "Man. You're so used to having other people do for you, aren'chu?"

"Damn, wha'chu so mad for?"

"I don't know!" she yelled. "You call me up at three in the fucken morning so you can come an' mess up my carpet with your poodle-shit life. Did you even think of asking about me? Maybe I have needs? Did it occur to you I didn't even scream at'chu for interrupting my beauty sleep?"

"Gah what a bitch you are."

"Thass right," she said, coming right up to him so she could spit the words right into his face. "I'm a bitch, an old fucken bitch, okay? Who knows what's wrong with me! I'm a woman, ain't I? They never make sense! Din'chu know that already? Maybe I'm just horny. Maybe it's cramps. Maybe my rollers were on too tight!!"

"Ah shit. To hell with this." Miguel waved her off, heading for the door out into the dark hallway.

"You walkin' out? All on your own?" She half laughed. "Ohh, I think you'll be back."

Miguel stormed down the hall, which got progressively darker and darker. He walked into a stone wall. He turned and made out what he thought was a doorway. He went into a dark room but from the sounds of his boots on tile he could tell he was in the kitchen. He doubled back, toward the light, and ended up in her bedroom again.

"Hello. You're back."

He leaned against the doorpost. "Get me the fuck outta here."

"I haven't heard the magic word."

"Please. Gawdamn."

"Thass better. You fucken baby. Now gimme your hand."

She led him back out of the dark and to the door, where she held on to his hand. "Aren'chu gonna kiss me good night?" It wasn't coy or cute but rather a serious question, her eyes still burning with anger. It was as if she was expecting him to be totally selfish, and was already disappointed. He pecked her on the lips quickly before she could respond.

"You been a great help," he said as he climbed the rattling steel steps.

"Oh fuck you."

"I'll call you sometime."

"Yeah, why don'chu do that."

He hadn't told her about the gun that Firebug had given him, which he was carrying. It seemed to weigh down his coat, to radiate warmth, so that he was always aware of it. He hadn't wanted to hear what she would say about it. He felt disappointed. She hadn't said a single thing he had wanted to hear.

He couldn't sleep that night. He kept getting up and going to the window to look down on his sleeping car. He was so restless he ended up going to the roof, its door usually unlatched and easy to open, rusty and creaky on old hinges. Up there in the cold wind, he stared down at the empty streets for a while, a few reluctant stars in the sky twinkling between thick black clouds. He took out his new gun and fired off a few shots at an ugly chimney on the roof. Man, the thing worked, had a nice kick; it sent bits of chimney chipping in sharp spinning chunks. Shooting the gun set something pounding a little faster in his chest. The noise died away but echoed off through the hills of tenements and TV antennas, like faraway thunder: a few moments of exhilaration, as if the whole world was at his fingertips, as if the whole world could be made to bow down to him. It was a solid answer, a real solution. It was only when he got back down into his apartment that he realized that the feeling was temporary, and that having his gun didn't mean shit. He was still powerless. So maybe some beat boy wouldn't get the drop on him. That was good. But his life was still out of his control. The gun didn't change that.

Did Firebug know about Spadgie's? Miguel, lying on Firebug's mat in the empty room, couldn't stop wondering. Man, the guy cleaned out everything. All he left was a box full of smelly clothes and a pair of old sneaks. No sign that a person had ever been there. He even took his goddamn bong. Maybe Firebug didn't know about Spadgie's but knew Miguel was in trouble, so he gave him the gun. Or maybe he knew about Spadgie's and felt bad, so he got Miguel this gun to at least give him a fighting chance. ("Well, how the fuck was I supposed t' know he had a piece?") Firebug could do his duty, relieve his guilt, and still act like he had nothing to do with it. (And if there was cash involved, he'd still get his cut.) Typical Firebug.

He went back to his room, to look down on his car. The sky was lightening up along the edges. If he stored the car at the municipal parking, he'd be a pedestrian again. Fuck that. Worse, it was an emotional thing. He wanted to be with his Baby for as long as possible. After the move, what? What would he do to his Baby? It gave him a headache thinking about it. He sat by the window and waited for the sunlight, his eyes stinging.

20

They were running through the apartment, barefoot and dripping, upsetting stuffed animals that sat all over the living-room floor like pylons in an obstacle course. As they ran, the cool air animated them and raised goose bumps on their glistening flesh.

He caught her right at the entrance to the bedroom. It was a fluffy dream-vision bedroom with thick white rugs and feathered boas dangling over the windows. His hands slipped on her wet skin, and she spun and jumped up on the bed, on all fours like a cornered animal, her back arched all catlike.

"I dare you," she hissed.

He jumped on the bed and wrestled her down on her back. She screamed and kicked and sent him tumbling off the bed. He climbed back up, holding her twitching struggling arms down, forgetting about her legs. In a snap she had maneuvered her feet under him and had sent him flying off the bed again. He climbed back on, pinned her down again with his body on top of her body, the two of them panting.

"Cheater," she spat.

He turned her over with those massive hands of his. "I'm gonna spank you." He whacked her quivering cheeks.

"Mothafucka!" She kicked out at him desperately, barely missing his balls. He rolled off the bed. She jumped on his back with a war cry, and then they started kissing and grunting like wild animals, falling into bed again, squirming all over each other.

"This is a crazy room," he said.

"Dolores is a hooker," she said.

The two of them froze on the bed.

"Yuch." Miguel leaped off. She jumped off, too.

"Take the blankets off."

"I'll get the pillowcases," he said, starting to pull when she collapsed in a mad laughing fit and told him it was a lie.

The apartment was big, spacious, and nicely furnished. It had three bedrooms filled with fluffy beds, thick rugs, plants, and beaded curtains. The large living room had one of those toy chandeliers that gave it a motel lobby quality.

"Yuh friends inta some weird shit," Miguel said, sniffing the sheets. Everything was scented with lilac or wildflowers.

"She works for some lawyer," Cristalena said, standing there all naked, staring at him with her big jailbait eyes. She liked it when he looked at her. His eyes would get all droopy. Like a cartoon ape. Magilla Gorilla. She laughed, hands on hips.

"So, you see somethin' you want, Magilla?"

The party had been boring.

They got there around seven-thirty. Rosa's house was full of young teenagers. Baggy pants were in. The girls were wearing them along with fat clunky shoes that looked like malformed elevator shoes from the seventies. The music was loud. Cristalena's aunt supposedly left to go dancing, Rosa said with a laugh, but she turned up later on in a pretty polka-dot dress that was very sixties.

Rosa herself was looking pretty stupid. She had on a red sparkly dress that was way tight her tits almost oozing over the top. She laughed all the time, her eyes swirling. Miguel sniffed around for the scent of smoke, but no deal. Only beer, wine, Champale, and tons of brown stuff that Rosa had hidden away in a cooler in her room. The screaming and yelling and dancing made Cristalena and Miguel want to leave really fast. It had surprised Miguel because he thought Cristalena would be in her element, but she seemed more determined to cut out to be alone with him.

She had been excited at first, her eyes sparkling as she cried out and hugged some girl she hadn't seen in a long time, introducing Miguel with a clutchy pride that warmed him up as she held him by the arm protectively. The girls swarmed around him like he was a door prize, their looks curious and teasing. Ten minutes into the scene, he had lost her, aware only of her laughter and chatter far away, around the bend, obscured by music. He sat by a table and stuffed chips into his mouth. Every time he spotted her in a group of screaming chattering girls he felt the tug, realized that if he hadn't known her, he would've made it his business to try and get her. She was just awesome pretty, and when she caught his eye, she would blush a little because she could see it in his face.

In twenty minutes Miguel had been introduced to a hundred people and he forgot all of them the minute they walked away. He couldn't believe how much older he felt, how distant. The party needed Jokey to poke holes in the wall with a police lock bar, and the Suarez Twins to open the sofa bed and hold their weekly fuck fest, side by side like good sisters, while Spider hung in all the corners like a mystic munchkin, handing out joints. The table by the stereo had the snow drawn in pretty white lines beside piles of tiny straws. Sounds of laughter and fucking and throbbing house music. This party was more like Romper Room.

Cristalena was feeling weird, too. She would appear out of a mushroom of faces smiling and laughing, and then she'd come over and pull him aside desperately. "We gotta get outta here," she'd tell him, breath scented with champagne. All night long she had talked about her "special plan," giving him that precious smile. She went into another room twice to make calls pertaining to her "special plan," and later ran up to him with a delighted hop. "Yes," she said, kissing him. "It's gonna happen. I got it all set up. Let's get this shit over with."

"But what it is you got set up?" He held on to her so she wouldn't escape, but she pulled away with a smug grin.

"You'll see, Magilla." (he says) "Whass this Magilla shit?"

She went through all the rituals like a trouper. There was a gift-opening ceremony that seemed to take ten days, with Taylor Dayne blaring from the stereo. Everybody was clustered around the large couch while Cristalena sat ripping boxes open, gift wrap fluttering everywhere.

"What about your boyfriend?" Rosa yelled through the peals of delight. "What about his present?"

Miguel turned red as he stood by the food table, still crunching on a few chips.

"He's givin' me my gift later, in private," Cristalena said. The room filled with screams. She didn't know about his surprise. She had gotten a skirt, a dress, two ugly blouses, three pairs of earrings, and two stuffed animals. She looked delighted with all of it, but nothing prepared her for the moment Miguel stood in front of her and handed her a slim little box. She stared at the package and then at him and the whole room grew quiet. Even Taylor Dayne stopped singing.

"Whass this?" She looked shocked.

"Just open it."

She looked at him, helpless. He laughed, enjoying the shock and surprise on her face as she tore open the box and caressed the fake-suede case, oohs and ahhs building.

"Gah Miguel, I'll kill you if you blew a lotta money . . ."

How was she supposed to know that the thing had been sitting in his closet for about five months? This was the bracelet Spider had told him to save for a real girl, and there she was now, flipping the box open. There was a collective gasp. She looked at him with her mouth hanging open.

"No," she begged. "Miguel, no . . ." She took it out as if holding a mouse by the tail, the thin line of shiny stones glimmering like electric lights.

He touched her cheek. "Can I put it on?" He loved the look on her face, eyes blank and mystified.

She got up, tears streaming from her eyes as he grabbed her trembling wrist and put the bracelet on her. When they embraced, the room erupted in applause. She was crying. When she kissed him, her lips tasted salty. "Now we engaged, okay?" She looked into his eyes and nodded desperately, hugging him before she started to sob. "No baby," he said, some of the girls laughing and coming over and cooing at her and caressing her arms.

The big cake had been set up on a TV cart so they could roll it in from another room as soon as it was ready. They turned the lights off and sang "Happy Birthday." It was so corny that even Cristalena was all red and sorry-looking. She and Miguel wolfed down three pieces. Then someone got the crazy idea that she and Miguel should dance a solo to that stupid song "Sixteen Candles." They danced real close and tight together and nuzzled and Cristalena started to cry again.

"You cry too much, man," he said. "Why you cryin'?"

"I love you."

"So why cry about it? Thass a happy thing. You should be like me, all smilin' an' shit."

"Why did'ju do it? Spend so much money on me? Those are real diamonds, right?"

"Yup."

"You didn't spend all your money?"

"Shh. Thass our money, okay? For when we live together. An' no, I didn't even have t' touch it. Don'chu worry about it, it ain't stolen or anything like that. It's just my way of sayin' . . . hey." Suddenly Firebug's grinning face appeared in his head and he felt sad.

"Hay?"

"Yeah. My way of sayin' hey."

"I look like a horse to you you gotta be sayin' hay t' me?"

"Yuh my wife now. You know that, right? Once you put on my bracelet yuh my wife. You hear that shit? Yuh my wife."

They started kissing so hard that the music stopped and all the lights came on, and everybody screamed and howled delightedly. They couldn't wait to cut out then. Cristalena chose the moment when Rosa got Raymond Cruz to stare at her legs as she sat on the couch. That's when she and Miguel made a break for it.

She gave him directions, turning up 156th Street. There were kids everywhere in heavy coats, girls carrying roller skates, posse boys in hats carrying sticks. This was all Miguel's turf. Was he expecting trouble? All those warnings about his car had him a little paranoid. They parked on Kelly Street, its quiet rows of brownstones making him feel safe, away from the chaos just two blocks up. She took him into a small private house that stood on the quiet tree-lined street across from a huge building that used to be a hospital. Miguel had had the shit kicked out of him by Ritchie just one block away and used to make his deliveries to Sammy and Joey two blocks down. Now he felt vulnerable, even though he had his gun on him. It was a funny bump in his coat.

"My friend Dolores lives here with some other people," she told him as she opened the vestibule door with her keys, laughing wickedly as they climbed up the rattling wooden stairs. "We used to be in school together. She was two grades above me. She felt guilty 'cause she couldn't be at my party, so I told her about you an' me an' she happened to have a vacancy."

At that moment they reached the landing. She opened the door like it was the secret entrance to their private playland.

He carried her in over the threshold. It made her start crying again. They had hardly explored the place before Cristalena suggested they take a bath. They both packed into the small tub and showered and bathed and fucked a little before she had run from him. Now he had her cornered on the bed again.

"Wait," she said.

He stopped what he was doing. "What?"

"We need music."

The bracelet glimmered on her wrist like a tiny light show. She got up from the bed and went over to the stereo that sat by the windows, turning it on and slipping in a cassette she had been carrying around all night. "Now this," she said, "is music to make love to." Miguel was sitting on the edge of the bed, reading the tape box.

"Tchaikovsky?" he asked. "Greatest hitsa Tchaikovsky? What kinda shit is that?"

"Shut up. It's classical music. People should always fuck . . . uh . . . Damn, you got me talking like that."

"Like what?"

"Shut up. It's classical music. People should always make love to classical music."

He smiled slyly. "Have you ever fucked t' classical music?"

"Well, no. But I figure making love should be like a real romantic thing, should have the right music, sorta soft an' flowy. Sure beats doing it to that hip-hop stuff."

"No way. Hip-hop gives it a kinda animal quality. Blacks make the best fuck music, man."

She grinned, waiting for the music to come through the speakers. "You can't say black," she said. "You have to say African-American."

"But I say black."

"You can't say that now."

"Why the fuck not?"

"Because you can't."

"But all my friends are black."

"All your friends are African-Americans."

"No they ain't. They ain't even been t' Africa."

She laughed quietly, gripping her stomach. "Nooo. Stop."

"An' what am I then? Nah, don't be laughing like that, turn around, I can see yuh asshole oooooh lookit. I'm serious, wha'chu gonna call me?"

She put a hand to her chest to restrain her laughter. "You, you're a Puerto Rican American."

"I thought I was Latino."

"Nah. You're a Puerto Rican American."

"How come I'm not a Latin American?"

Her eyes widened like she was amazed at his stupidity. "Hispanic is too much Spain. Latin American means Latin America. Puerto Rican American means you come from Puerto Rico."

"But I don't come from there."

"Stop that. I'm gonna hit'chu with something."

"I don't. If I do I came the long way." He scowled. "Puerto Rican American. What a loada shit."

"It's not shit, Miguel. It's people trying to find their own identities."

"I know my identity. I'm a spick. I like spick, okay? It tells me right away what I am. It don't confuse me into thinkin' I'm American. I'm a spick, okay? Thass how whites see you anyway."

She sighed as some soft music poured out through the speakers. "Man, I'm standin' here all naked an' shit an' all you wanna talk about is politics?"

"This music is womp," Miguel said, coming over to her and laying a loud series of kisses on the back of her neck.

"Well, you'll just do it my way now," she said imperiously. "I want some tender loving kind of shit. Not this fuck me fuck me pounding shit. Gotta have tenderness." She fell into his arms.

"You mean like this?"

He waltzed her around the room a little as the soft music started to flow smoothly over them. He sat her on the edge of the bed.

"Now I'm gonna show you something." He stepped out of the room and came back in with his bag of smoke and some rolling paper he had brought from the car. Her eyes got a little wider as he poured out some of the green spongy stuff and started cleaning it on top of a newspaper. "This," he said as he worked, "will loosen you up an' make you feel reeeeeeeeeal nice."

She grinned, her eyes curious. "No." Her toes wrestled with each other. "I don't know if I wanna do that."

"Oh, come on. Live. Take a chance. It's better than drinking."

"Why?"

"You don't piss so much. Come on, this is yuh birthday, ain't it? Come on, don't say no, I'll be right here, nothing bad's gonna happen. If you don't like it, we'll never do it again."

"But this means I'll really be living in sin."

He laughed and then she laughed. "Gah, you sittin' there all sexy naked an' fucken with me, an' yuh worried about bein' in sin!"

She just sat there grinning sweetly, not stopping him as he rolled the joint and licked it shut and held it up to her.

"Caterpillar!" he said.

"Gesundheit," she said back.

He lit it first. She laughed and made faces when he sucked smoke into his mouth, then blew it out and sucked the blue stream of smoke up his nostrils. It was really good stuff and Miguel didn't want them to get fractured, so they smoked just a little. He taught her how to suck it in and hold it and take little sips of air. She laughed and puffed and seemed determined to get it right. After only three good hits, she already had that soft pink glow around her eyes and was staring at him dreamily. They began kissing slowly. Each kiss seemed to last for a hundred years of soft touching and deep gazing. It was like being at the bottom of a pond, the water a pretty green ripple that sunlight couldn't penetrate. The music was tender and soft. She had just put him inside her when all of a sudden the music got louder and those cannons started going off. Miguel and Cristalena fell off the bed, laughing.

"You crazy nut," Miguel gasped. "You an' yuh classical music."

"It was working," she said drunkenly, slapping him away as she crawled over to the tape deck. "How was I supposed to know it was gonna explode like that?"

"You let me handle this," she said, rewinding the tape. They got back in bed and she grabbed hold of him, her face so smug as she worked him slowly with her hands and her lips and her tongue and then the cannons happened and then the explosions and she had to use a ton of tissue paper to clean the mess off the sheets.

"Wow," she said delightedly, "that was a big one!"

They dozed for a while, awakened by the loud Tchaikovsky piano concerto, its exuberant love tones making them tender and horny again. Two hours later, she was sitting on top of him, moving slowly, nibbling at his ears and passing her hand up and down his arms to check for goose bumps.

"Don't come," she said.

"You gotta slow down."

"We should try settin' a record," she said, covering him with her hair.

"Two hours already," he said.

"Are you tired?"

"Nah." He rearranged her hair.

They changed positions. Entering and reentering her was such a wonderful sensation: Once he was inside her he never wanted to come out. Inside was the safest, most dope feeling in the world, a forever pleasure that always ended too fast. It took a lot of effort for him not to come as she writhed and pushed against him, hips grinding, hair quivering over her face in twitching squiggles.

"Are you gonna come?" she asked.

"You want I should stop?"

He stopped.

"NO!" She whacked him on the ass, digging her nails in.

"YOUCH! Make up yuh mind then."

"Shut up. Fuck me. Come on. You won't be in there too long anyway." Her eyes were ferocious, an arrogant laughing wickedness in them. "You're gonna come, I can tell."

"Speak f' yuhself."

"Come on," she said, flicking her tongue at him. "Fuck me!"

He pulled out. "Roll over," he said. She turned and got up on all fours and pointed her lovely curvy ass at him. Going in was sweet, but he was gonna lose it all soon the way she was pushing against him, her back arching and spinning, her hair in flight as she began to cry out louder and louder.

"You want me to stop?" he yelled.

"NO!" She grabbed his ass as her cries peaked, her body twitching and rolling as her head sank into a pillow stifling the scream, her body tensing, her legs trembling and then stretching out.

After that they lay all over each other watching TV like zombies, nibbling on candy bars and playing with the remote. Around midnight, the phone rang. Cristalena answered it with a quick hop skip. While she talked, Miguel got up from the bed and walked over to the window, staring at the quiet dark street. He felt like he was in another world, as if he had been transmogrified into a human being. No more talk about posses, no more pickups and runs. No beeper. He was making some kind of transition, but how could he make it? Did Nelo really expect him to become a sixteen-year-old kid? Nothing could ever turn him into that now. Once you go into combat you're never the same again. Miguel had done things and seen things that most men walking the city streets on their way to cushy office jobs never would've survived. It made him feel contempt for all those people, for Nelo, who assumed Miguel was supposed to respect him as some kind of figurehead. Miguel didn't respect anybody. So far he had only seen people at their worst.

The meeting with Spider was tomorrow. Should he even show up? Amelia told him no. Even Ritchie said he should just skip town, already. Why was it that Miguel felt compelled to somehow break with Spider on amicable terms? Was it guilt? Was it a friendship thing? Miguel couldn't figure it out.

There was also the car.

If Miguel could talk Cristalena into living with him, he could keep the car. Sure, it was risky driving it around, it always had been, that was part of the thrill. But to part with it? Nelo would not keep the car. Miguel hadn't asked him about it, but he knew the guy would not take the risk. The car wasn't even really registered. What happens when its inspection sticker runs out? Miguel hadn't asked, but his license was worthless; he had no claim to the car. It was probably stolen. It came with Spider's world and he was starting to realize that if he left Spider's world he would also have to leave the car. If anything, it was the only real reason Miguel wanted to see Spider, to ask him about what options he might have. The car was a part of him. If he could hide the car or store it for two years, he could maybe get a real license and register the car as his own. But that was two years away; to somebody out on the streets two years away might as well be a fucken century.

Cristalena hopped on him from behind with happy laughter, turning him around and kissing him.

"That was Dolores."

"Hullo, Dolores."

"She's in Boston. Thass how we got to stay in her house, you see? She ain't coming back with her two roomies until tomorrow night. So we can spend the night!" She jumped on him and they both tumbled back into bed, even though Miguel didn't feel too happy. They snuggled and she brought him out of it, but when she started digging around for the word on his sour puss, he told her, let it all flow out of him in jagged chunks; then he looked at her like a wounded child.

"Why, Cristalena? Why you gotta be so goddamn sure we can't make it together?"

She sighed, rubbing his chest with her hands. "Ohh, Miguel."

"If I went out tomorrow an' found a place, would'ju live with me?"

"Ohhh Miguel. It might be possible. I don't know, we'd have to talk about it more."

Rent, food, furniture, clothes . . . Cristalena was still in school, he was a dropout . . . how would they get the money to survive? If she had to work she wouldn't be able to finish school. What about college? Was he going to go back to school? What kind of a job was he planning to get anyway? The questions spilled out of her. Miguel covered his head with a sheet and rolled away from her.

"Aaargh. You ask too many questions."

"They gotta be asked, Miguel."

"Don'chu ever take chances? What, you want everything to be all safe? I don't know anything thass like that."

"I wanna have a life, Miguel. I ain't tying myself to some sinking ship. I know that sounds cold, but I got plans, Miguel. I wanna go to design school an' make something of myself."

"Thass fine, man, but that don't mean we can't make it happen now. I know a lotta people done this."

"Yeah? An' how they end up?"

"Well, the girl gets pregnant, and the guy's never home 'cause he's out with the posse an' then the girl goes on welfare an' the guy maybe leaves huh f' another girl an' . . ."

"Look, Miguel, if you really quit this shit," she said sternly, "then there's no source of steady income. An' we'd need a steady source of income." All the girlishness was gone from her probing eyes. "Eight thousand dollars. Fine. That'll get us only halfway there. What'll we do for money? I can't leave school. An' you, you have to go back. I don't wanna marry some dropout."

It was the way she said it, the contempt in her words, that made him feel dislocated and unsupported. He needed her to go along with him, not argue.

"I din't know you felt that way," he said slowly, not looking at her. His face was burning.

"Miguel, I didn't mean to say it like that." She grabbed his hands and tried to get him to look her in the face. "Miguel?" She bit her lip. "I just want what's best for us. Even if it means we gotta wait. Why should we ruin everything now just 'cause we can't wait a while to do it right?"

"I just don't know why you can't trust me, why you gotta keep shootin' it down."

"I'm not!"

"You are!"

"I just want it to be perfect!"

"Well it can't be perfect. I don't know anything thass perfect."

"Well fuck you. Because we're perfect." Her voice broke a little. She was fighting it, squeezing his hands with the effort. "We're perfect just the way we are. We're two fucking kids, Miguel. We shouldn't try to be these big adults. We'll lose everything."

He was going to say something but she caressed his face, tracing his lips with her fingers. "Please," she said, "let's take some time to grow up first, please? I need time." She fell against him. They collapsed into bed, holding on tightly. A hundred feelings tore at Miguel at once; he didn't know which way to go. All he knew was her scented hair brushing against his face, the warm curve of her neck, the soft pillowy breasts. They lay there staring at each other without saying anything. The TV played to the empty room.

He was going to lose his independence, he was going to lose his freedom, he was definitely losing the car. He was going to be a sixteen-and-a-half-year-old now and live with TWO parents and have his own room and go to some school. He'd have to take the subway down to see her; they could go out on dates to movies and neck, but they'd have to phone home if it got too late.

They snuggled quietly, kissing softly.

"I'm gonna miss my car," he said.

21

He had parked the car three blocks away up a side street so it wouldn't be spotted. From there he walked many blocks out of his way to see if he was being tailed. The gun was a snug heavy bump in his coat pocket pressing up against his leg like a hard-on. Could everybody see it? He felt like he was on the beach and had to drape a towel over his crotch because
    because
    he had gone to the beach last summer for the first time since he was eleven (back then he was detailed to carry the heavy cooler while Mom carried the basket of cold chicken and Sis lugged the plastic buckets).
    THIS TIME with his new family
    Firebug
    Amelia
    The Suarez Twins (with two of their boyfriends, Sammy and Juice)
    AND the girl Miguel was fucking
    (that week)
    Deborah
    Or was it . . . ?

    Shoulder-length corkscrew hair all wet and coiled, coffee skin gleaming slick from sun from lotion he rubbed on QUICK GET MY TOWEL (how do women keep the spaces between their thighs so soft??), Orchard Beach THE SHINING STAR OF THE CARIBBEAN, smell that sand surf chuletas lechon bacalaitos frying on blackened grills in pots filled with bubbling oil, fat lady in a big white hat handing out tostones as if they were Bible tracts, every radio going full blast, kiddies scooting sand flying.

(Deborah jerked him off in the water.)

Amelia so cute in a red one piece her body so thin so elastic BUT her ass pokes up nicely, thank you—i.e., YOU KNOW SHE'S LATIN.

The Suarez Twins rubbing their poor unfortunate boyfriends raw on the sands draping towels over their privates but everybody on the beach could see, even the kiddies who giggled and kept coming closer while the lady with the tostones cried out to every angel in heaven to hurry up and come down and bring these twisted young kids some DECENCY some RESPECT some sense of DECORUM anything, she even gave them bacalaitos wrapped in a paper towel in the hopes that the crisp codfish patties would kill their sex drive.

MEANWHILE Firebug offers to help, he has been lingering around many of the flaming barbecues on wheels Miguel should've warned them about him but when he went over there and started fucking with that man's barbie, well, he started it. The explosion shot the ugly grill (with burgers still clinging) through a huge ugly plastic lounge chair that was still sagging from the weight of the fat lady who had been sitting there. Maybe they would've believed he was sorry if only he had stopped LAUGHING, juicy bloody ribs everywhere, clumps of dead burgers staining the plastic kiddie scoops that lay like discarded rifles . . .

AND THEN all those people got mad, too mad, so Miguel and Amelia (WHO were lightly buzzed from having toked some sweet weed) started packing up because THERE WERE TWELVE OF THEM, boxers in search of sparring partners.

They were laughing all the way back on the train

Suarez Twins shaking sand out of their hair their bikini tops and singing Madonna songs at the top of their lungs

(MAN those girls sure could swim real good bodies bursting out of their skimpy bikinis with their big fat culos and well-muscled tummies)

A joint between subway cars in the fading sunlight so golden brown the streets below like blinking images on an old View-Master reel

Arriving on Tinton all tanned all salty and smelling of summer and sunburned hair sacked out in India House, where Spider, so regal so short lay in his chaise lounge by the air con in the living room sipping his wine cooler and asking, "So, boys an' girls, how was the beach?"

It was like a family memory, a snapshot of the past. Miguel felt guilty, as if he were betraying a loved one. Walking the cold dark streets, he thought only of the good times he had shared with Spider—the crazy laughs, the parties, the small tokens of affection that kept him loyal. Spider was a big brother, a mentor, a guidance counselor that put the whole world in his hands. He was an inspiring general to fight for. He had been every image of family and sharing and teamwork, of power, success, and fame. All that had stood against the mundane humdrum WHITE world where Miguel felt like he didn't even register on the scale. It was a negation of THE AMERICAN DREAM or maybe a twisting around of it, like Spider was always "speechifying." "This is an American Dream idea I bet they didn't think about," he would drawl with his eyebrows flying up and down. Miguel learned he didn't need THEM. They could shove their schools and the 9-to-5 life, the work-hard-it-pays-off life, the read-a-book-and-get-ahead universe. Spider had made him feel like he was a master of his own universe. Too bad that Miguel had come to realize that in a sense they were all roaches, ruling their little kingdom under the kitchen sink, content to run out and devour crumbs until the fucken bastids came in and turned on the lights—then it was mad scurry time. Roaches. Ruling their under-sink world. Happy to feed on crumbs. Until that huge slipper comes down—

(SPLAT)

Miguel had to see him.

No way he could make Cristalena understand, or Amelia or anyone else. Even if it was stupid and dangerous he had to do it, had to know that despite the changes Spider was still a human being, that Miguel had touched his life and so had called for this last meeting. No one believed that could be true, but Miguel did. He had to. It was a family thing. You don't give up on family. Miguel still believed in him. Whatever Spider had done, Miguel had to believe there was a part of the guy that still cared, that felt remorse over the obligations and duties of business. It was that part of him that would come to see him to say goodbye. Because they affected each other. There was no way around that.

And if Spider tearfully asked him to stay, then what?

Miguel was determined to stick to his decision, but in one scenario he saw himself telling Cristalena he was going to stay in the biz "only a little while longer" just to amass some more cash for their future.

(Okay, it was just a query scenario.)

Because saying goodbye was always hard. It was the hardest thing in the world.

Walking the streets in his big coat, his upturned collar, he felt unprotected. Working for Spider had been like a safety net. Now he felt dislocated and vulnerable. He was just another putz on the street. The gun comforted him. It was in his hand, it was rock-hard, warm, and heavy, it was fully loaded and ready to back him up. He had never had a gun. It made him cocky to carry it. He knew why everybody had one now. The cop cars that cruised by irritated him.

It wasn't yet the "rush" at Spadgie's—on Sunday nights that was around midnight—and yet there were already people milling around outside the battered storefront, cars double-parked on Longwood. Miguel noticed a long black limo sitting under the el like a leopard waiting to pounce. It made his heart hammer in his head. It made him check his watch. Ten to ten. He was across the street and a block down. He could see everyone, the clusters of beat boys in their caps, baggy pants barely clinging to their hips, the girls chirping sweetly. The ratty-haired doorman was at his post in the same ugly brown coat, shifting his weight and glaring with his bloodshot eyes, his voice a throaty growl that reverberated up the street. There was no one around Miguel recognized as an enemy. None of the cars looked familiar, either. It looked like a pretty regular night at Spadgie's. Even that panting limo up under the el shouldn't be considered unusual for Spadgie's. Music throbbed through the door. Another party night; why should this night be any different? Miguel lit a cigarette. Okay, so maybe Spider did plan to hit the place, like Ritchie and Careta said. Who said it had to be tonight? Maybe Spider wanted to come down himself to put the fear of God in Spadgie, to remind him the boss was around and watching. Maybe it was going to be a kind of warning situation. Maybe he was already in there, having a private powwow with Spadgie behind the bar under the shimmering twitching dancing lights. (TEN O'CLOCK.) Maybe Spider was already in there. Maybe Spider was sitting in that fucken limo waiting to spot him.

(What?)

There were a frantic series of birdcalls, siren gull cries, high-pitched whistles. The boys on the street were signaling each other. Miguel waited. What was happening? The lights on the limo flashed twice. There were no Spider boys in sight. Was it possible Spider's operation had grown so big that he could use boys Miguel had never even seen? Impossible. Miguel had met most everyone, at least seen them, and he had a photographic memory for faces, for clothes, even for a certain walk and strut. The crowd at Spadgie's was always diverse. It wasn't a big hangout with the Spider boys. Even Spider used to say there was a "weird vibe" there. Spider boys stuck to India House, Columbia House, wherever the Suarez Twins went; but the Suarez Twins didn't go to Spadgie's. "Too far," Josie said, her gum clacking. "Too many fucken patos," Rosie said with that upper lip twisting in scorn.

Miguel decided to wait. Why be punctual? If he was early, it would be stupid to be there. Five or ten minutes late, and Spider would wait. And if Spider was late, Miguel could spot him going in. So he was going to stand right there and not move, thinking he had cornered a nice overhanging shadow that would cover him. But he had been spotted right away.

"Yo." The voice came from his right, and Miguel noticed there were two guys standing there in an even darker shadow. They were somebody's lieutenants. You could tell because they walked like the higher echelon and as they stepped into the lights you could see it on their uniforms— heavy coats, diamond belt buckles, their black caps tilted at exactly the same angle. One walked in front of the other, as if the other guy was covering him. As they stepped into the dull street light Miguel could make out the thin lifeless face of the guy in front squinting at him. His hands were in his pockets. So were Miguel's, one hand tensing up on the gun.

"Yo," the guy rasped, stepping up to him. "You waiting' f' somebody?"

Miguel stared at him and didn't say anything. Posses cleared the streets of people. After a certain hour they liked to think they owned the place. Miguel wasn't wearing colors. He wasn't in baggies or a cap. He had on his Marine coat, with the collar up. He had on his Spanish suede boots. The guy looked him up and down and then something clicked. His left cheek twitched.

"I know you," he said, without warmth.

Miguel recognized him too. "An' I know you, Beetle. How's tricks, bro'?"

Beetle shrugged. The cartoon character he was named after was cuter.

There was nothing cartoony about the lifeless eyes, the thick jutting lips, that twitch in his left cheek.

"Jus' checkin' the streets you know, doin' my patrol. We gotta big fucken party tonight, bro'. You here wif' yuh crew?"

Miguel smirked. "I'm waitin' f' my girl an' shit. Spadgie said he wanted to see huh do huh thing."

"Spadgie don't like women." Said with contempt.

"Well he like this one. She sticks a whole bottle of champagne up huh pussy. She makes it bubble. It comes out all foamy."

"No shit." The guy's cheek twitched. He wasn't moving.

"Yeah but I think I'm gonna go in. I don't want 'im t' think I stiffed 'im. If you see this tall skinny black-hair girl tell huh I'm inside. She'll be the one with a champagne bottle."

The guy nodded as if still trying to make sense of the story. Miguel left him there and crossed the street toward Spadgie's. Just as he reached the other side, there was a sudden roar, a car engine coming to life. Miguel turned in time to catch the black limo as it roared by, tires squealing dust churning lights cutting through the dark. It went past like an explosion. All Miguel caught was the design on the trunk, a huge "A" with wings attached. It looked like the patch symbol for an airborne division. For a moment, Miguel thought the car was going to lift off into the sky with wings flapping. Cheers suddenly went up around him, beat boys rolling fists and yelling.

"Fucken Ace, man," one of the boys near him said to another, who waved his hat. "He loves buzzin' Spadgie's."

Miguel felt a funny tremor. Ace? In that car? He noticed that the long sleek limo had U-turned down Longwood and was standing like a trembling seething beast with glaring headlights, as if trying to decide if it was going to make another pass. Was the guy looking for Spider? Was Spider already inside? It suddenly dawned on him that there was every possibility that Spider was already inside waiting for him, that maybe Ritchie had found out about the meeting and had set them both up. Maybe he had Spider all wrong right from the beginning. Maybe Spider was being honest. Maybe it was Ritchie who was playing the both of them.

His stomach tightened as he entered the place. The loud music boomed, immersing him in spinning slivers of day-glo light. He tripped down the wooden steps, hostile eyes glaring back; any one of these people could be working for Ace. Any one of these kids downing beers and lighting jays could be packing their pieces, waiting for that secret password, that special signal that will mean BULLETS and screaming and tumbling bullet-riddled bodies. Had Spadgie already gone over to the other side? Why not? But when Spider showed up, it would all be over. With Spider sitting there Spadgie would realize who was boss. Spadgie would shrink in front of him. Miguel could imagine the flabby frog-face changing color the minute Spider appeared at the bar with his thousand-yard GLARE. For some reason Miguel heard Spider using the same words he had thrown at Miguel in the stockroom at Franco's about riding for a fall. He could see Spider sitting there, lighting a cigarette and grinning.

"Ridin' f' a fall, bro'," he would say gruffly. Spadgie was shaking his head. He could hear Spider mumbling even over the music.

"Nah, Spider man, it ain't wha'chu think." Squirming Spadgie. And Miguel would be sitting right beside Spider, like his old lieutenant. It made him nervous to think about it. There was so much to say. How was it going to go? Was Miguel that much of a man? Was he going to tell Spider to his face? Was Spider ready to let him go?

Wall-to-wall bodies. A little push and shove. Gloria fucken Estefan raising hell with her cheap shoddy Latin POOP and lookit all the stupid fat-assed Latin girls swinging their well-greased hips. And how they writhe and swing and cream their panties for Rico Suave while he insults them and berates them! Miguel figured a little Guns N' Roses would clear the place out fast. He slowly made his way past big and burlies, past the pool tables, past a speaker blaring more Gloria, and then he could see the bar, way in the back. At first he felt a tremor, thought he spotted THE MAN sitting there all hunched and smoking, but as he came closer he saw it wasn't Spider, maybe a Spider double because the guy had the same army jacket, the same curly hair, but up close his face was drunken and disfigured by fistfights. There were only a few kids leaning near the bar, and there was Spadgie behind it, his arms crossed, his eyes locked on Miguel so intently that when Miguel noticed he blushed. Too late to change direction; Miguel walked right up to the bar, right up to where Spadgie was standing. There was a toothpick in his mouth. He gave Miguel an expectant look. Miguel only shrugged.

"I don't think you came here for a drink," Spadgie said, leaning closer so that Miguel would hear him. He smelled of cheap cologne and brandy.

"I'm waitin' f' somebody," Miguel said, as if he needed to verify it with someone. He was nervous and couldn't help fumbling for his cigarettes as Spadgie watched.

"Oh? Waitin' f' somebody? Who's that? Rico?"

"No. Not Rico."

Spadgie laughed silently, lips twitching with soundless ripples.

"I can't imagine who yuh here t' see." He pulled over a stool and sat, leaning over the table so he could stare right into Miguel's face. "After all, you ain't exactly one a' my regulars, now are you? I've seen you maybe three or four times. An' outside a' Spadgie's, well, I've never seen you without Spider boy."

Miguel lit his cigarette. His hands trembled a little. He decided to keep them out of sight but Spadgie had already noticed.

"Maybe you a little cold?"

"Nah."

"Yuh hands shakin' an' shit."

"I got a condition."

Spadgie let out another silent laugh, his eyes chinking up. "My my my, whatta pretty boy you are. You bein' here like this, why it jus' sets my mind alight." His face came closer, eyes widening as if about to swallow him. "Who you here t' meet."

Miguel didn't know whether to tell him. He didn't know if Spadgie was in on it. He didn't know if Spadgie should know Spider was coming. He shrugged with annoyance.

"I can meet him outside if you want, man."

"I already know who it is, little boy. You might think I don't got smarts, but I do, baby, I run this place, don't I? I don't like to think about what happens when little faggits cross me. Yuh Spider's girlfriend. The one with the car. The one he sent to check on Rico. Right?" He grinned. "An' now you sittin' here at the bar. Jus' like that." He was breathing heavy right into Miguel's face. Miguel moved back and Spadgie moved with him. "Now you tell me why you here before I call my boys."

"Maan, get off." Miguel shoved him back a little because he was tired of the man's breath in his face. It made Spadgie's face twitch with anger. He glared at Miguel, thin pale lips trembling.

"If yuh so hung up, why don'chu ask the man himself when he comes?" Miguel just blurted it out. He couldn't help it. He felt good when he saw Spadgie's face change yet again, the color draining from his puffy cheeks.

"Hol' up, hol' up," he said, stepping close again. "Spider's comin' here? Now? Tonight?"

Something weird was up. Miguel looked around him at the crowds of people, the clatter of billiard balls, the laughter of two girls who were spraying each other's hair with cans of spray glitter.

"What would make Spider come here?" Spadgie seemed to ask himself, but the confusion in his voice alarmed Miguel. It made him realize that there were too many things going down here that he didn't know about, that he was just a tiny nobody on a raft being rocked by high seas.

"Wait a minute." Spadgie grabbed Miguel by the coat and pulled him closer, his eyes searching him. "You sayin' that Spider's comin' here? Now?"

Miguel pulled his hand off his coat. "Yeah, he's comin' here now, dammit. Why else would I be here? We got some stuff to talk over."

Spadgie's eyes got glassy. They seemed not to see Miguel for a moment.

"He tol'ju t' come here an' meet him?" He seemed to have fallen into a trance.

"Yeah."

Suddenly Spadgie sprang into life. He reached under the bar for a tote bag. He unzipped it and took out a MAC-10 semiautomatic on which he checked the clip. Miguel looked around him but nobody seemed to notice. Spadgie stuck the gun back in the bag and zipped it.

"Whassup?" Miguel reached over and nudged him but Spadgie was on automatic, collecting his things from under the bar and dumping them into the tote's outer pockets.

"I'm doin' what you should be doin'," Spadgie said quickly.

Miguel felt the panic sting him. "Whass that mean?"

"Did he tell you he was comin' here t' see me?"

"Nah man, me. He's gonna talk t' me, bro'. He told me I should meet him here."

Spadgie grinned. It was like he had figured out the story at long last. He gave Miguel a quick tap on the cheek with his hand.

"Well then I'm gettin' the fuck. I don't know where you from, little boy, or even if you smart, but'chu gotta be the stupidest fuck if you think Spider would come here t' chat wit'chu. An' baby, when I don't like the smell I get my feets to move."

Before Miguel could say anything, Spadgie had shuffled off with his tote bag, disappearing into the masses of heads and caps and swirling lights. Miguel was trying to put the words all together in his head. Somewhere along the line he had made a mistake. There was something wrong here. His mind seemed to fight against the one possibility, the one painful prospect, that maybe it was true that Spider was going to kill him tonight.

"No way," Miguel said to himself, out loud. "No fucken way!" But he felt like he was running out of air. Spadgie was gone. Miguel turned from the bar and searched the dark bobbing seas of heads and faces. He felt hemmed in and trapped. And there was no Spider anywhere. He was walking. Away from the bar. He wasn't going to tell himself that he was whacked out and SCARED and feeling a metallic taste in his mouth like he would puke. He was simply going to GET THE FUCK. To hell with this shit and these crazy people and these gun-toting assholes. If he didn't see Spider between now and outside, that was it. He had waited. He had done his part. He had been faithful. The confusion about it hurt him, made his chest heavy. He still felt like he was a traitor, that he was running out on the team. But there were just too many questions. Miguel started working his way through the crowd. Everything around him was too loud, too much light, sound, and pushing. Suddenly Miguel was grabbed, huge fingers digging deep into his coat and pulling him back as if he weighed less than an ounce. In his backslide flip he grabbed a chair and crashed into the pool table, upsetting a bunch of people. Faces spun real quick and there was this one face in his, CLOSE. Miguel pushed the guy off. He looked vaguely familiar but only became REAL familiar after Miguel spotted that bitch Gloria leaning against the wall by the glittering strings of light in a tight red minidress and a great wad of gum that kept her chewing like a cow.

"So, we meet again," the guy said to him, his beer breath in Miguel's face. Was he still smarting from the cigarette Miguel had flicked in his face last time? He had to throw his head back just to look the guy in the eye.

"Get the fuck off!" Miguel pushed him away violently.

"Who the fuck you think you are comin' in here again after las' time like you think you can diss my girl, bro'? Like you think you can jus' come in here an' do wha'chu fucken want?"

"Maan get off!" The guy had him by the coat and wouldn't let go. Miguel turned and wriggled. Nobody around them even noticed. The pool players kept playing pool, the girl in the corner kept sucking face as Gloria stepped forward into a pink circle of light like an actress onstage.

"Man Miguel, you know? I swea' you got such a bad attitude. Like you so fucken rude. Las' time I was jus' tryin'na be friends, you know? An' you go an' blow me off like that. Did'ja hafta go insult my honor?"

"Look," Miguel screamed into her face, "I gotta lot t' do now an' I ain't got time f' this shit, so you tell yuh fucken fat-headed gorilla to go fuck himself, okay?"

Her eyes popped open as if he had stuck her with a cattle prod. He had freed himself and was now breaking through the faces, the bodies, the mad twirling lights that made it so hard to see when he got grabbed again.

"Who the fuck you think you are?" he heard in his ear like a mouse squeak before something hit him in the side of the head. It crunched and crackled, sent him crashing into a pool table, billiard balls sailing everywhere with little clacks. A million people seemed to go HEY MAN WHAT THE FUCK WHASSUP ASSHOLE as he turned and suddenly found himself dodging another punch.

What the fuck? He wanted to tell the guy because it was a simple story, really. OKAY, yes he fucked Gloria, several times it happened, but only because she had tits like two HINDENBURGS all squished together with giant nipples that really stuck out. She was dead in bed, did a lot of talking, chain-smoked, kept squeezing his dick until it was hard again. Good luck, bro', you can have her.

When the guy connected with a punch Miguel felt his whole face collapse. His nose went CRICK, his eyes SPROINGED, and he saw planets and stars like in the cartoons. Was he hitting the floor? Yes, he was sailing, falling against the pool table. He felt the crack of a pool cue on his head, heard one of the angry players yelling at him as if HE had started it.

Then the sound, like a large wave crashing onto a beach. At first it was like far-off thunder, a staccato cracking. Then the sounds swelled, clambering up one on top of another, metallic stuttering, wood cracking, or maybe it was like the sound that the jet spray from an open hydrant makes as the kid with the can directs the stream at the passing car. AND THEN IT BUILT—screams, girl screams, far, coming closer as if this was contagious, louder and louder first in a jar and then a stadium of screaming, pushing bodies and the far-off stutter becomes a deafening earsplitting blast that explodes rapid-fire. Suddenly glass was everywhere, shards frozen in midair like ice sculptures, chunks of wood, chairs tables bodies tumbling and the noise wouldn't stop, that rapid staccato growing louder. Coats flying, arms gyrating . . . Miguel felt bodies crash into him, hands grip him, hot stinging needles stabbing his cheek. He felt something slap him hard in the back SLAP HIM HARD IN THE BACK hard enough for him to feel a shudder, a spasm, that sudden nausea

oh God
I'm shot I'm shot I'm shot

Felt his skin SPLIT or was that his coat he was being pulled forward, pulled backward, he was falling, he felt a hundred sharp stings, a hundred punches and kicks and then
the splash of the wet
THE WET
splashing his face, splashing his hands, sticky warm wet another SPLASH near him, the sound like when you split a coconut with a hammer WARM SPLASH sticky wet

a cutting pain in his side and he gasped for air

oh God
I'm shot I'm shot I'm bleeding
don't fall don't
calm down try to calm

The firing was echoing through his head like an approaching subway train, the train pulling into the station with dark tunnel all around, and when he was sure the train headlights were gleaming big enough in his eyes
he jumped

•

•

It was all dark and the firing had gone away but there was crying. All quiet except for soft crying, girl crying, little child crying. Moans, choppy breathing. Miguel felt like he was at sea. He was at sea on a raft and then the panic set in when he realized he wasn't breathing he COULDN'T FEEL HIMSELF BREATHING there was someone on him.

There were sirens spinning closer. People walked through crackling glass, cop talkies hissing.

He felt calm. He didn't know why but his mind was being real rational even though his arms were trembling. When he tried to move a blinding pain shot through his arms and chest and something back there seemed to rip open and gush a warm flood down his back. Despite that Miguel felt calm enough to struggle with his arm and find his coat pocket and somehow he managed to pull the gun out of his pocket and he slid it along the floor and away from himself because do you know what the cops would do to him if they found it on him?

Spider was an acrid foul taste in his mouth tasting of bullets and steel and a deep hurt. Spider was climbing up the side of the building without a harness. He was all the way up on the roof in no time. He was waving.

Miguel clung to Cristalena through the swirling black nausea. He could see her screaming his name and clutching his lifeless hand. And when he saw her looking down on his bullet-riddled corpse with her face all torn up like that, then he felt sorry

then he felt like he had let her down

like he had never cared enough to spare her

like he had never thought this could separate them

he cried like a baby.

22

The first dreams had Spider in them. The dreams were immersed in dark colors and muddy textures. Miguel couldn't remember the story behind the images or where they had taken him. They were just snatches of conversation, little glimpses of the magic gnome scampering into a dark vestibule, disappearing between abandoned buildings, huddling under the bus-stop shelter on Prospect Avenue while rain pelted the dark street.

"I tell you what." He was sitting beside Miguel. The blessed scent of his car, his Baby. The Christmas lights under the dash blinked like black stars. Miguel could taste Spider's cigarette, the musky stink of his old army jacket. "Some people, man, they born t' be doctors. With a mission, like from day one. You can figure it out. There are people who are gonna die because he won't be there t' save 'um. He was born to save those people. You believe that?"

Miguel was in a stupor. After all, he had just been shot at Spadgie's and was under anesthesia. Drugs were flowing into his body through a jungle of plastic vines stuck to him. There was even something in his mouth. He was biting down and trying to figure out what it was.

"I said, do you believe in that?"

"Nah," Miguel said. His voice sounded like he was underwater.

"Well I know I believe in that shit. I'm just like that doctor, bro'. I was born t' do what I do. You get it? This was what I was made for. You can be sure I ain't savin' no money f' no college, boy. This is what I was born t' be. Fate. Destiny. All great men of history believe in it. A star. My star."

There was a flashing star and it was in Miguel's head and he was trying to figure out if it was a real memory of what happened or if he was just making it up. But it was a big star, flashing like a torch, spitting out bullets that smashed through bodies and tumbled out through tattered exit wounds that splattered paisley shirts and sent black caps spinning in torn strips. It was Spider's star.

They were rushing down streets together, Spider punching him with that crazy grin, and then he had an arm around him like they were buddy soldiers, and even though they were running for their lives there was still time for a little affection. They splashed through some frozen puddle that wet them through their pants and then they were crouching behind a parked car, peering through car glass at passing headlights that all seemed to be looking for them. They laughed and vapor rolled out from them in cloudy wisps that vanished into nothingness.

"That was close." Spider and Miguel laughed so hard that they were rolling on the hood of the car. They still had the memory of the bullets pounding into the riot gate behind them, of the crazy rattling and crackling and the gun barking and what a surprise it is, what a movie life to be standing on the street one minute sharing a joke and the next to find yourself frozen staring for a fraction of a second at a car that slows, at a gun muzzle poking from the back seat through the open window. It's like being in a war movie and hugging your wounded buddy, like being in a war movie and escaping by the skin of your teeth and then staring at each other in the cold, laughing, wiping at wet eyes and feeling crazy grateful.

"I tell you man," Spider said breathlessly. "I am the most fucken lucky bastid in the whole world, man. Pana. My pana. Comrade. Hermano." Grateful shimmers in his eyes as he looked at Miguel. It had been Miguel who spotted the car, Miguel who let out the yell and who gave Spider a shove that sent them both tumbling just as the gun started laying down its guest solo.

"I'm lucky t' have somebody I can trust." Spider was getting all mushy now sitting there toking, handing him the spliff.

"Yeah well, me too." Funny how goofy Miguel sounded when he said it, how unused he was to saying shit like that. Spider laughed and patted him on the head like he was his pet, and then they were stoned and singing some song from the seventies by K.C. and the Sunshine Band. Thass the way uh-huh un-huh I like it. Spider laid out two of his prettiest babes just for Miguel, the best smoke, the nicest, biggest room in Columbia House with the place empty and exotic with its rugs, its walls of beads and calaveras. Spider always knew how to say thank you. He gave and he gave.

"When you write this book about me," Spider instructed him late one night as Miguel drove him to Franco's, "I wan'chu should use my name— Spider. I wan'chu should write it so all these shits out here will know it's me."

Miguel laughed. "I ain't writin' no book, Spider, I tol'ju."

"Yes you are. Lookit'chu laughin'. You love when I bring it up. You like the idea a' thinkin' you gonna do somethin' else wit'cha life. I know you. This ain't enough f' yuh brains, right? So I'm givin' you this new assignment. An' when you famous, you'll know it was me helped'ju out." It was me formed you, it was me created you. The Lord giveth and the Lord taketh away. I made you, I can break you. This was gangster-movie talk, something from some movie Miguel had seen. He couldn't place it.

He was crying. His face was wet from the tears and he knew it before he had even opened his eyes. He knew a lot of things but he wasn't sure how. He knew, for example, that Spadgie was dead. He had almost gotten away all right, but he had hit the street with his tote bag right at the moment when it might've been better for him to have been behind the bar, ducking as shells slammed through it. Instead they caught him right out in the open. Miguel could see him spinning and struggling with the zipper on his tote before a barrage of slugs tore into him, making him dance and twitch like a crazy marionette. Miguel saw it all in his dream and later when he was told about it he couldn't decide if he had known before or after. He kept seeing Spider climb up that building, waving from the roof. There was no malice in his face, just determination. He was a man with a mission. He was born to do this, born to kill Spadgie and six other faceless bodies that would never groove to Gloria Estefan again. Born to rule the streets and make alliances and break them. Just like world powers and big corporations and successful businesses. It was all bigger than all of them. Miguel and Spider and all those other shadows, they were tiny pins on a map, they hardly registered at all. Their kind came and went. They didn't write about them or direct plays or paint murals about their lives. They were all walking shit. Whether they lived in the South Bronx or Bed-Stuy or Harlem or Los Sures. It didn't matter. They didn't exist. They were all lowercase people.

You get tougher and tougher and colder and harder until twelve-year-olds have eyes like grunts who've seen too many firefights, who've lived through too many ambushes, who bust caps at children and screaming gook mothers just because THE ENEMY IS EVERYWHERE, the only fun maybe a Zippo raid where you can watch them hootches burn, baby, burn. You learn to grow that exoskeleton so the hard knocks don't even show, tough tank armor with sloped sides so the shells slide right off. Miguel had failed. He tried growing the armored skin but he couldn't. Even little Jimmy with his nine was tougher. Miguel just cried. He cried his way right out of those dark swirling dreams, through dark alleys, running after Spider, trying to find him, to talk to him, to hear it from his own lips. Finally Spider was up on the roof of the building, waving, Miguel looking up at him with his hands clutching at the rough seamless brick.

"Well?" Spider motioned to him. "Come on up."

Miguel looked up at him, helpless. He couldn't climb. He tried clutching at the bricks and looked for little ridges, but there was nothing. He beat the wall with his fists. He was being left behind. He felt a strange panicky sensation in his groin. When he woke up he was in a bed in this room, his arms tangled in wires. He was on his stomach. There was a pillow in his mouth; He had been biting down on it. He was trying to roll over but couldn't. As he thrashed a sharp pain made him moan. The tears made it impossible to see. Then he was being grabbed. An overhead light snapped on, blinding him. Arms grabbing him.

"Stop that! Calm down!" It was a nasty woman's voice. He struggled to break free.

"Spider!" It was a hoarse scream from his insides. "Spider!" He caught a glimpse of a man standing by the windows. He looked like a ghost. He was smiling sadly. Miguel fell into darkness again, into a dark silence. When he woke again the man was there with his hands in his pockets, looking down on him.

"Spider," Miguel said to him.

"I know," the man said back quietly, fading into the onrushing blackness. No dreams, just Spider. Covering the walls like a huge shadow. By the window in a hunched silhouette. His favorite word, "pana," burning a hole through Miguel's head. When he came out of the black, he was choking with sobs, coughing with the puke. He was on top of the roof then, but Spider had pushed him off. Now he was just falling, falling, falling.

23

The detective's name was Sanchez. He had a kind face and large dark eyes like the black marbles that come with Chinese checkers sets. He spoke softly and when he got impatient he seemed to lose his breath. It wasn't anger; more like helplessness. His face was the first thing Miguel had seen when his eyes focused on the blurry shapes in the hospital room. The overhead fluorescents hurt his eyes. Sanchez stood there by the wall in his wrinkled brown raincoat. He just stared and grinned a little as if Miguel should already know him. It was painful for Miguel to look at him. He was lying on his stomach and his neck was all cramped up. The doctor was peering down at him and adjusting the bandages on his back. Miguel felt like an insect in a jar. He had a couple of IVs in him. A nurse kept checking them.

He spent four days on his stomach. Taking a shit was a logistical nightmare. His chest caved in with pain, one arm was stiff and useless, and he kept tangling himself in his IV tubes. A big black nurse yelled at him, snorting like a bull.

"You ain't supposed t' be movin' around on yuh own. You sit yuh ass in that bed an' don't be movin'. Nobody tol' you you could be movin' around, dear. You get back in that bed right now."

"But I wanna take a shit, man."

"Then you press that gawdamn button at the head a' the bed an' a nurse will come. You press that button, come on, dear."

"I can't even reach the button."

"You a real smart-ass kid, ain'chu? Now I see why they shot'chu."

. . .

"But I'm alive," he chanted to himself at night in the half-dark with light pouring through the open doorway. From the nurses' station a radio blared hits from the fifties while the women jabbered away like birds in a cage. The other two men in Miguel's room snored. The buses coughing and sneezing down on the street filled him with longing. He wanted out already. He was sick of the smells, of mouthwash and disinfectant and feet and vomit.

The doctor was a ruddy-faced guy with red hair. He was always munching on something. He would come in and peel away bandages and go ummm ohh hmm while Miguel lay there feeling too drowsy to talk. He only showed up early in the morning just when Miguel was starting to fall asleep because he could never get to sleep right away. He could never sleep on his stomach. He kept rolling over. Then he could feel things snapping in his back and warm liquids would churn. The nurse would scream at him: She put styrofoam pads on both sides of him so he couldn't move. He started crying. The nurse left him like that. Three hours later she came back and noticed his eyes were all blank and staring like on a dead dog. She touched his hair.

"Still can't sleep?" She took the cushions away and never brought them back.

The doctor didn't talk to him much in the beginning except to make cracks about how now he would get more girlfriends because he had been shot. (At least that's what his other Puerto Rican patients used to tell him.) It wasn't until the fourth day when Miguel was sitting up in bed that the guy told him he'd taken two .32 caliber slugs. They had tumbled into his back just below the neck, one of them a ricochet in chunks; the other nudged his shoulder blade just enough to cause serious pain and problems with his right arm, but that would go away. That was why every morning the doctor would take a wooden tongue depressor and run it up and down his arm. "Do you feel that?" he would ask through a mouthful of bubble gum. Miguel always felt it. He already had a highway of chalky scratches all up and down his arm. The fingers felt rusty and he couldn't make a fist.

"Don't worry about that. It'll go away. Just try to stay in one place and not move too much. Did you ever try these? They're like sweet gummy fruit sections made with real fruit juice." He held up what looked like a green slice of orange. He popped it into his mouth with boyish relish. "Here. I'll leave the box by the bed so you can have some. Watch some TV. Relax."

He wasn't eating much because he got nauseous. He always felt full. They were pumping him full of glucose. Without being able to do any exercise he was bloating up, getting flabby.

Sanchez was there before anyone: He was the dark ghost Miguel had spotted in his delirium. His voice was a soothing whisper. Miguel couldn't imagine the man ever yelling, but he had his own way of being pushy, like the time he drilled him about the car keys.

"So you were in a posse," Sanchez said, flipping open a notepad. "Tell me more about it, okay?"

"I wasn't in no posse." Miguel's voice was muffled by pillow. He was watching *The Jeffersons*, the TV bolted to the ceiling by the corner. It was hard for him to look up at it. He propped things underneath his chin and chest and the nurses kept taking the stuff away. "Flat, flat, yuh supposed to be *flat.*"

"So you weren't in a posse," Sanchez repeated. "How'dju get your own car then?"

Miguel turned his head slowly to look at him. "I don't got no car, man. Get real. I'm fucken sixteen."

Sanchez grinned. It was such a lighthearted happy grin that Miguel felt confused.

"What?" he asked.

Sanchez kept grinning. "I just think you're wonderful. I've been waiting a long time for you."

"Ahhh man I hope you ain't some fucken pato, bro'."

Sanchez laughed. "Have you ever seen *Casablanca*?"

"Nah. I don't travel much." Miguel had drooled on the pillow. It felt cold. He shifted his chin around to a warmer spot.

"*Casablanca*, the movie."

"Yeah I saw it."

"I always wanted to say that line: 'This looks like the beginning of a beautiful friendship.'"

Miguel stared at him. "Yeah, well. Keep dreaming."

Sanchez put his pad away and came around the bed, squatting down so they were eye to eye. "I don't know. I get the feeling we're going to be friends. It isn't every day I meet someone who worked so close to a man you could sort of say I'm a great fan of. I wouldn't say fan, I guess. Maybe that's the wrong word. Let's just say I'm a follower of the man. I know his work. I've been waiting for him to make his move." He winked. "You could say I have the man's poster on my wall."

Something in Miguel was starting to itch. "Wha'chu sayin', man?"

Sanchez whispered the name almost reverently. "Spider." It made Miguel look away from him.

"Ahh shit."

"He's the one got'chu that car, right?"

"Basta with that shit, bro'. I'm sixteen. How I could have a car?" He shook his head with derision but he still couldn't look Sanchez in the eye.

"You have car keys."

"What?"

"Car keys. You have car keys."

"You looked through my stuff?" Miguel's voice cracked a little as it climbed up an octave.

"Oh yeah. Sure."

"You people got no fucken respect."

This made Sanchez laugh so hard he almost fell backward and had to grip the bed for support. "You were holding the keys for a friend, right?"

Miguel was going to say that. He stopped the words.

"Well? Were you?"

"Sure," Miguel whispered into the pillow.

"Is that also his license you were holding for him in your wallet? Because he really bears quite a resemblance to you in the photo. Maybe you guys are brothers."

Miguel didn't say anything. Sanchez seemed ready to burst into laughter again, his eyes delirious, the smile wide and carefree. He was like a good friend making bad jokes. He patted Miguel's good arm, which was wrapped around his pillow.

"You get your rest." Sanchez stood up. "I don't want to ruin your family visit and it's almost time. I got me some other chirping birds to visit. I want you to remember this though: you're not a suspect. If you had been a suspect I'd be holding all your stuff in a little plastic baggie. You and me are on the same side. You could almost say we both work for Spider, right?"

The words left a strange impression. Sanchez left leaving Miguel feeling vulnerable. Just hearing the name SPIDER made him feel torn between wanting to be protective and wanting to spill everything. Who could he trust? Was he going to trust someone again? How much was it going to hurt this time? Thinking of Spider made his chest ache. Maybe it hadn't been Spider; maybe it was Ritchie, maybe it was Ace, who'd been tipped off that Spider was going to be there. But at night, when everything was dark, he knew it was Spider. He covered his burning face with a pillow.

Catarina was there right from the beginning. He remembered seeing her in the fuzzy dark after surgery when she stood outside the dreamy nothingness like a holy sentinel. Was she in a shroud? He thought he had dreamed her up, but she was standing by the windows in her black raincoat, her face expressionless. She seemed to be figuring something out, reliving part of her life all over again. She had been there the first time Sanchez had spoken to him as he swam to shore through a sea of anesthetic Jell-O. Sanchez had whispered in Spanish, short gentle questions that didn't threaten him. Miguel answered in halting Spanish until Catarina spoke up.

"Speak to him in English," she said, like a teacher correcting a pupil. From that moment on Miguel was always aware of her presence. Sometimes in half-sleep he could feel her hand on his hair. He couldn't say how he knew it was her hand. He just knew. The same way a baby knows.

Catarina helped him get to Cristalena and Amelia.

Cristalena came in with her hair all wet. She was carrying a large red stuffed dog. She kissed him over and over; their faces were all wet. Catarina coughed. They all looked at each other, Cristalena quickly tidying up her hair self-consciously. She waited for Miguel to introduce her.

"This is my wife," he said, motioning to Cristalena, whose face was frozen with wonder.

"My wife," she repeated to herself, looking at Catarina with a shared sense of shock.

"What?" Catarina edged closer.

Cristalena's eyes watered beautifully. The two women never formally said hello but Miguel soon found they were getting along as if they had always known each other. Somewhere along the line they had accepted each other. Cristalena hand-fed him sliced apples and orange slices. She slipped into bed beside him and they snuggled while Catarina sat in the pink plastic chair and peeled apples. The nurse screamed at Miguel.

"Get out of there, thass not allowed," she yelled.

Cristalena made like to get out of the bed but Miguel held her to him. "No," he said. "I need some warmth. I'm sick. I need this, man."

The nurse's eyes narrowed, hands on hips. "Well you wait 'til you get home to get your warmth. This is a hospital. Young lady you climb out of that bed or I'm callin' security."

"I don't see how this is harming anyone," Miguel countered, holding on to Cristalena. She was still trying to break free.

"Don'chu know there are rules against having anyone be in bed with a patient?"

"No. You show me where it says that."

The nurse turned and left.

"Miguel one, Lincoln Hospital zero," Catarina said, and then she put a slice of apple in Miguel's mouth. Grinning, she nudged Cristalena and put a slice in her mouth, too.

Amelia was different. When she came in the shape of the whole room seemed to shift in Miguel's mind. Her large eyes were wide and shiny and a little scared, hair pulled back from her face, her thin body lost under the huge coat she had on. She had wandered up and down the hallway twice before Miguel yelled out to her. When she spotted him she froze, her face soft and sad.

"Ohhh Miguel." She leaned over the bed and clumsily kissed him and touched his face and then she seemed to catch herself just as her movements got all frantic. Then she noticed she was being stared at and wiped the tears from her face, standing straight to face Cristalena and Catarina, who stood together by the windows.

"This is my best friend, Amelia," Miguel said.

Amelia looked at them both and nodded and then she choked back a sob and ran out into the hall for a moment.

Cristalena stared at Miguel. "Should I go an' get her?"

Miguel shrugged. "She'll be back on huh own."

Catarina was about to step out when Amelia came back in, wiping her face. "I'm sorry," she said. "It's nice to meet you. I'm just all shook up. Thass all."

It was Amelia who saved the car. He had parked it about four blocks from Spadgie's. He'd spent that first night swimming through the anesthetic fighting the nausea and wondering about parking regulations and tow trucks and having his car dragged away. Then Sanchez made that crack about the car keys and Miguel couldn't stop thinking about it. He had to save the car. There was every possibility that he was going to lose it anyway, but right now he had to do something. When Amelia came in, he already had a plan. He made Amelia lean down close so he could whisper, but the room was too quiet and Cristalena and Catarina heard every word.

"Take my car keys. Take 'um an' get the car. Please. Get somebody to hold it 'til I get out."

Amelia sighed. "But Miguel, I don't drive."

He stared at her. He knew she was reluctant for different reasons. He knew instinctively that she wanted him to forget that car, to just drop it. It was a link to the past. To Spider.

"Save my car," he said, squeezing her hand. "Please. Take the keys an' the license too. Before that fucken cop comes back."

"Miguel." Cristalena's voice trembled. "Forget it. You told me the cop knows about it. Don't do this. You could get in trouble."

Miguel didn't seem to hear her. He pumped Amelia's hand, his arm trembling with the effort. "Please. Hide it. Hide it."

"No Miguel, no." Cristalena got up from her chair and scooted over to his side. "What are you gonna tell the cop?"

"Why don'chu leave that to him?" Amelia asked her softly, like an older sister who refused to get emotional.

"Are you the one thass gonna be in trouble with the cops? Huh? Are you the one they'll arrest?"

Amelia stood straight and tall, staring calmly into Cristalena's hysterical eyes. "I'll do anything for him," she said. "Anything."

She took the keys and the wallet from the drawer in the night table and removed the license. Catarina didn't say anything, though her face looked troubled, eyes darting from Amelia to Cristalena, who stood trembling, wounded.

Amelia leaned down and kissed him on the cheek tenderly, touching his hair.

"Don'chu worry," she said. "I'll be back." Her black flats clacked away quickly. Cristalena seemed to be clutching herself, looking at the doorway. Catarina stood by Miguel and grabbed his hand, her eyes probing him.

"Now you tell me exactly what this is all about," she said. "I want every last detail."

. . .

The next time Sanchez came in, Catarina and Cristalena were there. It was weird. Catarina kept breaking in to ask if he was a suspect. Cristalena kept asking if Miguel wanted to change channels on the TV. Sanchez took it all in stride. Miguel liked the way he handled it. He could tell the only reason he came during visiting hours was so he could check out the family. The guy was casually doing his homework. He started asking Catarina questions about him right then and there. Catarina dodged and parried. She was very vague about everything. It touched Miguel to see it. Finally she seemed to lose her patience with Sanchez.

"Look," she said, rising from her seat. "I think if you are going to press charges against my son or something or view him as some suspect then fine, tell me so. But don't come in here and question us like you're building a case. My son is a good boy. He's been in some rough shit but he's a good boy."

"A good boy into some rough shit."

"That's right. Maybe my husband and I . . ." She paused and seemed to gather up some steam. "Maybe my ex-husband and I didn't provide a good home for him. Maybe we're to blame. But I know that much about him. He's a good boy."

"Did you know he was working for a crack lord? Delivering drugs and collecting money?"

She stepped closer as if blocking him. "Are there charges against my son? Because if there are, I will get a lawyer and then to hell with your questions."

Sanchez looked serene. "There are no charges. I'm just asking you if you were aware, that's all. Did you know your son was driving his very own car?"

Catarina laughed, crossing her arms. "That's the stupidest thing I've ever heard."

Sanchez didn't say anything. He went over to the drawer and took out the wallet. He was simply going to show her. He opened the wallet and looked in it and his face changed a little. There was no license. He looked puzzled and bemused. By the time he had sifted through the keys he had realized what had happened. He put the stuff back and came over to Miguel.

"What happened to the car keys?" He seemed to be enjoying this. Miguel couldn't figure him out.

"What car keys?" Miguel couldn't hold down the wisp of a grin. Cristalena, sitting on the other side of the bed by the pleated curtain, choked back a burst of laughter and looked away.

Sanchez put his hands in his pockets and sighed, giving Catarina a weary grin. "You should know very well that if Miguel were a suspect of any kind I would've confiscated all his belongings. The things he did out on the street don't really interest me. I'm really after bigger fish here. But you know the license was there. And so were the keys."

"The car keys belong to my husband," Catarina said without batting an eyelash. Cristalena and Miguel both looked at her.

It even threw Sanchez off a little. "Pardon me?" He tapped one of his ears. "I'm getting old. I keep hearing all kinds of weird stuff."

"My husband gave my son those keys. You see, when my husband was young his father died of a heart attack."

"I don't understand."

"My husband worked with his father in a grocery store. He was closing up when it happened. My husband took him over to the car, they had this blue Plymouth, but his father had misplaced the keys. Now, my husband knew how to drive, he had a permit, but what was he going to do with no keys? If he had had a pair of keys on him, his father would not have died maybe. So my husband has this thing, he gave my son those keys. Call it superstition. Call it a kind of tradition he's starting."

"Call it short story writing." Sanchez was smiling from ear to ear. He looked like he had had too many drinks already. The smile made it impossible for Catarina to go on. She seemed breathless. Sanchez looked at all of them, a clumsy admiration on his face. He came over to Miguel, who offered him a slice of apple. He took it and popped it into his mouth.

"I'm going to see you tomorrow," he said as he exited, "without the support players."

The next morning he was there. Miguel was groggy, staring up at the fluorescent lights resentfully. Every fucken morning they turned them on and wheeled in rubber food he couldn't eat. The black guy in the bed to his left kept farting. The guy on his right couldn't stop throwing up. Three nurses wrestled with him trying to get him into the bathroom before it happened but he managed to let it all out before they made it, and now the two nurses were in the room cleaning it up and cursing.

"You fucken pig," one of them was saying. "Cun't even have the decency."

"He did it on purpose, Regina, you sarrit."

"Just clean it," the man said from the bed in a weary rasp. "Just do yuh job an' clean that shit."

"You do this one mo' time an' you gonna clean it."

Sanchez arrived during all this. He shut the curtains on both sides and sat down by the bed. He looked a little sleepy, just like Miguel.

"Your mother's a good woman," he said, crossing his legs and leaning back.

Miguel stared at him. "You ain't no cop. You fulla shit."

Sanchez smiled. "Oh yeah? An' what makes you say that?"

"I don't know. You ain't like no cop."

"An' how's a cop supposed t' be?"

Miguel smirked. "White." He felt stupid after he said it but that's what came out.

"There are plenty of Latino cops, bro'."

Miguel knew that. He thought of the one that sat next to him in that cop car, so wordless and powerless and fawning. He seemed to be going along. Nothing to offer. It didn't matter that the guy was a spick. It was really just a uniform. "Besides," he added, "you haven't threatened me. Cops always threaten. Maybe you should smack me around some with yuh macana an' shit."

Sanchez took out a pack of gum and offered him a stick. "I don't have to threaten you, Miguel. I've been waiting for you for a long, long time. I'm sorry it happened this way, but here you are."

Miguel chomped on his fresh stick of gum. "I don't get it."

Sanchez leaned closer, eyes shining. He pressed Miguel's arm.

"Give me Spider," he whispered. "I want Spider."

The color left Miguel's face. He pulled his arm away with a slow twitch. "Get away with that shit," he said weakly, looking up at the blank TV screen.

"Look, this is serious. Seven people died Sunday night. You and fifteen others were wounded. These aren't the little leagues. This hospital is packed full of posse boys. There are even posse boys downstairs in the waiting room. They're all talking about Spider except for you. Why?

Don't you think I know about you? Some of those kids know about you. I have little scraps, but they add up. They add up so good I know you were in good with Spider. Tight. This was his big moment, Miguel. He's on the way up. I want to chop him down. And I want you to help me."

"Yuh crazy."

"Crazy? You're the one who's crazy. Spider sets up a hit like this, his biggest hit ever, and you're right there? Why? Fucking guy could've iced you. I wish you would tell me. There's usually a reason behind everything this guy does. Why would he set up this hit and have you be on the scene? I don't get that, and I don't get why you'd want to protect him. Spider's sleaze, Miguel. He's a murderer. You going to let him get away with that? You can help me put a stop to it."

"Yuh crazy man. You can't stop it. The world is fulla Spiders. Some a' thum wear cop suits."

"Some of them get elected President. So what. I don't care about that. All I care about is my little part of the world. I grew up on 149th Street, man. Back then we didn't have this crack shit. We had street gangs like the Spanish Mafia. I know these streets, man, I've seen what's happening. I want to do something about it." His face changed, all determination and fanaticism. He was totally serious now and making his pitch. "Miguel, you've got brains. You don't need this shit. I've been tailing this sonofa-bitch Spider for three years, hearing about him, watching him go up. A lot of bodies lead right to his doorstep. Now he's done it, he's stepped out where I can see him. This is your chance to do something positive, Miguel."

"My chance to get my head blown off." Miguel couldn't look at him. He felt like he was throbbing. One of the patients flicked on the TV. It was *Bewitched*. The goofy theme music swirled into the room.

Sanchez fell back into his chair. He had gotten too excited and was trying to calm down. He cracked his knuckles and that lopsided grin reappeared.

"At least you have a good family to protect you. Most of these brats only have their posses. A lot of them are talking. They want to nail Spider. They say it was him. Two of them even know you. They were wondering how it was you were at Spadgie's on the night of the hit."

"Maybe I wasn't so popular after all."

"That's not what I heard."

"Well why don'chu just tell me wha'chu heard all at once so I can deny all of it?"

Sanchez laughed. The nurse appeared at the door just then with a wheeled cart full of dressings and gauze and tape and tiny scissors.

"Man." Miguel scowled. "Here comes nurse Rat-Shit to change my fucken dressing."

The nurse didn't hear him, but Sanchez kept mouthing RAT SHIT over and over again until it struck a chord.

"Nurse Ratchet," he said, looking at Miguel.

Miguel grinned. *"One Flew Over the Cuckoo's Nest."*

The nurse shooed Sanchez away. He returned later in the evening when the room was packed. Catarina and Cristalena and Amelia were there, with Nelo in the background looking fidgety.

Amelia kissed him and whispered, "Mission accomplished." The car was safe. He closed his eyes when she said it, thinking of Spider and Firebug. Amelia was a piece of that life, standing there in front of him. In a strange way he felt bound to her, attached forever in a way that would probably scare Cristalena. She could never really know about them. She seemed to know it. When Amelia was in the room, Cristalena would grow quiet, solemn-faced as if at a funeral. She was torn between being beside him and giving him space. Sometimes when Amelia was there she would come over and grab hold of him possessively. Other times she would scoot off so fast Miguel thought she was angry, but she would smile passively and search through the bag of fruits and goodies good-naturedly, throwing Amelia glances as if to watch her progress. When Amelia spoke to him, she leaned close to his face. They whispered to each other. It looked awfully intimate. Catarina and Cristalena both stared.

Amelia hadn't said "I told you so." She didn't say anything at all. She knew he was hurting. She waited for him to bring it up. That evening when she told him the car was in good hands, he shut his eyes and his lips trembled a little. When he looked at her, he said, "Looks like Spider stuck me." She tried to smile but it cracked at the edges and two silent tears streamed down her face. He grabbed her hand and wanted to say a million things before the tears blinded him, but nothing came out. At that moment he felt he had to talk to her, to pull something out of himself and present it to her as proof that he had learned, but it didn't happen. He just held her hand fighting the sobs, and then Cristalena rushed over and embraced him and hid him and he lost Amelia under the warmth, the blue silk blouse, the hair, the hands that softly stroked him. And when he looked up at Cristalena she was crying too, for a different reason.

"Oh God," she whispered against him. "You're so far."

"Nah," he whispered back. "I'm right here."

"Nah. You're far."

Later Nelo asked to see Miguel's keys and when Miguel produced them Nelo slipped two car keys onto the ring. He gave them back and looked at Catarina, whose eyes were loaded with tears. She hugged him. After that he didn't say much, kept tripping over chairs and grabbing Miguel's bad arm. Miguel felt he was nervous about the cops questioning him or something. When Sanchez blew in, Nelo's face changed color. He quickly excused himself and vanished.

Sanchez didn't come to ask questions. He smiled at everyone and nodded all around and then came over to Miguel and handed him a big book.

"I just thought you might like reading this," he said a little shyly. Miguel looked it over, flipping through the pages. It was a new book, pages crisp and white, not torn and musty like all his secondhand books.

"*Native Son?*"

"Yeah. It's a book written by a great black man, Richard Wright. I think you'll like it. I just wanted to drop it by. I'm already late." He checked his watch, already retreating toward the door. "I will see you tomorrow. Enjoy."

Miguel sniffed the pages. He loved the smell of a new book.

"You didn't have to do this," he said.

"I did. All you got is the week-old copy of *People*."

Miguel held out his hand. "Thanks."

Sanchez looked like he hadn't expected the offering. He stepped over and shook hands, and then he was gone.

24

It was as if they didn't exist. On TV there was nothing on the South Bronx until this MURDER AT SPADGIE's deal. It became one of the biggest crimes in the city, but the noise only lasted a couple of days. All of a sudden they were interviewing kids in posses, toothless grinning midgets in eight-ball jackets who felt like war heroes. They walked reporters through the rubble, they showed off their guns, even taking one lucky white journalist up to a roof to show how they sniped at people. "Something's wrong with our kids," an ABC-TV special report moaned. A documentary, "Tough Turf," was put together by a blond reporter named Deborah Horville, who interviewed posse girls. They discussed fashion and man-catching tricks, bragging about stab wounds and beatings while a super-hyped hip-hop music sound track blared. The mayor made a speech. "We must take our streets back," he said, and then flew off to South Africa to visit with Mandela.

It was in *New York Newsday* that Miguel saw Spider's name in an article written by an investigative reporter who quoted Sanchez. "Spider is the big man now," he was quoted as saying,

> and there might be no stopping him. He made his move, cut down the opposition within his camp and set himself up firmly as the king pin. He might've been playing along all this time, working for one of the big east coast suppliers, but he was biding his time, setting up his own op. Now that he made his move like this there'll be no double-dealing

> him. It sends a clear message out to the streets. This is the
> kind of slick maneuvering that the big distributors look for
> in a major street dealer.

"Spider will love it," Miguel told Cristalena, who was lying in bed with him in his new room. He was living with Nelo and Catarina now. Cristalena could visit, but if they were together in his room the door had to remain OPEN. There were a lot of new rules.

Catarina had bought him a new bedroom set while he was still in the hospital. He came "home" to an empty bookcase and a new stereo and a big, comfortable bed. He stared at it all like it wasn't his.

The first thing he did was have Nelo drive him over to the apartment so he could get his stuff. Nelo had a nifty green Jeep 4×4. Miguel had dragged Amelia along. As Nelo took the last of the stuff downstairs the two of them stood in the empty apartment, holding hands and walking back and forth through the empty rooms.

"Where do you think he is?" he asked her as he slumped into the creaking car seat. He held up the old pair of sneaks that Firebug had left.

"I don't know." She shrugged absently. "I bet he's doing real well. There's always gonna be work for him." The two of them were amazed at how little they felt for Firebug, as if realizing how much more friendship entailed, how much less they had gotten from him. Miguel took the fake petunias down. His money was still hidden in the paper backing. He took the entire window frame and brought it downstairs to the jeep.

"You're bringing that?" Nelo's face wrinkled up.

"Yeah." And he hung it in his room.

Amelia was back in school, sitting in on classes and spending days in the financial aid office trying to clear up the mess. She took him with her one cool day, dragging him around campus, into the huge library, the dilapidated lounge with its stained cushions, the bookstore, the gym.

"This is where you should be, Miguel. In school." Her eyes glimmered. She had cut her hair short like Prince Valiant's. "They have an equivalency program."

"You don't get it, do you? Catarina wants me to go back to junior high. She registered me at some school. I'm gonna be goin' back next week." He looked totally miserable. She petted him.

"Ohhh baby, it ain't that bad. Get back into the swing a' things. Relax. You got free room an' board. You can live the life of a teenager with eight thousand smackers under his mattress."

She took him into the cafeteria, a large ugly hall with long thin tables and some of the worst fries he had ever tasted in his life. Within seconds his stomach was rumbling.

"You don't get it, do you? The fact is I don't wanna be livin' with no Catarina. I don't wanna call huh mommy. I don't wanna talk with Nelo about football scores. I don't wanna be a high school boy. Don'chu see I'm beyond that?"

"Jesus. Stop yelling."

"I can't help it. There you are all happy an' tellin' me I should be chill about everything, but I'm not chill. I hate this shit. Now I gotta start my life all over again, just when I had something goin' . . ."

Amelia pounded the table with a plastic salt shaker. "Thass bullshit! You didn't have no life. That shit you were in . . . that WE were in, that wasn't life. THIS is life, Miguel, look around'ju. People strugglin' to make it without havin'na deal rocks!"

"Zah. Buncha book geeks."

"What?"

"Fucken faggits. They ain't gonna get there. You know that."

"You shut up with that. You're really startin'na piss me off, Miguel. You must have a real short memory. You're lucky to be alive an' now you sound like you wanna go back."

"I didn't say that."

"Oh well wha'chu sayin' then?"

"I'm sayin' get real. You know an' I know things in this place are all stacked against us anyway. Why play along? At least on the streets I had a sense a' my own . . . I was in control a' my . . ."

His eyes lost their luster as he grappled for the words to say what he couldn't explain anyway. He looked at Amelia helplessly.

"You still miss Spider," she said sadly.

Miguel looked away. "He gave me something, man." And yes he missed the life: He missed his car, his apartment, the laughs with Firebug, with Spider . . . Suddenly he came to life again. "I'm sayin' I wanna get out on my own already. Me an' Cristalena. I wanna move out on my own. I ain't fit t' live like some sixteen-and-a-half-year-old brat. I wanna be my own man."

Amelia sighed, drowning her fries in ketchup. "I don't think thass possible. I think you'll have to be realistic."

"You sound like Cristalena."

"Well maybe the girl got some brains after all."

"Don't diss my woman."

"I ain't dissing your woman. I like her. I think she's really nice. She has a sweet disposition. And brains, she has them. But you guys ain't ready to live alone yet. Give it some time, man. You just got out of the frying pan. Try to relax."

But there wasn't much time to relax. The hospital smell was still in his nostrils when he was enrolled in a nearby junior high school. At first they weren't sure where to place him, so they made him take a battery of tests. That day he didn't speak a word and locked himself in his room. "I don't care!" Catarina yelled, banging on his locked door when he wouldn't come out to dinner. "As long as you're in school, that's all I care about." Soon Miguel was rising up early and marching off to school like an obedient putz, patiently putting up with the metal detectors at the door. The classes were all overcrowded. In one case he ended up sitting on the windowsill right over the radiator vent. It suited him fine. He could look out the window at the passing trains. The school was painted gray and black, with barred windows like a prison. He hated the kids, too. They weren't South Bronx, just snottier, beat boys so stylish with rad haircuts and round-rimmed nonprescription glasses. He fixed his hard, contemptuous stare on them, and they left him alone.

"Miguel, I can't stand this," Cristalena told him one night on the phone. Miguel was on the extension in the kitchen. It was past midnight already, so he was waiting for Catarina to come out of her hole and say, "Isn't it a little late for you to be on the phone? You have school tomorrow." Which she did often.

"I can't stand this shit eitha. Listen, you got our money, right?"

"Yes. I hid it. Miguel, my parents called in a psychiatrist."

"What?"

"I have to see this lady at school every week."

"Shit."

"I need to see you, Miguel."

"Me too."

They hadn't made love since the shooting. One weekend when he couldn't take it anymore he booked a hotel room at the Prospect, a seedy place on Hunts Point. They didn't tell their parents anything. "I'll be out late." "I'm stayin' over at a friend's." That was it. Sure there was yelling when they returned to their homes late Sunday, but being alone together was worth it. They stripped and lit candles and had a bit of smoke and fucked. They bathed together. They touched as if discovering each other for the first time. They clutched and hid under blankets. They dozed, watched TV, and ordered pizza from a place across the street, dreaming about living together. They left a pyramid of sticky tissues in a corner for the cleaning lady.

"They're trying to convince everybody I'm insane, even the school people," she told him as they snuggled. "I don't know what I'll do if they cost me my job, Miguel. I'll die without it. It's really the only independence I have. I don't know what I'll do without that money."

"Shh. Don't worry. You got four thousand dollars."

"Thass our money."

"Thass right. An' I'm workin' on it. We gonna live together, Lena. Ain't no doubt about it."

"But we only got eight thousand dollars an' my rinky-dink job."

"Don't start that again, please. I thought'chu was comin' around. Din't this weekend prove it to you? Damn, it proved it to me." He pressed her close. "We gonna move in together. I'm workin' on it right now. I can't stand this shit. I already passed through bein' a kid. Now I gotta be a man."

Her eyes looked large and doubtful.

"Don't say it," he said.

Something about the way he said it made her flash. She suddenly pulled away from him. She walked over to the window and began dressing.

"What?" He tapped the bed. "Whassup, where you goin'?"

She glared at him.

"I already have one father, Miguel. I don't need to move in with another one."

"Whass that mean?"

"It means we gotta be a team." Her face colored with hurt. "I thought'chu said we were a team, that we hadda work together. I thought we were always gonna be equal. Now you're lying there ordering me around."

He sighed, beating his thigh with his fist. "I'm not, I swear."

"Yes, you are. You wanna go do it all your way like if I don't exist. But I do exist. An' if you really cared about us being together an' all this shit then you would ask how I feel about it."

Miguel's face fell. He looked like a little boy who was being punished. He made a sudden movement toward the other side of the bed and let out a groan. His shoulder was still taped up, his arm still a little rusty. Sometimes it bled if he moved around too much.

"All right," he said. "Tell me how you feel about it."

She approached the bed quickly, trying not to gloat. "Well," she said, "I don't think we're ready yet. You know I love being with you, Miguel, but we should wait a little bit. At least until we're sure."

"Fine," he said, his face indecipherable. "Take off yuh panties."

"I would love nothing better than to live with you, Miguel."

"The panties. Off."

"You're my forever honey."

"My opinion on the matter is take off thum damn panties now an' come over here."

"You should maybe say please."

"PLEASE!"

She peeled off her panties and jumped into bed. It was so easy to speak with their bodies and skin and hands and lips. Words were no good, only kisses worked. Later they lay all exhausted, melted into each other like gooey sticky ice cream. Delicious warmth and safety. They intertwined bodies and fingers. They knew about each other. They were the same soul. And yet they were different. They had to respect each other. In the world Miguel'd grown up in you start with backyards and rubble lots and then you conquer girls. You get your way with them and you learn that's the way, in life you are supposed to get your way. The woman is supposed to know where she's at, where she BELONGS. It was all in his blood. To be THE MAN. The woman just did what the man said. That was respect. Tradition. Yet Miguel was throwing it all away, the ghosts of a hundred million Latin machistas all hanging their heads and cursing him.

"I'm sorry," he whispered in the dark forest of her hair. "I didn't mean t' order you around."

"Me neither," she said. They kissed again and that was all that mattered in the world.

The next day he met Amelia. He had planned to tell her that he and Cristalena had had it out and that he had won. He was hoping to tell her that they were going to live together and that was that, but the situation was still unresolved. He met her at the Parkchester train station after school and took her for a bite at a luncheonette nearby. Amelia seemed taller, her clothes looser, her laughter more carefree. She gave him a hug that warmed him for the rest of the day.

"You little shit, lookit'chu," she rasped. "Check out the book bag!"

"Shut up. They make you carry these stupid books. If you don't bring 'um, they—"

"What a little student you are."

"Nah."

They ordered cheeseburgers and fries.

"I can't get over how you look. All happy an' shit. Not like how I look at all."

"Mmm. You look fine. How's Cristalena?"

"Good. But she won't agree t' live with me now."

"Good girl."

"Wha'chu mean, you agree with that shit?" He scowled. "Shit. Women. You all think alike, man."

"Hee-haw, get the big Latin macho here thumping his chest. You might think it's macho, pal, but the only reason a gorilla thumps his chest is because he's nervous. Diane Fossey found that out."

"Diane Fossey? Ain't she the bitch did that movie with Liza Minnelli?"

She smirked. It was such a sweet look on her face that he wanted to kiss her. She wagged her finger at him, even though she was delighted.

"Oh no, you don't. You have Cristalena. I ain't that kinda woman."

"Just a peck. On the lips."

She laughed. "On the tongue, you mean."

"Man thass gross."

"You know I love you, Miguel." She squeezed his hand. "You helped me. I don't think I'd be here right now if it wasn't for you."

"Oh, right."

She looked sincere. "It's true."

"Well then, we're even."

"Ohhh, the food's here!"

A tall skinny guy in a soiled apron placed down their platters. Amelia began to salt her fries and his, too. "So tell me whass so goddamn important tha'chu gotta drag me from my line at financial aid."

He watched her a moment. "Well, it's this Sanchez thing." He lifted his burger and prepared to bite but put it back down on the plate. "The guy's been puttin' pressure on me to tell him what I know about Spider.

He knows so much, man, I don't believe it. I don't know where he gets it, but he'll say these little things to like, remind me, you know? He's been callin' me, an' now he's pushin'. He knows I was a runner, he even knows I had a '68 Chevy Impala. He don't stop askin' about it. But it's the way he does it, you know? He keeps tellin' me he loves Chevys."

"No shit." Amelia was stuffing fries into her mouth. "You know, we gotta talk about the car too."

"Wha'chu mean?"

"Well, you know." She swallowed. "Since the hospital, I had my friend Ramon take care of it. But he's sick of having your car. He has his own, you know, an' he's been parkin' it in his cousin's garage, an' his cousin's getting' all heavy about it. So he wanted me to ask you if you could take it back."

Miguel frowned. "Ahh man. Great."

"Can'chu get your father to hold it for a while? It's a great car."

"Nah. I'm tellin' you, he won't go for it. Imagine what would happen to him if he was drivin' the thing down 149th Street an' some a' the guys see it an' think it's me? They might bust some caps." A sudden grin appeared on his face. He started laughing. She punched him.

"Stop that."

"Well, it was just a thought. Anyway he won't go for it. I won't let him go for it. I don't want that man driving my car. It's my car. He shouldn't be touching any part of my life."

"I don't get this." Amelia stuck a fry in her mouth. "I thought you an' him were better now. Didn't he cover for you with his keys? I thought maybe he was coming around."

"Nah. I think Catarina made him do that. I don't even see him very much."

Yes, the guy worked hard. An exporter's work is never done. Somebody has to stay late at the warehouse and make sure those fake Gucci purses go out on time. He hardly ever came in before eight. A few words from behind his paper as he sat in front of the TV. Dinner. The kitchen table. Small talk. The family didn't used to eat all together. It was a new thing, Catarina's enforced familyness. Miguel just wanted to scoot off to his room with his plate. He was making the effort. There were times he tried to make conversation, but the man could only grunt or make a remark that always sounded like an underhanded insult. It felt like resentment. Miguel knew that feeling. It brought back memories of when his real father and Catarina used to fight. He didn't want to get caught up in that shit. He didn't even like Nelo. He wanted out. He massaged his temples for a moment, feeling overwhelmed.

"I don't know what to do," he said.

Amelia was still eating. It was like she hadn't seen food in a week. "I think you should really pressure your new pop about the car."

For a moment he glared at her. She stopped eating, looking around before letting her eyes confront his anger. What was it she said? Suddenly it was gone as quickly as it came, and he was desultorily tossing fries in his mouth, leaning back to stare out through the storefront windows as a train rattled by overhead.

It angered him to think of anyone driving his car. Sure, he could sell it. He could get nine hundred or twelve easy. The car was in good shape, fixed up royal, cams, hubs, a new transmission, his Baby was a sweetheart. It was his life that was in that car. With his own two measly fucken hands he had gotten himself a life where there was none. He'd created that car, mixed the colors, tested the scents, put it together with love and devotion, until it was an extension, a limb, an organ. Nelo would never sit in it, or look at it. Not Nelo, not anyone. The car was HIS creation. It symbolized his life. It symbolized Firebug, who fell asleep with the Suarez twins in the back seat one night (took Miguel two days to get that funky Firebug aroma out of the car). It symbolized Spider, sitting beside him as he drove through the streets Spider boasted of owning, if not now, well, soon, pana, soon, just stay with me, you'll see it wif' yuh own eyes, pana. Spider who presented it to him. Spider the father. The Lord giveth and the Lord . . .

"Miguel, whassup?"

Amelia brought him out of a trance. He stared at her and for a flash it was old times, Amelia slowly taking a hit in the front seat, Miguel kicking her out of the car. Miguel beating on the horn impatiently while she ran into a nearby vestibule for another glow. That hardness that used to be on her face was gone, gone, gone. It was the happy radiance that brought him back to the present. He wanted to be happy too, but he couldn't. There was the old life and the new life. The old life had a lot of shit attached but there was some happiness and freedom. The new life had nothing but shadows and fear and uncertainty. He felt powerless. He was sitting there looking at her and then she knew, somehow she knew what he felt. She grabbed both his hands and she squeezed.

"I know," she said tearfully. "But'chu have to let it go, Miguel. You gotta kiss it goodbye." The trembling in her voice reminded him how weak he was, how much he wanted to cry. She wiped at her own eyes apologetically, laughing softly. "Come on, eat," she said, "before I eat'cha burger myself."

That night he had a dream. It was a dream or a vision. In it he was walking down the street with Firebug, right down Prospect Avenue. There seemed to be no one else anywhere; the streets were empty and desolate. The big building on Beck Street was burning, and they both paused to admire the writhing golden tongues of flame, turning bronze in the fading sunlight. There were no firemen, no engines wailing, not even a crowd for the wienie roast. Firebug sat up on the hood of a parked Ford. He had his foot up on the bumper like he was going to make a long speech, his eyes hidden behind these rubbery goggles that he sometimes wore for the hell of it. Grimy-faced and pensive, his dark eyes took in the whole street.

"You listen," he said hoarsely, as if he had first had a few good drinks and a heavy smoke. "You listen 'cause I ain't gonna tell you again. Time is like that. Here today, gone tomorrow. Thass it right there, bro'. Fire heals, bro'. It is like a brother. It is like a father that hugs you. It eats away all the bad so that in the mornin' all you got are a few ashes to kick around. When I see fire I feel healed." He gripped his T-shirt as if he were about to take it off. "For me there ain't nobody been there but fire is there, fire burns forever. Don'chu f'get that. You should thinka me when you see a fire."

"I always do," Miguel said, a lump in his throat.

Firebug hopped off the hood and stood right in front of him. "Fire is really the best way t' say goodbye." He waved his arms around. "The Romans man, they used to burn their emperors in what they call a funeral pyre. They would lay their dead emperor or whoever the fuck on this huge pile of wood and they'd light it an' sing songs an' say goodbye, watch the fire turn yesterday into tomorrow." He paused, staring at the burning building, which seemed to burn continuously without being consumed, like a torch. In a moment Firebug was gone, disappeared. Miguel was alone on the bleak desolate landscape, alone with the burning building. When he woke up he couldn't remember if Firebug had actually ever said those things to him at different times, if maybe his mind had put it all together for him. It was such a real dream that Miguel thought he had actually been visited by Firebug. He spent the day in school like a sleep-walker. It was only when he got on the phone to Amelia that he came to life.

"About the car," he said, breathlessly, as if he had run the whole way.

"Yeah?"

"Come meet me again for a burger."

They were even sitting at the same table in the same positions. They were having cheeseburger deluxes again, only this time Amelia ordered onion rings.

"So whass this big time decision you wanna lay on me?" she asked as she popped rings into her mouth.

He grinned at her, a crazy daring flashing in his eyes. "It's about the car. I know what I wanna do about it now."

"You do?" Amelia seemed a little wary. "What?"

"I'm gonna burn it."

"Excuse me?"

"I said I'm gonna burn it. Like what the Romans used to do to their emperors, right? Like a sacrifice, a ritual. We could find some empty lot someplace and do it. That way my Baby lives forever the way I remember her."

Amelia seemed mystified. "A funeral pyre." Her voice was low with admiration. "What a beautiful idea, Miguel." She seemed grateful some-how, her eyes glistening wetly. "Ohh Miguel. What a way to say good-bye."

Her reaction relieved him. For a moment he thought he was going a little crazy. Now she reminded him that they were both from the same place.

"Thinka how much Firebug woulda loved it," she said tenderly.

"I miss him sometimes," Miguel put in, without telling her about the dream.

"Thass 'cause you didn't fuck him."

"But I thought'chu said that was the best thing about him!"

Amelia looked smug. "Thass before I found a real man."

"Op. Now whass that mean? You sleepin' around again?"

She hit him. He had said it so loud that people had turned to look at them.

"I just mean that sometimes we see something we have an' we call it good, without really knowin' what good is. I used to tell you you didn't know what love was, an' there I was giving it away to someone like Firebug. What a waste." She leaned closer, whispering. "One snuggling with somebody you love is worth a thousand fuckings from Firebug."

He felt touched, taking one of her hands. "I thought'chu had a boyfriend."

"Having a boyfriend won't make me a person, Miguel. I'm not waiting for somebody to come along an' shape me. I've become a sculptor."

He envied her sense of freedom, her confidence. "I wish I could say that. The only thing I feel I want to do I can't do, 'cause that stupid bitch won't let me!"

"Hey. Stop that. You're dissing your woman."

"Well I'm mad. Like I gotta compromise myself right outta business o' something. Why can't she just do it my way? Can't she trust me?"

"Why don'chu try trusting her? Maybe she's right, too."

"You women all belong to the same union! Look, I love huh but she don't know anythin', she's a little Miss Sweet. She don't know shit about it all. I'm the one saved up eight grand."

Amelia slammed down her burger. "Man, you sure got a whole fuck of a lotta nerve! Like that poor girl hasn't gone through the shit for you! A good clean girl like her can do lots better than end up with an ex-crack runner who's still tryin'na fool himself into believing he was ever in control."

"I WAS in control."

"You wish! It was Spider's game, start to finish. He played'ju, almost iced'ju like a little virgin. You fuck, going down there to meet him like you knew better than everybody! 'Cause you knew better, right?"

"You shun't be yellin' so loud, I can hear good."

"You fooled yourself back then an' I think you're still fooling yourself, Miguel. Give it up. The whole thing was a mistake. I don't think you see it that way. I think you're still wrapped up in it, in this sick street pride like you were your own man. Isn't that right?"

He was staring at her, his lips crinkling up slowly into a knowing grin, as if he was about to tease her. "Self-deception," he said. "It sure feels good though, don't it? It feels real good until you see whassup."

She caressed his hand. "Let it all go. Your little girl is right. You can only move forward when you realize where you been. You think because of where you were at that you're ready to go off on your own? Nah. You know that already, I can tell by the way you smiling, like you so slick. You think you figured it out without me, huh!"

"I KNOW I did all by myself, bitch."

"Lookit that cocky bastid. I guess you gotta right. You won something here, boy. You won the right to be sixteen years old again."

It was a nice speech. He held her hand and grinned. How was it that she could say all those things that he was thinking, word for word, the doubts, the questions, the decisions? She was amazing. Like a part of him that was outside of him.

"Give yourself some time, Miguel. Thass all. Give yourself some time to set it all up."

They rode back down on the train together, Miguel getting off at Elder Avenue. The two of them hugged and kissed like the war had just ended and he had just come off the boat.

"I love you, Amelia."

She blinked with surprise and crushed him with a hug.

"Me too me too me too."

He stepped off the subway car. When the doors closed she was staring at him through the window, her hand up against the glass.

"I'm gonna give it up," he said as the train rolled forward.

25

It was an empty lot way over the coal-black bridge on 149th Street just across the Bruckner Expressway, flanked by some squat factory buildings. From that lot—teeming with piles of garbage, glass, planks of wood, and cannibalized car parts—they could look out at the sparkling waters of the East River. Rikers Island stood like a fortified bunker behind a moat. Miguel parked the car, rubble and debris crackling and snapping under the cams. He picked a good spot, making Amelia and Cristalena run out onto the road to tell him if they could see him from out there. They couldn't. There was a tattered chain-link fence and half a shattered wall that kept the car from being seen. The line of trees held up empty branches but they added to the dense cover.

He had wanted both Cristalena and Amelia to be there. It was going to be the very last wienie roast. Amelia filled Cristalena in on the long wienie-roast tradition as they rode in the car for the very last time. It was a long joyride to Manhattan that turned into a picnic when they picked up some Kansas Fried Chicken on Hunts Point, went over the Triborough Bridge, and ended up on Randalls Island. There they stopped by the river to toke on a joint and think about the future.

"I'm gonna be a famous dress designer an' go to Paris," Cristalena said. The three of them lay on the grass leaning against the car.

"I'm going to become a therapist and have a lot of sex," Amelia said, making them all giggle.

Miguel took a deep breath. "I'm gonna testify against Spider an' get iced." They hit him for that one, punched and kicked and chased him from the car. Then they drove around and picked up some supplies: kerosene, popcorn, chips, and beer. Wienie-roast stuff. There was something else riding in the back seat, another piece of litter from his past life that had lost its usefulness. Miguel had taken the money from the backing of the fake petunias one day after he came home from school and found the thing sitting outside in the hallway with some other garbage. He desperately checked the backing before storming in to confront his mother, who was heading toward him with a box of old clothes. Her hair was wrapped in a handkerchief turban, her eyes impatiently defiant when she caught sight of him carrying THAT THING.

"What the fuck is my painting doin' outside?" he screamed. She put the box down and wiped at the tumbling strands of hair with a thick rubber glove she had on.

"Excuse me?"

"I think you heard me." His voice trembled as he paced, still gripping his "painting."

"I did," she snapped, her voice rising, "and I was wondering if I was going to pretend I didn't. Am I supposed to be scared of you now? How dare you walk in here and talk to me in that tone of voice?"

"Don't gimme that shit. Who tol'ju you could throw out my painting?"

"I'm cleaning up the house. I've been cleaning up all day, Miguel. I'm sick of seeing all this shit lying around."

"This shit wasn't lying around. It was in MY fucken room. What right did'ju have to go cleanin' up in MY fucken room? Huh?"

"I got carried away! How was I supposed to know that tin piece of shit is a painting?"

"I don't care if you think it's a piece a' shit o' what. It's MINE. You had no right to go into MY room an' throw out anythin' a' mines!"

"LOOK, I DIDN'T KNOW, OKAY? NOW STOP YELLING AT ME!"

She had almost thrown out four thousand dollars. He slammed his door and locked it and took the money out and hid it. Now the fucking petunias were going to go up with the car. The old life was over. He just didn't need it anymore. And Catarina and Nelo and all this shit had to go, too. He knew all that talk about him waiting and living like a kid again, but Amelia didn't know what it felt like to be trapped in a little boy's world while the big noisy ADULT world loomed just over the ridge. He had to go for it. Cristalena was sick of her life at home, too. Almost every other night they were on the phone, Cristalena in tears from another firefight with her parents.

"I'm going crazy," she whispered one night. "I think they're doing it to me, Miguel."

"You ain't crazy," he told her. "Do you see? We gotta get outta this. Look, I know it's hard an' all that, but we can do it if we plan it real careful. Like God o' somebody made it possible f' us to have eight thousand dollars to start with."

"I don't know," she said, but she sounded weaker. Now as they walked, as they kissed, as they threw each other glances, there was a secret message in their eyes.

Dinner table. Nelo munching quietly on fat juicy pork chops. Miguel picking at his, carving the slimy fat off the edge with his fork. Silence heavy. Forks scraping against plates. Catarina hovering, serving, dipping to replenish.

"I'm going out tonight," Miguel said.

"You are not." She dropped a lump of mashed potatoes on his plate with finality.

"I am," he said, dumping the mashed potatoes back into the glass bowl with a huffy clink of his fork.

"What? Again this shit on a Friday night? Are you going to have the decency this time to let us know if we'll see you before Sunday? Where is it you go, anyway?"

"Catarina," Nelo growled while masticating.

"None a' yuh business."

"None of my business! A fine answer! I knew this would happen! I just knew it!" Her voice arched upward and collapsed in torn tatters. "I knew you would ruin it! I knew it! Not even a month already—"

"You let him go," Nelo thundered, quieting her at once. "Just let him go. If he wants to, so what? Let him go. He's a man, isn't he? You'd think he was your daughter." The words spilled out with undisguised venom. Catarina instantly sat, clutching her arms, her eyes wide and stunned. Miguel took advantage of the sudden silence to make his escape.

That weekend he thought he had her. He could taste the surrender on Cristalena's lips, could see it in her eyes, but when he asked her she sighed and hugged him and looked at him as if she had seen the Holy Ghost.

"We have to wait," she said. "We have to be strong."

They sat together in their room at the Prospect, Miguel slumping into the bed like the spirit had gone out of him. She revived him. They fucked angrily, with a lot of hair-pulling, biting, scratching, and grunting. Grasping. Afterward they lay all moist and sweaty and tired and he started to cry. She didn't know what to do; she panicked. His crying frightened her, and she started to cry too. Then something happened in the moment he felt the most shrunken and powerless. She wrapped herself around him and cradled him. Then he felt how strong she was, how devoted. His little girl could take care of him. She was sturdy and willing and able to confront anything with him. After that it was like some strange wall had fallen. He looked at her and couldn't stop touching her, couldn't stop appreciating what it meant for her to be there. She had seen him as he was, scared and powerless.

"I'm sorry," he said, because he felt ashamed that he cried like that in front of her, all *mocoso* and broken.

"I'm not sorry," she said, and she didn't have to say anything else.

For the wienie roast, he gave Amelia and Cristalena bracelets, cute things with many dangling charms. Each of them was different. Amelia's had silver cogs and square coins, Cristalena's African beads and black roses. They all sat in the front seat for a long time, just watching the water shimmer, cold winds rattling debris and whipping up dust. Miguel had taken the hood ornament. (It was a big silver swan, set to fly.) Cristalena had the furry dice. Amelia scraped the letters off the trunk that said in pretty script IMPALA.

"Goddamn," she said, touching the dash. "The times we spent in this car." And she looked at Miguel a little longingly.

"The first time we were together was in this car," Cristalena said, almost as if she had to supplant Amelia's tender memories quickly. It was all getting too mushy for Miguel.

"Less do it," he said.

The girls spread a blanket out on a flat spot across from the car. They weighed it down with beer and one of the cans of kerosene so the wind wouldn't drag it away. Then Miguel took off his coat and wearily began to pour kerosene all over those beautiful cherry-red leather seats. Splash

splash and the stink tickling his nose gurgle gurgle like the seats were soaking it up, the can making gulp sounds. Cristalena yelled for him to be careful and not get it on his clothes. The wind was blowing toward the river, away from them. When Miguel tossed the flaming matchbook, there was a WHOOSH like an oven catching, then a low moan and a burst of orange flame that made Cristalena scream and pull on him. They hadn't really thought about the gas tank. There were a series of detonations, each with its own rolling ball of flame; then there were no more explosions. Cristalena was still holding him back because he seemed to want to get closer.

"We should move this blanket back some," Amelia said, and she started pulling on it.

"The gas tank's gonna explode," Cristalena warned, pulling on Amelia's sleeve. "Stay back, Amelia."

Amelia grinned, a little touched by her concern. They both dragged the blanket back.

A rolling cloud of thick black smoke drifted up. The three of them settled on a safe distance and sat on the blanket, sipping beer and passing the munchies around. Amelia made the toast.

"Here's to Firebug," she said, wind whipping hair against her face. She lifted her beer can and her moist eyes to the sky. "Here's to every gutter rat hollow-eye making a buck the sleazy way. To every crack girl and crack boy. To every twelve-year-old with a deucey-deuce and a packa jimmies." Her sonorous tones made Cristalena get the giggles. "Hoh mighty street god . . ." She waved her hands and stood up. Cristalena and Miguel both started laughing.

"Hey. This is a solemn moment here, kiddies." She waited for her audience to calm down. "Ah-hem. Hoh mighty street god. Please accept our humble sacrifice to you in place of a life."

Cherry red blackened. Cams blazing circlets. Wind lashing at the crackling tongues. Finally there was only black hulk and smoke pouring in dark spirals, slanting out toward the river, toward Rikers Island. There was only a small cluster of bright dancing flames in the back seat now, gnawing on the blackened springs. Miguel got up and walked over. He was in a private place, feelings flooding through him. Then he thought about Cristalena and their first ride together. How could he share the memory of her with Spider? But he was there, all over the car, a haunting father image, an empty-eyed ghost. There was this classical play about the son who kills the father. It's supposed to be a tragedy. Miguel looked right into Spider's empty eyes.

"You'll be back." Spider seemed to scorn him. "An' believe it or not, pana, I'll have a place f' you. What went down went down an' that was the past. We all make mistakes an' all that. So where do we stand? It's simple, pana. You an' me we bound together. We from the same turf. How far you think you gonna get without me, pana?"

Spider faded somewhere in the black smoke. Miguel had a heavy steel taste in his mouth. "Burn, mothafucka." His eyes glowered like the embers in the back seat. Suddenly Cristalena was beside him and then Amelia was on his other side and he had his arms around both of them, planting a splotchy kiss on both foreheads.

"I liked bein' with both a' you in this," he said, "but'chu know, this wasn't nothin' like the old wienie roasts. There were a lot more laughs."

Amelia wiped her eyes. "I'm glad it's not. It never should've been." She exchanged a look with Cristalena and they both laughed softly. It was like they had shared some secret woman-thought.

"Men are silly, ain't they?" Amelia asked her.

Cristalena smirked. "You mean *boys*, don'chu?"

They both looked at him but his eyes were lost in the smoky black. He suddenly snapped out of it and gave them a squeeze.

"Less get the fuck. It's time."

They walked off the lot and back onto the long, empty road. They did drunken kicks like a chorus line, they tottered and swayed but they weren't drunk—Amelia was carrying the remaining three cans dangling from their plastic gasket. The girls sang, not Miguel. They knew more house music than he did. When he started doing a Guns N' Roses song complete with lead guitar and feedback they started kicking him.

"So, Mr. Smarty, are you gonna take us out to eat? You shouldn't be such a cheap mother, man." Amelia slumped against him as they walked arm in arm in arm. He didn't say anything, only looked up at the bridge which they were slowly approaching. At the very end of it was a four-door brown car. It seemed to be waiting for them. Cristalena froze when she saw it.

"Miguel." She was breathless, fear in her eyes. She clutched his arm, pulling him back.

"Relax. I know who that is."

"Who is it?" This was Amelia, who had stopped walking, too

"You'll see f' yuhself."

The car was sitting on the road's shoulder, right by the ugly black bridge. The driver must've spotted them in the rearview mirror. As they got closer, a man stepped out of the car and leaned against it, lighting a cigarette and waiting. Cristalena recognized him first.

"It's the cop guy," she said.

Sanchez leaned against the car, his big coat flapping as the wind swept around him. He smiled at them warmly, nodding. They all stood facing each other for a moment.

"Out for a walk?" he finally asked. He had noticed the far-off smoke, he could smell the kerosene.

"Yeah. Good day for it." Miguel grinned. "I really liked that Richard Wright book, man. It was dope."

Sanchez stepped closer, his face lighting up. "Yeah, right? What I like about him is his ability to present us with the case of a young man who was born into a situation that he couldn't change. He couldn't help what he did. He just didn't know any better, and there was no one to teach him. Sometimes I feel like more Puerto Ricans should read it. We could learn so much from the black man." There was a childlike glimmer in his eyes that made Miguel laugh.

"When you called me I didn't know what to expect," Sanchez went on, hands buried in his pockets. "Last time I called you didn't seem so receptive. Suddenly you're inviting me to meet you. So I'm here. Was this just a social visit, or—"

"Nah. I tol'ju, I have somethin' f' you, an' I do." Miguel fished inside a coat pocket and took out a cassette tape. It was Spider's tape. He handed it to Sanchez, who turned it over and over looking for a label.

"I hope it's not rap."

"Betta than that. It's Spider. Yeah it is. No shit. Spider tellin' his own story. From start to present."

Sanchez looked a little stunned. He didn't say anything.

"I just thought . . ." Miguel paused, wind whipping hair into his eyes. "You gave me that book an' all. I figured I'd give you somethin'. I think yuh a bigger Spider fan than I am."

Sanchez stared at him. He seemed to be weighing the tape in his hand and making computations. He had started calling Miguel about two weeks before; their conversations were more like jovial chats than interrogations. That made a bigger impression on Miguel than if it had all been just straight cop stuff. So Miguel called him after making the decision. "Listen," he had said as if preparing a drug drop, "can you meet me tomorrow at two o'clock? I got somethin' I wanna give you." Now Sanchez stood there, looking pensive. "Well, thank you," he said, pocketing the tape and looking at them. "Can I drop you anywhere?"

Amelia and Cristalena both recoiled a little, pulling Miguel back.

"Nah man," Miguel answered, giving him his hand. Sanchez shook it and got into his car.

"I guess I'll be in touch." The wind carried ashes from his cigarette in their direction. He seemed reluctant to leave. He kept looking at Cristalena holding the furry dice. Miguel had a small bag slung across his shoulder, but it was open and Sanchez could see silver wings.

"Garage sale?" he asked.

"Ritual sacrifice," Amelia answered. That's when he seemed to realize he was out of his league. The car surged forward. They stood there until his car had scooted across the bridge with a soft hum and a flutter of taillights.

Miguel didn't know what was coming next. He didn't worry about having to testify against Spider because he knew Spider would never be caught. They would never nab him. It was like with Hitler: He was too important to be captured. He would die first. As for Sanchez, Miguel was going to take it day by day. No big decisions, no heavy plans. He was only going to walk along arm in arm in arm and watch their shadows snake along the sidewalk ahead of them so tall. There were no more posses in his world. There was only the three of them, walking away from it.

FOR THE BEST IN PAPERBACKS, LOOK FOR THE

In every corner of the world, on every subject under the sun, Penguin represents quality and variety—the very best in publishing today.

For complete information about books available from Penguin—including Puffins, Penguin Classics, and Arkana—and how to order them, write to us at the appropriate address below. Please note that for copyright reasons the selection of books varies from country to country.

In the United Kingdom: Please write to *Dept. JC, Penguin Books Ltd, FREEPOST, West Drayton, Middlesex UB7 0BR.*

If you have any difficulty in obtaining a title, please send your order with the correct money, plus ten percent for postage and packaging, to *P.O. Box No. 11, West Drayton, Middlesex UB7 0BR*

In the United States: Please write to *Consumer Sales, Penguin USA, P.O. Box 999, Dept. 17109, Bergenfield, New Jersey 07621-0120.* VISA and MasterCard holders call 1-800-253-6476 to order all Penguin titles

In Canada: Please write to *Penguin Books Canada Ltd, 10 Alcorn Avenue, Suite 300, Toronto, Ontario M4V 3B2*

In Australia: Please write to *Penguin Books Australia Ltd, P.O. Box 257, Ringwood, Victoria 3134*

In New Zealand: Please write to *Penguin Books (NZ) Ltd, Private Bag 102902, North Shore Mail Centre, Auckland 10*

In India: Please write to *Penguin Books India Pvt Ltd, 706 Eros Apartments, 56 Nehru Place, New Delhi 110 019*

In the Netherlands: Please write to *Penguin Books Netherlands bv, Postbus 3507, NL-1001 AH Amsterdam*

In Germany: Please write to *Penguin Books Deutschland GmbH, Metzlerstrasse 26, 60594 Frankfurt am Main*

In Spain: Please write to *Penguin Books S.A., Bravo Murillo 19, 1° B, 28015 Madrid*

In Italy: Please write to *Penguin Italia s.r.l., Via Felice Casati 20, I-20124 Milano*

In France: Please write to *Penguin France S.A., 17 rue Lejeune, F-31000 Toulouse*

In Japan: Please write to *Penguin Books Japan, Ishikiribashi Building, 2–5–4, Suido, Bunkyo-ku, Tokyo 112*

In Greece: Please write to *Penguin Hellas Ltd, Dimocritou 3, GR–106 71 Athens*

In South Africa: Please write to *Longman Penguin Southern Africa (Pty) Ltd, Private Bag X08, Bertsham 2013*